He had no h   tears, a shock

"Come," he offered, but she shook her head. He nudged her nearer. "It's not an order. I'm offering you my shoulder."

Shuddering, she leaned against him, her breath ragged as she fought for control. Twining his hand into her hair, supporting the back of her head, he soothed, stunned how easily the words came. There wasn't time for emotion, but he would do nothing else. Her body curved to his as time and sobs passed, his awareness moving from comfort to the sheer feel of her, from her loins to her head at the curve of his neck. And then her lips moved, kissed the base of his throat.

No other invitation was required. Warrick bent his head and captured her mouth, lifting her to him. It was like arriving somewhere familiar, comforting, until she reached up, her body pressing closer. The storm began, rain intensifying as the heat grew. He only wanted more. He started to draw away, and she followed. Unwilling to deny himself, he wrapped her close, swept his tongue through her mouth, and heard her soft whimper. Arching her to his hardness, he held them together. He had to swallow the moan in his throat when she gave a small squirm, her eyes widening in amazement. "I could take you now," he whispered against her ear.

She jumped, leaned back, her eyes wide and dark, her breath shallow. "I've never done this."

He searched the stable. "We're alone; the hay in the loft is soft. We could go there." But she was already shaking her head. Heated, frustrated, he heaved a sigh. "Is this what you did to Landgon, teased him to anger? It would explain the conversation."

She blinked, both hands bracing on his chest as she caught her breath. It was pointless to defend her innocence. He would never believe her.

"I'm a fool, but you're worse." She shoved hard, and he released her. Then she was gone, running through the rain and into the house.

BOOK YOUR PLACE ON OUR WEBSITE AND MAKE THE READING CONNECTION!

We've created a customized website just for our very special readers, where you can get the inside scoop on everything that's going on with Zebra, Pinnacle and Kensington books.

When you come online, you'll have the exciting opportunity to:

- View covers of upcoming books
- Read sample chapters
- Learn about our future publishing schedule (listed by publication month *and author*)
- Find out when your favorite authors will be visiting a city near you
- Search for and order backlist books from our online catalog
- Check out author bios and background information
- Send e-mail to your favorite authors
- Meet the Kensington staff online
- Join us in weekly chats with authors, readers and other guests
- Get writing guidelines
- AND MUCH MORE!

**Visit our website at
http://www.kensingtonbooks.com**

His for the Taking

SARAH PARR

ZEBRA BOOKS
KENSINGTON PUBLISHING CORP.
http://www.kensingtonbooks.com

ZEBRA BOOKS are published by

Kensington Publishing Corp.
119 West 40th Street
New York, NY 10018

All Kensington titles, imprints, and distributed lines are available at special quantity discounts for bulk purchases for sales promotion, premiums, fund-raising, educational, or institutional use.

Special book excerpts or customized printings can also be created to fit specific needs. For details, write or phone the office of the Kensington Special Sales Manager: Attn. Special Sales Department. Kensington Publishing Corp., 119 West 40th Street, New York, NY 10018. Phone: 1-800-221-2647.

Zebra and the Z logo Reg. U.S. Pat. & TM Off.

ISBN-13: 978-1-4201-0479-0
ISBN-10: 1-4201-0479-9

First Printing: July 2010

10 9 8 7 6 5 4 3 2 1

Printed in the United States of America

To Donna and Larry,
whom love has graced

Andrew Vladimir (1932–2008)
Dad, I miss you

ACKNOWLEDGMENTS

Hugs and thank you to my agent, Roberta Brown, whose guidance, wisdom, and friendship make the journey all the more special. Thanks to my editor, Peter Senftleben, and everyone at Kensington, who bring this book into your hands, and to you, the reader, for your kindness.

Chapter 1

1794
London

"Jump and you'll break your neck." Warrick halted, one hand raised in a plea he prayed would work. To his relief, the figure paused, coiled on the marble window ledge, and cast a glance toward him. He wasn't wrong. Trousers, a coat, and a man's cap pulled low over the face were no mask for the soft silhouette beneath, or the delicately curved face. This was a woman, although of the particulars, he had no idea. He would find out. Beyond, the oak swayed in the breeze; its long branches clawing upward were too thin for any weight.

"That branch wouldn't hold a child. I swear no harm will come to you, just come down." He waited. The only sounds were that of the men one floor below, their meeting still in progress. Whether he held her or she him, he didn't know. "Tell me your name."

"I'm sorry." She spun and made to leap.

He never gave her the chance. He seized her shirt and hauled her into the safety of his arms, dislodging her cap. Her hair cascaded to her waist, thick as it was full. Against the back of his hand it was pure silk, candlelight playing in the deep brown. Surprised by the richness, he caught back the desire to caress it. She was exciting and something deeper than desire stirred in him.

"Easy, sweet, we need to talk," he said, forcing his voice to remain calm. His reward was a sudden, sound kick in his groin. Locking hold on his prize, he stumbled into the carved desk. Her foot twined about his ankle, and she wrenched, then yelped as they went down together. A twist and she was free.

Sucking in a breath, Warrick sat up and found a letter opener shaped like a sword directed at his throat, the tiny point perfectly still. Needles of pain continued to stab through his loins. He gritted his teeth against them, glowering at her. From below, hurried footsteps sounded in the hall, then on the stairs.

"My friends won't be long. You can't fight us all off," he said. She glanced toward the window, where the curtains billowed, the air scented with spring rain.

"Please . . ." Her attention returned to him. She blinked. "I only wanted what's mine."

The desperation in her eyes chilled his soul, reminding him of a fox before the arrival of the hounds over a rise. "Tell me."

Her brow furled, and her lips parted as the door burst open to a man's shout. Light filled the room, then voices, as twenty men all rushed in. They were his assembly, and even though they included his father, the duke, they would follow his instructions.

"Do nothing," Warrick ordered over his shoulder and raised his hand, his eyes not leaving the woman's face. Beneath rubs of grime sparkled fire, and the echo of a memory. He had seen her before, but the details were missing. "What were you going to say?"

"It doesn't matter." With a sweep of her arm, she sent a

flurry of papers off the desk and over him. Catlike, sensual, and effortless, she was more insinuation of form than flesh and blood. She was onto the branch before he could lunge a second time.

At the window he watched her cling, toss a leg over a thin branch, and attempt to pull herself upright. Slipping, she tried again with success, and began to scramble down. "Damnation," he swore against the remnants of his pain and forced them into the background.

"I'll get her," called Trent.

"No, wait!" Warrick gave silent thanks as his friend halted before reaching the door. Good intentions were no match for the woman. "She's mine. Make sure she doesn't go another way." He ran past his father without a glance, awkwardly down the carpeted stairs, gaining with each stride. Through the lit hallways and across the blue and white tiles of the kitchen, he had no sooner opened the door to the garden when there was a snap and a sickening crash. He saw her hit the ground and roll; then she was on her feet, although how, he had no idea. She stumbled, teetered, and collapsed as he reached her, her breath in shudders. Anger ripped through him. Glaring at the crown of her head, it was impossible to tell if there was blood in this light. Touch revealed dampness, possibly from the drizzle, or something more sinister. "I should shake you for being a fool."

She swayed, tightened her grip, and looked up. "That would hurt."

"It would be far less than what your band of pirates has done. Three people died last week in smugglers' raids. That makes the total over forty." He paused and searched her face as she blanched. "Who is the organizer?"

"I don't know what you're talking about."

"Last week I spread the story I had found evidence that would send the smugglers to the gallows. I told everyone I hid it in my bedroom, but I made the story up. It was a trap, for you apparently. If you tell me what you know, I might be able to help you. Maybe you didn't realize what you were in to."

"I'm here with my uncle, no band. . . ."

She sagged, and the light from the torches showed her eyes green and brown, lacking focus but full of wisdom. "There'll be time for questions later, after you're settled."

"I can't stay." She hissed a breath, struggled to find her feet, but only leaned harder on his support as he started back for the house, tripping over the uneven cobblestones.

They reached the bottom of the stairs, and he knew they were at her limit. Warrick lifted her into his arms, her tiny sigh a bittersweet reward. She sank closer, the heat of her body and the scent of flowers and earth oddly peaceful. He had never held her before—he would have remembered this one—and yet she was familiar, he was more certain now than earlier. Memory rarely failed him, which meant more secrets. Beneath his hand he could feel her strength and spirit, even barely conscious, ruling out the ladies of the ballrooms.

Her head lolled against Warrick's shoulder, and she lost consciousness as Daniels arrived, his weathered face belying the seasoned finance minister. "She's hurt. Get a doctor." Taking the stairs two at a time, he strode down the hallway past portraits of proud noble relations and reentered his bedroom. A cold trickle of sweat traced the chill down his spine as he laid her in the bed, feeling her loss. His father moved to his side, but he didn't look up. "When I passed word I had information on the gang hidden here at the house, I thought I would catch"—he gave a shrug—"someone larger. She can't be much more than twenty."

"Villains can be any age or size."

"She doesn't look the part." Ivory damask pillows and comforter paled her appearance, the elaborately carved headboard of dark mahogany enhancing the effect. Warrick

fumbled for her wrist. "Her pulse is too fast." Skimming his
fingers over her head, he felt the rising welt. From either a
branch or the ground, it did not matter, the damage was
done. He ran a finger above a scratch on her cheek that
seeped blood. Her skin soft, her mouth fine, it could have
been a romantic caress except for the circumstances. He retrieved water, cloth, and basin from the corner and set to
work, dabbing and cleaning as he went, until he came to her
jaw. "I thought this was grime." Purple and black, the sinister bruise was too old to have been caused by the tree.

"Someone hit her."

"Rather viciously," Trent said, entering the room. "I've
sent the men out to check the waterfront. They'll come back
tomorrow at seven to report if she belongs to anyone."

"It would have been better if you hadn't done that. We
don't want to alert the smugglers we might have one of
them," Warrick said quietly.

Trent moved closer and studied the woman. "There's no
difference. By the time they act she'll be in the Tower, if not
already hung."

The man was his friend, and not hard by nature. Trent
was the third son and lacked the funding to do as he wished.
It had made him practical in all matters, except women. And
he did have a point: she would most likely be put to death,
although not as quickly as Trent predicted. For the first time
since he agreed to stop the smugglers, he had doubts on his
course of action. Fortunately his father distracted Trent.
Movement caught his attention, and he glanced down as the
woman's eyes fluttered half open. He continued his minis-
trations. "You took quite a fall."

"It wasn't supposed to turn out that way." She shifted,
tried a tiny stretch, and grimaced.

He gave her his most charming smile. "We'll start with
your name." Her eyes flickered in the direction of the duke
and Trent hovering nearby. "You might as well tell me; I'll

find out soon enough." He waited through her silence, meeting her gaze whenever she looked in his direction.

"Katherine Bane, but I prefer Karly," she said finally. Her gaze went to the ceiling, away from any of them. "You played a game of cards with my uncle last night. He lost a small miniature. In it was a portrait of my father, painted by my mother. I came to get it back."

Trent gave a loud snort. "You mean steal it back."

Warrick shot Trent a warning glare. "Angus Roberts never mentioned a niece."

"He doesn't relish the connection. Neither of us do." She blinked, her eyes becoming watery as she squinted to keep them from closing. "I'll pay you for it."

Warrick lifted both brows. He was not getting the answers he expected; rather than simplifying matters, everything had just become a great deal more complicated. "Wouldn't it have been easier to contact me, offer to buy it back, rather than climbing trees?"

"My uncle doesn't know I'm here. He wouldn't approve. I can't have him find out."

"Trent, go and fetch my greatcoat." When his friend returned, Warrick reached into the pocket, and withdrew the intricately etched locket from where he had stored it. "Is this it?" he asked softly. Her eyes lit at the sight of the small treasure, and he pressed it into her palm. "It's yours," he said and felt some satisfaction as her features brightened. Keeping her hand in his, he moved the cloth and stroked her forehead as she had slipped away again. He tried her name, but she was gone from him. Karly's face, which had shone only a short time before, remained as still as a porcelain doll.

"You shouldn't have given that back to her," Trent said after a long pause. "You had her for stealing. She would have gone to prison."

"I have her for far more when I'm ready." He paused, letting the irritation hang between them. "I chose to play cards with Angus Roberts because his brother-in-law is Patrick Bane, who spent time with the Barbary pirates. Their raiding tactics were similar to the ones being used by our smugglers."

Trent took a step forward, exchanging a knowing look with Warrick. "Patrick Bane was a pirate based in Bermuda."

"He died a couple years ago after attacking a British vessel, but his crew vanished." Warrick glanced at Karly. "There was no mention of a daughter."

The duke frowned, studying Karly, and shook his head. "You think she could be the one behind the smugglers?"

"She wouldn't be the first female pirate." Warrick searched Karly's quiet features for the secrets behind her lashes. He had told his father and friend enough. The hunch, that Karly was the key, would have to wait until he had facts or they would assume it was her figure that swayed his judgment. He couldn't be certain that it wasn't. Her presence captivated him. He wanted to know more, have her longer, learn and understand. Desire, unusually incarnated, seeped through his soul, but the words to explain were best unsaid. "I have a few days to find out before she can leave and go anywhere." He glanced at Trent. "If anyone does come looking for her, delay them. Father, I need you to take a closer look at Roberts's affairs."

"I assume you mean more than his finances."

They had shifted roles and it had been so effortless. His father had always been the one in command. Now, with the authority granted him by Parliament, it was his turn. Warrick studied the man he had known his entire life. Hard determination stared back, the same he saw in himself each morning in the mirror, and yet there was fondness. "Go as deep as you feel necessary."

"I'll make the inquiries."

Warrick moved to stand in the corner and rested his hand

on the strongbox as the doctor arrived. Perhaps it would be proper to wait outside, but Karly had almost escaped him once. Given the chance, she would most likely try again. He tried to be patient as the man checked Karly's limbs and head with slow, precise movements. When Warrick could stand the tension no longer he cleared his throat. "What is your estimation?"

The doctor cocked his head. "A nimble athlete. The damage could have been much more severe. She appears to be undernourished and already in a weakened state. The trauma has done the rest of what you see here. Keep her warm and give her laudanum for any discomfort, but not too much. Her brain will best set to right if left to heal on its own." He stood and patted Warrick's shoulder. "Do not worry, your lordship. She appears to have fire. Good food and rest will do wonders."

"You'll return tonight for any changes?"

"If you wish," the doctor frowned.

"Seven, no later, and I'll see she rests."

His father had stiffened, moving to the center of the room, where he waited while Warrick dismissed the doctor. "When do you plan to turn her over to the Tower and let her be questioned?"

"You know that would be signing her death sentence."

His father glanced toward Karly and shook his head. "I recommended you for this position against your mother's wishes. She's certain you'll be killed, but I know what it's like to be restless." He hesitated and turned to face Warrick. "Still, you are the future Duke of Berington. You've had your time at sea. Your assignment is to gather the information, no more."

"Tell mother that London ballrooms are far more hazardous than anything I'm doing."

The duke gave a soft chuckle. "Amanda Claridge, along with most of the available women in London, knows you will choose a wife soon. She wants to be a duchess. Besides, once you pick a wife, the man has the upper hand. In the end, it is the man's house."

It was Warrick's turn to smile, a relief after the tension of the past hours. "Yes, I see how well that works with mother." To his father's raised brow, he laughed.

"I made a mistake when I married your mother. I fell in love with her."

The world shrank to the room about them, and Warrick searched his father's face. "You regret that?"

"No," the duke said introspectively and sighed. "But tell her nothing. She knows me too well already." He gave Warrick's shoulder a squeeze and let go. "I'll send you word what I find."

As the duke's footfalls faded down the corridor, Warrick said good night and returned to Karly's side. Possible scenarios played across his mind. None answered all the questions and problems. He had much to learn if he was going to understand what brought her here. He held vigil as the light grayed, pinked and rays began to peek through the blue damask curtains. One touched the blanket, then crept its way, caressing a single strand, then another until gold, copper, and bronze framed her face.

Beauty was a woman's sword, and Karly was well armed. His father was right to be concerned as he rejected one plan after another, his mind returning to his father's cautions. At nightfall, Trent returned, his expression bleak, his golden hair askew from running his fingers through it. "You heard something."

Pursing his lips, Trent narrowed his eyes on Karly. Apparently satisfied she was asleep, he motioned Warrick to the far corner, his voice no more than a whisper. "Daniels spoke to the bosun from Roberts's ship, bought him a few pints. Apparently Roberts picked Karly up in Bermuda after a scandal there, something about an officer who is the brother-in-law of the governor. She was forced to leave, and Roberts was told never to return until she was gone. Two days ago, Baron Landgon was onboard Roberts's ship. Apparently they signed a contract. Karly is to be Landgon's mistress."

It took effort to mask his irritation. He didn't like surprises. "Anything else?"

"Her uncle took a hundred pounds for her—not a bad price to have a woman at your whim." Trent glanced toward Karly, as if assuring himself she was still sleeping.

"Landgon could afford more, but then again, he's eccentric."

"You mean mad."

"What would Landgon want with the daughter of a pirate, beyond the obvious?" At first he couldn't respond to his own question, even as answer fragments tumbled through him. She was pretty, lovely in fact, given the right circumstances. He had held her only briefly, and his body ached with the memory of her in his arms. Her impractical hair, cascading about her, haunted him, beckoning to be touched, caressed. A step of his imagination had his fingers speared, gripping with passion, with her beneath him, her lips parted. Uncomfortable, he chose the seat at the end of the bed and sent Trent out again, fighting to cool his blood.

Landgon's involvement altered the map; he was a known fop, unpredictable, with money, time, and a thirst for recognition. To him, Karly would be more than play or passion. She would be a tool and the project, ominous. He would have to change his plans accordingly, take a risk.

Evening passed; the doctor came and left. Warrick's resolve strengthened. Whatever the cost, Karly would have to remain with him until he had the answers. When her uncle sent a note the following morning demanding an audience, the time had come to act before she slipped through his fingers. Taking a seat at his writing desk, he opened the compartment, drew a piece of paper and a long breath, and began to write. The moment he finished, he sent the note and his gamble on its way to his royal highness King George III.

His answer came the next afternoon while he was studying charts of the coastline. He broke the royal seal and read it twice even though the king's command was simple and direct. It contained everything he asked for. What should have been pleasure felt like a stone. He sat, considering, until the sun slanted low through the windows, hurting his eyes. It was possible he was making a mistake, but she was as much his chance as he was hers. He entered the room and closed the door firmly.

Karly looked up, met his gaze, and froze. "What is it?" Dread shadowed her features as she watched him.

Lifting the letter and its seal into plain sight, he approached and sat on the corner of the bed. The memory of the wildcat who had pointed a letter opener at his throat was vivid, alive beneath her surface. He prepared for any reaction. "His highness, King George III, has given me permission to make you my wife. The wedding will be tomorrow." The words were out, and he waited. Silent, he watched her search his face, taken aback when instead of showing pleasure, anger, or frustration, she shifted away from him and toyed with the cover.

"No."

Although he had heard her clearly, he ignored the dismissal. "In addition, his highness has graciously agreed to an annulment once I am satisfied that I have learned all I need to know."

"The king cannot do that; it's up to the archbishops."

He quirked a smile, "The king has already gotten the approval of the Archbishop of Canterbury."

She jerked her head abruptly, and he paused, searching her profile. Whatever thoughts were warring within her had driven tears to her cheeks. Warrick resisted dabbing them away.

"I know you were to become Landgon's mistress. Are you in love with him?"

Her expression turned hard and angry. "I've told you before, I don't know anything. Forcing me to marry you will only bring you misery."

"It's the only way I can keep your uncle or Landgon from asserting a claim over you."

"I have things to do. I won't be your or anyone's property." She looked at him. She gave a shaky sigh and swallowed hard. "You should be grateful to be spared."

He leaned forward, catching her chin in his hand. "Don't cross me, Karly." He rose. "The Archbishop will be here tomorrow at eleven."

"The answer is still no."

Insulted by her rejection, he hesitated, tempted to argue. He was considered by many to be one of the most desirable matches in London. True, he was marrying her through blackmail and had no intention of keeping the match. It was to keep her uncle and Landgon's hands off her.

Warrick greeted the two men who guarded the house, and checked on the one in the alley behind. Karly wouldn't be escaping before the ceremony. *No* wasn't an option, but he would deal with that in the morning.

Chapter 2

It wasn't love; it never could be. Warrick Barry, Marquis of Ralstead, was a fantasy twined inseparably around her imagination. He was using her to an end. The truth made Karly almost sensible as she watched Warrick sleep, his dark hair tussled. Yet memories of Bermuda haunted her. Under a broad hat, her hair and face hidden, she had been one of many workers at the dockyard in Bermuda, toiling over *Moorea*, his latest ship. Pad in hand, she sketched drawings for the master ship builder. Though tempted, she had never once set the pencil to capture his image; it wouldn't measure close to the man. Warrick's eyes were dark brown with flecks of gold, as if day and night collided for one perfect moment. They were warm, filled with humor; she could look into them for eternity. That didn't make him her husband. She would marry no one.

She couldn't hate him, although he had refused to listen to her. The situation was impossible since she couldn't tell him the truth, beginning with her father's crew. Outlaws, they depended on her to keep her silence. They weren't the smugglers Warrick was looking for, but it wouldn't matter. They would be hanged as pirates. She would be too, no matter what happened. She would not take them with her.

Then there was her vocation, another liability. She had promised her father she would tell no one. If Warrick knew she was a pilot, that skillfully she could navigate any ship through Bermudan waters, what then? It was how her friends stayed safe, behind the reefs where no one could get them, not that anyone tried anymore. Hack and crew were harmless, taking only small foreign ships and fishing.

Karly skimmed her hand over Warrick's hair. Comfort surrounded the man, along with elegance and position. She had to make him understand and before tomorrow, before he insisted they speak vows.

Sliding onto the bed, she eased beside him and shook gently. He blinked and smiled seductively. "Hello."

His expression hardened, and he sat, glancing around. "How did you get in here? I have guards on your room."

Karly reached for his hand and took it in hers, patting it gently as if he were a small child. He closed, then firmed the grip. Aware of his power she forced her demeanor to be calm. "I went over the roof. I needed to see you alone before tomorrow. I promise I'm unarmed, no letter openers." She opened her free hand for inspection. When he frowned, she lay back against the pillows. With the sense of Warrick all around her, she tried to relax. It was like sinking into a cloud, soft, warm from his body, and scented with the heating coals and lavender. "I think best lying down," she muttered.

"And whose beds have you philosophized in?"

An emotional slap, she glared at him and gave a snort. Still, perhaps it was better if he thought the worst of her. "If I stare at the ceiling, I don't have to look at you." She turned her head and startled when he touched her hair, heat in his eyes. The fear hit like a blow, freezing her breath. As she was lightheaded, it was foolish to sit, and for a moment it was the memory of the commander above her, his breath foul, his face contorted.

"You misunderstand," she muttered and closed her eyes. "Karly."

His voice a whisper, she heard it twice before she peeked at him to find him stoic. The room chilled and she braced for the approaching storm. "I've been told I'm too impulsive." Karly swallowed against the quiver in her voice. "I realize that's hard to believe."

Warrick raised a brow. "I never would have guessed." Warrick lay down beside her, enveloping her hand in both of his. "What is it you want to say?"

Breathing out the panic, she forced herself to calm. "I am not helping Landon in any way." Steadier, breathing more easily, she scrubbed at the tickle on her cheek. Mortified to find a tear, she closed her hand into a fist and forced it back to her side. But the rest of the words, about Landon's murder of her father, refused to come. After what seemed like minutes, she gave up and went on. "If you force this marriage, I'll have to run at the first opportunity. It will look poor for you, even with the annulment."

"If you are not guilty, why leave?"

"You're trying to trick me. I've told you what I can."

He brushed a kiss to her temple. "I thought you weren't going to tell me anything."

A sweet wave of restlessness washed over her, leaving a wake of heat. Each pass brought new awareness of her body. Unfair enjoyment brought a sigh to her lips. "I know what will happen if you knew everything." He hesitated, and she recognized her mistake of saying too much. Pleasure was confusing her.

"You don't believe I can survive a little scandal?"

"Be serious. What will the king do when he finds you have no answers from me?"

"So you want to save me?" he asked and covered her mouth with his own. Unprepared, her lips parted with a gasp, and she tried to draw back. Before she could, he broke the kiss and stared down at her, brows together.

"Yes." She gave a sigh of relief, her cheeks hot.

"Who saves Karly?"

She was trembling, not with fear. The intimacy and the suggestions it raised were more frightening than the gallows. Images of Warrick's demise by her hand made her try to sit. His hold kept her still. "I don't need saving."

"Because you have Landgon to look after you."

Indignant, she bit back her first retort as the bruise on her face throbbed, the one Landgon had given her when she had refused to help him. But true pain came from the accusation, one she had never earned. "Stop it."

"You're very protective of the man."

Anger at the unfairness had her trembling against hysterical laughter. Cruel Landgon who had threatened, beat, and tried to blackmail her was the last one she would help, even if she hadn't promised her father not to reveal her skill as a pilot. To suggest she would allow him to fondle her, touch him back, made the bile in her stomach rise. She had never been claimed by any man, nor would she.

"You will never believe me." She tried to push up. "I'll go."

Warrick's arm moved across her shoulders, pinning her back to the bed. "Not until after the ceremony. I won't hurt you, but I wouldn't want to lose you at this point."

"I won't be used. Marrying me won't change that."

"But it will give me claim over you, and that's what matters."

"I could say no."

"You won't defy the king with your uncle standing there."

The royal order suddenly crystallized. She knew she had no choice. Defying the king was not an option. She could no longer run. Trapped for the moment, Karly did the only safe thing and rolled free onto her side, giving him her back. Now she would wait for her chance, in a match of wits as to whether he could stop her before she got away. "Good night, Warrick," she said and waited for him to grasp her waist. He never touched her.

She had intended not to sleep at all. She woke to find herself alone in the silk-draped bedroom, the daylight well past dawn. Across from the armoire, one of her faded blue gowns hung from the wardrobe, along with petticoats and undergarments. Beneath it was her trunk. Her uncle must have arrived. That Warrick wasn't here had to mean he had changed his mind, despite his noble cause. She sat with a pang of regret. Perhaps, when the danger was past, she would write him a letter and explain, not that it mattered. After today he probably would never speak to her again.

Karly pulled on her clothes and fumbled for the wooden brush at the bottom of the trunk. All that was left for her to do was run from Landgon. Although he was dangerous, she was sure Warrick would have been a far worse adversary. Braiding her hair into submission, she hurried down the hall to the sound of her uncle's voice in the distance.

Shoulders back, she tried not to think of the insults that lay ahead. Karly descended the stairs and entered the study, a room more wood than tapestry. Uncle Angus stood in the center, his hands planted on his hips. Dressed in white, his hair combed, his face shaven, he was a shadow of the handsome man he had been, before anger had eroded his soul. His eyes narrowed on her, and to his left, by the fireplace, Warrick and Trent stiffened.

"You're wearing a uniform," she noted.

"Baron Landgon has chosen to fund my next voyage. All his captains wear white."

Her balance wavered, the world seemed to tighten around her. Landgon had closed another door of escape. Her head ached, and she gripped the side of a delicately carved table.

Facing only her uncle, unable to smile, she did her best not to cringe. "I am glad you're here. I have imposed on his lordship long enough."

Angus drew himself to his full lanky height. He straightened his coat with a tug and smiled too pleasantly. "I would like a few moments alone with my niece. Please excuse us, gentlemen."

With a step forward, Warrick moved between them. "I'm not sure that's a good idea."

"It will be all right," Karly offered and made the mistake of meeting Warrick's gaze. Layers of concern and frustration had her nearly undone. Desperately, she blinked and gave a shrug, as if it meant nothing.

"I'll be on the other side of the door," Warrick said lowly.

She followed him with her gaze until the door closed with an audible click.

"Fell, is it?" her uncle said, breaking the spell.

"From a tree."

Her uncle's eyes burned red. "If you could see yourself you would give up such a lie. More likely spent the last few nights tumbling through every form of sin. That is what you are best at."

"That's not true."

"Have you looked at yourself? You have all the nerve telling me what is the truth when I can see it with my own eyes. I suppose the bruise on your face came from the tree as well?" He gave a snort. "You might be able to deceive these gentlemen into feeling sorry for you, but I know the way things are. I'm the one who had to come claim you in Bermuda, take you out of that prison for piracy, lewdness, and God knows what else. You've your lying father in you. That won't change."

Karly walked to the mirror and stared at her reflection. In the glass she was a stranger, beneath wild hair and gaunt features, scratched and bruised. The blue gown Warrick had provided hung too loosely over her breasts and hips. No sane woman would walk dressed as she had, but then she had left her wits at the base of the tree when Warrick had taken her in his arms. Her uncle's rants roared louder. She faced him to find he had darkened to near scarlet. "You never asked my story."

"When things go so far that the governor himself demands I get you off the island, your version is irrelevant. I thought it wouldn't get worse, but you've gone and blackmailed a duke's son to marry you. It won't happen"

"I told Warrick the same. He won't listen."

Roberts closed in, his face too near. "You're a slut, not a lady. I already made an appropriate agreement with Landgon. He won't appreciate being crossed, might even challenge this marquis for the sport of it. You're to belong to him."

Her throat closed, and she fought for breath to speak. "Bastard," was all she could manage.

She should have remained silent. Her uncle's face contorted with anger. She ducked to one side and tripped, landing on her hands on the plush carpet. Karly rolled and looked up, prepared to kick out as the door burst open. Warrick's jaw was set as he seized her uncle by the collar and sent him sprawling with a single punch. Then he was at her side, his brown eyes deep with concern. Relief mixed with worry.

"You shouldn't have interfered," she whispered.

"You're my fiancée; it's my right." Warrick glared at Angus.

Angus stumbled to his feet. "She's playing you against each other, my lord." He raised his hand to the spot on his chin where Warrick's fist had connected. "Whatever she's said, you should know she's already been tossed by a commander in Bermuda. She likely carries his child."

"She never mentioned a child," Warrick glanced toward her.

Karly looked between the men. She wanted to scream at them both for the unfairness of it all, starting with her innocence, which meant nothing since no one believed her. She needed to disappear. London was a big city. First she had to escape.

"I don't feel well." Grasping the nearby chair, she hauled herself to her feet. The ground lurched dangerously like a ship in the high seas.

"Sit, before you fall down." Warrick guided her into a chair. "I don't care about your agreement with Landgon. If you want to be his mistress, so be it. But first, I'll have the truth. Or do I have to send you to prison first?"

Karly shrank as far as she could, but couldn't make herself invisible. "I'll end up hurting you."

He touched her cheek lightly. "You believe that, don't you?" He ran his hand beneath her chin. "I'm stronger than I seem. Nothing is going to happen to me."

"I didn't mean hurt you physically, although that's a risk. Your reputation, your livelihood, your friends—I will be a nuisance, a problem, and you will be harmed."

"I have no choice, nor do you. As for the rest, you will have to trust I can handle it."

"Write to the king and suggest that he order me from the country. I will be out of anyone's reach and of no concern anymore."

Warrick's smile drew slowly across his dark brown eyes, until their warmth was hidden. "That won't stop the violence."

"No one can," she choked and glanced toward the window, wishing with all her might she was a bird, a longtail basking on the cliffs of Bermuda's South Shore. She would take wing and fly toward the sky, live at sea and be free.

"You haven't given me a chance."

Karly turned her gaze to his face. "You do not trust me, and I don't trust you either. We can't move past that."

"So be it," he said and stood up with her in his arms. She was cradled against his chest before she again found her voice. "What are you doing?"

"Carrying you to the parlor and the archbishop."

"I forbid it!" Angus exclaimed.

Arching her back, she attempted to kick free, to land on her feet. Her temper rose as Warrick held her. "Enough. I'm not a pawn for either of you." Flattening her hand on Warrick's chest, she gave a shove. "Put me down."

He obliged, but blocked her path when she started for the door. "It's this way," he said and took her arm.

There was no choice. She let Warrick lead her. They entered a marble room of glittering white columns, a prison with no escape. At the far end stood the archbishop, his robes black as a grim reaper. Whatever nerves she had left intact now stretched painfully against her skin, leaving her senses frantic. There was no hesitation in Warrick's voice as he answered the archbishop. Then it was her turn. Finding her voice took diligence. She heard the archbishop ask her again to take Warrick as her husband.

"Yes."

The service ended, and he faced her. Karly thought herself quick minded, but when his lips closed over hers, she could not build a coherent thought. Warmth turned to heat, and yet it was ever so soft. His kiss was a temptation more than a demand. Stunned, her lips parted. The bare tip of his tongue traced hers, whether invitation or reassurance, she wasn't sure. A giddy flutter began deep and spread to an ache that held as much pleasure as terror. She couldn't afford distraction. Karly drew back, her sight unfocused, his features blurred into what might have been his soul. His stunned expression vanished behind a mask of pleasantness.

One corner of his mouth lifted before she forced her gaze down to her wedding ring, twisting it absently.

"There, we're married. I'd like to rest."

Warrick slid his hands down her arms. "You haven't eaten and need your strength."

He led her to the dining room, bright and scented with roses. Dark wood held silver trays and plates, ornately decorated in an emblem of a horse and rider. The taste of neither lemon cakes nor ginger cream loosened the knotted threads in her stomach. Warrick's touch only tightened until she feared they would snap. Staring at a spray of flowers, she remembered dolphins playing off the bow of her father's ship. One had been caught in the fishing net and hauled on deck. Glistening in the sun it had watched her accusingly. She had begged for its release and won. Now she was the prisoner, not the dolphin, but things would not end well this time. As she ate, she surreptitiously considered doors and windows, making her plans. So caught in ideas, she startled when Warrick touched her sleeve and found her uncle standing beside her chair, his hat in his hands. Instinctively, she lurched to her feet and knew by her uncle's face that Warrick had also stood.

"Are you leaving already?"

"I must." He remained, turned his hat around once. "I've done all I can by you." He wet his lips and set his hat on his head.

"It was your choice," Karly answered.

Angus shoved his hands deep in his pockets. "So you'll begrudge me?"

She considered, but couldn't find any anger. She laid her hand on his white lapel. "Be careful. Warrick is wary of Landgon, as am I."

Her uncle's face hardened. "Stories about your betters will lead to trouble."

Warrick's hand firmed, but she ignored it. "Should we

have talked, I would have told you that smugglers have been raiding the coast, that Warrick is trying to catch them, and that he thinks I'm involved, through Landgon." She gave a sigh. "As it is, I'm tired, my head hurts, and I am going upstairs." She gave her uncle and Warrick a curt nod and withdrew, aware Warrick remained beside her. She ignored the rich furnishings, walking as if down a tunnel, until she entered Warrick's bedroom. Numbly she continued to the window seat.

"You owe him nothing, Karly."

"I'm not sure I believe that. He's my mother's brother, and she loved him very much."

"You did him a kindness."

She watched as her uncle appeared in the street below. Without a look up or back, he passed through the gates, turned left, and disappeared.

"I took a risk that I wouldn't anger you by revealing your plans."

There was the click of a lock. She turned and raised a brow as he approached to join her. "So this is to be my prison?"

His lips lifted in a small smile. "As if this room could hold you." She didn't move as he walked and stood before her, but when he bent to take her hands, she rose quickly to the side.

"Stop." She placed her palm on his chest.

"It's our wedding night."

Confused, she glanced about, at the sunbeams streaming through the glass. Then his meaning hit her. "You wish rights, even though our marriage is false." Her hands trembled as she moved around him to perch on the edge of the bed. She looked up as if retrieving a memory with no idea what to say next. She wasn't even sure she could lie believably, having never been with a man. All she had was the stories the sailors told, and those seemed impossible acts of contortion.

"I suppose you want to hear about all my lovers or just the last few?"

"None. I don't care."

"You're pardoning me, and I should give you your reward." Placing her hands behind her, she leaned backward, offering her neck and breasts. Dizziness rippled through her. She tried to sit, slipped off the bed and onto the floor, and dropped her head into her hands.

"Foolish woman." He slid his arms about her shoulders and beneath her legs and lifted her onto the bed.

"The world won't stop spinning. In the worst storm it was never this bad." Karly leaned closer until the top of her head met solid muscle. His hand touched her back, and she leaned heavily, letting his presence ground her. "I think I'm landsick."

He chuckled. "Look at me."

She obeyed to find his face close. If there was a man to whom she could surrender, it would be him. It was wrong. "I can't do this tonight." She rubbed her hand over her damp brow.

"Karly," Warrick began and, catching her behind the shoulders, pulled her straight. His expression turned grim. "I have never forced a woman. I am not about to begin."

The truth caught in the back of her throat—her virginity, her skill as a pilot, her father's death, all of it would be a relief to share with another. She had been alone so long, the words refused to come. "You are trying to get me to trust you."

"Is it working?"

She closed her eyes and curled on her side, facing him. "No."

"You're a terrible liar, Karly."

"No, I'm not—that's part of the problem."

"Until I decide otherwise, you belong to me."

"I belong to no one. I never have." She peered up, but he wasn't looking at her any longer. One of his hands was in her hair; the other was on a volume, which he flicked open and began to read. She didn't recognize the story, the English melodic and old. His voice resonated with words she almost understood, but they remained outside her awareness. If her head did not ache, if the bed were not so comfortable, she might have been able to sort it out. Her wits were her greatest ally. But since she had fallen, they were jumbled, although less with each hour. Giving in to the moment was sweet peril. For a time she could pretend she belonged in the bed of this man, listening to his voice and cherishing his care. When she healed, the illusion would have to be broken, by her own hand if necessary. She released her hold on the present and tumbled into the abyss of sleep.

Chapter 3

"I might have intervened with the prime minister, found another way to hold her. There were other options." Warrick's father, the duke, continued pacing before the marble fireplace like a caged lion, glancing only on the turns.

Deciding fewer words were best, Warrick remained where he was, in the center of the room. "This is better."

The duke shook his head and swore. He looked up and considered the man carved of stone, holding the mantel, its twin on the other side. "You would not have married this girl under other circumstances."

"Hardly a girl—her uncle says she's three and twenty." The duke stopped and pursed his lips. Drawing a deep breath, Warrick wet his lips. "I took the liberty of searching her trunk. The bottom of it was full of sketches, drawings, and precise measurements of ships in the British navy, several of whom have vanished, but not in these waters. Most were in the Caribbean."

"She's a spy."

"Possibly."

The duke drew closer. "Explain to me why you aren't sure."

"The evidence has to be stronger. Prison will simply hang her," he sighed, raising a hand to his chest. "I'm sure there is more than she's saying. Landgon's involved. It's worth taking the risks to find out what he's up to."

The duke worked his jaw, then placed his hand on Warrick's shoulder. "You are trying to save her. Don't give away your heart, Warrick. You don't know this woman."

"I've no intention of falling in love with her. She is connected, and that could mean all the difference. You have to admit, discovering Landgon is involved adds a whole new dimension to this mess."

The duke studied his insignia ring and remained quiet for a long while. "Landgon was at St. James yesterday, over his estate at Browley. Not a well-turned foot wrong, but I agree, he is potentially a problem. There is an air about him—I'd call it hunger." He eased a curtain aside and peered into the street. "Warrick, perhaps I was harsh, demanding you choose duty, but at the very least, promise to be cautious. Your brother William is very capable, but he has no interest in being duke. You're the heir. You're also a grown man."

"I'm restless, not reckless. I will be careful."

"That's all I ask. Do what you must."

"I could use your assistance. If you would contact my group. The nobility only—I'll handle my traders." The peace offering was transparent. He hoped his father wouldn't mind.

"Very well," his father gave him a brusque hug before leaving.

Returning to his study, Warrick retrieved the broken sextant and large portfolio of papers he had found in Karly's trunk. It was enough to send her to the gallows. He didn't expect she would tell him the truth; she was far too wary for that. What he needed was something plausible to build on. He got to his feet and carried the items under his arm.

He found Karly seated in the parlor overlooking the rose garden. Her shabby taupe gown left an impression of quiet defiance, her hair, unfashionable and wild, held by two small braids on either side of her head. He wished his father had seen her like this, with spirit and vitality. Her effect was like champagne. He wanted to savor more. He fought the urge and cleared his throat to announce his presence.

Her eyes fell to the item in his hand. He lifted it in full view as he sat beside her. "I found this in the trunk your uncle sent over with your things. Is it yours?"

"Yes."

Warrick nodded slowly and opened the collection of papers, displaying the first sketch and its notes. "The *Berwick,* British naval frigate, twenty-four gunner." He turned to the next page and the next ship. "The *Pelican,* British naval sloop, twelve gunner." He continued on, "The *Lady Ann,* the *Lancaster,* the *Amelia* . . ." Warrick paused, stealing a glimpse at her. He knew she was watching and listening, even though she stared unseeing across the room, her face pale. He continued, listing each of the ships until he came to the last page, which featured one of his own. "The *Celestra,* thirty-two gunner, merchant ship. You've accumulated quite a collection of information here on British naval and merchant ships. Where did you get it?"

"The papers are mine," she admitted hesitantly.

Warrick shook his head. "Let us try this again. Why are you collecting information on British ships? Were you carrying these for someone? Perhaps they were your father's?" With that she turned her head away from him. Warrick reached forward, catching her chin. "I need the truth."

"I like to sketch."

Warrick released her momentarily, and flipped the pages to a large drawing. Lifting it to show her, he clenched his jaw when she flinched. "I have no intention of hitting you," he said in a cool, sardonic voice. "This is the Naval schooner, the *Eagle*, but then you knew that. Six months past she was taken by a French frigate off the Bahamas. She was bound for Bermuda, her home port and coincidentally where you happen to be from. Treason is punishable by death. These appear to be evidence of misdoings."

"No."

"Tell me a more convincing story. You need to help me," he added, disappointed when she would no longer meet his eyes. "This morning I received a card from David Landgon, requesting an audience. He'll be here soon. Before he arrives, you need to tell me how all this fits in." Her full lips drew thinner as her eyes took an imploring quality. She shook her head slowly, and his heart sank. He set aside the book. With gentle pressure he managed to pry her hands apart and take one in his. It trembled.

"I . . ." Her head jerked up. "I saw you in Bermuda, when you were having your ships built. I'm from there."

"You can't find better than Bermudan cedar." He seized the grain of commonality he had been searching for. "My brother William should return any day with the *Moorea*. Would you like to see her?"

"Very much," she said and smiled and began detailing plants and animals from memory.

Careful not to ask too many questions, he tried to listen for what she didn't say, but it was hard not to be captivated. With fear gone, she shone for him, passion and light in her eyes. If that brilliance was ever turned on him, he would be lost completely.

"You miss Bermuda," he said, forcing himself back to the present.

"Very much." Karly looked up and bit her lower lip.

Warrick laid his finger on the bruised flesh, wishing it were his mouth instead. "You do that when you're nervous." He forced himself back to the topic and his touch away.

She got to her feet as the grandfather clock in the Spanish room chimed the hour. "Maybe we could go for a walk?" Without waiting for an answer, she started down the hall, but halted at the sight of a footman, announcing the arrival of Landgon.

Instructing him to be escorted to the library, Warrick offered Karly his hand and found her changed and stoic. "Stay beside me." She gave him a stiff nod, her eyes directly ahead as she walked, graceful as a swan, poised like a cat. This was different than with her uncle, and not the reaction of a woman preparing to meet her lover. Before they entered the room, he seized her hand and placed it firmly on his sleeve, then led her in.

Warrick had met Landgon only once before. The man had not improved. His thin mouth was just as devoid of color as before, made worse by the fact his entire wardrobe was white, from his boots, to his greatcoat trimmed with ermine in the style of King George. Beneath sallow lids he watched Karly like a man starved for a meal. His lips twitched in what could have been a smile, had his eyes shown warmth. Warrick smiled back and led Karly to a large wooden chair facing the sofa. Urging her to sit, he gestured for Landgon to return to the couch.

"Your request stated the matter was pressing. How can I be of assistance?" Warrick asked and moved to stand behind Karly.

"You will forgive the intrusion, Mr. Barry. I thought she had run off. I was relieved to find Karly was here, safe."

"I was fortunate not to lose her completely."

"Indeed?" Landgon asked with a lift of a brow and frowned hard at Karly. "How many times have I warned you to be more careful?" He swept Warrick a respective bow. "My apologies for any inconvenience she has caused you. I will gladly reimburse you."

"Hardly necessary," Warrick began and broke off when Landgon started forward. He had enough time to step in front of Karly before Landgon reached them, clasped his hand, and shook it heartily.

"You are gracious."

It would be easy to dismiss the man as mad. He had the bearing of a lunatic but the aura of a demon. It was then Warrick realized Karly hadn't spoken. She had remained immobile, her hands balled in her lap.

"Yesterday was my wedding. It left me in an excellent mood," Warrick said.

Landgon looked up and his pleasantry ebbed. "And who is the young lady?"

"Karly—she fell for me the moment we met, did you not, my dear?"

"I believe it was a few minutes later," Karly said, her voice a whisper.

Landgon became ice for several beats as he stared unseeing at Warrick. Then it cracked along with the man's veneer. "The daughter of a pirate married to the son of a duke. It has all the makings of a Shakespearean tragedy." Landgon walked to the corner table, lifted the brandy decanter, and poured a snifter. Swirling the amber liquid, he raised it toward Warrick. "My best wishes toward your happiness," he said and drank the contents, then tossed the glass into the fire.

"We appreciate your kindness," Warrick said and smiled. The conversation was not what he expected. "Baron Landgon, your note said your matter was urgent. How can I assist you?"

Landgon worked his jaw until he grimaced a dead man's grin. "I would like to borrow your wife, for a few months." He straightened and tented his fingers.

"Like a loan?" Warrick slid a hand down to her shoulder, surprised to find it steady. A glance and he saw her chin lifted in defiance. Here was the courage that had driven her up a tree and into his rooms. It would also get her killed. At what point she had moved past terror, he wasn't sure.

"Since we are both men of business, you might call it that."

"And what would you use her for?"

Landgon sat down in the chair across from them and tented his fingers. "She's from Bermuda, and I was considering a holiday. I need a guide. I promise to return her to you, better behaved even. I will even pay you six hundred pounds."

"Rent," Warrick said, furious. Landgon broke into a smile, then laughed and rose, lifting a hand to pat Warrick's shoulder, without a bit of regret for offering to discipline Karly. Closing his fist, Warrick drew back and punched Landgon in the jaw, sending him tumbling backward in his chair. He wanted to wipe the smile from his face. "Stay away from her."

Landgon fell with a curse and wiped the blood from his mouth, droplets spattering his coat. "You misunderstand me, my lord. I want to help you."

"You bruised Karly's jaw the last time you taught her how to behave. Never do it again."

Rolling from the chair, Landgon struggled to his feet. "She was insolent."

"Briggs, my valet, will show you out." Taking Karly's arm, Warrick lifted her to her feet and pressed her toward the garden. Past the tree Karly had scaled, he continued until he reached the farthest corner. Despite it being early spring, this section was wilder. He had asked the gardener to keep it like this. In London he could come here and not feel the crowds. He took her to the gazebo and released her.

"He'll be back. You had the advantage because he was impressed by your title."

"I hit him now because later it won't be as easy." He watched as she walked once around and halted, staring into the dark water of the pond. "You should have warned me before we went in there. Now I understand part of your mistrust for men in power. I'll wager this has nothing to do with you becoming his mistress, although he very well might have raped you in the process." Karly looked stricken and tried to pull back. Taking her arms, he held her still. "Are you trying to kill yourself?"

"No."

"Who drew the ships, and why?"

She laid her hand over his before she collected herself. "The drawings are mine."

He frowned at her, and she frowned back. "It makes no sense. Women choose landscapes, or figures, or horses. A nice flower is far more familiar."

"I lived by the sea my whole life. I can only sketch waves so many times."

"Except you not only sketched them, you noted facts and statistics on each one. Why would you do that? Simple curiosity?"

"My father loved ships. When he did not want to discuss anything else, we could always talk about the last one we had seen. Sometimes he would describe one to me. I would draw until I got it right," she said, her voice softened. "I also drew ships for the yards. It was how I earned money once father was gone."

"If that is the whole truth, why did you not simply tell me?"

"It won't matter. You and Landgon both just need me to get what you want. I won't be used by anyone again." She had not raised her voice, but her words reverberated through him.

"You're wrong. My goals are for the good of England."

"I know, but you will have to find another way that doesn't involve me." She whirled and fled to the house. He took a half step to follow and checked it. Trent would be there to make certain she did not leave. He needed to regain his composure. It was coming very near to shattering. That would be ruinous. With his help she had just fortified the walls erected around her heart.

Starting in the direction of the house he called her name, expecting no answer. He was not disappointed. He tried the greenhouse and continued from there through the various rooms, but there was no sign of her. Concern, anger, fear, and annoyance all slid through him. It didn't help that she had been partially right and he could have handled himself better. Communicating with women had never been a problem before; a smile and some charm had won him whatever he wanted. Not with Karly, and he wanted her. Warrick gave a silent groan at his private admission. Their night together had tantalized his imagination. She was already skittish, assuming the worst of him. If she could read his mind, she would know it was truth.

The shadows had crept the length of the rooms when she finally emerged, standing in the center of the foyer as if she had been there all along. He thought she might have been crying, but when he studied her, he saw no trace of tears, just sadness. He would have preferred the tears. If she would cry, she might let him comfort her. He could hold her again. Instead she kept her distance, remaining at the far end of the room.

"I was concerned about you," he said.

"You mentioned your ship will be arriving soon. Let me visit the *Moorea*. I will draw her for you and prove I am telling the truth."

"Tell me this: what would Landgon want ship drawings for? A reference, or does he plan to copy them, possibly steal them?"

"We didn't discuss it. I'm not sure he even knows about them."

Warrick shook his head. His first reaction was to give her paper and direct her to the scaled ship model in the parlor.

She could draw it, and if she was skilled, the truth would come out, that she was a spy or a conspirator. Neither made sense, however, even as the evidence mounted. It was too early to send her away. He wasn't ready. "As soon as the *Moorea* makes port, we'll go."

Chapter 4

Warrick had hoped to find solace in the stables. He was wrong. The scent of horse and leather couldn't clear his thoughts. Karly had barely touched her dinner and said almost nothing. It was possible she was worried about Landgon, but concern that there was far more at stake had him snatching up a polishing brush despite the fact Judgment's coat already gleamed, with no dust to be found. Murmuring to the stallion, he worked on, surprised when the animal's ears were no longer trained on him, but the doorway.

"Hello?" A shadow stepped clear of the others, dressed in a gown with curves and a sweep of long hair. "Karly."

"I couldn't sleep either. I saw the messenger come and go. Was it bad news?"

"Not at all. My brother's back. The *Moorea* will be at the Isle of Dogs tomorrow." Placing his hand on the stallion's neck, he continued to brush.

"That's good." She sidestepped into the lantern light, toward the wall.

Gray with a dark trim, her gown might have been for mourning, but he doubted it. Far too tattered, it had seen years of wear. He needed to buy her some clothes, even if their time together was short. Since she would most likely refuse his offer, he would send one of her old gowns to Fluke's Dressmakers on Church Street. They could use it for measurements. Judgment stomped his foot and Karly flinched. "You don't like horses?"

"I can ride, but I've never spent time with them. It looks angry."

Warrick extended his hand. "My parents breed racing horses. Judgment wasn't fast enough, so he's mine now. He won't hurt you." As if in agreement, the horse dipped his head to sniff Warrick's boot. With hesitant steps, she crossed to him, giving her fingertips then palm and closing her grip. Hands entwined, he placed them on the stallion's neck and felt the shudder of both. "Don't show fear. You'll make him nervous."

"What?"

Before she could step back, Warrick caught her waist and held her still. "He likes being stroked here." Placing their hands on Judgment's withers, he began to scratch, pleased as the horse lifted his head and curled its lip. "That's his way of smiling."

With her free hand, she stroked the neck. "They have personalities, almost like ships. I hadn't realized."

"Ships are tools." Stunned when she jerked free, he turned to face her.

"Instead of blood in their veins, they have wind in their sails. Ask any sailor. He'll tell you a ship has a life almost like a creature. They even call them 'she.'"

Passion laced her voice. He wanted that jubilance directed at him. Catching himself, Warrick lifted his hands in mock surrender. "You have your point." Removing Judgment's leather halter, he gestured her out of the box stall and closed it behind them. "And I believe you've spent quite a bit of time at sea."

"I want to prove to you about the drawings."

"That would be helpful." She was not paying him any mind however, now staring toward the window, as if she could see the drops of rain that tapped through the darkness. He lingered over her appearance. "Is there something else wrong?"

Karly looked back at him and gave a small sigh. "It isn't right that I am in your bed and you are in the back bedroom." She flushed and dropped her gaze to the floor. "Surely we can share your bed without disturbing one another, like the first night."

"That's not possible." Prepared to leave it at that, when her brows drew together, he stepped to her. A lock had drifted over her shoulder. Claiming it, he held it between thumb and forefinger, toying. "I wish I understood what was going through your head. One moment you're lying in my bed; the next, you're skittering away. I haven't done anything to frighten you, not that I'm aware." He considered her silence. "Someone hurt you. Was it Landgon?" Karly shied. He let her go, but followed her down the aisle.

"As much as you say you want to, you wouldn't understand," she called back over her shoulder.

"Then explain it."

"To someone who only knows how to command, it would do no good." She halted, whirled, her hand over her breast. "You believe I'm being willful, that if you are simply kind to me, it will make a difference. The truth is, I have no choice. I made promises that I can't break, won't break. That is my duty. Whatever you have to do to me, so be it."

He had no handkerchief, so he used his fingers to brush the tears, a shock against her soft skin, and opened one arm. "Come," he offered, but she shook her head. He nudged her nearer. "It's not an order. I'm offering you my shoulder."

Shuddering, she leaned against him, her breath ragged as she fought for control. Twining his hand into her hair, supporting the back of her head, he soothed, stunned how easily the words came. There wasn't time for emotion, but he would do nothing else. Her body curved to his as time and sobs passed, his awareness moving from comfort to the sheer feel of her, from her loins to her head at the curve of his neck. And then her lips moved, kissed the base of his throat.

No other invitation was required. Warrick bent his head and captured her mouth, lifting her to him. It was like arriving somewhere familiar, comforting, until she reached up, her body pressing closer. The storm began, rain intensifying as the heat grew. He only wanted more. He started to draw away, and she followed. Unwilling to deny himself, he wrapped her close, swept his tongue through her mouth, and heard her soft whimper. Arching her to his hardness, he held them together. He had to swallow the moan in his throat when she gave a small squirm, her eyes widening in amazement. "I could take you now," he whispered against her ear.

She jumped, leaned back, her eyes wide and dark, her breath shallow. "I've never done this."

He searched the stable. "We're alone; the hay in the loft is soft. We could go there." But she was already shaking her head. Heated, frustrated, he heaved a sigh. "Is this what you did to Landgon, teased him to anger? It would explain the conversation."

She blinked, both hands bracing on his chest as she caught her breath. It was pointless to defend her innocence. He would never believe her. "I'm a fool, but you're worse." She shoved hard, and he released her. Then she was gone, running through the rain and into the house.

He didn't touch her again until they reached the docks. Picking up the satchel with drawing supplies, he offered his hand. She accepted, a vague smile across her lips. Maybe the prospect of proving a part of her story was easing her mind, but he was in torment. There was so much to be said, but the docks were no place for such discussions. Mountainous piles of boxes, crates, barrels, and sacks piled around them, and everywhere there were people. Men, women, children climbed and clambered, with the sounds of work, the call of poverty. Overhead, seabirds screamed at the intrusion and in the distance, a forest of masts rose so closely together, you could almost cross the Thames without touching the ground. At the edge of Hounds Wharf sat the *Moorea*, and beside her, a double-masted schooner, *L'Ousterous*, on her stern. "It seems my brother caught another ship."

"I was looking at the *Moorea*."

"She is the prettiest in my fleet."

"And the fastest," Karly breathed.

Warrick raised an eyebrow and gave her a long searching look, at the confidence in her voice. "You do know your ships."

"I don't lie much," she answered solemnly.

He stifled a laugh at her outrageous words. She was beyond amazing. "Most of our trade is in spices, deals my father set up years ago when he used to travel to Constantinople."

"But your father is a duke."

"And I am a marquis, but some of us have professions, whether running our estates, investing, or controlling enterprises."

"I didn't realize. I assumed you sat, directed."

If her blush had not been so charming, her words might have bothered him. "To be a good administrator, you have to learn by doing. Father taught me the shipping business, and now it's William's turn," he said nodding toward the tall figure of his brother. The height of his father with the same blue striking eyes, William was hard to miss. He towered over most of the crew, resonating confidence. Warrick caught his eye and waved, and led Karly on deck toward the stern to where his brother stood, talking to a crewman on the smaller ship alongside.

With a chuckle, William slapped Warrick hard on the shoulders. "So this is why you sent me off on *Moorea* and stayed. I hear congratulations are in order. You must be Karly," he said with a deep incline of his head in her direction. "You are lucky I was at sea or I might have married her myself," he added with a wink.

Warrick frowned and met his brother's gaze, before turning to Karly. "William is a flatterer of the worst sort. You should know he has twice been challenged to duel, three times been confronted by angry fathers, and four times by ladies."

"Three times," William countered.

"Four," Warrick said.

"Clarissa did not challenge me. She was merely hurt."

"William, the woman came to Greythorne brandishing a man's cane and threatened to cave your skull, or something like that."

William gave Karly a wounded look. "I was young."

"You are still young," Warrick said with a sigh.

Crossing his arms, William leaned back against a barrel and clucked his tongue. "There now, you are giving my sister-in-law the wrong impression of me. The truth is, Karly, I'm the scoundrel. Warrick's the one with all the responsibility. It makes him cranky at times because he always has to do the right thing. He'd rather be out sailing if he had his way."

"You have ruined my impenetrable air."

With a shake of his head, William laughed. "That was gone long before, or she never would have married you." William gave a good-natured shake of his head and sobered. "Trent arrived an hour ago, rather out of sorts I'm afraid."

Warrick couldn't look at Karly. There had been far too much truth beneath his brother's good-natured teasing. His nature wasn't sedentary, but then neither was his father's. If he could find his way to adventure and dukedom, life might be far more palatable. "In addition to being a family friend, Trent handles the financial dealings for the ships. I'm certain he wants to get to work on the manifest for the *L'Ousterous*. Go ahead, William. I will settle Karly here on deck and be down shortly."

"I prefer the fresh air," Karly added when William scrutinized her.

Warrick led her to where the ropes had been piled while the sails were inspected. "Judging by the talent I saw in your book, this should be no more than an exercise."

"I will do my best," she said. She slid in a heap and rested against the rail, set the satchel on her lap, and peered up at him. "How long will you be?"

Warrick knelt to consider her, his instincts prickling. She stared back, her gaze never flickering. "Not long. If you need anything, the man in the corner beside the trunk is Wreck, the first mate. Tell him to fetch me."

She reached out and touched his hand, her thumb caressing lightly. "It is a ship. Nothing will happen."

If she meant to console, her words had the opposite effect. He couldn't place the feeling, but as he stood, his uneasiness grew. He crossed to Wreck, the weathered seaman cursing as the crew tied the riggings high above. Glancing toward an oblivious Karly, he reminded himself she had most likely heard and probably seen far worse. For the moment, it might be best to let her be, let her surroundings become somewhat familiar. It might make all the difference. Wreck looked up, his leathery face drawn into a question. "Keep an eye on my wife," Warrick said in a low voice, nodding to where Karly sat curled in a ball.

The old man gaped, closed his mouth, and narrowed his eyes. "I'm not a wet nurse."

For two years Warrick had learned the sea under Wreck's watchful eye. Long ago they had reached an understanding. "She's nearly gotten away from me, twice."

Wreck gave an exasperated sigh. "You're too gentle with women."

"Not according to her. I'll be below," Warrick said with a final glance in Karly's direction. Even with the hatches open, it was dark in the passages, the stairs narrow, the wood scented by the sea. He emerged into intense sunlight from the large windows along the stern, to find a desk and table where Trent sat, William beside him. "This can't take long," he announced.

William looked up from where he stood behind Trent at the desk and frowned. "Did you ask Wreck to watch her?"

"Wreck will do his best, but with her I'd rather not take chances. She is not what you would expect."

"Quite the pretty package," William said with a wink. "Did she really drop into your arms?"

Warrick slanted a look at Trent, who glanced away. "She did."

"Landgon is anxious for her?" William asked.

"Landgon tried to threaten me into giving her to him, as if she were a horse or dog. I'm sure she knows what the reason is, but she hasn't said."

"Nevertheless, the king had no business ordering you to marry the creature," Trent said.

It was near painful to remind himself his friend meant well. Trent was looking after Warrick's interest. His comments came from concern. "Careful," Warrick said, lowering his voice. "She's my wife. It's every bit his business since I am the one who asked. But Karly isn't the reason we are down here. It is possible the French are behind the attacks. Tell me about the *L'Ousterous*."

"We found her off the Isles of Scilly, hiding in the eastern islands. According to her log, she came from Calais. Her drawing matches the ship the lighthouse in Dover spotted. The French assumed we took her as privateers, nothing else." William gestured to the ream of papers Trent was considering. "There's what I salvaged from the captain's quarters. It appears to be manifests, a few letters, and some business. Nothing appears out of place."

He took his time to review, but in the end had to agree. Warrick glared at the mantel clock, its black hands reporting an hour had past. "Somehow the pieces fit."

Seated on the long table, William reached for a book and set it alone in the center. "Smugglers are using ships on our coast." He laid a second book next to the first. "Karly is the daughter of a Bermudan pirate who learned from the Barbary pirates. The smugglers are using tactics similar to the Barbary pirates. Karly's uncle works for Landgon. Landgon is interested in Karly." William studied the now line of books. "I agree with you. There are links, and they all point to the woman above. Father may be right. She could be a spy."

Rubbing the back of his neck, Warrick rose and walked to his favorite picture, a gift from Mr. Hasings, the owner of Northington Shipyard where the *Moorea* had been built. It had been used as a working outline and was an artist's rendition showing decks, cabins, beam, and draft from various angles, but it was the notes that tugged his notice and his heart lurched. "These are like the ones I found in Karly's trunk."

"I thought you said she wasn't really an artist."

The sounds from above became a din, with thundering feet and men yelling. "I need to go check on Karly." Warrick ran to the door. He took the stairs to find the *Moorea* shrouded in fog. Crossing to where he had left Karly, he closed on the hunched form only to discover a ruse, a blanket thrown over a nearby sack. Karly was nowhere to be seen. "Where is she?" he demanded as Wreck reached his side.

"She was here a moment ago."

Warrick surveyed the deck. He saw no trace of her. Wreck muttered an apology as Warrick shook his head. "She was waiting for the chance." Furious, he scooped a piece of parchment from the deck and unrolled it. His breath caught at the quick sketch of *Moorea* in Karly's now-unmistakable style, complete with notes in the corner. It was hurried, but it was identical to the yellowed one in his cabin.

Idiot, he chastised himself. He should have made the connection. The fact that she knew his name, her comments about ships, the drawing portfolio had all been clues right in front of him that he had refused to see. He had met her back in Bermuda. His mouth went dry at the memory. The *Moorea* was not finished. The artist had been working on a sketch for the riggers. He had stopped to ask him some questions, and Hasings had appeared immediately. When Warrick had turned, the artist was gone, but the eyes . . .

Footsteps sounded behind him as William arrived. Warrick called her name, circled the deck, and walked the docks nearby. The fog thickened, teasing him with wisps of gray and hints of shapes, but there was no trace of her. He returned to his brother and Trent.

William held out his hand. "Wreck also found this where she was sitting."

Warrick accepted the item and stared at her gold wedding band. His stomach clenched along with his fist. "I shouldn't have left her."

Trent shook his head. "I suppose that is the end of that. The king will grant the annulment without question."

"Ring or not, she is still legally my wife."

Trent rolled his eyes. "Until she gets to Landgon and he whisks her neatly out of reach."

"She's not a spy," Warrick sighed.

Trent exchanged a glance with William and squared his shoulders. "She's lied to you, fooled you with a sad story. I wanted to believe her too. The truth is, the reason the facts don't make sense is because you want her to be innocent. The fact that she ran proves her guilt."

William gave a solemn nod. "It does make sense, and I'm normally not the logical one."

Warrick angled a glance at William. He was squinting at the fog, as if with another look he might find some clue. For the first time since he had found her, reality hit hard. With so much against her, the truth was irrelevant. No one would believe her. He hadn't. Why should the others? "We had better start looking," Warrick snapped, handing the picture to Trent. Without another word he strode down the gangway, fear for her safety lengthening his strides. He doubted Karly even knew where she was going; she was merely running from a world that was decidedly against her. She didn't know London's maze of streets, people, and hazards. Anything could happen to her, and no matter the danger, he was certain she would not return to her uncle. Nor would she go to Landgon. No, she was leaving behind everything and everyone, including him. Warrick set off down the nearest narrow street, its cramped buildings closing around him in the growing darkness.

He had to find her before it was too late.

Chapter 5

Karly slumped against the cold stone building and sank into the shadows as the group of rakes approached, calling for her. In sight, the leader halted, his ghoulish face powdered, damp with fog, illuminated by a street lantern, and turned toward her. She couldn't breathe. Then his friends were there, cackling. The group moved on, their cries for their little "chit" growing more faint. When she was sure they had turned a corner, she bolted in the opposite direction, with no idea where she was headed.

It had been days, and she was still lost. London streets seemed to ramble and turn without any sense or planning; many appeared alike. Her fickle friend had been the fog. It simultaneously chilled and concealed her. There had been no sign of Warrick, but she knew better than to be relieved. He was not the kind of man who relinquished. Given the chance, he would find her, and the patience he had shown would be gone.

Her heart sighed as the shadow of his face drifted across her mind. She had tried to reason her feelings away. She should think of him less. It would make her life easier, but that would mean to forget. There had been good—his touch, the change in his voice when he said her name, the power beneath his softness. A woman could love a man like Warrick, and another woman would have the chance.

Across from where she stood she could see the soft lines of a tavern, its cheery windowpanes alight with a warm glow. Tempted as she was, she wrapped her arms around herself and huddled back. If she was discovered in there, she would be cornered. Besides, she was hardly the sort of customer they would welcome. Her dress was frayed, her shoes were soaked, and her hair hung lifeless over her shoulders. Harlots dressed better than she.

"Lost 're you?" a deep voice cracked close to her ear.

She took two steps in a single breath and stared in horror at the unkempt stranger, his straggled gray hair about his face, standing before her. "I'm looking for someone," she lied.

"I think not, Mrs. Barry. I think you're the one being looked for." The man broke into a toothless grin, "And I think I just earned me one 'undred pounds."

Karly began to back away. "A hundred pounds? For what?"

"For findin' you. That's what your husband promised for your return." He smiled, reaching out to grab her arm.

Karly spun and ran down the nearest alley, bursting into Covent Garden Piazza and a crush of humanity. Prostitutes, drunks, criminals, and every form of society mingled with gentlemen of distinction. Hoping to lose herself in the fray, she kept to the edge, only to be plucked at as she fought her way. She collided hard and peered up to find a stooped older man, his wig to one side, carrying a lantern. His face ragged and pockmarked, he stared darkly at her and opened his mouth to speak. She never slowed, even after she realized he was probably the night watch.

She spent the night in a stall, the scent of hay renewing quiet tears, her tears a balm tending the dull ache in her heart. Perhaps she should have tried harder to find a solution without breaking her father's wishes. It had become too complicated. Landgon's purpose and Warrick's involvement were both worrisome. Sleep came in bouts despite her exhaustion, and she was haunted by nightmares she could not whisk away.

The sounds of a hay cart roused her awake, along with the stirring of horses around her. Karly bade her time and listened until she was sure she was alone before crawling out. She pulled bits of straw from her hair, and ran her fingers through to neaten it. Then she stepped outside, closed the door, and left the stable yard.

She turned left, the brighter of the two directions, and made her way up the alley. A wave of lightheadedness swept over her, and she stopped until it passed. She needed something in her stomach, which was well past the point of protesting. Perhaps she could find a pub where she could wash dishes in exchange for a meal. She walked for a time before she saw one that might suit her needs. Pretty, with potted flowers around the windows, it almost seemed to be welcoming her. She avoided a large puddle and was just about to step up on the shoulder when a quick movement made her look up. She spotted Warrick at the precise instant he saw her. She was off at a full run when she heard him shout her name.

Dull and clumsier than usual, she skidded and fell over an uneven paving stone. Scrambling to her feet she disregarded his hails. But her hopes of a swift escape vanished when she rounded the corner and slid just below William's grasp. Doubling back around the alley, down a tiny tunnel, and over a bridge, she slipped on a wet board and tumbled into Warrick. He dragged her backward and held her to the wall.

"Let go!" Before she could break free, he used the entire length of his body to pin her.

"I don't think so." Presenting her with a piece of straw

from her hair, he frowned. "It looks like you were in a stable. Did you miss me, or Judgment?"

"Oh no, please, Warrick." There was no room to squirm. She met his gaze with all she had left.

"I've been searching London since you disappeared. You don't need to run anymore, I know the truth."

"Landgon told you." From over his shoulder, Karly saw a dark carriage pulled by four bay horses stop at the alley's end. She wished she could sink through the ground as the strength drained from her limbs. "It's to prison then, or are we going straight to the gallows?"

Without an answer, he lifted her into his arms in a fluid motion and carried her to the carriage, placing her on the red velvet seat. Then he climbed up beside her and drew the shade. With a rap on the roof, the carriage rocked forward. She gripped the wall to hold on. There were no clues in his face, and she realized she was too tired to care. There was no time left and only one thing she could do before her spirit shattered completely. Slipping from the seat, she knelt before him on the floor, one hand on his knee.

"I gave you the drawing as a token, since you already knew we had met before. The rest of the story is that I was working at the dockyards for money. My wages supported my father. When his letter of marque was revoked, he didn't know what to do. As he was a privateer, the ships and crews he took were brought safely to the Navy for payment. But he was a terrible pirate. He couldn't kill anyone."

The carriage lurched left. Warrick grabbed her shoulder, steadying her. "Landgon tells a different story."

"Of course, and being the honest man that he is, it rang true." She dropped her gaze. "Your sort are all the same. So long as someone has a title in their name, he can do no wrong, even when you know he's guilty."

"You're tired, or you wouldn't have forgotten I'm the one investigating him."

She seized his hand and held it. "Landgon is your enemy. When my father raided his ship, it was under a French flag. He wouldn't have attacked anything British. Ask yourself why a British baron would hide his nationality. I'd wager Landgon is behind the smugglers too."

"Your father's ship had an entire crew. If Landgon was concerned about someone turning him in, wouldn't he have murdered them all?"

"He might try." Her breath froze as the carriage stopped. She felt the brake engage, the box rock as the driver jumped down. Voices sounded about them, and then she heard the knob turn above the din of her pounding heart. Light shone in as the door swung open.

"Are you hurt?"

"No, I'm well," she snapped and looked away.

"Are you hurt?"

The sound of his voice, the lack of an assurance was more than she could bear, and she couldn't answer.

He laid both hands on either side of her face, directing her gaze. "You need rest; then we'll talk some more."

The tears she had managed to keep at bay welled and then broke. She swiped at them, but they wouldn't leave her alone. And then she saw the house, the courtyard, both familiar. "This isn't prison." He reached for her waist, and she batted him away. "You lied to me."

"I got what I needed. You did most of the talking."

Karly climbed down and peered about her, blinking at the gleaming windows, one hand over her mouth. "Why are we here? Take me to prison. I'm not afraid, I've been there before."

"We'll discuss this inside." He started across the courtyard and glanced back over his shoulder.

Behind her, the driver waited expectantly, two footmen beside the gate, and a wall around them. But she was too tired to run, almost too exhausted for the stairs to the first level. Anger gave her the power, even as her legs cried in protest. She would not admit weakness, half pulling herself using the banister. Instead of left, into the study, she followed Warrick down the back gallery and into a large closet adorned in green damask and covered with paintings and miniatures. Crossing her arms, she faced him as he closed and locked the door. "There's no reason for that. I'm too tired to do much."

He lifted a brow, circumventing her position to the far wall, and halted before a painting of the Atlantic, scrutinizing it. "Bermuda's a port with no real wealth. Why would Landgon be interested?"

"For the same reason my father used it as his base." She crossed and placed her finger on the map, between Bermuda and Europe. "All come this way from the Caribbean. They're full of everything from spice to gold. It's a fortune. I'm sure both the French and the Spanish would love to end privateer raids on their merchants."

Slowly he turned. "Capture Bermuda, turn it French, and the balance of power would shift."

"Landgon is the sort who could do it; I doubt anyone could stop him." Weary, drained, she sat on the black chair against the wall. She was an ocean away with nothing else to do. Placing her head in her hands, she closed her eyes and let the shards of her soul fall where they may. Tomorrow she would decide what to do next.

Chapter 6

There was no reason to keep her. Warrick had what he needed, but not what he wanted. He paced outside the door to Karly's bath as if he could outpace frustration. He had used Karly like a pawn. He had pushed too hard. In defense, he had little choice. He had bluffed. It had been a guess, not a trick. The confession was all hers. He had done his duty and could annul the marriage with a clear head, but his heart felt murky.

He stopped and listened. An unmistakable splash on the other side of the door assured him Karly was there. It was optimistic to assume a warm bath, fresh clothes, and a meal would remove the stains of terror. Sleep had brought her nightmares, and she thrashed in bed despite her condition. He picked up a book and tried to bury his mind in the pages while he waited. The words held no meaning and he flipped to the beginning of the chapter to start again.

Warrick felt her presence even before he turned. Framed in the doorway she had arrived silently, buried in his dark maroon dressing gown. She met his gaze and walked forward, her bare feet only just visible at the beginning of each stride. Everything else was hidden, including her state of mind. He rose to a hint of rosewood and forced a smile.

"I trust you feel much improved," he said and gestured to a covered tray. "Something to eat?"

"I was hoping you wouldn't come." She sank to the ground, facing the fire. "It would have been for the best."

He crouched beside her, but thought better and sat nearby. The flames highlighted the torment in her eyes, his fault. "We're going to cooperate."

Karly opened her mouth as if she was going to speak, but closed it, sitting quietly for a while. Lacing her hands together, she cast her eyes down and shook her head. "I cannot help you."

"So you said before," he frowned. Her vehemence warmed his heart—any emotion meant hope. "I missed you."

She exhaled a soft laugh that rippled across his soul. "After all the trouble I have been?"

"Perhaps that is the point. Boring you are not." Reaching into his breast pocket he withdrew the wedding ring. He caressed her hand and singled out her ring finger. "You are still my wife."

"By the king's command," she said as he slipped it on her finger.

Warrick gazed past her smoky lashes and into her eyes, which fascinated him. The nights she had been gone, he had seen those eyes in his dreams, but had not remembered the gold flecks. He moved closer, tucking damp tendrils of her hair behind each ear. "You accepted me as your husband. Therefore you have an obligation to me as well."

"Trickery, persuasion, and now bullying," she said, pulling free and wrapping her hands around her body.

He walked to the bed where he had left the strongbox and motioned for her to follow. Unlocking it, he withdrew the papers and looked up. He rustled them in her direction. "Here is everything written that I have gathered during my investigation." She gave him her full attention, moving closer. "Here is the chancellor's document authorizing me to act as necessary to stop the smugglers. A copy of the king's letter, ordering our marriage, and this," he said, laying the first aside and picking up another, "is from the Ambassador John Adams for the newly formed American government, granting his assistance. Based on your information, I've added reports of French movements, as well as letters and documents we have intercepted over the last three years. And finally," he pointed to the last five heavily creased papers, "what we found hidden on *L'Ousterous*."

"You acted on what I told you?"

"The Admiralty already has files. They sent over a summary this morning. Before I can order Landgon's arrest, I need proof. I need to make certain that when I make a recommendation, I have all the facts and all the culprits. We have no precise details on what his plans are, only your guess, which I believe is the most likely explanation."

Her hands unwound, and she cocked her head at him. "So I'm not the spy, you are."

Warrick set the papers down and sat on the edge of the bed. "William went after the *L'Ousterous* because she was mentioned at a party by the French ambassador when he believed no one was listening."

"A French ambassador discussing a ship at a party in England sounds like a decoy."

"The party was in France," Warrick countered.

"That's all?" she said as she searched his face.

He could spare her more questions but it was ludicrous to hesitate now. "His interest in you is still a bit of a mystery. It's more than lust."

Karly shook her head. "I'm sorry. I don't know," she breathed, her voice not even a whisper.

He cupped her face in his hands. "Anyone who deals with Landgon disappears or dies. You'll be next." With his thumbs he stroked her cheeks and brushed his lips over her brow. She closed her eyes. He kissed each lid before easing to her mouth. "I am worried for you." He frowned.

"So you have said, along with other things."

Her resolve had become a fortress, guarding her in nearly every form. He wasn't sure how to proceed. "We can resume this in the morning. I will leave the documents with you. Read whatever you want."

"You cannot expect me to trust you after what happened, and I'm not hungry," she said, glaring at the covered tray of food set out for her.

"Cook's excellent. She baked for you." He pulled the cover off and studied the rounds of bread, bowls of strawberries and pudding, and a pot of cream. In the center was a large teapot. Taking a seat on the sofa, he chose the nearest cup and poured for himself.

Karly hesitated a moment longer, then sat on the floor and claimed a roll, nibbling, her eyes on him. "She's very talented."

Taking a risk, he poured a second cup and offered it, glad she didn't refuse. "I should have been gentler." Awkward, he grasped a roll and bit in heartily.

"You have priorities."

Swallowing the food and his pride, he looked up. "That doesn't excuse brutality."

"You didn't hit me, beat me, or use torture. I'm not injured."

"I'm trying to apologize."

"I know." She studied her tea. "It isn't necessary."

Frustrated, he set down his cup and walked toward the door. "I'll be one bedroom over, if you need anything." Unwilling to face her or the pain that he had caused, he left her to the rest of the evening and morning, responding instead to an urgent summons from William.

* * *

He arrived to find an outraged customs inspector, his robust form stiff, buttons glistening in the sun. In his hand was a stack of papers. Before him, William stood arguing, while two other inspectors guarded the gangways, the brilliant sun holding no warmth. Warrick pasted on his most cordial smile and faced the leader, the one holding the Port of London regulations.

"Inspector Morgan, how may I be of assistance?"

"Your lordship can explain to your brother that we need the documents from both ships before either can be clear." He waved his hand, and the papers rattled in the breeze. "These rules cannot be broken."

"The paperwork is not here I am afraid," Warrick said as Trent arrived. "I have them at my residence. If you like, you can view them there, perhaps over a glass of port?"

"Not here?" The inspector bristled, and his eyebrows drew together in a large bushy line as his chest swelled, forcing his coat outward. "That is not the procedure. All seized ships must have their cargo cleared by our office first. We have five other ships waiting today." The man reddened and clutched the papers tightly.

The anger raw, Warrick regrouped, sliding a glance at William to be quiet. "Inspector, you have my sincerest apologies. I recall our last meeting. You've always been thorough. I will send a note immediately and request the accounting be sent to you. You can make yourselves comfortable in the great cabin."

"What, here?" Morgan blustered.

"I'll have some provisions sent, and you can relax."

"We have a schedule, my lord. I suppose we can take an accounting as you unload. It will take a bit more time, but I could send for two more inspectors. It will cost thirty pounds."

"Thirty pounds?! Your conduct is outrageous," William snapped.

Warrick nudged him before he could continue. "You should charge us forty." He shot William a look, silencing him. With a mock shrug he gestured toward Trent and the waiting French ship. "My man will show you the way."

"That was bloody clever. Father's right—you will make a marvelous duke someday." William watched as Morgan and his staff moved on. "You handle people brilliantly."

"Not all of them, unfortunately."

Shielding his eyes with his hand, William watched the men move on, the inspectors beginning their work and a crewman heading off to fetch more. "So where are the documents? I thought they were here."

"I took them to Karly. She's reviewing them as we speak."

"Are you sure that's wise, after all that's happened? She could sell them or blackmail us using any one of them. It took us a week to find her the last time."

For all their common experience, he had been sure William wouldn't agree. He had been prepared, but he waited before answering. It would be better if William reached the conclusion on his own. "She's better than that."

"I hope you are right."

"So do I. It's possible I've been too rough with her, that I won't get anywhere at all."

"But you handle women brilliantly." William winked and lengthened his stride to catch the inspector and join Trent, who was overseeing the unloading.

Warrick stayed on the fringe as cargo was brought up and placed in large stacks and piles about the deck to be opened, inspected, and logged. It gave him time to reflect and deepened his guilt. He might not have physically harmed her, but he had hurt her, cruelly. The thought that he might be no better than Landgon, using her toward an end, wouldn't leave. His mind was in the midst of the situation, or he might have recognized Karly sooner. Already on deck, the silence of the men made him turn, acknowledge a beautiful woman, and then look closer. Karly had spun her hair loosely about her shoulders and down her back. The soft green silk dress he had ordered accentuated her beauty, clung to the curve of her bodice and waist, and blossomed about her hips while gossamer white trimmed her neckline and arms. She might have been a visitor to St. James, except she lacked the necessary hat. He opened his mouth to speak when she caught the lapel of his coat in hands and buried her face against his chest. He drew her in and felt a rush of satisfaction that layered beneath a tumult of emotions at her appearance.

"You're trembling," he said.

"I needed you."

A chill speared his heart, chasing away any hope. "Is it Landgon?" Her answer was a tug at his coat toward the railing. He forced himself to calm and let her guide him before he could stand no more and stopped her. "You were to remain at the house. Why would you run off again?"

"I didn't run off. I came here."

"Alone," he said between clenched teeth and searched the dock to make certain he was right. None of his household staff was to be seen.

She shook her head and faced away from the group of men working on deck. "It would not wait. I read the documents you left. The rum from the French ship is booby-trapped." She blinked at him and wet her lips. "Do you understand? When you try to open it, someone will be killed. You need to warn them."

At first, he wasn't sure he believed her. But the truth was in her eyes, the set of her lips, her brow. She was frightened, for him. Warrick looked up and saw the inspector approaching, Trent dogging his side. "All right, follow my direction." He lifted his hand to the back of her neck, pressing his shoulder to her back as the men arrived. The curve of her thigh molded to his, as if the petticoats didn't exist, the suggestion of her flesh heating him.

"Is there a problem?" the inspector demanded.

Selfishly he tucked her closer, moving himself between her and the threat, and decided to keep her from the fray. Whatever had brought the knowledge to her, it would be between them, later. Better not to let the inspectors turn their attention on her. "This is my wife. I'm afraid she is rather emotional. Her cat just died. It was rather old, but females can become attached to their pets." Warrick placed a light kiss on the top of Karly's head.

"My apologies, my lady." The inspector whisked off his hat and gave a quick bow. "I lost a dog myself a few years back. Good creature, never set a paw wrong. With all due respect, sir, we must continue."

Warrick nodded, keeping his arm firmly around Karly's waist as his men moved off. "Stay here in case anyone's watching. I don't want people to realize you are the one who warned me."

She lifted her head to regard him with a frown. "Why should it matter?"

"Later," he hissed and watched as the men opened crates and boxes for the officer, who was checking and assessing each. When they reached the rum, Warrick released her and gestured William forward. The barrels stood in a long line and appeared, at first glance, rather unremarkable: American oak, fifty gallons, bound with six steel hoops, with *Ron* for rum marked in dark letters and the distiller's stamp. Nothing seemed out of place. Unsure, he glanced at Karly. Her fists balled; she stood with rapt intensity. Pursing his lips he studied the rum and scrubbed his chin. Then he took several steps away. "There's something wrong here, seems these have been booby-trapped," he announced. "Everyone should stay back until we determine the nature of the device."

"You are not serious?" the customs inspector blustered as he retreated along with the crew.

Warrick approached the rum with care. He knelt beside the cask to study the design.

"Why booby-trap rum?" William asked as nonchalantly as possible as he and Trent knelt by Warrick.

"I take it *she* gave you this information?" Trent added.

Warrick ignored the question and channeled his annoyance. Trent's doubts were becoming tiresome. Later they would talk. Instead, Warrick focused on William. "There is no reason, unless you were protecting something else. The grain on the wood is not consistent after the third ring. It appears as though there might be a false bottom hiding something beneath."

William stood immediately and retrieved a wedge bar, but Warrick caught it from him.

"Here now . . ." William protested.

"An older brother's prerogative. Besides, I do not want to be the one who explains to father if anything happens to you."

"If something goes wrong, you had better hope it kills you. Father won't be your biggest problem. Mother will."

Warrick met his brother's gaze. Through the chides and banter, he saw the fear and squeezed his brother's shoulder. "If we are careless, neither of us will have to face anyone save Saint Peter," Warrick said and glanced again at Karly. She had moved closer into the circle, her mouth drawn with tension and her cheeks pale. He waved her away, but she gave a terse shake of her head in response. There was no hope. She wasn't moving. Proud, angry, Warrick knelt and studied the cask, pointing to the bottom third. "Do you see the metal clip at the edge of the ring?" Warrick asked.

William nodded. "You think it is a trigger device?"

"I wouldn't doubt it. We need to be careful." Warrick glanced up at the group of spectators and found Karly chewing hard on her lower lip. She released it, crossed her arms, and returned his gaze. The woman was stubborn, but her confidence buoyed his hopes. She had come to him, despite all that had happened. He took the wedge bar and slid it behind the ring. With slow continuous pressure, he bent it apart from the cask.

"They're two separate drums," William said.

Warrick peered at the newly formed gap. "There's a hammer here that must create the spark for an explosive device. I think it's disarmed, but ease the bottom loose slowly," he instructed William and Trent. He placed his hands on both sides of the cask to steady it.

"You ready?" Trent asked.

Warrick gave him a nod, and they worked, lifting the top two-thirds of the barrel free. The false bottom was stuffed with straw. "What do we have here?" He avoided the disarmed explosive and reached for the carefully nested silver bottles. Lifting one, he stood and unscrewed the cap, sniffing, and shook his head. "There's no scent."

"The marking is the symbol for death," Karly said, having moved to Warrick's side.

"Death for opening or it is used for death?" Trent asked.

William shook his head. "Anyone opening it without knowing what they were doing would have been blown to pieces. It could be some kind of poison."

"So the rum would all be destroyed?" gasped the inspector.

"It is more likely water. Rum is too valuable," Warrick said. "Anyone trying to open it this way would cause a spark from these edges, and the entire top would blow in their face."

"You were right to be careful. Never can trust these French ships," the inspector said.

"The tap hole is likely rigged, too."

"I will have to impound these, your lordship." The inspector waved his colleagues forward.

Warrick frowned as they took up their positions. "Very well, just make certain they stay well guarded. Whomever they were intended for might try to retrieve them."

"Here in England?" the inspector said, lifting an eyebrow.

"That depends on how difficult they are to replace. Use care."

Warrick watched the man give orders to the other inspectors and then stride down the gangway. "He does not even know what is in those bottles."

"Perhaps you had better take Karly away from here," William said quietly. "Maybe Murdock might know something. This is his sort of trouble."

"You're leaving?" Trent asked.

Warrick held one of the silver bottles in his palm for Trent to see. He had all he needed to investigate further, but he did not want the inspectors to know he had taken one of the bottles. It would mean questions. "It's a bit dangerous down here for her, don't you agree?"

"I am quite well," Karly said and began to pull away.

Warrick cast a grim smile at William and Trent, then took Karly's right arm and patted it. "A bit more color in your cheeks and I will agree with you."

"But . . ."

"I would like you to come with me," Warrick interrupted, keeping his words firm as he showed her the bottle. Her eyes widened.

"A walk would do me good."

He led her off the ship and into London. They passed through crowds, and he kept her close, not merely as a precaution in case they were being followed. He knew he shouldn't be glad to have her with him. They were not in the best part of town, nor was she yet in the best of health. But he felt a twinge of giddiness, like a schoolboy with a crush. It was lunacy. Despite that knowledge, he reveled in it.

"How is it that you have never had a pet?" Warrick asked to ground himself. "Most ships have cats."

"Not ours. My father didn't like animals."

"What about you?" he asked as they backtracked. "Do you like animals?"

Karly knitted her brow and looked around. He saw realization in her eyes as she recognized his ploy. "I don't know any," she announced suddenly. She caught Warrick's stern frown and wet her lips.

Warrick dodged a group of men and a large puddle while he considered the sadness in her voice. "We've always had cats in the buttery and stables, horses, sheep, and cows in the barn."

"You sound more like a farmer."

He kept to the busy streets until they reached a more distinguished part of town. "In here," he directed and ushered her inside a coffeehouse, pressing her past the men gathered to take in the news and drink and into a corner table. With his body and the partition, she was shielded from view. Ordering two mugs of coffee from the nosy barmaid, he searched Karly's face intently until they were alone. "Tell me about the rum. It's important how you knew about the trap." Karly appeared distracted by the scene around her. He reclaimed her hand, stroking the back of it with his hand until she looked at him.

"On the manifest, the casks contained the code for danger."

Warrick frowned. "I didn't see anything unusual."

"It is rather obsolete," she said, shifting awkwardly, and tucked her hair back.

"You're hiding something, Karly. I can tell."

"You will start claiming my father is a pirate again, and he wasn't."

"I'll hold my tongue." He gave her what he hoped she would take as an encouraging look and waited.

The mugs arrived, steaming. She reached for hers, and toyed with the handle. Lifting it, Karly took a sip and set it down with a dull clunk. "The system works as a warning. Certain symbols are put in letters and words, but not in the right place. You can find them when you know how to look. It's a sort of courtesy among pirates. On the manifest, the rum was listed by containers, not casks. That told me where the danger was. At the bottom of the page was an inverted *y*, which meant death."

"So the question becomes: what is in the vials?" He removed the small silver vessel and toyed with it. "Any ideas?"

Karly shook her head, and boldly met his gaze.

He leaned back in his chair and considered her with care. "I'd like your help, not because of your father, but because you are good with people."

"Not in the same way you are."

"Precisely. They look at me as a lord. You are . . ."

"Common?"

"One of them," he corrected and assessed her reaction, glad when she turned reflective. "I will ask that you promise to stay with me. It won't be the best sort of town. Do we have a bargain?" The words were no sooner spoken than he hoped she might say no. He did not want her harmed, but it was too late to take back his offer. If he did, the fragile trust he had just forged with her would vanish. He had to wait and hope silently for her to refuse, but he knew it was pointless, even before she nodded. And his life just became more complicated.

Chapter 7

It was late morning, but no sun broke through this part of town. London Bridge to Graveshead was a labyrinth of unreality and warehouses, hidden beneath the vapors of mist and smoke. It was the heart of his business, though his sort rarely frequented this area, choosing the clubs and polished halls of the Exchange. Here Warrick learned about dealings long before they reached the marble halls uptown. Too much cargo, a payment that went astray, an unhappy paymaster all found their way here first, where his friends like Murdock waited.

It was selfish to bring Karly. Even with her background, she was out of place. But the way she held his sleeve, barely a touch that anchored her to him, was impossible to break.

"And now you get to learn one of my secrets." Warrick nodded toward the building behind the hops exchange. "It belongs to an acquaintance named Murdock Mooreland. I'm not certain what he called himself before that. He has been trading from this location for over three years—some of it legitimate."

"He is a friend of yours?"

"He helps me. I keep him out of Newgate."

"You blackmail him."

Warrick startled, then chuckled. "He claims to be improving his morals, and I give him the opportunity. He does try to stay out of trouble and succeeds most of the time. Truth is, he's become an excellent source of information."

"How is sound business operation a secret?"

"I met Murdock years ago when he was stealing from gentlemen's pockets, including mine. I caught him, and met his wife and three children. I found him work; he repaid me with tidbits." He opened the door and ushered her inside. Musty air laced with salt greeted them as they moved into the lair. The smell was followed by the dank draft from outside. Crates were piled to the ceiling, and as he walked he examined the emblems, of many countries, on the side.

"How anyone finds their way through here is a mystery," he said.

"A man would have to work very hard to build up this much trade in a few years." She slid him a sideways glance. "Unless someone was funding him."

"I may have offered him a loan, long since repaid." His voice trailed off as he spied a crack of light. A few more corners and he found what he was looking for. Hunched at a small rickety desk, Murdock was reading from a ledger almost bigger than himself. His hair had thinned, pulled too many times, and his face was nearly pressed up to the pages. From his perch, his feet didn't touch the ground. Warrick led Karly until they were alongside the figure and cleared his throat.

Murdock cried out, leapt from his desk, and inadvertently tossed his quill to the side. He peered around until his gaze settled on where they stood, clutching his chest. "That was cruel. It was, Markee. I startle easily. I do, always have."

"I'm surprised I was able to sneak up on you," Warrick said, chuckling.

"It's my ears, not what they should be. Got sick last month, and they're not the same." Murdock's eyes slid over

Karly before he brandished a large smile. "Did you bring me a present?"

"Karly is my wife. We were married a few days ago."

Murdock crossed to Karly and reached for her hand. To Warrick's surprise, she did not draw back. "Markee's a good 'um there. He'll take care of you, took care of me right well."

"Why do you call him Markee? That isn't his name."

"Aye, but I know him too well to call him lordship and not enough for Warrick. That leaves his title, Markee." Murdock raised her hand to his lips, brushed it, then patted.

Warrick cupped his palms around Karly's shoulders and stepped forward until her back pressed against his chest, warm and alive. "I need your help."

"In a moment—I've a treasure for you. Got it yesterday. Too fine for my lady but will match yours," he blurted and scurried back, a candle in one hand, disappearing from view.

"I like him."

"Odd, but I thought you might." Warrick followed Murdock's voice, which beckoned them until they reached several large and ornate trunks.

"Robbins brought these in. Came from a French merchant ship near Saint Martin bound for some fluffy female shop. Before you ask, all the paperwork's been filed, inspected it meself," he said, raising a finger toward Warrick. "Would make a lovely trousseau, judging by your . . ." He paused as his gaze wandered appreciatively over Karly's figure. A frown from Warrick turned his attention back to the trunks. He worked to open the first trunk, reached in, and drew out an emerald gown, offering it to Karly for inspection.

She touched the delicate fabric, finely brocaded, and immediately pulled back. "It's lovely, and I would ruin it."

"Why don't you look while Murdock and I have a word?"

He caught Murdock's elbow and drew him to the side. At first he watched Karly as she extracted a pair of silk stockings. Her blush was intoxicating. With a pretty tilt of her chin, she moved to the furthest trunk and continued her perusal. The collection would suit Karly. "How much?"

"For you, Markee, two hundred pounds."

"Robbins will have you on charges. I would prefer not to have to go before the magistrate yet again on your behalf."

"It's only been three times, and the last one wasn't my fault. I've been good." His face lit. "Laura would tan me if I was anything but."

"She's a good woman."

"I'd not trade her for my left arm. I owe that to you. Take the trunks. The deal's mine." He glanced at Karly. "You've done right by yourself, but you need to show her off better."

"Five hundred will keep you from trouble. My man will pay you with delivery." The matter closed, he reached into his pocket, removing the silver vial from the rum, and presented it to Murdock. "What can you tell me about this?"

Murdock's hand quaked as he accepted it and glanced over it once. "Looks like perfume," he said with an unconvincing shrug and tried to hand it back. "Put it back wheres you found it an' forget."

Warrick raised an eyebrow. "You and I both know this is not perfume."

Murdock paled. "This is trouble," he said and offered it again.

Warrick lowered his voice to a dangerous whisper. "An entire shipment of rum was booby-trapped and hiding vials like these. William intercepted it based on information overheard from the French ambassador."

Murdock rolled his eyes helplessly. "They're poison, Markee. Add a drop to ale and you guarantee death in hours. Each of these," he held up the vial, "has thirty doses in each vial."

"I appreciate your efforts."

He nodded toward Karly. "Don't you want to know about your lady? She's not long for here."

Warrick watched Karly examining a blue silk gown, its color rippling in the low light. "What have you heard?"

"Her uncle was hired by Landgon. Her father was a pirate, Bermuda and Caribbean mostly."

"None of that is new," Warrick said.

"Someone put a bounty on her, a thousand pounds, dead only."

Warrick stared at Karly in horror then in growing fury. He felt ill from the dizzying speed at which his mind was racing. "Landgon?"

"It's word of mouth with the Black Quay as the place to go with the body."

"Find me a name. I will handle it from there," Warrick said simply.

"I'll see what I can do," Murdock said at last and strode toward Karly. There he reached into the trunk and held up the first thing he caught. "You will be lovely at the theater in this."

Gaping, she accepted the sheer chemise. "Thank you."

Murdock dove his hand back into the trunk and withdrew a white shawl inlaid with threads of gold. "I'm a fool, and you, my dear, are gracious. I meant to show you this."

Warrick lifted one of the boxes Karly had examined and studied the brass sextant. "Nice instrument," he said and offered it to her.

"Is it?" Karly asked.

Warrick turned it over thoughtfully and gave her a deliberate frown. "There will come a time when the secrets will have to stop."

"Everyone has secrets, even you," she gestured about them.

"Mine won't get me killed." He took her elbow, escorting

her toward a distant corner. "Besides Landgon, who else knows you're here in London?"

Karly's lips parted. She gave a small shake of her head.

"That's not an answer."

"My uncle and Landgon," she said, frowning with confusion.

"If Landgon thought he couldn't get his hands on you, what would he do?"

"I . . ."

"What about the crew of your father's ship?"

"I told you, they're in Bermuda."

"But you can't be sure. They could be here. They could be the smugglers."

"I don't know any smugglers."

She started to turn from him, but he caught her arm and whirled her back, bringing her face within inches. Ready to challenge her about the bounty, he saw her fear. "They come ashore at night, bring knives, slice the throat of anyone they meet. Mostly they carry wines, since the tariff on them is the highest. Does any of it sound familiar?"

Karly shook her head. "They're in Bermuda. They wouldn't leave; they promised."

"And you believe them. I had best get you home," he said. He ushered her to a cab and pressed her into the darkness. As they rattled through the streets of London, he studied each nuance of her face and wondered what she could have done to warrant her death for such a handsome sum. He gathered his thoughts. Before he could reopen the conversation, he spotted the familiar, flamboyant coach with a team of palomino horses. Karly had already seen it, but he could still order the coach on.

"It belongs to Amanda Claridge, who had hopes of becoming my duchess."

"She'll be relieved when you explain the annulment

clause." Karly climbed down as the carriage halted, not waiting for assistance.

"It ended a while ago," Warrick said, wincing inwardly at the harshness in his voice. He followed her into the house.

"Your brother is in the library. Miss Claridge is in the kitchens, speaking to the staff," Briggs said with authority.

"Karly, join William. I will follow shortly," Warrick said, but she had already left. He set off for the kitchens, preparing himself for the worst. He was not far off. Amanda had placed the entire staff of the kitchens in a line. With a swish of her skirts she was prowling the formation like a general preparing for battle. She halted and, in a sweet voice, lectured on the ills of cool coffee and warm ale.

"Amanda, this is a surprise," he said quietly.

She spun and let out a gasp, pressing her hand to her chest just above the neckline of the bright yellow muslin.

"Warrick! I was wondering when you would return. The staff and I were just having a chat. I hope you don't mind, but while I was waiting, I noticed a few things. I decided to take care of them for you."

"I heard," he said.

Her smile became brilliant. "Come and have something to eat. You must be famished." With a forced merry air, she glided to his side. Locking her arms through his, she led him toward the dining room, where she pulled the doors closed. "I missed you." She draped her arms around his neck and raised her face to his. Their lips met before he could speak as she stroked his mouth with her tongue, seeking entrance.

He gripped her shoulders and set her from him, his irritation thrumming in his ears. "How's Andrew?"

She lifted one shoulder and frowned. "I haven't seen him since that night. It was outlandish behavior, I know. I believed all of his flattery, every word. I never meant to hurt you."

"I doubt you thought of me at all," he said, remembering her on the garden bench, her legs on either side of Andrew Kent, head thrown back.

"You were jealous, poor darling."

"Actually, the emotion was more relief."

Amanda swept closer with a half turn. "You're clever, and I heard, married." Pursing her lips, Amanda perched on the chair and bent slightly forward. She poured the tea with a practiced hand. Straightening, she offered it to him as he sat across from her. "Have you known her long?" she asked while she poured her own cup, took a bit of sugar, and set it down.

Warrick took a sip before answering. He thought of his first glimpse of Karly, hidden beneath grime and all that had occurred since. Dull did not suit her at all. "No. Not long."

Amanda lifted her cup and balanced it neatly, tilting her head with a dramatic sigh. "My father thinks this is an attempt on your part to bring me to heel." She set the cup down and reached for his hand. "You know we are a good match."

"Your father found out about your lovers then."

Amanda turned to ice, frozen in place for a long beat; then she set her cup down and clasped her hands together. "None of them have a title. You do. It's as simple as that. I heard your Bermudan girl doesn't have one either. So if you marry me, my father will be happy. I'm sure your family will be more than satisfied with my dowry. I will even let you keep your new friend."

"And you will go back to your 'friends,' I suppose."

Amanda smiled, her blue eyes melting away the frost. "There, see, we understand each other."

"No, Amanda, we do not. But I do have one question.

After your father ordered you to come here and sort things out with me, is there any chance he took a bounty on my bride?"

She rose quickly. "My father is a viscount, not a villain." Amanda clasped her hands in front of herself, pressing her bosom farther forward still. "Warrick, dearest, I don't want to quarrel," she began.

He intercepted her before she could embrace him a second time, and kept his gaze up, away from her breasts. "In that case, I'll call for your coach." He walked toward the door, opened it, and waited. Amanda remained motionless, trapped between seduction and outrage. She approached with a sway in her hips, coming near, giving him time to appreciate each curve. When she was close, she leaned into him and brushed against his chest, caressing his cheek.

He was not unaffected by her earlier kiss. His body recognized a beautiful woman, and his memory recalled their past. But there was no more than the hollow remnants of what he had once considered reasonable comfort. "Good evening," he said gently. She pulled back, and he saw the anger behind her blue eyes. With a lift of her chin, she swept out of the house. Warrick heard the clatter of the horses' hooves in the street. He entered the foyer to find William leaning against the marble statue of a thinker in the corner of the foyer.

"Where is Karly?" he asked, glancing around.

"With Trent. He seems to be warming to her." William straightened his tall frame. "Amanda guilted you."

"She was disappointed," Warrick said and quickly reviewed what he had learned.

"If Karly serves no other purpose, getting rid of Amanda would be well worth all the trouble she has caused."

"You speak of Karly as if she were no more than a pawn," Warrick said and sat in front of the fire.

"You're rather fond of her. Are you sure that's wise?"

William scrubbed his chin. "The best spies are masquerade artists. And she is hiding something—information she may never share."

"Everything, everyone is new to her, including myself. She seems to want to do right, provided I can keep her alive." He sighed. "She may not live long enough to make any difference."

"Has it occurred to you that this bounty could be a ruse as well? She could have made it up herself or had her uncle order it to deflect your suspicions."

"To fool me into thinking she has an enemy, and thus let my guard down? Yes, it has."

"She could be an assassin. Landgon's clever. He could have sent her to win your confidence. She kills you and Landgon loses his biggest opponent."

"You would not avenge me?" Warrick smiled.

"This is a serious conversation," William said and sat in the leather chair across from him. "Of course I would avenge you. Get her out of London to a place where she has fewer options and get the truth."

"I have the investigation. I cannot simply leave."

"Both Trent and I are here. We will follow your directions and then join you in a few days with our discoveries. At Greythorne you will have Mother and Father as extra eyes; they will help discover answers, then you can annul the marriage," William said in a logical tone. "You've got a tiger by the tail," he quipped. "But an intriguing one, I'll grant you that."

"Suppose I choose to keep her?" Warrick glanced up the stairs.

"There are prettier women."

"I haven't seen one since I met her, but it's more than her appearance. I keep asking myself if another wife would suit me better, and the answer's always no."

"It's only been a few days. Could it just be you're angry at Amanda?"

"I never loved Amanda."

"Do you love Karly?"

It was the hardest question. "I can't say yes, but I'm not ready to say no."

"Let me ask you this. Why didn't you tell her about the bounty?"

"I was angry, and I thought I was keeping her safe."

William cracked a grin. "Love doesn't always come in a moment."

Chapter 8

"William's right," Karly said, breaking the silence that rested between them. "I could kill you. It would be easy. I sleep in the next bedroom."

Warrick looked up from across the carriage. "Why not now? We're alone. Afterwards you could disappear into the forest. No one would find you."

"I'm lacking a letter opener." She faced the window of the coach, hating the anger. Warrick had defended her to his brother. Still, their words haunted her.

"How much of last night's conversation did you hear?"

"All of it. Eavesdropping is quite useful. You only tell me what you want me to know." The air felt like rain, and she longed for it. Rain would mirror her mood. Then she could walk outside and cry, and no one would be wiser. Tears came far too easily these days. She hated each one but today she could make an exception. She should be numb after the last few months, but her heart wouldn't settle. A cry would help.

Warrick rose and slid beside her, pointing out the window. "There's Greythorne."

A great house etched into view, immense, spreading onto the land like a stream through the middle of a clearing.

Trees flanked either side, dotting the park and thickening around clearings and pools. Wild and untamed, the place had a plan at work. She couldn't sketch it from this angle but the grandeur was clear. "It looks old."

"Greythorne was near ruins when my father bought it. He added a wing and landscaping and updated the interiors. It is more imposing from here, but the inside is warm."

Whether it was the thought of the duke or the house, suddenly she couldn't breathe. "I'm going to take a walk, before we arrive," she said, yanking the door open.

Warrick ordered the carriage to stop, and she averted her gaze, and started for the small copse. "Alone, if you please," she called over her shoulder when he followed.

"That would not be wise."

"I need to clear my head. We're in sight of your parents' house. Nothing will happen."

"Karly," he began softly.

With an impatient wave, she stormed away with more indignity than she felt. Neither the sky nor Warrick would accommodate her anguish. She needed to cry in peace at the injustice of her accusers, her hunters, and the pain that wouldn't leave her, even here. If she let loose the misery that darkened her soul without reining it in, it might calm. She pressed on, following the ridge. She caught occasional vistas of Greythorne in the distance amidst an array of chimneys. Something rustled to her left. She froze as two deer burst from the brush and bounded down the slope. They had not reached the bottom when Warrick was at her side, his pistol drawn.

"You mean to shoot the bounty hunters then, or is that for me?"

His chin came up. He stared at her for a long silence before sliding the weapon into his pocket. "You should have spoken last night."

"One wrong word from you and I'm placed in prison.

I've had to use every bit of diplomacy, almost selling myself in the process, yet I would do it again." She turned and collided with his outstretched arm, and let him guide her to his shoulder.

The tears did come then, and so did the rain, washing over and through her. His gentleness only made it worse, or was it better?

When she lifted her head, Warrick was soaked, time long passed. "I was certain revealing everything would only make things more difficult."

"What is your plan then, or don't you have one?"

"I do, beginning with our marriage. Come out of the rain."

How to explain the feel of fresh air in her lungs, the return of nature that she had missed in London? "Just a bit longer, please?"

He paused, then gave a reluctant nod. He took her hand and led her around a large boulder that turned down a narrow path. It dove down the face of the slope into a private alcove, once a simple stone outcropping. Now there was a small fountain, a bench and vines for privacy. Sheltered from the weather, she made no protest when he gathered her again close.

For a moment she could forget they were at odds and surrender to safety. He would not harm her, of that she was sure. It hadn't pained her to bare her soul before him; his quiet words were comforting. Men weren't like that, at least not around her. She gathered every shred of logic she could manage and patched the open wound in her heart, taking deep breaths until she was again solid. "I don't normally lose control."

"It's time you did. You've been holding tight for too long, not without reason."

Karly sank onto the bench and didn't move when he tucked her hair over her shoulders. Across from them the fountain splashed, and water meandered down the wall into a small pool. It was silent, the rain masking the sound. If only she could drown the sound of her racing thoughts as easily. "You should annul the marriage soon. The damage will be less that way."

"How very philosophical of you."

"Will I need to sign anything?"

"No, the matter is entirely in my hands. All I need to do is ask. It will be dissolved within the week. But I don't believe I will." Shadows deepened and then were gone from his face, but they never seemed to leave his eyes.

She sensed danger, from him and from within her heart. She needed to guide the conversation, before the path became more treacherous. "The rain is slowing."

"Stop running from me."

His voice was like liquid silver in her veins. He stood before her and touched her lips with his finger, then languidly traced their outline. It was all Karly could do not to move or speak. Her body began to tremble with want of words. She could not go back; she could not break the spell he was casting. His touch advanced slowly past her cheek until his hand massaged the nape of her neck. She heard her own sigh and felt the tension ease, replaced by a delicious warmth that spread outward. "I won't fall in love."

"You love easily, Karly. That is why you hurt."

"So you intend to hurt me." She remained immobile while his lips stroked the curve of her jaw.

"To do that, you would have to be in love with me."

"I'm not. I can't . . ." she said hesitantly as his gaze met hers. The words were coated in regret before she had even spoken them. "A marriage between us couldn't work."

"You aren't willing to try? Admit you want me."

She did want him. A simple word, a change of direction, and she could remain like this, with him. He didn't hate her; he was offering a place for her to belong. And when he discovered she was a pilot, that she had sailed on the pirate ship, helped them more than by providing sustenance? Forcing her mind quiet, she lifted her hands to his shoulders and nuzzled his neck in return, his masculine scent tantalizing her.

His mouth closed over hers before she could continue, his tongue seeking entrance and an answer to his statement. She gave in and tasted the salty sweet pleasure of him. Her balance faltered. In the circle of his embrace he guided them to the stone bench carved from the rock face, seating her in his lap. Her toes barely touched the ground.

She closed her eyes and pressed her forehead to his, savoring him. If he was cruel, angry, demanding, and harsh, she could turn her heart to steel and lock her mind against him. But against his care she could do nothing, not even breathe normally.

"Karly," he whispered.

She opened her eyes, prepared to plead once again for his compassion. But when she saw his empathy, she fell mute. He was as unprepared for this as she was. Karly lifted her hands, cupped his face, and kissed him, opening her secret heart despite herself. He did not move while she tasted and touched the curve and slope of his incredible mouth. She was beginning to doubt her boldness when his hand touched behind her neck, tunneling into her hair, and his lips parted. This was different. He demanded more, pressing further and with greater urgency. She heard his groan and answered with a shiver. He tugged her deeper into his arms, his lips trailing along her face and cheek, then tormenting the delicate skin of her throat.

Karly lifted her chin and gasped when he nibbled lower. His mouth teased where fabric met flesh. If she was going to stop, this was the time. His kisses battered her reason, his touch massaging her breast.

She needed to say something brilliant, but her thoughts fell away with the fastenings of her bodice. She would accept the consequences tomorrow. He was the right man, even if the time was wrong. His passion made her feel alive. He didn't love her, but he did care. And he was her husband; he wanted to stay her husband. She quieted the rest of her rational mind. He paused with his hand on her bared breast. Braving a peek, she found him gazing up at her, a gentle smile upon his lips. And then he lowered his head, his mouth closing over her breast, and she moaned, barely registering her own voice. The warmth of his touch scorched hot as it traveled through her body and tightened between her thighs. She tried to calm her breath as he began sensual circles working inward, their thoroughness excruciating, tantalizing, the experience and sensations completely new. Karly feathered her hand through his black hair and clung to his coat as his tongue flicked, then suckled her nipple.

"You needn't be afraid of me."

She laughed softly and shook her head at his incomplete grasp of the situation. "If I was smart, I'd be terrified." What he kindled within her—that was her source of bittersweet terror. "This is not about fear."

He pressed a kiss on her temple. "Will you trust me?"

"I don't suppose you have an easier question?" she asked.

Warrick raised an eyebrow, his grin widening. "An easier question? Perhaps," he said huskily, reaching under the hem of her gown and dangerously close to her wall against the world. He placed his hand on her calf and traced upward along the curve of her leg, over the silk stockings, until he reached bare skin. "That's a question?" she gasped. He said nothing, nibbling her earlobe before continuing his journey along her thigh. He finally stopped achingly close to the core of her desire and massaged slow sensual circles into her flesh. Trembling in anticipation, she turned her head, and he lifted his.

Her breath heavy in her chest, she tripped over an explanation and tried to gather her thoughts. "I won't be tricked."

"I want you to stay," he said, his voice firm.

"I'm not sure." She pulled her bodice back and turned for him to relace it, prepared for a refusal. He said nothing, his hands gentle, a kiss to her shoulder. Tucking her sleeves and waist and smoothing her skirt.

"I am starting at the beginning with you," he said, his breath ragged, "or close to the beginning, before you lost all trust in me."

"I haven't." He frowned so sternly she almost laughed despite the circumstances. She offered her hand. The corner of his mouth lifted. He raised her fingers to his lips and kissed them.

"Some men meet their fiancées only a few times before they wed. We're beyond that."

"Warrick," she drew a breath and considered telling him all, but thought better. What he had already said would be made irrelevant. Even if he accepted her involvement, her lies, a duchess was not a pilot. "It's damp. Will you escort me to Greythorne?"

"I am trying to show you a bit more consideration," he said quietly. When she did not move, he came to her. "It is possible I have pushed you a bit hard. It was not cavalier of me."

Karly shook her head but accepted the gesture. "I am beginning to wonder which part of you is real."

"All of me is real, but you should heed that part that is trying to find its way to you. If we stopped dancing around each other and started dancing together, who knows what could be?"

"I can't dance," she whispered and averted her gaze.

"Then walk with me," he smiled.

"It will make things more complicated."

"But you are not alone in dealing with them."

"You still don't understand."

"Not yet, but I hope to."

There was so much sincerity in his voice, his eyes, and his manner, she believed him. But doing as he asked would not be simple. She was in her own way.

His was the touch she wanted to remember, savor, and cherish when this business was all over. His was the kiss she wanted to remain in her dreams. But he had not taken; he had given. That was worth some measure of trust. If she expected nothing from him, then he could not disappoint her. From their vantage point she caught sight of two figures as they stretched over the lawns on horseback.

"Those would be my parents. Mother's in the lead," Warrick said.

They turned and vanished behind the building, and were still walking their horses when the carriage arrived, despite the rain. She remembered the duke, tall, muscular, and filled with power. The duchess was petite with hair a cascade of black curls and Warrick's eyes. Arms linked, horses on either side, their lips touched, broke, and they halted, the woman taking the reins as the man stepped forward, blocking her.

"I come in peace," Warrick said, opening the door.

"We didn't recognize the carriage." The duke clasped Warrick's hands; the duchess dropped the horses' reins and kissed his cheek.

Beneath her feet, the stones crunched as she listened to the greetings, caught the curious stares, and curtsied as the duchess faced her.

"Jonathon told me Warrick had company."

"Karly Bane," Karly said quickly as the group before her exchanged glances. It didn't matter they were as wet as she, or that her dress was nearly as fine as the duchess's. They were a wall, different, and she would never belong, not here. Guilt at what she had promised only hours before clawed at her conscience, and Warrick's eyes narrowed. Extending her hand, she shook the duke's fiercely. "I was wondering where I could go to change."

The duchess returned to the mounts and lifted their reins. "Warrick, the second floor, next to my bedchamber is prepared. I'll be along shortly, once I tend to these two."

"Karly and I are married."

The duchess dropped her chin, her gaze on Karly. "In that case, take the blue rooms and closets."

It was all Karly could do to curtsey a second time on shaking legs. Into the house, the grand staircase and gallery were irrelevant. Passing doors that had no meaning, she let Warrick guide her into a place where the fireplace was bigger than she was, servants bustling about, tending to curtains and blaze. She rubbed her hands and held them before the flames, but it was no use.

Chapter 9

She should have refused the truce, spurned Warrick's advances and dove for the streets at her first opportunity. This was lunacy. She couldn't even bring herself to unpack her trunks. She could see them through the doorway to her right, untouched, setting at the end of the enormous four-poster bed of carved spirals hung with silk curtains of ivory and blue for privacy. It was meant for her. Warrick's trunks were visible too, to her left; his room was just as imposing. Karly rolled her eyes at her own foolishness and froze. Even the ceiling was painted in a statement of both art and intricacy with a pattern of stars, clouds, and what looked like angels, although she wasn't sure. It was over-whelming.

The knock at the door warned Karly it wasn't Warrick; he would have simply walked in. No, with luck the maid had returned to rescue her from her plight. "Come in," she called. Warrick's mother entered, dressed in a rich burgundy silk. Petite, but with an air of unmistakable majesty, she glided into the room, closing the door behind her. Unsure what to do, Karly curtsied awkwardly. Her voice dropped to a mere whisper. "My lady."

The woman studied her face and then approached. Karly's heart hammered louder as the distance closed.

"To you, I'm Jaline, and you're Karly. We're family, and I'm not much for titles." She continued into the room and halted in the center, then turned. "I hope this room is comfortable. Blue is Warrick's favorite color, and the view is one of the best in the house."

"It is perfect," Karly said and attempted a polite smile.

Jaline blinked and gave an elegant nod. "You should know I ordered Warrick and Jonathon to remain downstairs so we could talk," she said in a lilting voice.

Karly waited for her to continue, but Jaline had retrieved a very large pillow from the sofa. She placed it on the floor and sank with all the grace of a drifting feather. She arranged her dress, and looked up expectantly. Doom and despair circled Karly's head, but she followed the older woman's example. She tried to emulate the movement, her landing far less delicate with skirts billowing about her. Karly slapped them down, then realized her error and flushed, peeking at Jaline, who was smiling.

"I have lived amongst the English for"—Jaline paused and gave a small wave into the air—"a long time. I have never gotten used to their fashions."

"Corsets make it hard to breathe," Karly said and wished she could relax.

"I remember the first time I was forced to wear full English dress. It was for an elegant dinner when I was nine. My stepfamily was quite proper, but after a few minutes of trying to stay seated in my chair, I slipped off, right under the table."

Karly giggled, her hand flying to her mouth respectfully. "What did you do?"

"The worst thing imaginable: threw a tantrum. I declared to the entire party that the floor was so much more dignified. After all, that was where the Sultan sat. Then I stomped out of the room." She paused, tipping her pretty face to one side as she considered Karly. "I didn't come here to discuss fashions, although it can be a rather entertaining subject. I wanted to talk to you."

"Yes?" Karly said, her voice just above a whisper.

"I know you care about my son. I see it in your eyes. It concerns me that you have not confided in him about your circumstances, for your sake."

Karly's thoughts scattered around her, along with the last traces of warmth in her cheeks. For an instant she felt light-headed and set a hand down to steady herself. "You speak your mind clearly."

"I've had to, and I've been where you are. When I met Jonathon, there was little I could say. There was a part of me that thought that his attraction was based on the mystery, that when he knew the truth, he would let me go."

"He didn't."

Jaline smiled wistfully. "The fear was very real, because at some point, I fell in love with him. Warrick does care for you. It occurred to me that you are harboring an affection for another man, not this Landgon, perhaps someone in Bermuda. If that was the nature of your problem, you might appreciate a woman to speak to."

"You might very well understand better than most."

"My secret was my riding. It sounds ridiculous here, now, looking back on the past, but I didn't want Jonathon to know. It almost tore us apart, almost killed me."

Karly reached for Jaline's hand, finding it an anchor despite its delicacy. "There is no other man. I wouldn't hurt Warrick. I promise you that."

"And the pain that he'll feel if a bounty hunter kills you?"

"You are most direct," Karly said.

Jaline gave her a gentle smile. With her finger, she nudged Karly's chin up. "I am also a good listener."

"It can't be my father's crew. They wouldn't harm me.

They're back in Bermuda, so the ship that William caught has to belong to some of the smugglers."

"You are certain?"

"I am."

"Have they ever killed anyone?" came a man's voice from behind her, Warrick's voice.

Karly spun to find him in the doorway, the duke with him. She wouldn't lie, so she linked her hands and looked down.

"That would be a yes," the duke answered, "but then so have I."

Karly studied each of them around the room. The more she said, the worse it sounded. She had done her best to explain herself. Those final months in Bermuda before her uncle had arrived were a terrifying blur. In her dreams she still found herself back in the cell, Commander Farris standing over her, his face contorted by rage. She braced for more questions when she heard the duke clear his throat.

With a sweep of her skirts, Jaline rose. "I have been outnumbered far too long. It's time there was another woman in the family." Jaline gave her an appraising look. "Besides, I know a good heart when I see one. Dinner is in an hour. Do not be late."

Karly blinked up in surprise, as Jaline moved to the doorway "There are not many horses on ships. I learned to ride when we were ashore, though I can't ride sidesaddle. If you'd like company, perhaps tomorrow, we could talk more."

Jaline gave a soft laugh as she eyed her husband. "I never did like sidesaddle, either. Nine o'clock, the stables, ladies only."

"Karly has a bounty on her head," Warrick began.

Karly opened her mouth to answer, but Jaline waved her silent. "Greythorne's safe, and no one will be expecting her out on the trails so early. Besides, Warrick's entourage is here. With so many dukes, earls, barons, and admirals, it will be quite safe."

The duke remained, his gaze lingering on Karly's face. "While you are here please, for all of our sakes, use the stairs, not the windows." He gave a small wink before following his wife.

Karly looked down at her hands, afraid Warrick might see the torment in her eyes, and the truth deeper. It still wasn't love, she assured herself. It was too soon for that. But Warrick's face, his touch had replaced all others. It was better he never know it. "Your mother was worried I am in love with someone else."

"I told her that wasn't the case, but she wanted to hear it from you."

"She loves you very much." She realized her mistake when he turned away from her for the fire. "I apologize. Men don't like to talk about such things."

"Tell me about your friends in Bermuda."

Karly sidestepped him and the question. "I want to get ready for dinner, dry my hair, before I have to face your friends. Maybe they won't recognize me." She gave a sweep of her arm toward her skirts.

"No one is going to question you tonight, Karly. That isn't why I brought you here. The group meets every few days to discuss developments. Right now, it's Landgon they are interested in. Another French ship was taken. Again Landgon was mentioned, but there was no rum onboard, or should I say, poison."

"Why not just arrest him?"

"Because," he said, taking her hands in his, "I'm not sure if he's the leader or a pawn. If he's leading, it would end whatever was amiss, but if he's a pawn, the players would find someone else, the arrest would be a warning, and I would have to start over again to discover the plot."

"You believe this is larger than smuggling?"

"Much larger." He gave her a quick smile. "I'll wait for you on the stairs."

She dressed and wanted to believe their reassurances, but when Warrick covered her hand with his own, her confidence wafted away like the evening's conversation. A small meal of bread and cheese would have sufficed. The drawnout presentation of soup, followed by wine, then meats and more wine made her head swim. The other guests, men she recognized from her intrusion at Warrick's, were busy talking around her. Knowing the players, she sensed danger, and avoided their questions.

Karly eyed the clock, then the door. The servants entered with yet another course, this time tarts, puddings, and creams. The conversation turned to piracy, and she slid her hands into her lap, then felt Warrick's cover her own as another course arrived filled with dried fruits, cakes, and more wine. To others, they were newlyweds, she mused. It pleased her. Odd that through everything, he, who had held her against her wishes, was her anchor. His words earlier that night gave her strange hope. The chill that had shadowed her vanished.

The duchess called her name, her expression grave. "You look quite exhausted, and we are supposed to ride tomorrow. Would you like to retire?"

Karly was on her feet the next instant. "Thank you." Warrick rose and accompanied her back to their rooms. She thought he might return downstairs, but he walked into his bedroom, leaving the door ajar. In her chamber, she found her trunks had been unpacked for her, her clothes neatly arranged in the armoire. Choosing an eyelet-laced sleeping gown, she slipped behind the Chinese screen and undressed.

She considered her bed as she passed it, but continued on. Tonight, she would be his wife and feel what that meant. Their interlude in the garden must be finished; then she could move on, forward or wherever it may lead. It was simple. Curiosity and desire, the want of him, the need to know more about him drove her. She accepted it without further questions as she spotted his neck cloth on the bureau. He must be changing. Karly went to his bed, threw back the blankets, and burrowed beneath them into the middle. Seated, she neatened everything, and waited.

Warrick emerged in a slate gray dressing gown, parted at the center, tied at the waist. Beneath, she glimpsed white linen and a tie. He hesitated, then approached, stopping within reach and glancing from her to the door. "You're ready to sleep after the journey?"

"No. Come, I warmed the bed." She reached up, and he removed his wrap, his gaze locked on hers. Odd that he should appear more powerful still without his coat. In a simple white nightshirt, he was more male to her than with the padding of fashion. He lifted the cover, and she slid over, her boldness weakening. He watched her as he settled, and offered his shoulder for her to rest her head, his chest to rest her hand. She took his invitation, and with her hand, stroked from his neck to hip, no lower.

"It is rather uncomfortable for men when women are this close."

Beneath her hand he stilled. "Who told you that?" he asked, his voice crisp.

Karly took a steadying breath, wondering how much she could tell without revealing all. He gave her power to continue. "My mother died in childbirth. There was no one to watch me, so I spent time on my father's ship, the *Triumph*."

"And you talked about men and women sleeping?"

"Hack, my father's second in command, told me. When we were in port, men were allowed to bring women to their bunks. He said men don't sleep much when a woman is near to them. That sometimes it hurt."

Warrick tilted his face to look at her. "You should consider there are better sources to learn about relations than on ships."

"I understand how everything works," she said confidently.

For a long moment, he said nothing, claiming a lock of her hair, winding it around one finger, then releasing it. "If someone knew how a ship was rigged, would they know how to sail?"

"Sailing is a far more involved endeavor."

"So is making love, but no one's ever done that with you, have they? It's been a physical act only."

Karly's lungs felt small. Warrick had spoken so easily. He didn't mind the conversation, so to correct him, explain her ignorance, might ruin his openness. Propping on her elbow, she peered at him. "Tell me."

His expression became sober, and he searched her face. "I would rather show you."

Karly thought of the women she had heard below decks. Some cried, others screamed, but the most frightening were the quiet ones. If she was ever to learn, she wanted Warrick to show her. He would complete what they had started in that alcove. Studying the depths of his brown eyes, she heard the answer in her heart first before it made its way to her lips. "I wouldn't trust anyone else. I want to know what it means to be with you."

He studied her, then with a powerful surge, rolled her beneath him, covering her legs with one muscular thigh. His elbow brushed her breast through the fabric of her gown. The small ache she had felt earlier returned between her legs. Just as quickly, he gentled. His breath was hot on her shoulder. He seemed to waver on her words. Then, he lowered his mouth to hers, and she opened, unsure.

A caress and kiss, as unhurried as if every part of her mattered, she mattered. He moved over her face and neck, exploring, inviting, and she reached for him. Taut, hot, he was alive and fluid, a paradox of strong and tender. Untying the ribbons of her gown, his gaze never left hers. She didn't refuse him. She sat and slid the garment off her body and offered it.

"You're beautiful, Karly."

Content, she shimmied back to his side. His hand crossed her thigh, and her restlessness intensified, knotting inside her, tightening her awareness. Soft words murmured in her ear were hard to believe, but they soothed, gave her confidence. When he touched her sensitive folds, Karly's mind froze, and she panicked. Without thinking she arched, heard Warrick's sharp intake of breath. She forced herself to calm. "I'm all right."

He stroked her hair and kissed the bridge of her nose. "I promise it won't be bad this time."

His words and concern filtered through her reasoning. She frowned up at him and had a flash of honesty. They were so close, she had to tell him the truth. "This is my *first* time." Mortification at discussing this at all began to burn her cheeks. Awkward, she placed his hand on her mound and thought past the sensation, hoping he would continue. Tenderly he slid his arms around her waist and held her close, kissing her neck. Through the gap in his shirt Karly touched the bare skin of his chest, curling her fingers through the soft hair. His erection touched her leg. She jumped, returned, and drew a breath. "You surprised me."

With a kiss to her temple, he traced a necklace of kisses along her collarbone. "Don't apologize."

"Don't stop." She arched closer and, sliding her hand beneath his waist, invited him.

"Not yet. We take this journey together."

Before she could ask what he meant, his kisses lowered until he found her breast, tormenting it with lips and tongue. "I like this," she moaned as a new ache hardened with exquisite clarity into need. "There's no pain."

Turning his attention to the other breast, he slid his hand lower, entering her with a finger, and the ache changed, the sensation grew. Quakes of pleasure rolled through her, and she held on. Warrick was her tether. Here it did not matter what she could and could not say; all that mattered was what she could and could not create with him.

He sat suddenly, pulling off his nightshirt with ferocity. It was her first glimpse of the whole of him. She thought of his earlier compliment. "You're beautiful, Warrick."

He gave a low, rumbling chuckle before kissing her. Sinking into the blankets, she enjoyed the feel of his skin to hers. He moved, and her readiness melted away as the full force of his arousal brushed her legs, then nestled between them. She wanted this, she reminded herself over and over as he kissed her. He broke their kiss and looked at her with concerned and puzzled eyes.

"You're shaking."

"Am I?" she asked. She prayed he would not stop now. Her body might forgive, but her heart would not. She was so close, and then he eased into her. Steeling her body, she closed her eyes and braced. His hand was on her jawline, caressing her cheek with his thumb, and for a moment she thought he would retreat. She opened her eyes as he thrust, her cry inadvertent at the crisp and personal pain, the intimacy of being next to him carrying her through. He paused immediately, his face just above and filled with concern.

"I told you not to believe the rumors," she stammered.

"Yes, you did," he said and caressed her cheek. "I'm sorry."

He rose above her, kissed her brow and temple, and then called her name.

"It doesn't hurt anymore," she said. No longer frightened, she reached around him and caressed her hand over his muscled back.

"It never will again, I promise you."

Even joined they were too far apart. She lifted her head, and he found her kiss halfway, pressing her back into the pillows. He began to move, and the ache returned, but it was no longer sharp. Being this close to this man, she could think of no better place, no safer place. She felt him shudder and turned her head with concern as he clasped her tightly.

"Are you all right?"

When he didn't answer, she touched his forehead, grateful when he looked up.

"Never better, Mrs. Barry," he said, his voice heavy.

She would pretend that she could relate like this, touch like this, love like this for the rest of her life. That nothing else would ever matter. It was at best a fantasy and at worst a lie, but one she could tell herself tonight. With luck it would last, but she didn't believe that.

Chapter 10

It was wrong for her to sneak out of bed. Warrick would be disappointed, possibly irritated, but she couldn't be late. Jaline was expecting her. Karly dressed quickly. With her boots in her hand, she crept across the common room and stopped midstride. With a sheet wrapped about his waist and dawn's light streaming in the window from behind, he was haloed in what she decided was perfection. His upper torso was chiseled, like a Greek statue, only this was no statue. Her body tingled at the memory of just how real Warrick Barry was.

"Your mother asked me to go riding, remember?"

He raised an eyebrow at her and approached, one hand holding his cloth. "Disappearing after a night of pleasure is hardly polite."

"Nor is making her wait," she managed as he stood before her, one hand on her neck, lightly caressing her chin, the other still clutching the makeshift covering.

"Can you sit on a horse?"

She grimaced and considered her sore body. "I took a shot of brandy."

"I meant, can you ride well enough to not fall off? Or was that talk about sidesaddles all bluster?"

His concern was genuine. She couldn't tease him for it. "I don't bluster. There was a long period I lived ashore."

"Alone?"

Karly wet her mouth as she considered the question. "At times," she said and made to walk around him.

He blocked her path, his expression becoming stern. "I appreciate your past loyalties. Things are different now. When you return, we need to sort out the truth. Help me protect you."

For a moment she could only stare. "I'm late." With her fingers she reached, yanked the sheet out of his hands and fled. Odd that she should feel guilt. Waking in warmth with Warrick's body spooned against her back, she had not wanted to move. She did not want to pretend she was not happy. In her dreams her nightmare had been replaced, although it still hovered on the fringes of her mind. Last night she had been the longtail bird of her imagination, only she was not alone. She had found her soul mate. It was Warrick. Despite everything, he had brought her to his family's home. They had not turned her out. They had accepted her. Together they had danced in the sea breezes, together for life as longtails were.

She had not realized how desperately her heart craved him. She could think of nothing more wonderful than a lifetime of waking next to him. His gift of not pressing her made her want to give in return. But how could she do that and honor her vows?

She entered and was greeted by two dalmatians, who bounded to her side. Rubbing the dogs behind their ears, she continued in search of Jaline. She found her halfway down the second aisle, only she was not alone. The duke stood, watching her prepare her horse. Karly stopped, but he had already turned his head. His slight smile at her presence confirmed her suspicion that something was on his mind.

"Sorry I am late."

Jaline peeked from around the corner of a stall and smiled broadly. "I thought you would enjoy riding my horse, Sultan."

"Your horse?" Karly asked while admiring the lilt in Jaline's voice.

"I will bring this big fellow. He's only four years old, and the experience will do him good. Sultan is in the fourth stall on the left. There's a groom there to help you."

"Thank you," Karly said quickly and hurried on. She heard the duke follow, but did not turn. Reaching the stall, she was forced to wait while the groom finished, the duke standing beside her, much taller than Warrick and even William. She rocked herself onto the balls of her feet, saw him frown at her, and stopped. "He's a beautiful horse."

"Yes, he is."

"Thank you for allowing me to stay here."

The duke gave a slight incline of his head, holding her gaze as he did so. "I have two sons. You are my first daughter-in-law. Of course you should stay here."

"Taking into account that I became your daughter-in-law under poor circumstances, you are being very considerate."

The duke gave a throaty laugh and grinned down at her. "You are a realist then?"

"I am not certain I know that word, but if it means I like to see things as they are, then yes."

"I am a realist too," he said gravely.

He was vague, but she decided his tone was a warning. Karly lifted to her full height. On the tips of her toes, she could not look him in the eye. She settled for her best attempt. "I would never harm Warrick."

"I didn't think you would," he said, his voice gentle. He cocked his head at her and dropped the smile, his expression grim. "I believe this is taking a far greater toll than you are willing to admit." He raised an eyebrow and waited for her to comment. When she said nothing, he continued. "My marriage to Jaline was not a conventional one either. She had the same haunted look in her eyes. I nearly lost her for it."

Her heart in her throat, Karly glanced to where Jaline was leading a large black horse from a stall. The duke leaned forward slightly and lowered his voice. "When things begin to crumble, give Warrick the chance to help you. I trust him above any other man I know, and not just because I am his father. He is a good man and will make a great duke."

"I know," she said, wincing at how distant her reassurances sounded. With relief she took Sultan's reins from the groom and followed Jaline into the stable yard, patting the dark bay's neck. No sooner were they in the clear, she swung astride. The duke never left her side. She turned and gave him a quick smile. "Thank you for your words."

"It was Sultan's grandfather, Galip, that brought Jaline and I together."

"Oh?"

"It is a long story, but once I made up my mind, nothing that happened would convince me otherwise. Barry men can be oddly single minded."

Karly pursed her lips and blushed. "Thank you," she said. His blue eyes sparkled, and he bestowed her with a genuine smile. Turning Sultan, she trotted after Jaline, slowing to a walk beside her. The morning was crisp, dewy, and sparkling bright, but she could not relax. Every step they took she was prepared for Jaline to resume her questions, and as the silence stretched down the lane and onto a perimeter path, her nerves strung tighter. Sultan began to prance, most likely responding to her tension. Karly gave him a light rub on his neck. "Do you think he would like a morning run?" she asked, surprised how loud she sounded against the stillness.

"You don't mind?"

In answer, Karly leaned forward. Keen, Sultan sprang into a gallop, nearly unseating her. Clutching his mane, she tucked herself to his body. Wind rushed and tore at her skirts and hair, yet she felt secure. Years of riding ships' riggings must have helped. Glancing over her shoulder she saw Jaline, her eyes bright, and she leaned lower, encouraging more speed as they gained the ridge. Higher up than before, she could see Greythorne in the distance, before they plunged into the ravine on the far side.

Sultan splashed into the stream with a crack, sending water rivulets flying in a spray of wet rainbows. Thinking of the uneven bottom, Karly drew him to a walk and beamed as Jaline came up beside her. "He's lovely."

"Shush, his ego is large enough already," Jaline laughed. "And you are better than you led me to believe. You ride rather well."

Laughing, Karly fell in step as Jaline took the lead. Up the river bank, they followed the edge until the horses did not blow each breath. Then they stopped, allowing the animals to drink. Sultan began pawing playfully at the water. Karly was so amused by his antics that when he tossed his head and pricked his ears at the far bank, she thought it was more of the same, until something whooshed past her ear. She heard it again. Sultan spooked, and Jaline's horse reared. Karly watched in horror as Jaline tumbled off to one side into the stream and her horse fled at a full gallop back in the direction they had come.

Karly half dismounted, half fell into the knee-deep water, landing next to Jaline. She seemed dazed, her hand covering her shoulder around the shaft of an arrow. No one was in sight, but they were not alone.

"Come on," Karly urged, suppressing panic at the sight of the water turning red. Jaline was hit, and they were easy targets, with only Sultan blocking another shot. They were unprotected and alone. If their assailant wanted them dead, he could step out of the brush and finish the job, and no one would be the wiser. Partially assisting Jaline, Karly dragged her to shore, still clinging to Sultan's reins, grateful the horse gave no trouble or indication of wanting to flee. A few more steps and they gained the cover of brush, but not before another arrow passed with a whoosh. For all the distance she had gained, they were barely camouflaged.

"Go for help," Jaline muttered.

Karly lifted Jaline's head into her lap. "I need to stop the bleeding."

"If he comes after you . . ."

"I brought my letter opener for such an occasion," she teased when she heard a branch snap. Grasping a fallen limb, she rested Jaline on the ground with care and rose, holding her weapon at the ready. Moments passed, and when no one emerged, she dropped it, and sat next to Jaline.

"Is he gone?" Jaline asked.

"I'm not sure." Lifting her skirt, Karly ripped her petticoats into strips and tied two together at a time. "This should stem the bleeding. When the doctor comes he can remove the arrow."

"I'm not squeamish. Take it out."

"If I do, I might make it worse. I know it hurts, but it would be better to wait," Karly explained as she wrapped the shoulder, leaving the arrow securely in its victim. "With my help could you get on Sultan?" Ebony eyes blinked in confusion, and Karly repeated herself, grateful when Jaline nodded weakly. Helping her sit, she gave Jaline a moment to get her bearings before helping her to her feet. More time passed as she steadied herself, gaining strength, and they limped toward Sultan, who was happily munching on leaves a short distance off.

"Down, Sultan," Jaline ordered.

Karly's jaw fell as the large horse dropped to its front knees, then folded its hind legs until it was lying down, and waited. After she helped Jaline onto Sultan, she heard her command the horse, and it got to its feet. "How did you do that?"

"When you're small like me it helps if the horse will meet you partway," she said, her voice not rising above a whimper as she studied the landscape all around them.

Seizing the reins, Karly broke into a jog and heard Jaline gasp with pain. She had no choice but to slow. It was possible they were alone, but she would not feel safe until they were at the stable, and perhaps not even then. Each gust of wind, brush of a branch, or rustle of a leaf crackled her brittle nerves. Soon she had a headache. The marksman had not shot again, but he could be waiting. What he might be waiting for only made her stomach churn harder.

Once, she was sure she was lost and paused, but Sultan continued and she let him take the lead. If there was going to be an end to this waking nightmare, it was only by moving forward.

She thought of Warrick. He had hurt her, but did he realize why? She had never explained. Her last words to him had been in frustration. At his direction his parents had welcomed her. In retrospect, she could have taken the hand he was offering and worked a bit harder. It was possible she would never have the chance if their assailant or an accomplice was waiting somewhere ahead.

Karly heard the hoofbeats approaching at a gallop and turned to Jaline. She heard it too, her eyes wide. From the sound, the horses were nearly at the ridge. There would be no chance to react. Karly pressed her finger to her lips and led them off the path. Glancing for a weapon, she found nothing nearby. She thought of the limb she had dropped when the riders burst into view and thundered down on them. She knew the face of one of them in an instant and cried the name of her husband, "Warrick!"

Warrick's horse skidded to a halt. Before he could dismount, Karly drew Sultan behind her. "Your mother's been hit by an arrow. She needs a surgeon."

"It's not bad," Jaline protested.

Jonathon slid from his horse and gave the reins to Karly, taking Sultan. "Ride Venture home," he ordered. The next moment he was in the saddle, his arms wrapped around Jaline. "Lean back, sweetheart," he instructed her and turned Sultan toward home and into a rolling canter.

"Karly, stay next to me," Warrick ordered, circling her once while she mounted Venture.

"The marksman left, but we might still be able to catch him," she began.

His expression turned to fury. "We're going back. Don't leave my side."

"This is my fault. If it hadn't been for that bounty . . ."

Warrick held his finger to his lips, commanding silence. Keeping up was not difficult. Warrick flanked her stride for stride. Keeping her mind from finding all the reasons why this was her fault was not so easy. When they reached the stable, Karly spotted Jaline's riderless horse being walked by a groom. The men from dinner, the ones who had been there the night she had broken into Warrick's house, stood about, their stares of accusation directed toward her. Jonathon ordered someone to get a doctor as he carried Jaline toward the house. Karly slid to the ground, and Warrick's arms were around her. "I'll be fine; Jaline is the injured one."

Warrick cupped her chin, his eyes nearly black with intensity. "Are you hit?"

She told him what she could. As she described wrapping Jaline's shoulder, her throat tightened around her breath.

"He was aiming for me. I should have been hit, not her. I didn't even realize what was happening until it was too late."

"Why did he leave? You were alone. He could have killed you." Karly recognized the man speaking as the one named Daniels.

"I don't know," she said in a hoarse whisper as Warrick's eyes swept over her and lingered on her face.

"We'll wait in the long gallery." He gave her his hand, leading her down several corridors until they reached a room ten times as long as it was wide. There she sat at the far end with Warrick by her side. He did not ask her any more questions. He covered her hands with his own and stayed, his silent company more comfort than any speech. Staff came and went quietly, their mood solemn, blame clear on their faces.

It was dusk when the door at the far end opened and the duke gestured them to enter. She found Jaline with good color, her manner bright and looking as she had before their ordeal except for the sling draped over her left shoulder. Unsure of approaching the bed, she took up a position at the end. There was no accusation that she could see, but the guilt hung over her shoulders like a blanket. "Your horse is unharmed," she told Jaline.

"It is lucky for me you are clearheaded in times of danger, or we might have been killed."

"There should have been no need," Karly began.

"Then the fault is mine," Warrick interrupted. "I brought you here, and I allowed you to go out unprotected."

"I'm afraid since it is my home," Jonathon said, "anything that happens here is my responsibility."

Karly looked from one man to the other. "What neither of you is saying is that it could have been me. William already said I was an assassin. The ride was my idea. How hard would it be to believe I had arranged for Jaline to be hurt, to dissuade you from your investigation? The men out there already think it. You would be foolish not to."

"Jaline's been hurt before, on a ride, in that vicinity. Someone might have known what happened and tried to recreate the crime. If you were behind it, you would have needed an accomplice," Jonathon said.

Warrick linked his fingers and looked directly at her. "The last time you spoke with your father's crew was months ago. You have no way of knowing where they are. You admitted they killed before, even if they were squeamish about it. Perhaps your friends became nervous about what you might say and decided to come after you, or warn you."

Karly drew away, raked her hand through her hair, and regarded the small party. She needed proof of her innocence and had none. Lacking answers, everyone was doing their best. She opened her mouth to speak and closed it as Warrick looked away. His opinion, his feelings, his confidence mattered. Tonight, emotion was heavy around her, and the weight of it squeezed the last of her confidence. Distance was what she needed, even though it would rip her apart. Lifting her shoulders, she dipped a small required curtsey before leaving the presence of the duke and duchess. Then she looked at Warrick. There was nothing to say. Without a word, she turned and left, closing the door gently behind her.

Chapter 11

Warrick muttered a curse as he spotted the bit of purple atop the crumbling wall. Through the pointed arch doorway, he braced a hand on the stones, shielded his eyes against the sun, and studied her predicament. Perched with complete calm, Karly sat, feet dangling, all but hidden from passersby. It was tempting to call to her, but her last fall was too clear in his mind. He might startle her. She was mostly cornered, unless there was a tree within grasp. From his vantage point, he noted several and cursed again. First he would control his temper and get her down; then he would strangle her.

She hadn't run—that was the most important consideration. He had decided if he hadn't found her by four, he would ride for London and begin the search by dawn. Warrick blew a breath and took three stairs, then three more. Unable to look down as the ground fell away, he kept his eyes on Karly, his impulsive, stubborn, secretive, foolish wife.

She was not the kind of woman who inspired deep sentimental attachment. The chasm of misunderstanding was too vast. Thoughts of her gave him no peace, mainly because he wanted her yet again. The last time hadn't been nearly enough, and he wasn't sure how many times would be. His boot scraped, and a stone bounced down the stairs, hitting the ground below. He studied it and pressed his back to the wall until the wave of vertigo subsided.

"I'll come down."

Jerking his head in her direction, he saw her swing back and start toward him. One of Murdock's finds, her gown was a brocaded floral. "You promised to stay in the house."

"You searched the grounds; there's no one here. Besides, from up there I can see someone coming from quite a distance. I saw you."

Her tone had been wrong, choked. "You were asleep last night before I came to bed. I missed you next to me."

"I faked rest. There was work to do." Karly slipped her arms about his waist and laid her head against his shoulder.

Hugging her to him, he palmed the back of her spine and felt her tremble. Nothing could have terrified him more—first the heights and now the emotions. "What is this about?" he asked and cocked his head to see her face.

"I have something for you." Karly withdrew to the stone slab bench and sat. He joined her as she flipped up the hem of her dress. He caught a glimpse of the curve of her legs while she fidgeted. It was impossible to not remember how silky those legs had felt, their feel against his skin. Karly withdrew a neatly folded piece of paper and replaced the gown. "Take it," she said and handed it to him. "Keep it safe."

Charcoal lines caught his eye. "You went up there to draw Greythorne?"

"Something far more useful I believe."

Warrick glanced at the item in his hand and again looked at Karly's anxious expression. He unfolded the document and smoothed it on his knee, revealing Bermuda before him, coves and beaches, reefs both hidden and visible. Wrecks, deep channels were outlined, and there were notes where currents were particularly strong. "You made this?"

"Please don't start that again." She chuckled softly and pointed to several points where an *X* crossed an arrow. "I was thinking about all the pieces you found, and I have a theory. It's"—she paused—"most unlikely, which is why I believe it's what they're up to." She rose, walked to a gray half wall, and leaned her back to it. "What is this place?"

He studied her. Strength through uncertainty seemed to be her way of coping. What had upset her had been set aside for business. But if there was a point to her meanderings, he couldn't see it. All he could see was her, the curve of her figure, the gleam of her hair. He had wanted to caress and stroke her, learn more before facing the morning. It wasn't possible out here, not for lack of privacy. She could be in his arms, but her spirit and thoughts were elsewhere. "It was a castle belonging to a Saxon prince. You enjoy history?"

"It depends on whose," she gave a gentle smile. "There's a family of foxes using the area in the back as a nursery, and in the corner wall are snakes."

The beauty of her company, of her relaxed presence made him want to drop the paper and take her into his arms. Concerned she would resist, withdraw, he began to read over her work.

Karly moved to his side. "I have highlighted the areas most vulnerable to attack from memory, but things do change. And it isn't complete. You should check current charts," she said in a rush. Taking her lower lip between her teeth, she began to chew. Warrick placed his finger on her mouth and gave her a stern frown.

"A bad habit," she murmured. "Please don't ask me why or how I guessed."

Warrick swallowed all the other questions in his throat. How she arrived at her conclusions was not relevant at the moment. It upset her. A return of yesterday's accusations would get them nowhere, would take them backward. "I said too much. I shouldn't have gone so far. I was upset."

"Your mother was hurt."

"You were too—maybe not shot, but there was pain. You blamed yourself, and I was so angry, I let you." She drew him into his arms and could feel her heart thundering against his chest.

"It was understandable." She closed her eyes, throwing back her head. "I hate being here because it hurts and I hurt others."

"You've done what you can. You'll continue to do whatever you feel you can." As she looked at him, he touched his forehead to hers. "Let's go back to Greythorne."

Her fingers caught his coat, her knuckles turning white. "I wanted to seduce you."

Surprised, he lifted his head to get a better look at her. No teasing sparkled in the hazel, only serious wonder surrounded with uncertainty. Warrick's heart leaped against his ribs. He could let her, so easily. "After the ball, when we have more time and privacy." His mouth dry, he held her hand, kissed the back of it. "Thank you for the map."

He led their way through the pines, down the hill, and into Greythorne. Her trust, so quietly bestowed despite the storm, was a precious link. The small squeezes she pressed into his hand were like squeezes of his heart. He studied her out of the corner of his eye, certain the next moment she would not be there, and then he noticed her shoes. She had worn her old slippers, plain and brown. Desire to run was that close to the surface. It was too soon. Pleasuring her mattered. To do otherwise was to risk everything. What he needed was a distraction before they reached the bedroom and he lost control to her touch.

Entering the main door, he turned in the direction of Jaline's apartments. It was impossible not to notice the look of disappointment on Karly's face as he left her in a flurry of maids. Meandering through the grounds until the party began, he dressed and forced himself to appear unconcerned, joining his father in greeting the guests as they descended from the line of carriages. Gowns and jewels glittered against all the marble and crystal Greythorne had to offer, its halls alive with light and beauty. Unconvinced by his act, the duke motioned him to a side salon, drew the door shut, and folded his arms expectantly.

"We should be out there."

"I would rather not have to explain to your mother the round of social calls she will have to make to right your insults. You ignored the Viscount of Spenceport completely and called Lady Downes *sir*. Not that I am fond of either, but you're wearing your worries tonight."

"Mother never cared for those rules," Warrick said, feeling the guilt.

"And yet she respects them when possible," he said with a half smile. "What happened with Karly? And may I remind you, lying to your father is a sin."

Warrick quirked his mouth. "I was not going to lie. Nothing happened. I have a feeling something is wrong."

"Did you have another argument?"

"She was upset and then accommodating. She drew me a map of Bermuda with directions where she thought someone might land." Warrick pulled the document from his pocket. Initially he had intended to leave it in his rooms, but changed his mind. It was too explosive, the ramifications reaching across the Channel and into war. He offered it to his father.

"I realize she's an artist, but it's rather unusual for anyone to be aware of these sorts of details, especially a woman," the duke said.

"She spent most of her life at sea, but I agree with you."

The duke shook his head. "Even so, it's rather unusual."

"She drew ships," Warrick frowned, studying the document.

"That makes more sense than this."

"She took refuge with pirates, and clearly she doesn't want me to know how much time she spent there. I'm guessing it was most of her life. Pirates would be keenly aware of the strategic inlets around the islands."

"It would explain some knowledge, but wouldn't pirates have certain locations that were the most desirable? Why learn all the inlets? She has noted over forty, two of which are near settlements."

"Are you trying to persuade me I should be more worried, or are you trying to alleviate my concerns?" Warrick said with more fervor than he intended.

"I think you are making progress," the duke said with a nod, and opened the door to the ballroom, pausing to scan the crowd. "Your mother and Karly are at the far end," the duke began and lowered his voice. "Go and keep them out of trouble."

Within a single step Warrick drew up. "I apologize for being distracted."

"I understand, better than you think. Go."

He searched as he walked. The crowd had to number in the hundreds. From the landing of the great staircase, an orchestra played. Silks and laughter, crystal and gaiety crowded his senses. There was a gap in the throng, and he caught sight of her. In the ivory ball gown Murdock had sold them, Karly shimmered. He preferred her hair down, but tonight, up and about her face in a chestnut mass with tiny ringlets, he thought he had never seen it more beautiful. She had captured the admiration of several men. A local gentry said something funny, and Karly raised her hand to cover her mouth, her eyes bright with amusement. The nape of her neck exposed, his fingers longed to stroke her just there. This afternoon had ended abruptly, somehow, so he had to assure himself they had time later.

He was halfway to his goal, oblivious to those around him, when Amanda Claridge stepped in his path, her chin tipped up offering anyone who chose an unencumbered view of her bosom, her nipples barely out of view. Warrick gave her a curt bow.

"It is always a pleasure to see you at my parents' parties."

"I came to see you," she laughed softly. "Don't appear so worried. Perhaps there is a place we can go for a private discussion?"

Even in the middle of the ballroom with a crowd milling about them, a personal conversation with Amanda was a mistake. She was quite capable of causing a stir. "I was on my way to see my bride and my mother. You may join us if you wish," he said with careful politeness and a quick bow, then continued on his way, not checking to see if she was following. He reached Karly a few minutes later. Kissing his mother's cheek, he kissed Karly's next and noticed her breasts were pressed sweetly against her bodice, out of others' sight. It didn't matter. He knew their touch, their taste. Tonight, he would learn more. His mouth went dry. Then he met her eyes. She gave him a smile that whisked through his senses like a summer breeze.

"I am sorry I am late," Karly said.

"No apologies, the wait was worth it."

"You can thank your mother. Without her assistance I would have been at least another hour."

"Surely you didn't insist—the duchess's arm is in a sling," Amanda said as she joined them.

"No, of course not," Karly said, flushing.

"It's really not difficult—the fashions I mean. Hair is my bane; it never wants to do what I want." Amanda gave a toss of her head. "Fortunately I've found a wonderful ladies' maid. I'll send her to you, so the duchess can rest."

Warrick needed an excuse to distract Amanda. What he found was Trent already in a bow, asking her for a dance. With barely a word of consent, Trent swept her onto the dance floor.

Jaline sighed heavily. "Amanda is not terribly pleased how things have turned out. I didn't realize she was so interested in you."

"She wasn't," Warrick said, feeling he had to clarify for his mother.

"Good." She gave Karly a small push toward Warrick. "Go and mingle lest our guests feel you are neglecting them. I must find your father before he finds me first."

"I believe her arm is hurting her," Karly said when Jaline was out of earshot.

"My father will make certain she uses care. Come," Warrick said quietly. Aware of the admiring glances from men they passed, he introduced her, but monitored the conversation, keeping the subjects light. Poised, charming, and elegant, she handled herself with grace and bearing as if she had lived amongst the peerage all her life. He knew it was a role, one she was managing well. After they had eaten, he could see the strain and guided her away from the admirers, toward the dancing hall.

"Warrick, no."

"It is appropriate that we dance," he said, continuing on. She shed him, slipping through the doors to the garden and into the night air. He caught her before she made the terrace, prepared for some excuse but not her pale cheeks and wide eyes. He touched her brow, but it was cool.

"I'm not ill," she whispered and continued farther along the terrace away from prying eyes. Then she stopped abruptly, and he nearly crashed into her.

Karly took a deep breath of the evening air. "Do I smell oranges?" she asked, and looked to Warrick for an explanation.

Taking her hand, he led her off the stone patterned terrace and down the wrought-iron stairs toward the walk and the shelter of hedges. He saw what he was looking for and halted, pointing toward a tree. "They were my mother's idea. Oranges were halved and filled with wax to make candles." He turned to face her and paused in admiration. Karly had closed her eyes, inhaling deeply, enjoying the scent. As they drifted open to regard him, she smiled shyly and then looked away. He nudged her chin up until she looked at him. "You are beautiful," he breathed, lowering his other hand around her waist and stepping to the music. To her credit, she did not miss a step, graceful as if she had spent her time in the finer ballrooms of London. "You can dance."

"Naturally, although it is easier on a flat piece of earth than the pitching deck of a ship."

"Your father brought a tutor onboard or a governess?"

"Neither. I had quite the repertoire of partners."

"I believe I'm jealous." She paused and tilted her head so prettily he began to plot how to smuggle her upstairs without notice of the guests. "I figured out a long time ago, from the way you talked, you had spent more than passing days onboard ships."

"There was Harding, Ned, James, Martin, but Nick was my favorite. He was from Greece, ran away from his family's farm for adventure. I think he liked it as much as I did."

Warrick wondered if she realized her eyes changed from hazel to emerald when she was happy. "Your father's crew sounds like a most unusual group. I wager you were lovely even then."

She bit her lower lip and shook her head. "I was a hellion. I think my father told them to dance with me just to keep me in sight and out of the rigging. You shouldn't laugh. I may have to challenge you to another duel, though of course I will need a real sword."

"I believe you," he chuckled. "And I hope I'm never on the receiving end of one of your duels." He brushed his lips over hers, before raising his hands and cupping her face. The difficulty was putting into words what he was not certain of in his heart. He wanted her safe, he wanted her in his bed, but these things she already knew and they were not what she needed to hear. Swaying beneath the stars with only the moon as a witness, there was much he could say, but that would not make it right. Someone called Warrick's name, reminding him of his immediate responsibilities. He broke their kiss. "When the party is over, there are some things I need to talk to you about. Can we continue this later?"

"Later," she whispered and kissed his cheek.

With Karly on his arm, he met old friends and spoke of horses. The world outside Greythorne melted away. Bright as a bride and as clever as he ever imagined, she sparkled, the bloom in her cheeks high, almost feverish. It was the heat of the evening, the heat they made together, with too much clothing. Upstairs, he would remedy that. He nodded to an admiral and his wife, but when he took Karly's hand for another dance, she seemed even more strained and almost a little frightened. Warrick bent closer to whisper in her ear. "What's wrong?"

"Yes," she said breathlessly and then blinked as if coming out of a dream. "There is a small matter with my gown. I will go see the upstairs maid and have it checked."

He started after her, but she whirled to face him directly in his path. "Really, Warrick, it's a loose seam. I will get it repaired and be right back." She took his hand, gave it a quick squeeze, and hurried into the crowd.

It happened so fast, he watched as she made her way, footmen in red opening the doors at the far end and then closing them, his view of her gone, replaced by Amanda, who raised her glass and started in his direction. Changing tactics, he singled out Lord Thoughton and his wife and dove into a discussion of their latest renovations. By the time Amanda reached them, he had turned the conversation to varieties of water foliage, and her eyes glazed quickly. Given a few minutes, she would politely lose interest, Karly would return, and the night could progress.

Chapter 12

It took willpower not to tremble, not to fall apart as Karly searched for her father. There was no mistake. He was alive—a guest holding a glass of wine. His blue eyes had met hers in a bland, almost uninterested stare, but she knew better. It was as if the months had never passed, and were mere hours, only he was thinner than before, paler from lack of sun, and more drawn. His hair was short, cropped in a new style, and combed. With a slight incline of his head, he had motioned toward the rear gallery, then slipped from view without a ripple in the crowd.

There was no chance he was here on invitation, no chance that Warrick knew of his presence. He would have told her, would have handed her father over to the magistrate—and possibly handed her over as well. Karly drew to a halt. No, she would have been safe. Warrick would have warned her. Bane had to know he was in danger, and still he walked into the very heart of it. Bold as he was, he was relying on the subterfuge of his death to avoid discovery and it prompted her to wonder why.

Entering the hall, she glanced up the stairs. The party overwhelmed the scene, and couples passed behind her. Continuing past the doors and rooms, some open, others hiding murmurs and soft whispers, she disregarded the inquisitive stares from those she passed, checking as she went. More than once she surprised couples in intimate circumstances. She was prepared to deny she had seen him when she noticed the door to the tapestry room was ajar. Her pulse in her throat, Karly crept forward and slipped inside.

A single candle lit the far end of the room, a lone silhouette by its side. It all could be part of a dream. She hadn't come this far to find her imagination playing tricks. Her face warm, she wondered if she was well and then the figure turned and her heart leapt. "Father?" she asked and took a small step, then another. He opened his arms, and she ran, hugged him tight, and kissed his cheek. "You're more bone than muscle." Tugging at him again, she kissed his cheek.

"How many times have I told you, it's Bane?" His voice broke as he stroked her hair.

"I'm sorry."

"No matter, child, and don't cry. All is well, I promise it is," he soothed before roughly holding her away from him. His eyes flickered across her face, and his expression turned grim. "Tell me about the pompous bastard who brought you here before I see to him personally."

The strength of his voice, his annoyance, made her smile. "No, we start with you. They said you were dead."

"You don't think I would let Landgon kill me? It would make him too proud. Bastard. Better to take my own life than let him have it."

"I don't understand. If you weren't dead, where have you been?"

Bane shook his head, wiping the tears from her cheeks. "Never underestimate an Irishman."

"You're not Irish," Karly said. She frowned as he coughed

and wheezed to catch his breath. "And you shouldn't curse so much."

He pushed her hand away when she rubbed his back. "My grandfather was Irish, and I speak as I choose, damn it." He drew up, coughed, and wiped his hand across his mouth. "As for my death, I know a few tricks, and have friends who hid me well. Circumstances being what they were, I thought it best I stay dead, until things could be worked out. I thought I was doin' right, except when I went to find you, I discovered you had been turned over to Angus. I couldn't very well go telling everyone I was still around, so I came to London."

"You've been here in England? For how long?"

"A while. I was looking for you on the quiet. No one knew anything, and I had given up hope when I saw the announcement in the paper, stating you'd off and been married to a pompous Marquis of Someplace and his family here at Greyrock." His voice trailed off as he looked around the room and sighed.

"Greythorne," she corrected. "Warrick Barry, Marquis of Ralstead."

"That's what I read."

"Father, I mean Bane," she corrected, taking a deep breath. "It's good you're here. Warrick needs your help, my help. He'd found evidence that Landgon is involved with the French. The information isn't clear, but I believe they want to invade Bermuda. I want to tell him what I know, about my abilities, but I promised you. . . ."

"Yes, you did," he interrupted. "And that's a promise never to be broken."

"Landgon knows, I'm sure of it. Someone from the crew must have told him."

"Son of a . . ." Bane shot a glance at her and scratched his head. "He's a toad. Most likely Thomas; I was sure prison would break him."

"I should have confided in Warrick."

"No. If he was to find out you're a pilot, you'd be hanged. Women aren't supposed to work on ships. I'd be hanged for letting you learn. The crew—Hack, Bug, Nick, all of them—would be strung up because they know our secrets. As for Landgon, he won't admit anything that would give away his own plans."

"I didn't tell him. I know my duty." Karly pressed her lips, considering him for a long moment before continuing. "But now that you're here, things might be different." She cocked her head at him. "You already know what Landgon's up to."

Bane released her and waved his hand between them. "Aye, and you're as bright as always. You figured it out without seeing what I have."

She caught his hand, searching his face; his scowl told her much hadn't been said. "You have to tell Warrick what you know."

"Warrick, is it?"

"It is in his best interest to help you, to stop Landgon."

"If I wanted to meet him, I would have introduced myself rather than sneaking in the servants' entrance. No, child. Best if he thinks I'm dead. Your Marquis wants to build more houses like this one. He's interested in how to fix things, not find the truth. His kind is never interested in the truth of people like you and me. No one can help me right now."

"You're wrong."

She felt his anger shift like the wind. Then it vanished. "I only came here to make sure you were doing well. I have plans of my own, to find the crew and help them move on. I'll make things right, and I'll not be burdenin' anyone to do it," he finished.

"Now that I know you're alive and that I was right about Landgon, I'll break my promise. I'll help Warrick, before it's too late."

Bane grasped her shoulders and gave her a small shake. "Don't be foolish. You weren't onboard when we took and unloaded Landgon's ship. He's not merely passing information; he wants to rule the island."

"Why would you say that?"

"Hack and I removed two metal safe boxes." He leaned closer. "It was gold."

"No one noticed you carrying something that heavy?"

"We did it in the dark, and I had already opened a cask of rum. No one was paying attention to us. In the smaller one was a letter signed by the commander of the French Navy himself. The coins were for paying for militia and guns."

"And when Landgon heard, he came after you looking for it, and tried to kill you."

"I was injured. The lady who sheltered me spread the rumor that I died shortly thereafter. That way, when Landgon tried to question anyone, I would take the blame. No one would be the wiser."

"Except Landgon came after me."

"I hid the treasure in your favorite cave. It was good and dark. It's not possible he could find his way back without my help, or yours."

"That explains much." Karly suddenly felt nauseous. Her father was not evil, but somehow he had lost his way through this mess. It was up to her to bring him back to reality. "The crew and I were thrown in prison for the unauthorized taking of that ship."

"It was better than letting Landgon know the truth. You know as well as I do that, save for good luck, not one of them is even close to being a good shot, let alone much of a pirate. They would have been hunted down and killed within a week. No, better to let them think I took it. Hack kept his silence, couldn't find his way back if he wanted to, and I set up traps just in case the wrong person tried," he wheezed.

"So you knew Landgon's plans but you did nothing?" Karly asked, angrily.

"I hid the money. Without it, he can't pay for any troops, now can he?"

Karly shook her head in disbelief. "You could have warned the governor."

Bane began to pace a short line. "Would that be the same man who called me a pirate? The one who threw ye in prison? No, I'd not be going to the governor. And I didn't tell you so he couldn't use you."

"Instead, I've become extremely valuable. Not only can I pilot, but I know where and how to get the gold." She shook her head. "But then, if I'm better off alive, he wouldn't be the one to put a bounty on me."

Bane clenched his jaw and muttered a curse, then raised a hand in apology, coughing hard. "This Warrick is below useless, letting Landgon speak to you and a bounty be called. I should be on me way, before anyone's the wiser. Someone might find the man I borrowed this from," he grinned and plucked at his suit. "I had to make sure you weren't being mistreated. Once I get settled, I'll send word where you can find me. In the meantime, you stay out of sight." He sighed, then, kissing her cheek, started for the French doors. "I must say, you do look elegant dressed up so prettily, thought it was yer mother when you first walked in."

Karly struggled with what to do. Her father meant well, but his reasoning was flawed. With his health failing, she needed more time. He needed her. She had lost him once. She might be able to prevent it happening again. Warrick could help, but Bane would not believe him. With the letter and the gold she would prove his innocence. She was risking Warrick's trust. Having abandoned him, he would likely rebuff her. But he would do what was right when it came to Bane. "I'm coming with you."

Bane turned to her in an instant. "Not likely." He jerked his thumb toward the ballroom.

He wanted her to leave. She had no intention of letting him walk out of her life so easily. "That was not a request."

"How far do you think you will get in that dress? In that color you'll be spotted before we get halfway across the lawn."

With a decided wrinkle of her nose, Karly reached for the sideboard and removed the pair of silver peacocks. Whisking off the dark tablecloth she wrapped it around herself. "Better?"

"I'm not traveling in the best of circles. You said this Warrick has been looking after you. I've never been much good at it. You are safe here."

It was growing late. She would not win this argument. Instead she made for the small door that led into the garden. "If we take horses, we'll make better time," she whispered.

"You're as stubborn as yer mother."

"I'll consider that a compliment." She swept outside and down the perimeter path. "We'll find your proof, and then we'll tell Warrick and you'll let him help you." She saw his eyes flash and raised her hand. "Or, I can simply begin screaming, and we can take our chances." She heard him mutter a curse. "Is that a yes?"

"It's not fit to be repeated," he answered, then took her hand. "Come on, there's not much time."

Across the lawn they hurried, taking the far side around. Leaving the house, she could not bear to look behind her, not while her heart was so firmly set forward. But as they crossed the courtyard, she searched the many windows for one more glimpse of Warrick. He would be waiting for her, and she would not return, not for a long time.

"If he means that much to you, go find him."

Karly listened past the sounds of the party. "No one will be around the back of the stables at this hour. All the visitors' horses are at this end," she said, pointing at the darkened building.

Bane shook his head. "Better than horses, there's the butcher's wagon, and he's getting ready to leave. We can sneak aboard and ride it all the way to London." Before she could answer, he took off at a run, following the hedgerow. Then he crossed to the cart and climbed inside.

Karly scrambled up beside him into the deep straw that smelled strongly of livestock. A hand clamped over her mouth, and another seized her from behind. Someone grabbed her legs, and she was tossed face first into the darkness. She tried to scream and bite as a cloth was dragged across her mouth and tied securely. Beneath her the cart began to move. Ropes bit into her ankles.

"I'm sorry, Karly. It's for your own good," Bane said from somewhere in the murky darkness.

Karly felt him gather her hair as he had when she was a little girl. She yanked away.

"Try and get some rest. It's a long ride," Bane said.

She fought, and when he tried to soothe her, she kicked. Beneath the gag, she cried out. The cart shuddered as the pace picked up, but she continued her efforts. He began telling her stories through the darkness, of places he had been. His cough and wheeze disappeared, no longer needed to garner her sympathy. She blocked him out. With each passing hour his voice grew tighter, and yet he rambled on as she worked and night turned to day. She refused to meet his gaze. Mercifully dusk came again. She could see nothing. Exhausted and sore, she had no choice but to slacken, her wrists slick with blood.

It was dark when the cart finally halted and the gate opened. She waited for Bane to climb down and coiled herself to spring. Before she could, she was hoisted like a bag of flour by the two men who had tied her up, and tossed down at him. She listened to them talk, and tried to make sense of her environment. They were at the riverfront, the dark shape of a schooner docked nearby. Bane carried her aboard, across the deck, and into the shadows below. Dank smells seared her nostrils. She choked, trying hard not to breathe. Stench of an unkempt ship and unwashed sailors grew as they traveled down the dreary passage, ending in the cargo hold. He lifted her. She squirmed and tumbled hard to the floor.

Pain lanced her shoulders from lack of use, but she refused even a whimper. She had shared enough of her suffering. She would share no more. Besides, Bane was arguing with the men, and for the moment she was an afterthought. Then it was over, and Bane approached, knife in hand, and cut her gag, then set to work on her bonds. Once free she wanted to yell at him. Instead she drew as far away as she could, lest she strike him and make matters worse.

"I need your dress."

Karly glared at him in warning as he hunkered down before her. "I think not."

"A gown like that will fetch a handsome sum, and we need money. I brought some of your old things," he said, retrieving a nearby bundle revealing her old gowns.

"You went to my room at Greythorne," she said, understanding for the first time how well planned her kidnapping had been. "Did you read about the marriage in the paper, or was that a ruse too?"

"I did not want to deceive you, but I had to get you out of there, away from him."

"Tell me the truth! You owe me that much!" She saw the men's heads whip in her direction, but she didn't care. She was watching Bane.

"Mind your tone; I'm still your father," he snapped.

"Yes, you are," she said and looked away.

"Here, girl, don't cry. It's for the best, you understand,"

he said, eyeing the two men. "I need your help; I couldn't take a chance on his lordship of Greyrock."

"My husband," she blinked.

"What kind of a man marries a girl without her father's permission?"

"You were dead!" Karly staggered to her feet and saw the men tense. She ran her tongue across her lips, and faced Bane. "You want the gown?" She began unbuttoning it in front of all three of them. Bane started to protest, but she was too furious to be logical. Lifting it above her head, she all but threw it at him. Clad in her undergarments, she was barely covered. She glared at her audience, daring them to comment, before grabbing one of the old gowns and tugging it over her head. "Good luck selling it, just leave Murdock alone."

"Murdock?"

"He's a trader at the docks. He's trying to make a decent living. He pays too much so people don't feel cheated. Leave him out of it." Facing the wall, she sank to the floor and rested her head against the wooden planks. Her ploy to involve Murdock was obvious, maybe too much so. Hopefully it was so obvious they would think it impossible she would try it, and would take the gown to Murdock. He might recognize it as one of the ones he had sold Warrick. He might be able to tell Warrick who sold it to him, if everything went in her favor. Then it was a question of whether Warrick would actually come. He needed her help, but if he thought she had run away, he might not. Then there were her drawings and her evasions. By now, might he not have had enough?

Karly wrapped her arms around herself in misery. The probability of things falling in her favor were close to nil. Her father touched her shoulder, and she jerked away. "No." Curling up, she closed her eyes, heard him turn the key in the lock, and prayed for oblivion.

Chapter 13

It was the worst ball Warrick had ever attended. Every woman he glanced at reminded him of Karly. Over a week, she had been gone. He hadn't looked for her; he refused to beg any woman to return. He had given more to Karly than he had to anyone in the past, and now, it was uncomfortable. He closed his eyes and when he opened them, William had appeared, his last golden-haired offering missing. "I'm not in the mood."

"It's not what you think."

Warrick shook his head. "I don't want to think." He eyed William's wineglass.

"Suppose I told you I might know where Karly is. Would you want to know?"

"No." Circumventing his brother, Warrick strode outside, following the columned path in a half circle until he reached the winter garden. There he chose a bench at the far end of the large round pool and listened to the fountain as he cleared his head. He still wasn't alone. There was a rustle, a bit of color at the edge of his vision, and he turned hopefully. Amanda emerged, two glasses in her hands. She settled next to him, a gap between them, and wordlessly handed him one of the glasses.

Accepting wasn't difficult, but drinking was. His throat tight, he sipped as the torches played, and raised his gaze to the figurine in the fountain. She was naked, body taut, breasts lifted, arms outstretched, the water playing over her long, impractical hair.

"You miss her."

He did drink then, half the glass, but the tannins held no pleasure. "She was entertaining."

"She was also beautiful," Amanda added quietly.

"Yes, she was." He dragged his gaze to her and searched her face. "And you were jealous."

"You were in love with her; you never were with me. It was hard to accept." Amanda paused for a drink. "I don't think it any secret I want to marry you. I may not be as exciting as she was, but I can be kind."

"I've seen it, with your brothers and their children." He laid his hand over hers. It was warm, but it held no warmth, no pleasure. Years appeared in an instant. He could almost see children, Karly's children with his dark hair. He looked again at the statue and rose. "Excuse me, Amanda. I need to find William." He set the glass down and started at a walk, broke into a run the moment he turned the corner. Bursting into the ballroom, out of breath, he spied William between the Lastrum twins, one on each arm. He nearly plowed him over.

"I was wondering when you would come find me," William said, grinning.

"Don't be conceited; what do you know?"

Kissing each lady's hand, William gestured Warrick with him out of the ballroom, down the stairs into the courtyard. Along the line of carriages, they stopped at William's while the coachman jumped down and opened the door.

"We're leaving?" But Warrick's question was answered when Murdock stepped down, clutching a brown paper package.

* * *

As Warrick studied the vessel, he found a new emotion taking control: dread. There had been no sign of her, although he had recognized Bane from Karly's locket. Active as she was, he could not imagine a circumstance that would keep her below deck unless she was in trouble, injured, or dead. Anger at Bane kept him focused. A duel would be too polite. For slipping into Greythorne, Warrick wanted to punch him. For taking Karly with him, he would fight.

One of Admiral Howarth's lieutenants rushed up and saluted. "We're down to three guards."

"Everyone is ready then?" Warrick asked, exchanging a glance with William.

"They'll sail soon. We have no choice but to be ready," Admiral Howarth said. "Try not to worry, son. If your lady is in there, we'll find her."

Warrick pulled his pistol from his coat. "I intend to come with you."

"Very well, but my lieutenant gives the orders."

Warrick gave the man a nod and watched as a small group of officers moved toward the stern of the ship. Then he followed the black-draped lieutenant toward the bow. Scouts were up the bow lines and onto the deck before a single cry was uttered. Riding the crest of men, Warrick tried for the doors below. Twice he was stopped by pistol fire as men swarmed onto the deck. Then he saw Bane appear and disappear below. Warrick fell to the deck and rolled his body. He made for the door, skidding down the steps. A pistol cocked, and he ducked as splinters exploded above his head. From behind him came shouts of reinforcements.

Down here, between decks, he could see little and hear even less over the ruckus above his head. A door rattled from the right passageway, and he aimed toward the sound.

"Give it up, Bane." His answer was the scuffling of feet. Dropping the pistol, Warrick dove at the sound, slamming into fabric and flesh.

"Where's Karly?" he roared and hit Bane again. Bane grunted and fell limp. Ice balled in his stomach as footsteps rushed from behind; the lieutenant carrying a lantern illuminated the scene into a grayish nightmare. Bane snarled to life, knocking Warrick into the wall and scrambling down the passage. A pistol roared, and Bane collapsed along with Warrick's hopes.

"Don't fire! He has to help me find Karly." Reaching Bane, Warrick saw the dark stain by the man's shoulder. Turning him over, he stared hard into the cloudy gaze and forced his voice to remain calm. "Where is she?"

"She said you were bright," Bane muttered and closed his eyes.

Warrick gave him a small shake and repeated the question when there was a muffled cry from nearby—Karly's voice. He sprang to his feet. "Call again!"

"I'm in here!" she answered. The third door to his left rattled.

"Get him to a surgeon," he ordered as he ran, threw the bolt, and swung the door wide. Karly tumbled forward into his waiting arms. Touch, the feel of her body to his, was all encompassing. It stole his breath. Clasping her tight, then tighter, he didn't dare close his eyes, lest she vanish and her presence become a repeated dream. "You're safe."

"You're here." She buried her head against his shoulders, clinging tight.

There were problems, but all doubts disappeared. More than obligation or affection had brought him here; how to handle the emotional repercussions would be his burden and hers as well. Their relationship had changed, although he wasn't certain when, but more than a vow bound them. Lifting his head, he studied her, paler, tired, more beautiful than he remembered. There was too much he wanted to say; pride and awareness held him back.

"Where are you taking Bane?"

The mood shattered as sounds filtered back, and those around him became clear again. Warrick glanced at the naval men. They had Bane on his feet, his eyes open, his color good. Apparently the faint had been yet another ruse. Disgusted, Warrick looked down at Karly. "He's going to Newgate, where he belongs."

"But I went willingly. You can't send him to prison. He'll die."

"Then we're no worse than when we started," Warrick snapped, and then he saw her raw wrists. "He tied you up?"

Karly didn't argue; she buckled, her knees giving way. He followed her to the ground, softening her landing. He had been prepared for banter, or to carry her if necessary, but surrendering? Relief tainted by worry filled his heart. He fought an inner battle to remain calm. "Why would you go with him?"

Karly peered up at him. "I told you he's innocent."

"Innocent men don't run and hide."

"They do when no one will believe them. I was going to help him."

"You are making this difficult. It looks as if you are part of all this," Warrick vented in frustration.

"She's got nothin' to do with this," Bane hissed.

Warrick's control fractured as he looked into the older man's face. "I don't know, nor do I care what side you are on anymore. You could have gotten her killed, for trusting you and believing in you. If that bears any weight, I suggest you consider very carefully what you do and say next."

Karly grabbed Warrick's lapel and jerked him to her. "Landgon wants me because I'm a skilled pilot."

"Karly, don't!" Bane shouted, holding his shoulder and struggling.

She closed her eyes before continuing. "Landgon found out. That is why he wanted to hire me from my uncle. I can guide any ship around any reef in Bermuda. That was how I made the drawings of the island. Those ships I drew are based on ones I've seen in St. George's harbor. You may investigate. They all docked there."

Bane let out a yelp, but Warrick ignored him, and turned to the admiral. "I need to get her home. She's overwrought."

Karly plucked at his wrist. "There's more—a box, with documents and gold. I'll help you find it if you promise me you won't send him to Newgate. I won't leave without your word."

Her threat meant nothing. He could carry her without effort. But her adamant pleas tore his resolve to send the man as far from Karly as possible. "He's a pirate," Warrick said, keeping his voice gentle as Karly shook her head vehemently.

"If I may suggest," began the admiral, "I will take Mr. Bane to the Academy. We can keep a watch on him while we sort this out."

Warrick found himself at a loss. She was shivering. He wrapped her in his arms. She bent her head and hid against his shoulder, waiting for his decision. He lifted his gaze to where the men stood guard over Bane, poised and ready. "Thank you, Admiral."

"I will make certain he speaks to no one except you or me."

Karly shuddered harder, and Warrick tightened his hold as Bane was led away. Thankfully, the man said nothing. "We'll discuss the rest of this from home." He made to carry her, but she pushed away and got to her own feet, bracing one hand on the wall.

"I will manage."

There did not appear to be much keeping her upright, except willpower. She was protecting her father, no doubt, trying to make the situation look less dire than it appeared.

Warrick thought he had pieced together Karly's past. He should have known there was more. She made it as far as the gangway before her strength gave in. Lifting her in his arms, he carried her to the waiting carriage. As the horses moved off, she told him of the ships she had piloted, her time working for Mr. Hasings, and her life amongst the pirates. Through bouts of dizziness, she did not stop. It was difficult to hear of the hardships, but he willed himself silent. But when she came to her life after Bane's supposed death, he noticed the story took a leap forward. One moment she was in prison with the crew, and the next, she was on her uncle's ship. "How long were you in prison?"

"I didn't keep a record. Uncle Angus arrived. You know the rest."

"He was in Bermuda when he was sent for?"

"No, he wasn't."

In his head he estimated three months, if everything had worked in her favor. From the haunted look in her eyes, it hadn't. At the house, she didn't object when he carried her to the bedroom. She tried to undo the stays of her gown, but her hands shook and she plodded toward the bed.

"I am going to help you," Warrick promised.

"I did not mean for any of this."

"I realize that now." He leaned her against him and unbuttoned her gown, slipping it over her head and feeling the warmth of her skin. She was back in his arms. Their bonds of trust were in tatters, but she was here, alive, willing, soft. He removed her petticoats, and found no stockings. Had it been winter, she would have been ill. Taking her clothes to the dresser where he had first seen her in her desperate search, he set them aside. Much had changed since then, but not Karly's resolve. She believed in her father's innocence, and that meant something. Despite all that had happened she had remained steadfast and loyal. Next door, the sounds of servants died, a door shut, and he knew they were alone. "There is a bath waiting. I'll help you."

She laced her fingers with his as he helped lower her into the warm water, keeping her wrists clear. Her silk chemise became translucent, her breasts and body visible. His blood heated at the memory of their night together. It had been more than coupling—making love he could call it, savoring their tenuous bond. He wanted more, now, to climb into the tub with her and keep her there in passion, rebuild the frayed edges of their relationship until the base was strong and they could continue. It was out of the question—she was exhausted—but his imagination had taken him too far. His body hard, he didn't speak, afraid his voice would betray his arousal. He took the bottle of powdered soap, opened it, and poured it into his hand. "Wet your hair. I'll wash it." She sank beneath the surface of the water and sat, pushing her hair from her face. Warrick began to work, keeping his gaze fixed on the gold-flecked tiles on the wall and his touch on Karly. There was no substitute: the statue, another woman, a memory would not do. It was her, this, he thought, running his fingers through her chestnut hair.

"I have made matters worse," she whispered.

"Your father is alive. That is a great help." He had to stop when she turned her head to look at him. "I'll deal with it in the morning."

"What do you plan to do?"

"I plan to finish helping you and then get some sleep." He helped her out of the tub and into a robe, by the fire, where he wrapped her wrists with soft linen. "I will send a maid to help you dress and get to bed. If you need anything, I will be in the library."

"I wish you wouldn't leave."

There was need in her voice. It gave him hope. "I can't stay, not yet, but I won't go far."

He left, wandering restlessly through the house as anger

spread through him. All she had said, in a rush, could have been told before. He understood why she had waited, but it burned him that she had. Several times he tried to sit, but took to touring until he was interrupted in the salon by William. "Where is Bane?" Warrick asked his brother.

"Secured in a locked room on the second floor of the Naval Academy, and I must say it is a good deal nicer than that hole he tried to sail in. I doubt that ship would have made it down the Thames. How is Karly?"

"Better now that I'm taking care of her." He pursed his lips and closed his fists, wanting to hit something.

"Bane asked after her."

Warrick gave an ungentlemanly snort and entered the library. "He can ask all he likes. If he wants to speak it will be to me or the admiral. He nearly killed her. Her wrists are in shreds from where he tied her."

"Apparently Karly tried to escape, to come back to you. He wanted to prevent it. From his point of view, you kidnapped her."

"Naturally. I'm a marquis; what would I know about his life?"

William chose the chair near the door and settled into it, resting his hands while he regarded his brother. "I meant to compliment you, for hitting him in the shoulder rather than killing him. That took a great deal of restraint."

"He has crucial information," Warrick muttered.

William's eyes narrowed, and then he nodded his head slowly. "Right."

"He wanted me to tell you that Karly agreed to come, but when they got to the cart, he had her tied up. He didn't think she would really leave you."

"He was wrong," Warrick sighed and sat at his desk.

"Bane is convinced that you are simply using her," William sighed.

Warrick opened the middle drawer and pulled out the

letter. "Then he would be very glad to read this since it would rid her of her obligation to me." He handed William the document and waited for the reaction.

"The king sent you an annulment order?"

"When Karly disappeared, I assumed she wanted to go. I wrote him and asked that he 'unharness me from overwhelming hardship.' That arrived the next day." He leaned back in his chair, the creak of the leather not at all comforting.

"Sounds as if you have the matter well in hand," William snorted and got to his feet.

"You have no notion what I have been through for her already. I care for her. I admit it. The feeling is not mutual."

"Then by all means, brother, sign the paper and get rid of her. If you truly believe she does not care a whit for you, then you have every right to be free from the hell that would come from living with a woman such as Karly."

"You have no idea what you're talking about."

"With all due respect, Warrick, neither do you," William said and started for the door. Halting inside the threshold he again turned to face Warrick. "I am fond of her, nearly as much as I am of you."

"I should overlook what has happened?"

"You should weigh everything very carefully. If you do, that paper will be the first thing you burn in your fire."

Warrick listened as William retreated deeper into the house. Tucking the letter in his safe box, he locked it. Then he pulled out the broken sextant he had discovered in Karly's trunk that first day. It had been hers. The signs were there, had he only read them properly. It did not cancel her deception, but he did feel guilty he had not solved the puzzle. He carried it with him and returned upstairs. Karly was seated before the fire, threading her fingers through her hair. Her bare feet peeked out from under her sleeping gown, and an empty tray sat beside her, morsels all that was left. She had not bothered to wear a wrap. She glanced around as he entered and followed his progress toward her. "I could have been anyone."

"I hoped it would be you."

He searched for the appropriate response and did not trust his voice, so he remained silent. Taking a seat across from her, he listened to the sound of crackling logs while she held his gaze. Her eyes were fields of uncertainty as she waited patiently. "You will be glad to learn your father will be fine. I plan to question him tomorrow."

Karly looked at her hands and slumped her shoulders. "You don't want me to go."

"And you are going to ask me to take you."

"He thinks you're using me. I can correct that. I told him what you were trying to accomplish," Karly added quietly.

Warrick remembered the instrument in his hand. "I believe this is yours," he said and gave her the sextant.

"You're disappointed I didn't tell you earlier."

He had to break his gaze because he didn't want to lie. "You did what you thought you had to do. I'm furious, I think you're biased, and I believe you're irresponsible. I also can't see questioning Bane without your help."

"I'm sorry."

"I know that too." He reached out and took her hands. "I'm glad you're all right."

She rose, walking to the bed and sliding beneath the covers without another word. After a moment, he followed, just as soundlessly, taking a seat on the bed, desperate not to break the contact. "What am I going to do with you?" he whispered and returned the sad smile that played on her lips. Her eyes drifted closed as he caressed her hair, her breath softening into a rhythm, her hand resting by her face. So peaceful, the week might not have happened, except the scars were there, on her arms, in his heart.

Chapter 14

Answers about their surroundings would calm her nerves. Warrick had barely spoken to her all morning. He was polite, but not much more; the gentle night was long gone. Arches soared, and painted cherubs flew about her head in the mammoth building Karly had first mistaken for a palace. The Naval Academy was meant to intimidate anyone who entered and did its job to perfection. She felt humbled and disoriented.

She could have learned her trade here, had she been a man, born of the right family with the right connections. From the stunned looks of the officers they passed, the only reason she was welcome today was because she was accompanied by Warrick.

One long gallery turned into another. It seemed they had circled the entire courtyard or grass and marble when Warrick rapped on a lacquered door and escorted her inside. The uniformed man at the desk rose, greeted them, and vanished through another door at the end of the room. Minutes passed before the door opened again, admitting a beefy graying man in a heavily decorated uniform. He greeted Warrick first, then removed his great plumed hat and gave her a quick bow.

"I am Admiral Howarth, and you would be Lady Ralstead. I understand you claim to be a trained pilot."

Karly's thoughts stumbled over her title. No one had addressed her as "Lady" before. It sounded too odd for her to own. "Please call me Karly. I am not trained, but I do know Bermuda," she admitted and saw the admiral and Warrick exchange glances.

"You will forgive me, but I need to test that. I am responsible for our naval operations in that part of the world, and pilots are of special interest."

"What would you like me to do?"

"It's rather simple," he said, showing her into his office and to a large map on the wall. With his index finger he broadly traced the perimeter of the hook-shaped island. "Suppose I was sailing an eighteen-gun schooner, and I wanted to land unseen. Where would you direct me, and how would you get me in?"

Karly looked to Warrick. He wore the same expression he had all morning: a stoic mask. Her violation of his trust had come to this. "What is the vessel's draft?" she asked.

"We can say it's twenty feet."

She let his gray watery eyes bore deep into her, accepting his challenge. Karly faced the map. She moved forward until she could no longer see Warrick, even from the corner of her eye. Whether he was angry or pleased, she didn't want his reaction to distract her. "Not knowing the ship, the wind, or the crew, it is rather difficult. I suppose I would bring you in here at Basch Cove along the South Shore, away from St. George. The rocks are high enough to hide your masts."

"It is also full of reefs."

"You are correct, which is why you need a pilot." She clasped both hands behind her and faced her judges. "You do not believe me."

The admiral smiled dryly. "I'm sure your information is

accurate, but it could have been attained through many channels."

There was no harshness in his voice. He seemed a factual man. She couldn't fault him for stating an obvious concern. "It is also possible I overheard it in a conversation and am just repeating it now."

"Are you?" the admiral asked.

Karly faced Warrick. His brown eyes appeared black, fathomless with thoughts she wished they could talk through; the rest of him was as if carved of stone. "No. I am telling you the truth."

Warrick broke his stance and gave a slight nod. "Admiral, would it be possible for us to see Bane now?"

"I will take you myself," the admiral said, giving Karly an appraising look.

She assumed they would have another long walk ahead of them. Instead, they turned one corner and entered another office where two guards stood on either side of an ordinary door. Saluting the admiral, the men pushed it open. Karly entered to find another two officers in full uniform. Bane lay in the center of the empty room in a large cot. A small table with water was nearby, and a large window threw light on the whitewashed walls. Had it not been stark, it would appear cheery. It was clean, and the air was fresh. She sat beside Bane as he turned to regard the small group. Then he looked at her, and searched her face.

"What do you want, Karly girl?" he asked.

"Not this," she said, indicating the bandage on his shoulder.

"How many times have I told ye not to worry about things that are not in your control?"

She took his hand and held it between hers. "Father, I need to talk to you. The chest you took from Landgon's ship. I need to know how it is protected."

"That money is for the crew. They earned it pure fair. If certain people had not taken away our license," he said, glaring at the admiral, "then they would have been able to keep it."

"It's not the gold I want. It's the documents you mentioned."

Bane let out a half laugh, half cough and shook his head. "I see ye are back to strength and have found your sense of humor."

"I am not joking."

He removed his hand and laid it across his chest. "What I said to you was meant to stay with you," Bane muttered blackly.

Karly closed her eyes and steadied herself against her father's growing anger. "I know. I have kept my word to you as best I could. Circumstances have changed," she continued. "Surely you must see that."

"All I see is a daughter who would rather warm a man's bed than a father's heart."

She sat so straight it felt as if her spine might snap. A tremor of anger started around her heart and spiraled outward. She felt a hand touch her shoulder and looked up to find Warrick beside her. "Had you declared that booty and had it been legitimate, you and the crew would have only received a portion. That is the nature of being a privateer."

Bane clenched his jaw. "Some is better than nothing."

"And freedom is better than prison," Karly said with cold, measured words.

Bane rolled toward her and narrowed his eyes. "Did he hurt you? In prison, did . . ."

"You've changed the subject," Karly said, interrupting him. How she had let the specter of Commander Farris into the conversation she wasn't sure. The man was in Bermuda, supervising the fort, not here. A trickle of sweat slid down her back at the prospect of her nightmares returning. It could have been worse, she reminded herself. He could have raped her. But he had tried to frighten and blackmail her, no more. "We were discussing the documents. They might incriminate Landgon."

"By now someone else may have taken his place. The French may have a new plot. The documents could be worthless."

"Once this is exposed, the embarrassment to the French will be so profound that no one will dare. Besides, if it is as great a sum as you mentioned, I doubt they will be able to duplicate it so quickly," she said, thankful to be back on course. "In exchange, I would like to make a proposal." Karly slanted a glance at the admiral. "The crew will be allowed to divide the gold. All charges against you will be dropped, and your license will be reinstated."

The admiral coughed, or did he choke? Elaborately clearing his throat, he dabbed his mouth with a handkerchief. "Treason is not my decision."

"To have stolen property from a traitor is not a crime, Admiral. My father has done England a great service if his efforts thwarted Landgon in any way." She turned back to her father. "The provision is that you must help with what you know."

"And I am to trust you on your word?"

"I have not lied to you. You made me promise to remain silent of my trade if something happened to you. I did as you asked."

"This is what happens when you spend time with too many fancy Englishmen."

Karly bowed her head. With Warrick behind her, her father in front, she felt as if she were in the vortex of a tempest.

"I need those papers," Warrick said.

"What say you?" Bane demanded of Warrick. "You're willing to part with a box filled with gold for a few papers?"

"I have my own condition," Warrick answered.

Bane raised his eyebrows. "By all means go right ahead. A vivid fantasy is all the grander."

"Someone has placed a bounty on Karly. I want the truth: what you know or even suspect, everything. If you lie, I'll know."

Bane's mouth grew thin, "You think it is someone against me?"

"You were thought dead. There would be little in revenge. But you have been to London before. Tell me what you can so that I can deal with this threat."

Lifting his hand, Bane cupped Karly's cheek. "For all the mischief you cause, I can't think of any enemies." Then he raised his gaze to Warrick. "But I would not put anything past the Roberts family."

"Angus Roberts?"

"Angus is my wife Caroline's brother. I was thinking of their parents, Karly's grandparents."

"Why would they hate Karly?" Warrick asked.

Bane gave Karly a long, calculating look. "We did not part on good terms. I met Caroline when she came aboard my ship. Dressed as a lad, she was asking for work. It wasn't long before I discovered her identity. She had run from home after her father had arranged to marry her to a butcher. We fell in love, and soon she was pregnant with Karly. We rented a small room in St. George, and Caroline took a position stitching sails. We intended to make it honorable. We published bans, and I went to sea to earn a bit more. I wanted to buy a proper home." He cleared his throat and took a fortifying breath.

"What happened?" Warrick asked.

"I was gone longer than I expected, the winds and all. When I returned, Angus had carried Caroline to England." He narrowed his eyes and made a fist. "By the time I caught up to them, she had given birth and died. Mr. Roberts had refused to call a midwife. Didn't want anyone to know

Karly existed, or that I did for that matter. They handed her to me and told me they never wanted to see either one of us again."

Warrick frowned. "And since then, have you met?"

Bane shook his head. "I hate them. I blame them for Caroline's death as much as they blame me." He took Karly's hand. "Don't cry, Karly girl."

Bane had never told her the whole story. Only that her mother had died giving birth. Karly got to her feet. It was too late to hide the tears, so she pretended they weren't there. "Draw me a map, and I will keep my end of the bargain." With that, she strode past the soldiers, through the doorway, and past the second set of guards. At some point she began to run, lifting her skirts when she nearly tripped.

It was midday, and the streets weren't crowded. She dashed across several without checking for carts. A splash of green caught her eye, and she veered into and down the forest path when Warrick called her name. It occurred to her this was not his first call. It was more effort to stop than to continue. She fell into a brisk walk as he drew alongside her. Together they passed large trees that had seen far more interesting things than her. The sound of stones crunching beneath her feet became irksome. She wanted silence and took to the grass. When they reached a small lake, she stopped and looked both directions, trying to decide which way. Neither made any difference.

"He never told you about your mother to protect you," Warrick said in a quiet voice.

"I know. It was a long time ago. I shouldn't care."

"And yet here we are."

She twisted toward Warrick. His arms were open to her. She risked meeting his eyes, and the world fell away. It was all she could to do to hazard a step. He met her partway, pulled her to him, and wrapped her in his arms. "I don't know what happens next," she said.

He kissed the top of her head, then her brow.

"I know I shouldn't have made all those promises," she said.

He caught her chin and lifted her face. With his thumb he brushed away her tears. "I will make it happen."

It was all she could do to nod. She wished for calm, but it was several minutes before she could speak again. "I shouldn't have left until Bane gave his word."

"When you're ready, we'll go back. Let's give him a chance to think."

She wanted to forget what Bane had told her. In her mind she had imagined her grandparents. They had been graying and kind. Their voices had been husky and soft. Her grandfather had smoked a pipe, and her grandmother had smelled of cinnamon. She kept to herself as they returned to Warrick's house and during dinner. Trying to be pleasant, she pretended to be positive about the weather, fashion, and William's observations about changes during his absence. London was busier, women dressed more outlandishly, the air was darker. She agreed with it all with half her attention until the subject turned to the *Moorea*. The rush of thoughts halted, and she blinked into the present, seeing the plate of meats before her and the men seated around the table. "Are you planning on sending her to sea?" Karly asked, settling her gaze on Warrick to her left.

He set down his fork, but looked first to William, then Trent before meeting her eyes. "I'm taking her to Bermuda to get the evidence. It's what I have to do."

"Without Bane's help, it will be difficult." The words had to be right when she asked her next question. She faltered. "I can go with you."

A long silence fell. Then William sat forward, rested his elbows on the table, and cocked his head at Warrick. "The charts on the *Moorea* need updating. Not to mention the fact we could use a good pilot. That is, if you are inclined to bring her aboard."

"You were banished by the governor, were you not?" Warrick asked.

Her heart skipped a beat, and fell. "Because of what Commander Farris said, yes. He was in charge of the fort where I was housed."

"Not for pirating?"

"You think I'm still lying to you." She held up her hand when he started to say something and shook her head. "I haven't given you much to trust, I know that. I'm telling the truth. You have every right not to believe me. I wouldn't blame you. I'm asking for the chance to prove myself."

Warrick tented his fingers, letting a minute drag. "You can come. I will handle the governor and Commander Farris, if he shows himself. Before we sail, see what Bane will tell you."

"There is one concern." Trent leaned in, and set his glass down. "I am not sure the crew will accept a female pilot."

William shrugged. "They care about remaining alive. If she is skillful, they'll accept her. Which reminds me— before you leave, you'll need a few more hands; several men just finished their contracts."

"I'll handle it," Trent answered.

Karly pushed away from the table and stood. She waved her hand dismissively when the men began to rise with respect. "I am going to get some rest. I will try to talk to my father tomorrow. Good night," she said, not hiding her weariness.

She didn't wake until dawn. During the night, Warrick had spooned against her, his hand over the curve of her waist. She nestled closer. There had been times over the past few days that she had wondered if she would ever be in his arms again. Better still, he had offered to let her pilot the *Moorea*. She had a place and position, and he had accepted her. She took one last memory and slid from his touch. Choosing a simple gown of flowered silk, she considered what words she would use to persuade her father. But when they arrived at the Academy, she was no closer to an answer. She faced Warrick. "Let me speak with him alone."

"I will be right here," Warrick said, and brushed her cheek with a kiss.

She greeted her father properly and seated herself much as she had the day before, taking his hand.

"You look improved," Bane said.

"I am."

"Yesterday . . ." he began.

She didn't want to revisit the story of her grandparents. "In a few days we are sailing to Bermuda to get the chest you mentioned. I came to see if you have instructions on finding it."

"You are asking me to trust this Warrick of yours."

"I intend to help him either way," she said, began to chew her lip, and stopped. "It would be easier with your guidance. We might be able to stop this whole plot."

"And what is your share?"

He had not always been this way. As much as he played the old warrior, she remembered the happy merchant. With time, perhaps she might see that side of him again. "Proof that my father is the admirable man I have told Warrick about."

Bane gave a small snort and reached under the pillow behind him. Handing her the folded piece of paper, he closed his hand over hers. "Not as detailed as one of your maps, but it's the trail as I remember it, and how to work your way through. The traps aren't exactly clear. Some are mine, but two were already there."

With relief she studied the paper. He had meant to help her all along. He had marked the positions well, noting each with his own code. "Set by whom?"

"Dunno. I managed not to spring them, but I don't know how they work. When you have questions, think of what I would have done."

Taking his hand, she gave him a smile. "You've done the right thing today."

"I've made a terrible pirate. But then you knew that."

"Yes, I knew that. Be safe," she whispered, and leaned forward, kissing him gently on the cheek. He lifted a hand to her shoulder, holding her close before releasing her and capturing her gaze.

Warrick had not moved from where she left him. The concern on his face was slow to ease, even when she showed him the map. "We can go over it on the *Moorea*." As they stepped into the sun, Karly glanced sidelong at his handsome profile. It was his eyes that drew her, but from this angle she couldn't see them. So she studied his mouth, jaw, and hair. Knowing she cared for him gave meaning to the confusion within her. He had to care for her, although she wasn't sure what that meant.

Her distraction was complete. She saw a rough-looking man by her side just as his hands closed around her waist. Another clamped over her mouth. She was dragged down the tight alley with walls so close she could almost reach both simultaneously. Karly saw Warrick struggling against two assailants. Planting one foot, she managed to kick out and succeeded in throwing herself off balance. She saw Warrick break free and heard his call, but his path toward her was blocked, the larger of his two assailants swinging with full force at him. Warrick dodged, his reflexes quick as he punched hard.

Karly saw the flash of the knife and concurrently her own death. The man behind her tightened his hold around her waist and raised the weapon to strike. She didn't think, just acted, grabbing the knife, her hand closing around the blade. Pain shocked her, and steel tore into her flesh, but she held fast, even as her own blood flowed, threatening her grip.

Warrick stumbled as the second man punched him from behind, while the first had armed himself with a knife as well. Tactically, she closed her eyes and feigned a faint, letting her full weight sag and fall, her captor dropping her with surprise. She landed hard and heard a man shout, but didn't look. Her plan, albeit flimsy, needed to be precise. Peering through her lashes, she saw her nemesis pause, then bend over her.

"Get the body," came an unfamiliar voice.

Her moment had come, and she took it. Kicking up with her legs, she knocked him to his side and jumped to her feet. She grabbed a board within her reach and whirled, holding her makeshift weapon at the ready. Not prepared to give in, he lunged. She swung, catching him by the ear with a loud whack, while evading his outstretched hand. She swung again and hit, catching him on the other side, and skittered again out of reach.

He roared, his hand to his head, and poised for another pass. Gathering herself like a cat, Karly waited. Warrick shouted from behind her, and her heart turned over. She said a silent prayer he was unharmed, but she couldn't turn, her adversary too close. Unexpectedly he shifted his gaze over her shoulder, and then he ran. Straightening in disbelief, arms suddenly closed around her from behind. She twisted, trying to wrench free. "No!" she screamed.

"Karly, it's over," Warrick breathed against her cheek, reaching for the board. "It's over," he repeated, "Let go, sweetheart."

He had called her sweetheart. Stunned, Karly let go and lay quietly in Warrick's arms.

Chapter 15

There was so much blood, Karly's blood. Warrick hoisted her into the carriage and climbed up, seizing her hand.

"It appears worse than it is, or could have been," Karly said, her voice eerily even.

"I need to wrap the wound, stop the bleeding." He released her injured hand and flipped up her skirt. Karly pushed it back down, froze, and removed her objection. From her petticoats he tore strips, tied two together, and began wrapping. "Hold this," he ordered. She closed her free hand tight and around his work.

"Three more should be enough."

Warrick did not look at her. He was distracted by the sharp turn of the coach. "Not the townhouse, the *Moorea*— it's closer," he told the driver. Karly laid her head in the crux of his shoulder. While he could no longer see her face clearly, her eyes were open, her expression thoughtful. "I think I should ask what's going through your head, before I find out the wrong way."

"We should go back, warn Bane."

Warrick shook his head. "There might be more. You are already hurt. Besides, it wasn't him they were after. It would be better if you rested until we reached the *Moorea*."

"You have a theory."

"Yes, which I'm not ready to share."

Karly sank back down, her body contouring to his. But her gaze stayed watchful, filled with calculations and suppositions. He let her be, saving his comments for a future conversation. He would get her safe, then contact the admiral. Possibilities were endless. The attackers might have nothing to do with Karly or Landgon, but his instinct said otherwise. They returned to Bane's comments about her family, Angus, and the grandparents. If Bane had read the announcement of their marriage, the grandparents might have as well.

Reaching the *Moorea*, he steeled his arm around her waist, ignoring her protest, and started up the gangway. Giving orders for word to be sent to William and Trent, he called for Wreck and took her into the great cabin. He saw the man's scowl as he turned. It vanished in the next breath, when Wreck caught sight of Karly. "Two men attacked us. She's hurt."

"Seems as if I'm not the only poor wet nurse," Wreck said tightly. As Karly sat, Wreck pulled a small table and set it to one side of her. "Get my supplies. I'll watch her."

He took orders from no one, save Wreck. It was too deeply ingrained; the man had trained him at sea. Warrick broke into a run, sliding down the stairs. He found the worn gray bag at the foot of Wreck's bunk. Without breaking stride he was back in the cabin while Wreck was still loosening the makeshift bandage. He untied it gingerly, careful not to jar her.

"Brandy," he ordered.

Pouring a snifter, Warrick handed it to him, and he passed it to Karly, who shook her head. "It gives me a headache. You drink it, or Warrick."

"I'm no maid, and this ain't a ball," Wreck frowned. "It's for the pain."

"Whiskey or rum, then; they're easy."

Wreck's eyes flitted to Warrick. He left, returning with a pewter mug. "Rum is never a problem," he said and thrust it to her.

She drank in three long drafts and dabbed her mouth on the corner of her sleeve.

With a raised brow, Wreck took the mug and thrust it back at Warrick. "Better?"

Karly nodded. Her cheeks burned from rose to red.

"Not many skirts can swallow rum like that." Wreck didn't look up as he examined the hand, turning it one way, then the other as fresh blood seeped free.

"I lived at sea for months at a time. It's safer than water."

"Smart lass," Wreck said with a nod of approval toward Warrick.

Warrick wished he could chide. His heart wasn't in it. Her hand in his, he placed it on a towel. Then he took the bottle of brandy Wreck handed him, and poured it over the wound. She cried out for the first time since the incident happened, started to jerk away, checked herself, and shuddered.

"I'm sorry," she said, her eyes bright with pain. "Perhaps I should do it."

"Not your own hand," Warrick soothed. "It's too deep. The bandage must be tight."

"Wrists are bad too," Wreck muttered, changed his hold, and continued his work. "Tell me what happened. I love a good spar."

Warrick recounted the attack, more to himself than to Wreck, mulling the details over in his mind. "While you rest, I have some things to attend to."

Karly got to her feet. "I want to come with you. He's my father."

"I'm not going to the Academy." It was not an answer she

would accept. He didn't want Karly's company. Not on this errand. He couldn't have her trying to follow him either.

"Mayhap you'd take a bit more rum, for the pain." Wreck offered Karly a second full mug. Sly in his reasoning, Warrick waited while Karly drank, the smile on Wreck's face growing larger. Wreck handed her a third and raised an empty mug to his lips. He waited for Karly to imitate him. "To a quick recovery."

Finishing her gulp, Karly coughed and shook her head.

Wreck topped her mug yet again. Warrick gave Wreck a small shake of his head. She didn't need any more. Drunk, she would fall asleep and likely wake with a vengeance. It was only a matter of time. Her words were already slurred.

"I am far sturdier than you give me credit for," she said.

"I'm sure you are," Warrick answered, taking the mug and lifting her to her feet.

She waved her index finger. "I know how to fence, and not that tiny little sword I used when we first met. I can fight with real blades, sharp ones too."

"Oh?" he asked, leading her by slow steps toward his quarters.

"I did not have a fancy instructor. My teachers were sailors, but don't call them pirates or I'll have to trip you."

"I will be very careful."

Karly's expression became serious. She halted, leaning the full weight of her body into his. "I learned to fight because I had to and it's a good thing." She shuffled in his hold and held up her bandaged hand. "It's not the first time I kept myself from being hurt. I fought off Farris too."

Warrick followed her gaze to Wreck, pretending her words had no real meaning. The name was familiar; Farris was the commander of the fort. "Farris had a knife?"

"No, but he was bigger."

"Why didn't you run?"

She shook her head. "I was locked in the cell. Nowhere

to go. I get nightmares, but they aren't real." Her voice slurred.

He touched her brow and traced his finger along her hairline before lacing his fingers deep into the silk. "No, they aren't. If you have more, come to me. I'll chase them away."

She reached up, hesitated, and touched her lips sweetly to his, her body, an invitation she pressed against him. Warrick heard the door close. They were alone. A few steps and they were at the edge of the bed. A tumble and he would not be able to stop until he had all of her. It was what he wanted, needed. As close as she was, it wasn't enough. Nothing would be.

She touched her face, and when he saw the bandage, his passion quelled. Later. All would wait until then when it would be both of them, undisturbed. A nudge was all she needed to sit. He did not expect her to hold on, her grip on his collar fierce. Landing with one arm on either side of her head, her body beneath his, Warrick pushed himself to his feet. "I can't now." He wanted to douse himself in a barrel of cold rainwater. He knelt by her head. He brushed his lips to her temple and urged her to rest. He watched her eyes drift closed. Striding into the main cabin, he pulled off his coat, exchanging it for the clean one over his chair, and then stepped to the wash basin, splashing his face.

"I'll watch over her," Wreck said.

"I know you will, and I won't be long," Warrick said distractedly.

"If you're going for who attacked you, you should take company."

"The men are gone by now."

"Take this," Wreck called and held out a pistol.

Accepting the weapon, Warrick gave Wreck a grim smile.

* * *

Inquiries led him down paths and streets until, within a period far too short to calm his temper, he found himself standing in front of the home of Phineous Roberts, Esquire—Karly's grandfather. What had once been a whitewash exterior was now a dingy gray and the accenting planks of deep brown had cracked. Windows were dark except for a flicker of light from deep within, behind gossamer curtains. Stepping onto the landing, he noted the tarnished brass plaque, an advertisement for Roberts's services, and knocked hard.

At first it was quiet, and he wondered if they had simply chosen not to answer. Then he caught the distinct sounds of someone approaching, followed by the creak of the bolt being drawn. The door swung open, revealing a woman's pale face. Cocking her head suspiciously, she regarded him with mild interest and no surprise. Without a question or comment she widened the door and allowed him to enter the dim foyer. Traces of Karly were hidden in her features. The shape of her face was the same, the height, and perhaps the hair, now gray, had once been a brilliant brown.

"Mrs. Roberts? I'm here to see your husband."

She nodded silently and motioned for him to follow. The hall was narrow, its elaborate wooden paneling pulling the walls closer still. Reaching the end, they entered what was perhaps a study, perhaps a breakfast room. Here there was at least some sun filtering through windows that peered over an inner courtyard. Woods dominated and darkened, and Warrick could not help feeling as if he were inside a large ornate box. In the corner, well ensconced in the largest chair in the room, an older man sat buried behind a large book. Warrick halted with thinly veiled irritation. The man finally removed the obstacle and regarded him detachedly.

"I must apologize for not sending word of my visit, but time is a bit short," Warrick said.

"What do you want, your lordship?" Mr. Roberts said harshly.

"Since you know who I am, you know what I want."

The elderly man closed his book with a snap and set it down with an echoing thud. "I told Angus you would demand a dowry if you could. Found out the girl's history, did you? Well, you're wasting your time."

"You are mistaken. I have no need for nor do I want your money."

"What then?"

"You will leave Karly alone. She's in my care now. She isn't bothering you, nor will she."

"I beg your pardon?"

"Keep your distance. I understand that upon your daughter's flight, you declared you would make her pay. You will not use Karly to extract your revenge."

"How dare you! I have taken nothing out on Karly!" the man shouted, springing to his feet. "I've wanted nothing to do with the brat."

"So that's why you let Angus handle everything? Perhaps you are not aware of the sort of man your son has turned into? That he is under investigation as a possible conspirator in treason? The facts are, you turned a blind eye, even when he neglected her. Is that how you have kept your conscience clear?"

"He swore he never laid a hand on her."

"He's a liar. When I met her she had a bruise the size of his fist on her cheek. As for you, neglect is its own form of abuse, Mr. Roberts."

"She's not my responsibility."

"That is correct; she's mine. If you can't bear the thought of her, that is your burden. Leave her alone, and I will make sure the two of you never cross paths. But call off your bounty for Karly's death. Revenge will not bring your daughter back."

"How dare you tell me about my daughter! You didn't even know Caroline. I have no use for the chit. That doesn't mean I want her dead."

Roberts was outraged and shocked. It was not the reaction of a guilty man. "The men who attacked us this morning weren't yours?"

"If I wanted her dead, I could have dealt with her as a babe. Angus could have dropped her overboard before she ever made London. Of course I had nothing to do with the attack."

"Phin!"

Warrick turned toward the shout and saw the gray-haired woman in the doorway, her face deathly pale. The room fell silent except for the ticking of a large cracked clock on the mantel.

Karly's grandfather slid the book toward himself. He caressed the volume, appearing to take some comfort from the rich leather binding. All the while his eyes never left his wife. "Is she injured?"

"What concern is it of yours? You wanted nothing to do with the 'chit.'"

"Is she hurt?" Mrs. Roberts echoed, moving forward and gripping a large wooden chair, her knuckles white.

"They cut her hand. We managed to run them off before they could do much more."

Mrs. Roberts relaxed, her eyes closing as her shoulders sagged. "Praise be."

"*We?*" Mr. Roberts asked, his eyes flickering between Warrick and his wife.

"Karly stayed by my side and fought back," he said and looked between the two. No, they were not guilty. "Do you have any idea who might do this?"

Mr. Roberts cleared his throat. "She lived her life among pirates; anything is possible."

"The attack was here in London. The bounty was here in

London. If you think of who might be behind it, I expect for you to send word." He pulled his calling card from his pocket and tossed it on the table. "Other than that, I expect for you to give Karly peace. Now, if you'll excuse me, I have taken up enough of your time." His gaze traveled from Mr. Roberts to his wife, and then, starting for the door without another word, Warrick showed himself out.

Chapter 16

Withdrawn was not what he expected her to be after getting her drunk. It was more than a hangover. Her change in personality, so drastically different from what he was used to, made him suspicious. Explanations about her grandparents would have to wait. She was hurt. He hoped the news he had told the crew she was to act as pilot would improve her spirits. It didn't. A trip to the nautical shop made no difference either. Warrick watched Karly pore over the charts, selecting some, discarding others, squinting. Despite the rich lavender of her gown, she appeared ill and stressed. "Does your head hurt?"

"The pain left hours ago."

She offered only short sentences, with no further explanations. He knew he had been right. She was angry. "Are you up for one more errand? I wanted to stop by Murdock's before we sailed. Your sextant is broken, and you admired the one he had. You do need a sextant, do you not?"

"There isn't one onboard?"

"You should have your own."

Her gaze drifted to the left. He wished her thoughts were words to help him prepare for what was to come. She was up to something, but her thanks were quiet, and her con-

versation with Murdock held no clues. They returned to
the ship to find William and Trent directing the steady
stream of supplies for the voyage. Karly headed directly
below, and although he was inclined to follow, he chose to
wait. Some time apart might make the difference and give
him a chance to think as well.

The sun was low over the river when he decided enough
time had passed. They'd have dinner together, a talk, and he
might even apologize, if the right opportunity came along.
Warrick froze in the doorway to the great cabin in disbelief at the apocalypse before him. His entire collection of
charts was strewn throughout the room, unfurled on his
desk and tables and stacked on the floor. Books propped
some, others were rolled in piles, a few stood in the corner,
and in the center was Karly. "What are you doing?"

"Organizing your charts," she said, her voice as distant
as the wind. She hastily rolled the map she was studying.

Picking his way across the floor, he came to stand beside
her. "What do you have there?" She offered the roll, and
he took it, opening it to a familiar sketch of Grand Bahama
Island and the surrounding waters. "We're not going to
Nassau."

She sat down on the floor and spread the map in her lap.
"I was reading it, before the new ones are delivered."

"But you've taken them all out." He gestured around the
cabin and noticed a small pile, clearly maps of the Caribbean islands even from here. A knot formed at the base of
his spine.

"As the pilot I am responsible for all charts. When one
is needed it must be immediately accessible." Reaching for
another roll, she dropped her head until her hair curtained
her face.

Her words were rushed. He frowned again at the chart in

his hand. "Bane had mentioned taking the crew from Bermuda. This wouldn't have anything to do with his plans, would it?"

"No."

The muscles in his jaw tightened, and he counted silently to five before responding. "You're going to run again. Admit it."

Karly reached up and tossed her hair back, tucked it behind her ear. At first she stared, her mouth pursed. Finally she released a shuddering sigh. "We are too different."

"I see."

"I tried because I . . ." She broke off, her gaze shifting around the room. "I thought I could help."

"Which you are."

She shook her head, looking down at her hands. "No."

He advanced carefully and knelt a short distance away. "You were glad to be back. What's changed?"

"I know about the annulment."

There was no mistaking her anger now. He started to take her hand, but she shifted out of reach. "I told you I wanted you to stay. We settled that at Greythorne."

"Trent brought your personal papers onboard. Your letter to the king was on top. The king's answer was underneath. It was hard to miss. Your annulment was granted; all you have to do is sign." Her voice hitched, her hands made fists, and she glared at him.

He had forgotten. Her presence had distracted him, as had the mission, his work. Never would he have been so careless, nor had the stakes been higher. "I wrote it after you ran off. It was the third time, and I was angry."

"It was not intentional."

"I didn't know that." Warrick flexed his jaw and looked toward the aft windows. It had started to rain, washing the colorful scene on the Thames to gray. "Bane had no right to demand so much of you, after what he's done. He could have come to me; after all, you risked everything for him. But even though he didn't, you should have. I would have listened."

"You're right, which is why the annulment from the king is for the best."

The pain was acute, as if she had stabbed him with a knife. "Don't you want to stay?"

She got to her feet and lifted a handful of rolls in her arms. "I will put everything back where it was before."

"Use whatever system you were planning; you can explain it to me when you're done." He went to his desk, covered with charts. He was tempted to shove them off and onto the floor. As a compromise he pushed them to one side and picked up the offending letter. The privy seal of his royal highness was a beacon with no pretense of being hidden. When he had asked Trent to bring his personal papers to the ship, he had assumed they would remain in the box. That they hadn't made no sense, not that it mattered. It didn't change the facts.

The wording of the letter was no help. *Damnation*. It must have been cruel to read. He probably should apologize, but she would not accept it, not right now. He placed the letter to one side and began sorting. Karly returned to her task, using some method he could not work out, and he suppressed the urge to watch. His feelings were raw, as were hers; the great cabin was large, but not large enough.

It was dusk when she excused herself for a walk on the deck. He did not go with her, although he was tempted to check, make certain she was still there. Instead he summoned Wreck, who introduced a cabin boy of no more than twelve. "Matthew here knows how to stay out of sight. He'll keep watch on her."

It was underhanded, but he agreed. Seated, he went back to work and left the door open. It took time, but he rose, walked to the honeycombed cabinet where she had been working, and began to study. There was order here. She had replaced his pile with neat sections, maps listed by the area they covered. Her work was impressive. Reaching the Caribbean he paused with a finger on the map and strode back to his desk.

She returned with a plate of dinner, as candlelight shone about the cabin. Taking a seat by the window, she ate in silence and managed not to look at him. He watched as she pushed roasted chicken about her plate and mouthed a few bites. "I won't order you to stay."

Candlelight played across her hazel eyes and lit them in gold behind dark lashes. His admiration drifted to her mouth and down, over her figure to her hands. Then he imagined what it would be like to never see her again, never have the chance to talk with her, to solve this.

Karly stood. "I should finish," she muttered. "Excuse me."

He poured wine for each and followed her. Flashing her a half grin, he stood beside her and offered her the glass. "Tell me about your system. I tried to make sense of it."

Her head jerked. She looked at him, then strode to the cabinet. "Everything's in place." Karly stopped and turned to face him. "And you're clever. It isn't possible you couldn't understand it."

"Tell me anyhow."

After a brief hesitation she gave a mild shrug. "I thought I would place all the maps of Europe together. They were catalogued by who is friendly and who is not. Now they are alphabetical."

She was not asking for his opinion. Warrick gave her a nod and offered the glass a second time. This time she took it.

"I said I wouldn't order you not to go. I'm not going to beg you either."

"I wouldn't want that."

He waited while she took a sip, watched the moisture as

it clung to her mouth. "I want you here. It's not the same without you." Warrick reached out for her hand, halting short of his goal. It was Karly who bridged the distance by placing her hand, palm up, inside of his. He raised it to his lips, then pressed it to his cheek. "Is there anything I can say that will change your mind?"

Karly slid her hand over his and lowered his touch just above her heart. "Words are just that."

"Then I'll show you."

She placed her hands on his chest. "We've already done that too."

He bent to her anyway, meaning a light kiss, a touch of his heart. It hurt, the feel of her close and so far away. Acute pain began to burn deep, but he savored it. It meant he was alive and she was here. Resisting taking her in his arms, he kissed over her cheeks, to the curve of her neck, along the jaw. Then she slipped away, but she didn't go. Standing before him, her back to the cabin, she locked her gaze on his, and then raised a tentative hand to his jaw. There she paused, her touch light, delicate, almost nonexistent. It rumbled through him.

She stopped and waited. When he didn't move, didn't take command, she slid her fingers into his hair, bolder, and kissed the corner of his mouth only. He reached for her but she evaded him.

"Let me try." She rested his hands on the table. "I'll set the pace—no king, country, Landgon, father, or husband."

A ball of desire, need, and understanding formed in his throat. There was nothing to say, so he nodded, resting against the table, and simply let her. Cautious, she unbuttoned his coat, then tugged his shirt free. Raised on her toes, her mouth to his, she gave, beckoned, demanded, undoing him just a bit more with each pass. It was cruel heaven, allowing any woman complete control.

God he loved the feel of her. He was trapped between her

and the table. Her passion caught him by surprise as she pushed into him, aligning her body intimately with his, but so tender. Reckless wonder and he didn't want it to stop but had no idea how to make it continue. She held the moment, reached lower, and held him in her hands. Warrick moaned and closed his eyes, trying to keep control.

"It's too much?"

He jerked his head from side to side, hoping to mean no, but she removed her hand and he looked at her. "With another woman, I could have managed to resist, but not with you."

"Have there been many?"

He gave her a half smile. "You're all I want."

"I'm not sure what to do next." She eased to stand beside him. "You could take over."

"We could go there together."

She placed her hand on his hip and began to knead. "If you meant what you said, about wanting me, show me."

He lifted her on a whim, set her onto the table, lavishing her. Never expecting her in his arms again, exploration was a gift. She winced, and he moved them to the comfort of the bed. A kiss silenced her question, and then he worked lower. She was pressing her sweet heat closer, but it was too soon. Warrick parted her thighs and knelt between them.

"What are you . . ." Her question broke into a gasp as his mouth closed over her.

As he soothed her with his hand, driving her with his tongue, her calls of his name grew lower, huskier, and she shook. She began to tremble as he carried her up into pleasure, then again. Her hand stroking the back of his head became insistent, beckoning.

"Come back to me."

He eased beside her, between her legs, but it was she who arched to him in silent plea. One shift and she was around him, the ecstasy immediate, hot, and possessive. There would be no other, couldn't be, and to tell her that was the most foolish thing he could do. Silence on the matter was the only option. For now, there was the ecstasy of the moment, the joy of their joined bodies as they tumbled amongst the linens and between paradise and ecstasy.

Warrick gave a long slow thrust. She tilted her head and arched her spine. Pressing his lips to the curve of her throat, he nibbled to her earlobe, seizing the tender flesh between his teeth before flicking it with his tongue. He drew another slow thrust. That was all he could stand. Heated power rose within him. It was all he could manage to keep his rhythm steady and hold on. Karly wrapped her arms around his shoulders.

"Warrick?" Her muffled cry came moments before she pressed her face into the hollow of his throat.

"I won't let go," he answered. Karly gave a small gasp and stiffened, trembling. Joining her moments later, he held on. "I won't let go."

Chapter 17

Karly had everything in place for what could be her death. It was risky, but if Landgon believed she had a fake map, he would come. Murdock's chain of information had worked once in her favor. There was no guarantee it would succeed a second time, even though she had been clear in her note, blatant in her description. Her excuse, that she wanted her own funds, was plausible, but no one with any sense would believe she actually had created a map of all her knowledge of Bermuda. Landgon, however, was desperate. He would be panicking, not thinking clearly. If she succeeded, Warrick would have the evidence to have Landgon arrested. No one else would be hurt.

There was still time to tell Warrick. He wouldn't approve. As much trouble as she had already caused, this would be her gift to him: Landgon, along with a confession. Besides, he would want to know why she was sacrificing herself. She wasn't sure she could lie, not after last night. Anything less than the truth, that she loved him, would sound hollow. If her plan didn't work, there was no one but her to blame. No, she would hold her own counsel until either Landgon appeared or the ship sailed.

She closed the door and began her inspection of the

Moorea, board by board. It had been years since the ship had left Hasings's shipyard. Each rigging and tie needed to be studied. She was responsible if there was a difference between the ship in her mind and the one beneath her feet. Taking her time, she caught the irritated stares and mocking whispers meant for her to hear. She paid them no mind.

Wreck was another matter. He never bothered to whisper. He avoided her completely, ignored her questions blatantly, and walked away from her twice. It was a complete breach of command, and the others were watching. Gone was the surgeon who had cared for her hand. She was an untried, unproven pilot who had been given a post without earning it. To complain would make matters worse. She resolved to say nothing. Karly focused on what she knew, and what she didn't, she would find out.

She paused at the base of the mainmast and stared up the riggings to the crow's nest. It was a good seventy-five feet in height. She called to the one sailor aloft, but he didn't respond. To drive the point home, he struck up a conversation with another sailor on the deck to her right. Karly circled the mast, assessing what she could from a bound sail. Turning, she caught the eye of several crewmen, each looking immediately away. Then she spotted Wreck, with his arms folded, watching her. The slow smile on his face was a dare to ask him. Lifting her chin, Karly accepted and walked up to him, keeping her gaze as steady as his.

"Good morning, Wreck. I was wondering if you would tell me, when the sail is up, how many loops does it have?"

"Loops?"

Male laughter rippled about her. "Perhaps my term is not the correct one. How many stays are there holding the main to the mast?"

"Oh right," he said loudly. "Those little bows we make to keep the sail all pretty."

"Precisely."

"A *pilot* doesn't need to know that."

The exaggerated use of *pilot* was meant as jest for the entire crew to enjoy. She gave them a moment to enjoy their wit and drew a deep breath. "I didn't ask what a pilot needs to know; I asked how many stays were on the mainsail."

"Best ask the captain. If he feels like it, he can tell ye. Or climb up yourself. I won't stan' in yer way."

Karly heard another swell of laughter, a bit louder and less cautious. "Thank you," she said, and headed below. Mutters crested in her wake. She blotted them out, although she knew their meaning. The men assumed she was going below to consult with Warrick. The men assumed she had been pushed too hard. The men assumed wrong. She entered the cabin she and Warrick shared. Slipping off the blue silk, petticoats, and stockings, she pulled on Warrick's trousers and tied them with a belt made from a cravat. While they were far too loose, they would have to suffice. Buttoning one of his linen shirts over her chemise, she wound a handkerchief around her bandaged hand for extra protection.

The slippers she had were far too slick. She shed them. She had spent much of her life barefoot. England may not be as warm as Bermuda, but this would not take long. Glimpsing herself in the mirror she frowned. Gone was the lady. Even in Warrick's fine clothes, she appeared wild. She could only imagine how she had appeared to Warrick the first time he had seen her. Unable to fix her hair, she secured the wisps with a clip, and returned to the deck.

The men had resumed work, although a few paused as she passed. She did not acknowledge them. This was not a game of manners. They already knew she was there; even those who did not look up knew. Either she would prove herself or she would fail. Swinging onto the railing and over the rigging, she began her climb, focused on the job. Her hand ached before she reached halfway, as the thin rope ladder chafed her bandage. Soon it began to throb. Continuing, she reached her goal without a slip.

Her hand felt as if it were going to split. Somehow the initial wound never was this bad. Karly held it up, and the blood drained down her arm. The pressure eased, but the pain did not. From this height she had some privacy. The crew below could not see her. She searched for the man who had been in the crow's nest but he was gone. She studied the skyline of London along with its bridges, ships, and people. All were live subjects on some giant canvas that belonged only to her.

When the agony ebbed, she set to work. First she checked the main, and then surveyed the mizzen mast and the foremast as best she could from her vantage point. If she was well, she could have swung across. Under the circumstances that would be tempting fate. Climbing down would waste too much time, so she set across a pair of ropes, surveying the aft sail, before descending and landing softly on the deck.

Karly took a deep satisfying breath and turned, ramming into Warrick's chest, far broader than she recalled. The hope that he wasn't angry burned barely long enough for her to raise her eyes to his. Almost black, his eyebrows drawn, he was glowering at her, with Wreck standing to his left. She cleared her throat. "I was taking a quick check. You have one loose fitting, four on the main. The others are in good condition. Of course I haven't been up to the fore."

"You won't be checking the fore, not with your injured hand. Why didn't you ask Wreck? He would have told you."

Wreck's gaze was on her, but she didn't meet it. "He was busy."

"He also happens to be the first mate, and in charge when William and I aren't on deck. You should know better, especially with your background."

"I'm sorry."

"Sorry?" Warrick grasped her wrist, and turned her hand. Dark splotches of blood had worked their way through.

"Yes," she sighed. "Now, if you'll excuse me, I would like to change and clean up." Her cheeks burned as she strode to the great cabin. No footsteps followed, and no voice called for her. She was grateful, craving peace more than consolation. The gentle scent of cedar, the creaking of the ship, and the calls of the men above were enough to ease her nerves even before she reached her destination. She breezed in and closed the door behind her, anxious for a few moments alone. A noise from behind surprised her, and she turned in time to see a flash of white before Landgon clamped a hand over her mouth as her breath turned into her scream. Propelling into the wall, he pinned her. Karly bit hard, and the cold steel blade pressed into her neck and stilled.

"I'll kill you and sleep well tonight, or you can live and listen."

Her plan had worked all too well. Karly narrowed her eyes in response and gave a faint nod. Her human gag was removed. "How did you get aboard?"

"I wore a coat and followed the supplies." He gave a low chuckle. "No one even questioned me—they were far too busy watching you. Tell me where it is, and I will be on my way."

His eyes could have been striking, his mouth full, if he didn't sneer. Cruelty had warped his features and mind, his muscles weak on a bulkier frame.

"There's no map," she rasped, her heart pounding painfully against the knife's edge. Landgon's blow was immediate and harsh. She had no time to prepare. Staggering as his palm struck her chin upward, she lost her balance. Before she could fall, he seized her by her forearms and forced her again into the wall.

"Let's begin again," Landgon hissed. "I want your Bermuda map. Not one you bought at McKinton's. The one you made to sell."

Pain pinned through her head, needles and flashes of it sounding like tiny drops of glass against her skull. The plan had worked, almost. If she could remember the second part, he would leave.

"You're mad."

"And yet I can kill."

"I am an amateur artist."

"You are an accomplished pilot."

With a burst, Karly surged forward, bringing her knee hard toward Landgon's groin. He slid to one side, blocking her, and laughed. "If your key had been easy to find, I would have been gone before you returned." He snatched a chart off the nearby table. "This is a very nice chart of Bermuda, but I don't want a nice chart. Where is it?" he demanded, his eyes glinting with an extreme light.

"Leave." She was ready this time when the blow came and tasted the blood. It took all her willpower to not cry out when he slammed her into the wall.

She had to struggle to pull a breath into her lungs. That did not stop the ringing in her ears. Her memory returned: the fake key she had made was nearby. She just had to get him to steal it. It was time to make her "slip." She glanced at the drawing of the *Moorea*, the same one that had told her secret to Warrick. She looked again, and then she met Landgon's gaze. He was smiling with cruel satisfaction. She prepared for another strike, but he released her, letting her slide to the floor with a whimper. Then he followed her instructions as precisely as if she had called them aloud. He turned the picture and removed the folded piece of parchment. Opening it, he looked at the fake map and refolded it. Only he didn't make his escape. He came back and knelt by her side, touching her cheek with terrifying gentleness.

"It would be a shame to leave you here," he told her, his

voice slow and soft. "We have just begun to know each other. Since I have the map, our relationship could be of a more private nature, like your uncle had in mind."

She stared at him, horrified, as his fingers drifted lower, cupped her breast, and squeezed.

"And when you grew tired of me, you could throw me overboard, or poison me. That is, if you have any to spare after you reach Bermuda."

Landgon grinned but removed his hand. "Bane has a witty daughter. Excellent. So you've discovered my purpose. The poison will prevent bloodshed, surely you can see that. The populace will be quite safe because I will need them. I'll only kill the officers. You have no love for any of the officers. You rejected Commander Farris when he offered to make you his mistress. Then again, what is a commander of a local fort? When this is over I will be the very king of Bermuda."

"That's why you're doing this, for titles?"

"You should be able to understand what that means— a title stole your father's legitimacy, changing him from a privateer to a pirate with the stroke of his pen. Men like your marquis and the Duke of Berington rule England and much of the world. The best people like you and I can do is save enough to become a baron, only to have it snatched on a whim." He shook his head. "I vowed I would rule my own destiny. I am offering you a chance to be a part of that."

She was losing ground quickly. If she could delay him long enough, Warrick might find him here. "You don't have the money to pay those soldiers. My father stole it. That's why you were after him."

"He made things difficult, but not impossible. I'll wager you could help me find it."

"No."

His eyes narrowed on hers, and she sucked in a breath to scream. As he covered her mouth, she kicked wildly. In the end, it made no difference. He was stronger. She said a silent prayer. Dragging her to her feet, he tried to lift her, and she twisted violently. Like a rag doll she was shoved hard, her head echoing an odd noise as it hit the wall and a thousand shards of light shattered before her eyes, before all went dark.

Chapter 18

She was doing what he had asked her to do, pilot the *Moorea*. Karly's display had not been a slight against him. Warrick knew her better than that. It was the shock of finding her dressed in his clothes at the top of the mast, but then, he had met her dressed in men's clothes.

Warrick clasped the railing tightly. It should have occurred to him she would be thorough. She said she was good. He really had no complaint. As for Wreck, the man had been surprisingly quiet since Karly's departure. He wouldn't even look at him. Wreck could have stopped her, but didn't. No doubt, one of his tests by fire that had worked, thank God.

The crew had the right to test her, and she had the right to prove herself. His nerves might not survive, but he had the feeling Karly would. Of course, before he saw her, he needed to gain control of his frustration. He was powerless in this process. He helped Trent check the cargo, inspected the riggings on the front sail, visited the hold, and reviewed the supplies. Karly had not returned, but his frame of mind had improved.

It was time to go and find her, to check her hand or kiss her, whichever came first. But with each step, his frustration returned. What would he do if the challenges escalated? He could not stand and watch her risk her life in a game of wills. He halted in front of the great cabin. Perhaps he was not ready to approach her. He could wait until she emerged. She might want to speak to him then, and the conversation would go better. Unfortunately that could be in front of the crew, which would make matters worse. He drew a long breath and was about to turn around when he heard a crash. The handle wouldn't budge. From the other side, he heard a man's voice angry and low.

Warrick kicked, and the molding splintered. A second kick and it shattered. Torrents of papers, files, and charts blurred the room into a picture of disarray. He saw it all in an instant, including the man dressed in white kneeling over a bundle of material, but he moved on to the chestnut hair. Bile rose in his throat as he recognized an unconscious Karly. "Landgon," he growled.

Landgon rose slowly, the knife glinting his hand, and let Karly slide to the floor. "I warned you she was a mistake."

It was possible to break the man's neck with a single blow. Warrick flexed his fingers in anticipation. "She is my mistake to make. What the hell are you doing here?" She might still be alive. Landgon had been crouched over her, but he might not have finished. Karly may have been at Landgon's feet, but her life was at his. To win this encounter, Warrick had to lull Landgon into a sense of security and power.

"Grown on you, has she? I have to admit, you have done nicely with her. I didn't realize she would turn out so well. Although marrying her was really quite extraordinary. Really, Warrick, a man of your status should have more sense."

"Status does not rule my life."

Landgon gave a throaty laugh. "You have no idea, or you would protect yours better."

Warrick could have laughed as well. He understood status, and the pressure of it far too well. The man before him was not worth the explanation, but he needed time to wear him down. "Is that what all this is about, status?" Warrick asked.

"You wouldn't understand." Landgon shook his head. "If you did, you would have been at your father's seat by now. You would have married an heiress, someone who would bring your family more power, not an indigent waif. Power is lost on those who don't appreciate it."

"So that is why you are willing to betray your country, for power?"

"As I said, you wouldn't understand," Landgon said, his voice iced with malice.

Landgon was too far away for an effective assault, and the man was armed. He was prepared to act.

"You had power once, but you threw it away," Warrick said.

"I had nothing."

"A house and a shipping company are not nothing."

"I had no title and no future. When I tried to make my move, Parliament rejected my application."

Warrick saw a flash of movement as Karly's foot disappeared beneath the trousers she was still wearing. She was alive. Warrick wanted to breathe with relief. He did nothing. Landgon was watching him closely.

"You asked for a monopoly on trade to the South Caribbean."

"Enough," Landgon said and gave Karly a swift kick.

Warrick would get Landgon away from Karly. Then he would pummel him. He channeled his anger and began a slow circle around the room.

"You won't get off this ship."

"I can't afford a mistake. And now I won't have to," Landgon boasted, patting his pocket. A paper rattled inside.

"A mistake or another mistake?" Warrick said in an even tone. "It seems to me you made your mistake when you chose the wrong side of the Channel."

Landgon dropped his smile, his mouth forming a thin line. He took a step forward and balled his fists. "You're like a parrot, Warrick, repeating the same thing, 'King and country.' Not all of us have the luxury that wealth affords a certain few."

"Only a few of the very worst use any excuse to justify their treachery."

Landgon glanced down to Karly and pushed her with his boot. "She's not worth it."

"She's worth much more. You, on the other hand, have nothing to recommend you."

Time ground to a halt. Landgon's eyes blazed fury. Another moment passed, and he lunged. Warrick managed to block his jab, but the knife nicked his shoulder. Pivoting, Warrick coiled his muscles to strike, except Landgon didn't turn. He continued at a run to the end of the cabin. He flung open the small door to the captain's balcony. In a single movement, he was over the side, landing in the Thames below with a splash. Warrick followed, gripped the railing when a shot fractured the wood above his head. He watched helplessly as Landgon scrambled aboard a waiting rowboat, his men ready at the oars and already pulling for the opposite bank. A second man aimed a pistol and fired. Warrick ducked to the side and heard shouts from the deck above. Landgon was out of reach.

"He was too much of a coward to fight you."

The voice was Karly's. Warrick spun to find her standing beside him, her expression grave. He yanked her into his embrace and held her tightly, winding his hand into her hair. She was trembling. Her heart pounded a ferocious beat against his chest. He set her back and skimmed a critical eye over her. "How badly are you hurt?"

"I'm not."

"You're . . . what the devil were you doing?"

She reached for his shoulder. "You're the one who's hurt," she said, her voice quivering.

"I'm fine," he said. "You, on the other hand . . ." He lapsed into silence and traced her cuts and bruises. He stopped at her neck and the outline of hands about her throat. "I should have killed him."

"He knocked me unconscious. It didn't last. I'm glad you came when you did." She shuddered. "He was going to take me with him. I didn't plan on that."

It was hard to be angry when she was alive, but he was sure it would come. He gave her what he hoped was a stern look as he waited for an explanation. It could not be as bad as what he was imagining.

"Don't frown so cruelly. I was brilliant. He wanted my key, and I gave it to him."

His anger began to build. "Your key to what?"

"Bermuda, much like the one I gave you at Greythorne, only far more detailed."

"Karly!"

"It wasn't a real one." She swayed, and he caught her to him, his eyes searching hers. "I told Murdock I wanted to sell one, so I could buy you a gift. I hoped Landgon would find out. I even told Murdock about the deliveries to the ship."

"Why would you do such a thing?" he asked, his voice hoarse.

"It's a ruse. He thinks he's trumped us."

Her tone told him she didn't understand why he was furious. That didn't stop the emotion that surged through him. He wanted to shake her. "You may be an excellent pilot, but your judgment regarding your personal safety needs adjustment." William burst into the room with six sailors, all armed. Explaining in brief what happened, Warrick guided

Karly to their personal quarters and before their full-length mirror. His hands on her shoulders to steady her, he met her eyes in the glass. Maybe if she could see what he saw. He watched her study her reflection. Her hair was askew and dried blood marred her beautiful features. There was a fresh bruise spreading across her cheek where she had been struck and her neck bore a cut from Landgon's knife.

"You can't keep trying to do this alone."

She turned in his arms, away from the apparition and toward him. "The idea was a good one. When he tries to use the map, his ship will breach on a reef. He'll never make it ashore. I know it was a risk but I thought it had merit."

"Why was he going to take you with him?" She tried to look away, and he caught her chin. "Karly, tell me."

"Entertainment," she said, her voice barely a whisper. "Do you really think I'm worth all this trouble?"

Warrick cursed to himself. "You heard that?"

Karly nodded as color darkened her cheeks. "I regained my wits quickly."

"Your ego seems quite well fed after your demonstration on deck. Things won't always go your way. When they don't, what will happen?" Her gaze flickered, and then fell. He scooped her to him. "In answer to your question, yes, you are worth it," he said softly against her hair.

"It's not that I don't trust you," she said in a quiet voice.

"You feel it's much to ask of me," he finished for her.

Karly looked absently around the cabin. "I don't understand why you even want to try."

Warrick took her hand and placed it over his heart. "Is this reason enough?"

"I suppose you're entitled," she said quietly.

"On occasion," he said and combed his fingers through her hair. "Are you certain you're all right?"

She straightened and gave him a quick smile. "The

sooner we get under sail, the better I will feel. We can warn the island and find that chest."

"You must rest. Considering your hand, that bruise and your head—"

"What will people think?" she interrupted.

"They'll think you're every bit of trouble."

"Or that you're a tyrant."

He gaped at her. "Indeed?" He waited, and she shifted, her cheeks flushing bright red.

"I'd tell them they were wrong."

"There's hope for me yet," he said and gave her a lopsided grin, but her face fell.

"I wouldn't let anyone think badly of you if I could help it."

"Don't go losing your spark. I am beginning to enjoy it."

She closed her eyes as his lips brushed a kiss on her forehead, only to jump away at a loud knock from the adjacent room. He went to investigate. When Karly trailed behind, he blocked her. Relieved to find Trent, he lowered his guard. "Is there something urgent?"

"Angus Roberts is here with a woman who says she's Karly's grandmother. They'd like to see her."

Karly drew beside him and touched his arm. "I want to meet her."

He had told her as little as possible. Having experienced enough at their hands, he had not wanted her to suffer any more. Mrs. Roberts had seemed genuinely concerned for Karly. It could also be another charade. The wrong word could cut deeper than the knife had. "I am not certain that is a good idea."

"It is all right," Karly said.

"I am not sure it is," Warrick corrected and turned to her. "Haven't you been through enough today?"

"We sail tomorrow. Besides, you will be there. Nothing will happen."

She was right of course, but Warrick hated the idea. Had Trent held his tongue and spoken to him in confidence, he would have said no. Now he had two items to discuss with his friend. "Give us a few minutes, then show them in," he said and held Trent's gaze until Karly's touch dragged him away. A tear clung to her cheek, another sat poised to follow its path, and her eyes shone bright in the dim light.

"I've never met my grandmother. Why would she come here?"

"You do not have to do this."

"In a way I do," she said and turned, again seeing her reflection in the mirror. Karly gave a long sigh.

"Once you wash your face and put on a fresh gown, it will not look so bad."

"Of course it will, but there is nothing to be done for it."

She was right. He did his best to stay between her and the mirror. When her hands shook too much to be useful, he finished her stays and buttons. Finally he took her hands in his and ran his thumb lightly over her bandaged hand. "It will be fine. I won't leave you, and they can't hurt you."

Karly gave a solemn nod and returned to the dreaded mirror. With her hand she stepped around him and inspected her improved image. "I can do this," she said with a steadying breath.

Warrick offered his arm and guided her through the narrow doorway and looked first to Angus. While he appeared very much as he had the last time Warrick had seen him, the lines around his eyes were not as pronounced, nor the scowl on his brow. In his arms he held a wooden case. Mrs. Roberts pressed her palms together and then to her lips as Warrick stopped their progress. "Mrs. Roberts, Mr. Roberts," he began and gave a curt bow. "This is my wife, Karly."

Karly watched as the woman faced her, her hands clasped in an unspoken prayer over her lips, her face paling.

"I'm Karly. You asked to see me?"

"Yes," Mrs. Roberts began, breathlessly. She appeared unsure, as if she wanted to say something else. After a pause she smiled ruefully. "You resemble your mother, more than I expected, except the eyes."

"So I've been told."

"I brought you something." Mrs. Roberts opened her arms to Angus, accepting the lacquered chest he was holding, and proceeded to place it on the table nearby. She retreated a step and flickered a smile. "This was your mother's. I saved it after she left. When she died, I wanted the memory of her. Warrick mentioned you were here; I decided perhaps the memory was better in your hands."

Warrick flinched. He hadn't expected to be named; he hadn't expected this at all. He hoped the revelation wouldn't send Karly into a withdrawal any more than she already was. "That's very kind of you," he said politely.

Karly released his arm and crossed to where the chest lay. Intricately painted in bright colors against a black background, it was a sailing ship, detailed down to the twisted ropes of its rigging. She traced its outline with her fingertip, considering whether to speak, act, or walk out. Making up her mind, she reached for its tiny gold key and opened the box. Brushes, paints, oils, small bottles, and assorted tools greeted her, all neatly arranged. Their condition was immaculate, tenderly placed, and pampered. "Her supplies?" she said.

"Caroline cared for this set a great deal. When she left, she took nothing. They've been sitting under my bed, but they are really meant to be used." Mrs. Roberts paused and then nodded, taking Angus's arm. "We should go. You are due to sail shortly."

She was almost at the door when Karly called after her. The pair halted by the door.

"Thank you."

Mrs. Roberts released Angus and faced Karly again. "When you are ready, you will come and visit," Mrs. Roberts choked.

Karly didn't move again until they were gone, their footsteps no longer audible. "Why didn't you tell me you had visited them?" she asked, glancing at Warrick.

"I went after you were attacked." He saw her surprise but looked past it toward the window and cleared his throat uncomfortably. "I told them to leave you alone, along with a few tidbits of the woman you had become. I didn't think Angus had done justice impressing them with the fact you were a beautiful, talented woman who deserved to be left to live her life."

"You threatened them?"

He shot her a quick glance and shrugged. "At the time I thought they might be responsible."

"And now?"

"Now I think they are trapped by their own mistakes. As for your uncle, I believe Landgon hired him because he wanted someone who wouldn't ask questions. Your uncle is quite comfortable in that role." Warrick sighed and faced her. "I didn't think she would come here."

"I understand," she muttered, withdrawing her hand from him. "If you will excuse me, I would like some time to myself."

"Of course," he said and heard the slam of her heart before the click of the door. He should have told her. Once he had decided the Roberts family were not to blame, he should have sat down and taken her hand. Explaining what he knew of her family would not have been easy. Her face when Bane had blurted the truth about Caroline's death had been evidence of that. But it would have been better from him than from anyone else. Mrs. Roberts had meant well, but Karly was a stranger to her. In some ways she was a stranger to him, but a precious one. It had been selfish on his part to pass over the truth. He did not want to see the pain in her soul as she fought, yet again, to find her footing. The door opened abruptly, and he turned, prepared to lecture Trent, only to find William.

"We should sail as soon as possible," Warrick said.

Frowning, William entered the room and closed the door. "Karly nearly ran me over on her way to check the fittings again."

Warrick started for the door. "Alone? We don't have time to search the streets of London. . . ."

"I have the watch keeping a very close eye on her," William said and crossed his arms, raising an eyebrow. "I don't suppose you want to tell me what is wrong?"

"I would rather not," Warrick answered, tapping a poorly positioned chart into place.

William gave a small nod and pursed his lips. "When I first heard of your marriage and of whom you married, I wondered if you had gone mad."

Warrick grunted and leaned against the wall, eying his brother, "And now?"

"Now I think you have found a woman to spend your life with. Father looks at mother like that."

"That may not be in Father's best interest."

"You're smitten."

"That may not be in my best interest. Karly saw the annulment grant."

"How?"

Warrick shook his head. "It doesn't matter. She wants to go. I may not be able to stop her, no matter how smitten I am."

"Perhaps if she releases you, she will let me have a go at her. She is rather striking. I don't believe I have seen prettier hazel eyes than hers. And her figure is admirable. She is rather muscular from working on a ship, but her curves are luscious."

His voice drifted off as Warrick stood squarely in front of him. "You want me to hand her over to you like some family heirloom?"

"Only if you don't want her."

"She's a woman, not a piece of silver. Besides, you would never manage to keep up with her; she'd be hurt, or killed within a week. And as for her figure, I suggest you keep your admirations and flirtations away from my wife." The fierceness of his warning hung between them, and yet William looked amused. Warrick stared at his brother, his eyes narrowing.

"You're not really interested in Karly, are you?"

"I think she's a perfectly lovely sister-in-law."

Warrick shook his head and raked his hand through his hair, then peered up at William. "I should have sent you to sea for five years instead of six months."

"My flirtations are harmless," William said with an exaggerated shrug. "Besides, I wouldn't get far. She's in love with you."

Warrick stood straight and searched his brother's face. The teasing was gone. William's blue eyes had gone deep with serious reflection.

"She told you that?"

"She doesn't have to. I have eyes. You enter a room and you are all she sees. You touch her, she blushes. And when you speak, she listens carefully."

"Except when she disagrees," Warrick added.

"She may be in love, but she's still got spunk. You wouldn't want to lose that, would you?" William asked, raising an eyebrow.

"No, heaven help me," Warrick said softly.

"I have battled for enough fair hearts to know a hopeless cause when I see one."

"She's making plans to leave me when this business is over."

William frowned, looking in the direction she disappeared. "What are you going to do?"

"Stop her."

"How?"

He didn't have an answer. "She should want to stay."

"When father starts raising a horse, he spends as much time with it as possible, so that in the end, it can't imagine life without him, and it stays."

"Karly is not a horse."

William rolled his eyes. "Consider the principle."

"I understand the principle, and the advice."

"Take it for what it's worth. I'll be on deck if you need me."

Watching him go, Warrick could remember his mother's stories, how she knew she loved his father when she couldn't imagine her life without him.

"A horse wouldn't climb up the mast of a ship," he muttered.

Chapter 19

She wouldn't admit it out loud, but she and Warrick were connected. He was no longer merely a companion; his moods, his body, his spirit were all a part of her, a part she had come to cherish. She loved him, she was sure of it. But there was more to settle, and if her instinct was right, there wasn't much time.

Warrick stood flanked by William and Trent, alert as the Thames pilot maneuvered the *Moorea* from the dock. Lines ran from the *Moorea* to two small boats in the middle of the river. She could see the men onboard pulling, their rippling muscles taut with the strain. Warrick's muscles had strained during their passion. Hers had too. Through the desire she had glimpsed ecstasy. Denying it was not possible. Tempering it was proving harder than she could have imagined. She wondered if he yearned for her the way she did for him each time they met.

The *Moorea* wavered, like a bather uncertain how cold the water was, then crept away from the dock and into the Thames. More orders were shouted, and Karly felt the first creak as the *Moorea* came to life. A flock of gulls cried and soared alongside, begging for scraps. Good-byes were shouted and waved and they were freed. Time passed before she caught the first whiff of salt. She saw the ocean beckoning, and she beamed with sheer joy at it all. She felt Warrick beside her. With the sun on her face, she was not ready to turn. Discipline brought her pulse under control. When she finally met his gaze, his expression was companionable. Disappointed, she had wished to find a trace of the same meanderings that plagued her heart on her face.

"What do you think?"

Karly glanced around the deck. She studied the mainsail, the foremast, and finally the aft. "She's rigged too tight." Karly quirked her mouth in amusement as his expression became blank. "That's not what you meant, is it?"

"You're correct," he said.

"I think she's a beautiful ship, and I think a great deal of work lays ahead." Her answer seemed to sadden him. She was about to ask him why when he gave her a curt nod and walked to the wheel. It was harder than she expected to not go after him.

She spent her days noting their position. At night she worked diligently on a sketch of a ketch she had seen days before. Small and elegant, she had memorized its lines. Placing the charcoal to the paper was a distraction. It did not erase the pain in her heart, but how was she to repair the damage? Karly slept without an answer. The nightmare returned that night. Farris had her in a corner, his hands planted on either side of her head, and he leered down, his face twisted. She woke in a sweat to find Warrick in the small cot at the other end of the cabin.

She dressed in the tiny captain's closet, collected her drawing supplies, and went on deck. She wandered to the bowsprit. There she sat with her legs dangling on either side of the ropes and managed to escape with the help of a school of dolphins. They had arrived before her and were playing in the bow wave beneath her feet. Voices of the crew behind her were swept away, their presence hidden by the entrance to the decks below. From her perch she could hear nothing but the wind.

A dolphin leaped into the air and spun, followed by another, its gray body glistening in the sun, followed by a glimpse of pearly pink. She laughed, then tried to remember the last time she had laughed out loud. "I don't suppose you'll join us all the way to Bermuda?" she asked the dolphins.

"What did they say?"

Karly looked up to see Warrick standing on the deck above. With a fluid movement, he grabbed a rope and swung under the railing. Hoisting himself onto the beam he left safety behind. He paused before finally making his way out to her side, sitting carefully. "Not much. We were comparing notes on the weather. I suppose I was caught up in watching them. Did you need me?"

Warrick blinked at her. "I missed you. I forgot how quiet it can be up here."

"You should try up there." Karly pointed toward the mainmast.

Gripping her arm, Warrick shook his head at her. "Use two hands to hold on, please?"

Karly gave him a quick nod and turned her interest to the creatures playing below. "You don't like heights, do you?"

"I don't like you and heights. You can help me by not climbing the riggings."

"Because so many sailors have slipped and been killed falling under the ship, I know."

"Karly . . ." he warned.

Holding her hands in front of her, she grinned. "I won't climb the mainsail."

"Stay on the deck whenever possible and use both hands on the ropes."

Karly held on and gave him her best guilty look.

Breaking into a soft laugh, Warrick shook his head at her. "That won't work. Save your flirtations for a more appropriate occasion. How is our position?"

"Good. The wind is excellent. She's a fast ship, but then, you knew that."

"Yes, I did."

"You really missed me?" she asked, and regretted it the moment it passed her lips. She sounded like an infatuated simpleton. Asking had opened the door to a conversation she wasn't sure she wanted to have. It could turn terribly wrong and most probably would. "I mean, I'm sure you missed me. You were looking for the readings." Karly pursed her lips and looked away. She doubted he had accepted her hasty recovery. Her words had made little sense. When she again faced him, she found not mockery nor humor, but serious contemplation.

Getting to his feet, he reached for her. "Let me help you. I wouldn't want you to knock your sore hand."

"It's healed nicely," she said. He would not be swayed. She steadied herself, let him take her forearm, and felt his strength flow to her. His power balanced her, and she climbed over the first rope. With one foot in front of the other, she waited for him to stand on deck before she made her way. His hand touched her waist, and she startled. Karly tried to adjust, became tangled in the ropes, and slipped with a cry.

He caught one arm and grabbed the other as she fell. "Hang on."

She heard his order over her pounding heart. Of course she was going to hang on. Did he think she would let go? Warrick leaned over the ropes and guided her toward the beam. He steadied her while she tried to get a leg up and over it. It took several tries before she finally managed to seat herself. "I've got you; untangle yourself."

Karly did as he instructed as the ship rose and fell above the sea. Her leg was twisted to one side, and she had to tip her body to work the snare. Warrick's hold was like a death grip. Strong and steady, she was as secure as if she had been holding the ship itself. She freed herself, and he half assisted, half dragged her to the deck.

"I know. I should use more sense," she said.

Warrick stared at her, slack jawed, then wrapped her in his arms.

She hoped he wouldn't let go for a long time. Her wish was granted. He didn't let go at all. "I hate petticoats," she said, trembling, shaking her skirts in displaced anger. "They don't belong on ships."

"Apparently not."

Karly rested her head on his shoulder and waited for the lecture while trying to stop the tears her own fright had conjured. His long silence made her nervous. She peeked up at him. Worry etched his face. His hand wound up her neck into her hair, cradling her. She sank closer, closed her eyes, and fell into bliss. Her heart was so full of joy at being in his arms, she forgot where they were until someone shouted above their heads. She followed Warrick's gaze to the crow's nest, rotating in his hold.

"Did you hurt your hand?"

"No. Warrick, I'm sorry."

He stroked his knuckles lightly over her cheek. "It was an accident, but please be more careful."

"I promise."

"Then enough said."

Karly stared at him in surprise that there were no angry words to be found. If he wasn't upset with her, why did he sleep elsewhere last night? Unless he had resigned himself to their eventual separation. That would explain much, and break her heart.

"I should get to work. I wouldn't want to get us lost."

Pursing his lips together, Warrick tucked a loose strand of brown hair behind her ear. "Not much chance of that with you on duty. I'll join you there in a bit. I need to take care of a few things up here first."

Heading toward the quarter deck, Karly glanced over her shoulder. Focused on the spot she had fallen, Warrick unfastened one of the ropes and reworked it to allow for access onto the bowsprit. She halted and watched as he made a zigzag pattern, providing an effective barrier, his dark brown eyes full of concentration, his mouth thoughtful. She could imagine their feel, touch them if she wanted. She turned and nearly collided with William.

"I was looking for my brother."

Embarrassed to be caught admiring Warrick, she blushed. "On the bow," she said and slid past him before he could say or ask anything else.

Chapter 20

"No!"

Karly's muffled cry made Warrick's blood freeze. His heart pounding, he burst into the cook's galley, prepared for battle. But instead of mortal peril, he found Karly doubled over in laughter behind the long table. Wreck, the only other person present, stood in the center of the room with mirth in his eyes. Wreck, who had complained at the thought of having to look after her for a few minutes, was entertaining Karly as if she were an old friend. She covered her mouth. Then she saw him. Karly sobered immediately.

"What's this about?" Warrick asked, bemused.

Coughing, Wreck waved his hand in the air in a nonchalant gesture. "Just an old story, one you've already heard," he said, crossing to the large wrought iron stove and lifting the steaming kettle.

While it clearly required attention, Warrick was certain the pot had been that way for some period, its existence a convenient excuse. He looked from Wreck to Karly, who sat hidden behind a large mug of tea, her eyes bright, and shook his head as the pieces came together. "I would think you would have grown tired of that tale."

Wreck smiled and threw Karly a wink. "She married you.

She has the right to hear it." He poured water into a cup and wrapped his hands around it before continuing. "Now where was I?"

"Warrick had run on deck naked," Karly said in a low voice.

Warrick gave a loud snort. "Did you explain the pirate ship had come alongside silently? There was no warning. The first we knew of them was when they came over the rails."

"Aye, and you were asleep, William on deck and it was his first trip. I got past all of that," Wreck said.

"And it was hot. The Caribbean in the summer is extremely hot," Warrick added.

"It was hot," Wreck said and rolled his eyes, set the mug down, and bent toward Karly. "Warrick bursts onto the deck naked carrying a pistol. The pirate was so stunned, he dropped his pistol, but there're all his mates right behind him. So it's a face-off."

"Not precisely," Warrick said, crossing his arms. "I had a standing order that if we are boarded, the guns are to be opened and ready. The pirate had nine on him."

Karly's gaze moved between the two men. "At close range, you might have sunk both ships," Karly said.

"I wasn't going to turn the *Moorea* over to anyone," Warrick said with a frown.

"It's my story," Wreck said, drawing his bushy brows together. "Warrick gets himself dressed, and they get into this duel over who gets to keep which ship. He's fighting and doing a bang-up job, when William, who's trying to help, gets behind him and they both go over the rail into the drink."

Karly looked from Warrick's reddened expression, to Wreck in shock. "What happened?"

Warrick shrugged. "Wreck screamed, 'Your Majesty!'"

Wreck leaned forward and lowered his voice as if confiding a secret. "Before we had sailed I had heard the pirate in The Black Gull. His mates were teasing him about not being able to swim. He was not the brightest, but had a fast ship, which is why he had been able to do as well as he had."

"He had also followed you from the tavern to the *Moorea*, which is how he decided to come after us," Warrick said.

"There was only one tavern in Old Town and everyone could see the ships in port," Wreck sniffed. "The pirate jumped in after Warrick. He wanted to be able to demand a nice fat ransom."

Clearing his throat, Warrick glanced up at Karly. "We saved him, in exchange for his surrender."

She grinned, almost laughed. "It is quite unusual to find a pirate who cannot swim."

"You would be surprised how many seamen can't," Wreck said.

"I'm an excellent swimmer, always have been," she said and grinned at him. "It's a good story. No wonder you like telling it again."

Wreck pulled a long sip from his mug and set it down. "I had best get to work on deck." With a nod to Karly, he hurried out the door.

They had forged an understanding, for which Warrick was grateful. There would be no more challenges up the masts or through the rigging. There better not be. "I missed you this morning."

"I woke early."

"You were quiet, too quiet. I didn't hear a thing," he added with reflection.

She touched his hand. "Too quiet?"

"Knowing our history, it is disturbing you seem to be able to sneak out."

Karly shook her head and fiddled with the plates on the

table, stacking them with no apparent system. "We're at sea. Where could I go?"

"Do you still want to leave?"

She stopped moving and bent her head. "Excuse me," she said. Before he could elaborate, she was gone. But he had seen the raw pain in her eyes. He hated that look. Warrick rose and followed her to the great cabin, locking the door behind him. She had unrolled a large chart and spread it on the table. He recognized the hook of Bermuda. He noticed the tremor about her shoulders—but she didn't look up. She remained where she was, tracing the coast with her fingertip. Whatever had upset her was still battling with her spirit. "How do you remember each bay and how to get in? Don't they change?"

"Yes and no. While they are always different, like people's faces, once you have met, they have a certain degree of familiarity."

"But you use some charts."

From behind her curtain of hair she glanced at him. "Storms or wrecks alter the coast. That is why I study. I am surprised you don't use any charts. You're lucky you didn't run *Moorea*'s hull through a reef or get stuck on a sandbar."

He was more interested in her tone than her words. Granted, her explanation was interesting, but not as much as she was. First, he had to get her focused on him. "Planning your every move doesn't always work for the best either. Sometimes you're better off working on intuition," he said, keeping his voice gentle.

Karly looked up. She whisked her hair over her shoulder and gave him a critical look. "And sometimes your intuition can lead you astray. A second plan is necessary to fall back on."

"Fall back on, or hide behind?"

Her fingers tapped the table. "You would want a pilot who doesn't read maps?"

Warrick rested his hands, palms down, on the table. "I want to know what upset you this morning." Karly blinked and turned, knocking the chart from the table onto the floor. She stooped to retrieve it but stood too quickly, knocking her head with Warrick's. Off balance, Karly tumbled toward the deck. He caught her against his chest, and landed on his shoulder on the large Oriental rug, cushioning her fall. With a twist he rolled and knelt beside her. She was not moving, her cheeks void of all color. "Go slowly," he warned when she tried to sit.

"I've fallen from trees before, remember? This was nothing."

He didn't like the tremble in her voice. She had fallen far worse, but this had frightened her. "Perhaps we need to work on your balance."

"My balance is fine, except around you."

"Then in the future, I'll tether us together. That way I know you will be safe," he deadpanned.

"I'd love to see you try."

Warrick slid down beside her and propped on his forearm. "That can be arranged."

"May I get up?"

"We just got here." She moved as if to shake her head, while at the same time parting her lips. He kissed her, not quite certain what to expect. She was soft at first, beckoning, opening her mouth to him, and touching her tongue to his. He felt her desire, her hands at his waist and in his hair. He moved closer, let her feel him, and heard her small groan as her fingers plucked at his sleeve. She wanted him. He knew it and grew all the more aroused. But without explanation, she broke the kiss. Warrick nuzzled her neck and heard her sigh, but she stiffened.

"What happened this morning? Why did you leave?" Warrick asked.

"It's not important."

"I thought we agreed to try harder."

"We also were sharing a bed, which you moved out of."

"I moved out because you have been having nightmares." He felt the jolt travel her body. Time was her enemy and his friend. He shifted to one side, resting his hand over her waist, his head in the crook of his other arm, and waited. Listening to the sound of the ship against Karly's uneven breath, he wondered how long it would take this time. He played with her hair, arranging it around her shoulders. She had changed so much. Strong and independent, confident and self-sufficient, she could manage on her own. She had done it so far, albeit marginally. But this wasn't a battle over her abilities. It was an open invitation for her to enter his life, one she could continue to refuse. Temptation frightened her, dependence even more so.

She released a shaky breath in frustration. "It's silly."

"Yet you're shaking," he gentled, cupping her cheek.

Tears began to spill, and she turned her head. "There's nothing you can do."

"I would like to hear the rest."

"I thought it was gone." Her voice broke. She drew a shaky breath before continuing. "I suppose going back to Bermuda, knowing I will have to face him again, is why it returned."

"Who is he?"

"I will deal with him. I have in the past."

"You won't be alone. Does this man have a name?"

Karly pursed her lips and gave a quick shake of her head. "You don't have to defend me."

"His name," Warrick said. He already knew she would not answer. He was also certain he already had the answer. She had given him that piece of the puzzle when she had been so tipsy on rum: Commander Farris. If she didn't remember, it was probably for the best.

"You need to let go."

"I'll help you up, but I'm not letting go," he answered, bringing her to her feet.

"Has anyone ever told you you're too stubborn for your own good?" she sniped. "It's not humorous." He caressed her cheek as she fidgeted, avoiding meeting his eyes.

"I'm here. I will remain here. I'm part of your life, as you are of mine."

Karly flattened her hands to his chest but didn't push. "No, you're not. The annulment, remember?"

The power in her voice surprised him even as her words confused him. Warrick placed his finger to her lips. "I was angry and foolish, but mostly hurt that you would disappear yet again. The letter is gone. It should have been gone before you ever found it. I threw it overboard."

Her mouth opened in a quick intake of breath. "You threw the king's letter overboard?"

"Yes. I suppose I did. I never should have asked for it in the first place," he sobered and skimmed his hand over her shoulder.

Karly shook her head. "It's not that simple."

"Yes, it is," he softened. He teased her earlobe with a tender kiss.

"I want to trust you, but so much has happened."

"I promise I won't hurt you."

"You will hurt me," she said and gave a small gasp. "Don't you understand? I care about you. How can you not hurt me?"

It was brutal honesty, her emotional core. He didn't know whether to be thankful or awed. Warrick swallowed hard and stared deep into her eyes. Her words had only skimmed the surface to the depth he saw there. So much she would not say, so much he could not say . . . not yet. She would never believe the tangibility of it. Despite all he had done to undermine her tender feelings, she had given them to him. Warrick shook his head at her. "I will not hurt you again."

"You don't know that."

"I know what I want."

"You said that before."

"I will repeat it until you believe me. I'm falling in love with you." Karly placed her palm to his cheek. She watched him, her gaze hard and deep. If she would not hear him, he would show her. He took her hand and led her back to the bed. But Karly slipped away. She pressed his shoulder and him into the bed. Lifting one leg over him, she straddled his body, her gaze constant.

Stunned at her forwardness, he stared up at her. She was still dressed, her hair loose around her, and she looked so innocent. But his body did not want to hear tender musings. All it cared about was how incredible she felt. She brushed her lips across his, and kissed him before she lay on top of him, molding herself to his body, curve to muscle. Promising nothing, she took possession of his body, exploring him with her hands and mouth. It took iron control not to roll her under him. She removed his shirt and breeches, her mouth tracing the path her fingers took. He was not sure he could stand much more when she again lay on top of him, her fingers curling through his hair. He reached to hold her, and she brushed him away, raising his hands over his head and leaving them. He needed to say something before he wouldn't be able to say anything at all. When he opened his mouth to speak, she placed her hand over it.

"No. Words can be a problem with us."

She was right, but he wondered how much she planned, how far she would travel. He knew she was testing him, but she was also testing herself. He had to let her. Let her know he was hers to do with as she would. Tiny strands of trust, faith, and hope had been woven from her heart to his. They were tenuous at best, and yet he could feel their tug. It wasn't enough, but it was a beginning, something he could strengthen if given the time, and time was against him. It would run out, and she would run, unless somehow he could convince her otherwise. When she took him into her mouth he lost all coherent thought. His hands reached for her. He balled them into fists of control he was not certain he could sustain. Then the heat was gone.

He opened his eyes as she again straddled him. He could not stand any more. He placed his hands on her thighs, holding her. Suddenly she stopped, her expression becoming uncertain. Not trusting his voice, knowing she didn't either, he reached for the curve of her spine, and brought her to him, ravaging her mouth. Her fingers dug into his shoulder, her kiss hard and sweet. She rose over him, came down, and arched her back, driving him into her with a ragged moan. He could no longer feel the swell of the ship beneath him, only the woman above. His will shattered, and he heard Karly give a soft cry. She collapsed to him and pressed her face against the hollow of his throat. The wonder of the moment sealed permanently in his mind.

Chapter 21

Karly batted the tickling sensation on her cheek. It returned, and she tried again. When it came back, she opened her eyes to find Warrick's mischievous ones twinkling down at her. In his hand was a lock of her hair. He reached down and caressed her with it. He moved, and the sun hit her face, forcing her to squint.

"Good morning, sweetheart."

"Morning?" Karly repeated in confusion. "The last I remember . . ." She lifted her hand to her breast, and her voice fell away as her cheeks grew hot.

"I remember that, too. It was one of my favorite parts of the evening," he said, grinning.

His body against hers, she could feel his breath expand his chest, his skin warming her own. His arm rested over her waist, and his hand splayed over her hip. He was wonderfully exhilarating and comforting at the same time.

"I didn't have any nightmares," she said with surprise.

He propped himself on his elbow and frowned down at her. "It's time to tell me about these dreams."

Warrick was the kind of man that would want her to stay safe, away from danger. He might even send her back to

England. The small clock on his dresser chimed the hour, and she rolled, then sat quickly and peered at its tiny face.

"I missed my watch. I should have been on deck an hour ago!" she exclaimed. There was only one way out of the bed: over him. The side she was on was firmly attached to the wall. Karly drew the blanket around herself and tucked her legs underneath. "You need to move."

"I will give you until we reach Bermuda, but then I expect you to tell me what these dreams are about."

"All right. Now if you would, please?" she asked, not hiding her annoyance. With luck, in two weeks he would be far too busy with the situation in Bermuda to remember his request.

"Gladly," he breathed and reached for her, pressing a light kiss to her bare shoulder.

She closed her eyes and sighed with pleasure as his lips whispered soft caresses across her skin. "No. I mean I need to get past."

He chuckled and captured her injured hand in his, holding it lightly. "Wreck is taking your watch for you. We both agreed you needed your sleep."

"You planned this?"

He murmured assent against her skin. When she didn't relax, he drew her into his arms and laid her back, stroking her hair. "I was up a couple hours ago, and we talked then. It's the captain's prerogative to see the crew is well rested." He traced a kiss from her shoulder to collarbone. "Besides, your responsibility is once we get closer to the island."

His arousal brushed her leg, and her own desire heated. She wanted to make love to him too. What would it be like to remain here for the entire day? Her thoughts began to slip into ecstasy when they snagged on the feel of the ship. At first, she assumed it was only an odd wave, but her instinct itched with warning. She slid from him and listened to the message the sails and beams were trying to tell her. "There's a storm not far from here."

"I was on deck an hour ago—the sky was clear."

Karly remembered the white birds that had flown behind the *Moorea* yesterday. For hours they had trailed the ship, then at dusk they had settled on the mainmast. They were longtails, seabirds "Are the longtails gone?"

"The long . . . the what?"

"The birds that were resting on the mainmast, are they gone?" He appeared speechless, and she shot him a deliberate frown. When he didn't respond, she followed his gaze down. In her excitement she had dropped the blanket and was naked from the waist up. She lifted the blanket, wrapped it as best she could, and tucked the loose end between her breasts. Then she gave him a dainty shrug.

"Perhaps now I can concentrate."

She dropped her chin with embarrassment, but he caught it between his thumb and forefinger, lifting it.

"It's a good thing when a husband finds his wife attractive to distraction."

Karly inclined her head and slid to her feet. "The *Moorea* is already starting to roll. A storm is coming soon."

"We could pass to the south of it."

Even as she met his eyes, she knew he did not believe that. He rose and dressed, hurriedly buttoning his shirt. She was not as quick, her bandaged hand more cumbersome.

"Let me help," he offered, getting to his feet.

Her eyes took him in at once in every detail, from his muscled broad chest to his well-sculpted loins. Her breath caught in her throat. She realized with mortification she was staring. One glimpse of his expression and she knew he was very much aware of her perusal. Facing in the opposite direction, she lifted her hair and waited. Eternity seemed to pass before she felt his hands on her shoulders and then the clasps of her dress.

"I'll get the hang of all these trappings one of these days," she said quickly, unable to face him. "Thank you."

"The pleasure is mine."

"I'll be on deck," she said, heading for the door, when he called her name. She turned reluctantly, to find him wrapped in his robe. "Yes?"

"Take your bearings while the weather's good. If it turns I'll expect you to go below deck immediately."

"If I were in simple trousers, I could stay on deck even when the weather turned."

"A simple gown is more appropriate, for everyone's sake."

He did not understand, so there was no reason to respond. Propriety made no sense when there were practical matters at hand. She could argue and perhaps win, but that would take time, and there was none to waste. There would come a time when simple trousers wouldn't fit. Her mind drifted inward. How would her body change? Warrick touched her elbow. She jumped, then saw the shadow of concern on his face.

"I'm going," she rushed. Taking her instrument bag, she ran topside.

The smell from the galley made her stomach turn. Too much time on land had robbed her of her sea legs. She would try a biscuit and tea later, once things settled. Their conversation had left so much unsaid. While the late morning sun was still bright, dark clouds were visible in the distance. Watching the sky, she took her readings and noted their speed. At the first sound of thunder, Warrick was beside her.

"Finish up your duties and get below."

Karly worked quickly as the late morning turned into an eerie twilight. Lightning and thunder chorused, and the wind began to rise. White spray danced along the tops of waves and over the deck, hissing menacingly at them and making everything slick. Securing, tying, and bracing anything that could move, she stayed next to the crew, kicking off her slippers to help her footing. Warrick would stop her. She wanted to be ready when he did. She saw his approach, followed by Wreck and two other crewmen; there would be no private conversation.

"You've done enough—get below. Have Wreck rewrap your hand; it's bleeding."

Arguing with the captain would not do. Other crewmembers were already heading down the stairs. She nodded, helping to tie cannons. Continuing all the way down to the belly of the ship and its kitchen, she passed several men working in silence to store tools, pots, pans, and knifes safely. She recognized Jenkins struggling to secure two large casks. He was one of the new hands who had been brought onboard in London. Inexperienced, he couldn't tie a simple knot. She had heard him say he had been to sea before, but she doubted it. He probably was desperate to leave London for whatever reason—a bad love affair, money, debts, or worse. She didn't trust the look in his eyes, but she knew how it felt to be a newcomer. With work to be done, she set personal feelings aside and went to him. "If you can hold the lines, I'll tie down," she offered.

"I won't trouble you," he growled.

"It's no bother," she began when he flipped the rope at her face. For the second time in a day, she remained silent. A woman's assistance was not always welcome, but she was a member of the crew. Certain respect was required, but the storm demanded that there be no distractions. With a final tug she finished the cabinet and watched Jenkins walk off. Her hand ached, and from the corner of her eye, she saw red. The wound was seeping again. Constant use had given it no time to heal.

With each roll, the groans and creaks of the ship grew louder, harmonizing with the moan of the wind. The

Moorea fought hard, shuddered, tilted and then surged ahead. Experience separated the new crew from the old as seasickness began to take over. All were having trouble keeping their footing. Karly soaked cloths in a half bucket of rainwater and offered them to the sailors, trying not to worry about the men fighting just above her head. Warrick would be fine; she had to believe that. The door flew open, and a man buried in a gray wool coat entered. Water streamed off him as he made his way to the long table and collapsed on one of the benches. She grabbed dry towels, hurried to him.

"What's happening?"

The doused sailor accepted the towel and blotted the water from his face and grimaced. Pale except for the blue tinge about his lips, he coughed and looked up as Wreck approached.

"What's the story 'bove?" Wreck asked.

"It's quite a fight; riggings keep breaking loose," the man said and coughed again.

"I'd best go help," Wreck muttered.

"Me, too," she said, but as she started to follow, Wreck blocked her path.

"I think not."

"I handle storms well."

"And at causing a few, from what I've seen. But orders is orders. You stay, I'll go." He patted her hands. "Don't worry, I'll watch after 'im."

She wanted to argue, but this was a ship. Down here, Wreck was in command. Karly rubbed her damp palms together as the ship swung and trembled, righting itself reluctantly. She reminded herself yet again the *Moorea* was well built. Hasings had designed her for seas far worse than this. He had inspected each timber before allowing it to be placed and used only the best Bermudan cedar. If she stretched her mind enough, she could smell the fresh wood and hear the calls of the men as they built her. But with each crash of thunder, her nerves frayed a bit more.

Warrick knew his way around a ship, as did William. But men were sometimes swept away. A wrong step, a loose rigging, a rogue wave had all claimed the lives of the best sailors. Cold fear churned in her stomach and caused a fresh sheen of sweat to break over her skin. Needing a distraction, she returned to work, drawing to keep her mind occupied. It almost worked, until a loud crack sounded directly above her head. The ship shuddered, as if in fear, the eerie sensation traveling up her spine. She handed the cloths to the nearest sailor. "Keep handing these out," she ordered and strode out the door, prepared to yank free of anyone who tried to stop her.

The stairs rocked and bucked. She had to pull her way up to the deck and gasped at the sight before her. The sky was black and brutal, while lightning cut the horizon in two in hues from yellow to blue, the thunder roaring its encouragement. Karly squinted against the pelting rain and staggered forward. She saw Warrick and William fighting to keep the *Moorea* into the wind. The few men on deck scurried and clung with lines tied to their waists. Death was no more than a wave away. To her left, Trent worked furiously on a pile of tangled lines and splintered wood that had once been a piece of rigging. She fought to his side, grabbing his arm as he started to slide. "Hang on," she cried over the wind, only to have him haul her flush to his body. A wave crashed, drenching them and threatening to take her with it to the depths from which it came.

"Get below!" he roared.

She ignored him, and set to work on the debris. He seized her arms and whipped her to face him.

"That is an order!"

"I'll help—then we'll both go," she answered without looking up. The *Moorea* lurched, and she planted her feet.

His glare burned the top of her head, and then he set to work.

"It's caught farther up. You stay."

She watched him fight toward the bow. He was a man of the earth, not of the sea, and his good intentions would get him killed. Hand over hand, she held on and followed. Together they found the knots holding the wreckage. Seawater had swelled it immobile.

"Do you have a knife?" she asked.

"Here," he said, thrusting a small flimsy pocketknife in her direction.

Even though she held tightly to the netting Warrick had made of the bowsprit, she had trouble keeping her footing. The waves caught the ship, lifted it high, and dropped it heavily into the sea. Wrapping her wrist around the rigging to hold on, she cut away the ropes. Another wave washed over her, its cold hands tugging her sideways. Her feet slipped, but her grip held. She managed to cut halfway before her sore hand began to ache from her efforts. When they reached Bermuda, she would find Trent a proper knife.

She switched to her injured hand, holding the rope to steady it. The bow lifted and crashed, a large wave rolled over her head, and dragged her sideways into the railing. Her eyes stung with the saltwater. Karly blinked them away, and tried to find her footing. The next wave hit hard, but she held on. Suddenly she was dragged backward by her skirt and over the side. She opened her mouth and screamed. Then it was the sea's turn. Bitter and angry, it grabbed her, choking her mouth and throat with saltwater. A wave loomed high above her head and smashed down, beating her below the surface.

She clawed upward, gasping for air, and looked for the *Moorea*. The ship was close, but when she bent to swim toward it, her petticoats snaked around her ankles like living creatures. A wave pushed her forward, lifted, and then slammed her into the side of the ship. Stunned, Karly slipped beneath the surface, recovering in time to scrabble back up. Another throw might kill her. She shoved hard, and then struck out away from the hull. Her dress fought her every stroke, binding her legs and making each subsequent kick more difficult. She could feel her strength begin to ebb. The ship was slipping past her.

Karly let out a desperate cry, almost a sob, with Warrick's name on her lips and heard an answering shout. She tried to lift her head, and again lost the surface. She reached, paddled, and kicked, making no progress. Opening her eyes to darkness, terror clamped her heart, and for a moment she wondered if it would stop completely. Her legs wouldn't move, as if tied by ropes, and her lungs were bursting when she was dragged upward and broke the surface. A flash of lightning and she saw Warrick beside her.

She tried to ease her burning lungs by coughing. The water resisted, tossing her like a bit of driftwood and choking her breath. Her legs were useless, and there was little she could do. She focused on simply keeping her head above water while Warrick pulled her to the *Moorea*. She saw a rope, and she grabbed it, looking up. A ladder flapped and swung against the ship. It was her only way to safety, and it was impossible. Her legs remained tangled in the petticoats. She tried to explain, but seawater filled her mouth. He pointed upward, and she shook her head. "My legs," was all she could manage. With a nod he was gone.

Horrified she turned full circle, nearly letting go, when his hand touched her legs beneath the surface. She jumped, but resisted the urge to kick out. Both of his hands had her now, and they traveled higher up her thigh, tugging hard at the fabric, but it wouldn't budge. He reappeared and clasped her to him. His hands tugged her dress up, and then closed about the bare skin of her thighs. If the situation had been less dire, she'd have a clever retort. Right now she was desperate with no breath to spare.

"Reach in my belt. You'll find my dagger. Don't drop it."

Fumbling against her numb fingers, she followed his instructions, sputtering through another mouthful of sea-water.

He pulled her arm through the rung and then held her gaze. "Wait here and hold on tight. I won't leave you," he said, and again vanished below the surface. She felt a hard pull and nearly slipped. Clamping her mouth closed, she forced her breath through her nose and felt him cut at her petticoats, fighting for her freedom. Twice he resurfaced only to take a deep breath and vanish again into the sea. Then they were gone, and he was again at her side.

"Climb!" he shouted over the noise of the storm.

Karly stared up the long wet ladder, and started her ascent. She managed three rungs when her grip slipped and she fell into the sea. Warrick's grasp was like iron, and she found herself again at the base of ladder but no longer as certain. Wrapping her injured arm around the outside of the rope and through it, she used her forearm for leverage. Again she slipped at the third rung, only this time, it was into Warrick's arms she fell, banging her ribs.

"Take your time."

Karly glanced over her shoulder at him with his arms on the rope on either side of her, waiting for her to continue. Panting hard, she nodded, climbed two more stairs, and stopped. Her legs shook with effort. She looked up to find that the deck seemed farther than when she started. The ship tossed. Although they had managed to get out of the ocean moments before, they were dunked and lifted clear, the wild storm offering no break. "I can't."

"Yes, you can. Climb."

She gained a few more feet before her strength failed. Her knees would no longer bend. Terrified to tell him and unable to proceed, she huddled and pressed her face to the rope in dread. His hand touched her cheek. "I can't make it."

"Turn around and face me," he ordered in her ear.

The sharpness of his tone gave her enough momentum to turn. She was surprised to see his alarm. She wished she had the words to reassure him and herself.

"I'm going to carry you. Just lean. I'll do the rest."

It was an order, but she defied it, for a long second. Placing her cheek to his, she pressed to him, pressed the feel of him to her heart. Then she brushed downward, dropped the rung, and did as instructed. He caught her against him and draped her over his shoulder, securing her with his arm across her calves. Karly lay completely still. If she moved, it would not only be her death, but Warrick's too. Tense, bracing with each movement, they reached the top, and she was pulled over the railing into William's arms. Shivering through the blur, William was setting her in a cocoon of blankets in the great cabin before she found her voice. "Where is Warrick?"

"He's right behind us," William said, wrapping a blanket about her shoulders.

"No, he's still on deck."

"I'm right here," Warrick countered and knelt beside her. "Which is where you were supposed to be."

"I heard a crash."

"There were a lot of crashes. Storms do that."

"I know what storms do, remember?"

"Then you should have sense enough to tie a line around your waist, in case you were accidentally washed overboard."

Karly watched William discreetly exit. She drew the blankets closer and tried to take a deep breath. A racking cough seized her. Warrick bent her over his arm and rubbed her back.

"What is obvious is that you can't seem to follow the simplest instructions. You go about what you think is best, and dismiss orders, even those given by the captain."

He was right. On her father's ship she would have been disciplined. "I'm sorry," she said with little enthusiasm.

"You're lucky to be alive to apologize."

"I was trying to help, I did ask Trent."

"As a seasoned sailor you know it does not matter what Trent says. Everyone must follow my orders."

"Don't save me next time."

"There won't be a next time," he seethed.

He was right and she was wrong, but her composure crumbled. She felt the anger well within her. She knew it was partly due to the fear that remained in her system. She had only just escaped drowning. But even knowing she should remain quiet was not enough to stop her.

"You won't let me help, yell at me when I do, and lecture me regarding my methods. I am a seasoned sailor. I've probably spent more time at sea then you ever have. I've told you petticoats were a problem on a ship, but you wouldn't listen."

"I gave an order."

"Which I tried to follow. I thought there was trouble. If that's the case, the pilot's place is on deck. If I hadn't been wearing a dress, I could have swum and climbed up all by myself."

"So you are blaming me for you falling off the *Moorea*?"

"No, it's my fault. I should have never agreed to any of this." No longer able to look at him, she tried to unbutton her sodden dress, but her fingers shook too violently for any progress. His hand covered hers, and she jerked it away. "I'm perfectly capable. As captain, you have other things to do."

She expected him to argue with her, but he didn't. Instead

he got to his feet. Above the storm, she heard the cabin door shut and he was gone.

She tried not to care. The ship lurched in time with her heart. For a moment, she thought she would succeed and not cry. There was no use. Sobs tore through her. She gave in, letting the storm inside take over, no longer willing to fight.

Chapter 22

Warrick studied Karly's half-eaten biscuit and glanced toward the side chamber door. She was sick again. Not that it had slowed her. She rarely rested, proving herself as sturdy as any member of the crew—almost. She was strong, but not if she didn't eat. If he kept her quiet, it might help her feel better. Since the storm they had finished what repairs they could until they reached Bermuda. There they would need a shipyard to repair the *Moorea*. Hopefully she would recover quickly once they reached land.

The door opened, ending his thought process. It would be better to say nothing to her. Saying something would only wound her pride. He watched her cross to her trunk, open it, and frown. Then deftly she reached in and withdrew the pair of trousers. He pretended to be occupied with the chessboard before him. When she crossed the floor, he waited until he could no longer hold the ruse, then glanced up. "Those are for you," he said offhandedly.

"You are giving me a pair of your trousers?"

"I had them altered by the ship's stores. They needed to fit. Can't have them falling down in the middle of the deck."

"That wouldn't do."

"So why don't you get dressed and play me a game of

chess? You do play, do you not?" He watched her expression drift from uncertainty to wariness and fought not to react.

"A little."

"Excellent. I had my board brought up from the hold. With things quiet, I thought we'd have a match."

"Things are quiet?" she hedged.

There was a light wind and calm seas. The repairs from the storm had been completed and the crew was hard-pressed for diversions. Quiet was an understatement, but he did not elaborate. She shrugged and approached, eyeing him as he held out a chair. Warrick took the seat across from her and replaced the elaborately carved wooden set. "These were a gift from my mother. She taught me to play when I was only five."

"I hope you have improved since then."

"I will let you be the judge. Ladies take the first honor," he gestured.

"White goes first," she corrected.

Warrick carefully rotated the board, placing black before himself. He smiled inwardly when she lifted a delicate brow and then bent her head. Move to countermove she played, taking the first game and then accepting his challenge for a second. Giving her a second quick win, he saw the frown and realized his mistake when her hazel eyes danced emerald as she regarded him.

"Checkmate," Karly said, tilting her head brazenly.

He examined the board. "So it is. You are most accomplished at this game."

"If you really considered me good, you would have played to the best of your skill, not hand me the win."

He mocked surprise, but she didn't blink. Acknowledging his ruse with a shrug, he began resetting the pieces. "Can't a husband let his wife win?"

"No, he can't. It's a false victory, so it's no victory. I

might as well not play." She got to her feet. "Thank you for the diversion. I would like some fresh air."

Warrick caught her hand before she could pass by, and she halted. "I'll open the window here," he said. She waited, and shuffled, appearing nervous. "When the stakes are high, I never hold back," he said with an arch of his eyebrow.

"Honor is not enough?"

"I prefer something more finite."

"I see. So, the clothes were to whet my appetite for a truce. You needn't worry. I'm not angry. You don't need to make peace with me."

If she could hear her tone, she would change her declaration. Warrick decided to let it stand. They were talking. That was a start. "They aren't peace offerings. I am looking out for a member of my crew," he retorted. She flinched as if struck, his words inflicting more sting than he had intended.

"I am well, I assure you."

She started to move, and he stood, taking her shoulders. "Wait. Think of them as considerations. You were right: on the deck of a ship when you are working, petticoats have no place."

"I should have obeyed orders," she said blandly, staring at his chin.

"And I should have listened to reason," he said, hoping he had not just sent her scurrying behind her emotional wall. "Will you play another game of chess?"

"Will you participate fully?" she asked and met his gaze.

"I promise to do my best." She moved away, and he released her, waiting while she resettled in her seat before reclaiming his own. "What are the stakes?"

"I usually play for sport," she answered and moved her knight.

"I want something else. During the repairs, I damaged my right shoulder. It won't set right on its own. If I win, I would like you to rub my sore muscles since I can't seem to make any progress by myself."

"You're hurt?"

The change in her manner, from her voice to her entire being, was instant, like tiny ice crystals melting with the first breath of sun on a spring day. There was so much there, he had to hold off the temptation to bypass the dialogue and simply kiss some sense into her.

"I want to win your services, without any stipulations. And if you win, I'll teach you to take the helm of the *Moorea*."

Her hand paused above the board, clenching the rook, her knuckles turning white. All irritation vanished from her face.

"You mean I'll stand next to you."

"No. Your hands on the wheel; I stand next to you." She studied him, motionless, except her eyes.

"The crew will not likely be pleased."

"You won't be in command. You'll be at the helm. I'll still be captain. If that's not worth anything to you—" Her hand caught his across the table, and he stopped talking. She gripped him hard, most likely harder than she intended; her emotions were clear in a simple touch.

"I accept, but you have to do your best to beat me."

He consented with a generous bow. Karly waited, considered her options, and then set to the game. She was intent, but she also smiled good-naturedly. It was the challenge that captured her. He liked that. She was also very good, her strategy a combination of a well-thought-out approach combined with practice. All the makings of an excellent pilot were there on the board before him—thoroughness, concentration, and a clear understanding of multiple elements. There was also her weakness: she was predictable. Odd that in life she bordered on reckless, and yet here, that quality was absent.

He was the opposite. In business he took risks, but in his personal life he preferred security and predictability. She was his complement, and in the same breath, his opposite. A strength that could be built on, or a weakness that could tear them apart. He saw it all clearly and it was his move. He took it, willingly, seizing the moment and taking her by surprise, from the look on her face. He was able to eliminate her defenses within four moves, locking in his victory before she could formulate his approach.

"Checkmate," he said, emphasizing the second word. "Did that qualify as me using my skill?"

Karly shot him a lopsided smile and leaned forward, studying the pieces. She looked up and shook her head. "I walked into that one."

"It's an easy strategy to overlook."

"Hardly; it was brilliant." Karly got to her feet. "We had better go to our quarters. I'll be able to work on your shoulder there," she said and headed for the door leading to their chamber.

"Now?"

"Unless you have something more pressing? Your shoulder is not getting any better."

"Now will suffice," he said and followed her. He would let her control the situation, whatever her plan, however difficult that would be. She closed the door behind him and approached slowly, her eyes on his chest. "Is something wrong?" he asked, glancing down.

"No, not wrong. This would be easier without your shirt. It's in the way."

"I can take it off," he offered.

"Please," she said and stood to one side and then retreated behind the screen.

Unbuttoning the garment, he removed it. He heard a soft cough and looked up to find her watching him, dressed simply in her chemise. It was his turn to feel uncomfortable.

She was as timid now as she had been passionate the last time they made love. She was still getting used to him. That would take time.

"I didn't know you were going to change," he heard himself say, his voice huskier than usual.

"It will be easier this way, and it keeps the delicate silk from wrinkling." She took the shirt from his hand and laid it over the nearby chair. "Now sit on the bed with your back to me."

Warrick swallowed hard, and followed her directions. He tried to remain stoic as her hands first touched his shoulders, then sang over his bare skin. Her simplest touch was so much more, an erotic dance down his spine. He shuddered involuntarily, disappointment replacing sensuality as suddenly the connection was broken and her touch was gone. Turning his head, he gazed at her. Her eyes were wide, stunned, her breath deep. He balled his fists to squelch the urge to draw her into his arms and press her through the conversation they so desperately needed.

"That was wonderful."

Karly blinked as if returning from a distance and then frowned. "Are you certain? I thought I hurt you."

"No," he soothed. With her index finger she made a small circle on his skin and reluctantly he tore himself away, settling in his original position to better allow her hands to move over his tired muscles. Hot and urgent, he felt his desire battle with the pain as she concentrated her efforts on his right shoulder. Applying a small amount of pressure to the tightness, she kneaded slowly and with progressively more strength. Control helped him through the pain. He lay down, and she followed him.

As she altered her patterns, the sharpness gradually disappeared. He was able to relax into her touch, nearly a caress. He eased to his left and patted the empty place beside him.

"Did that help?"

"It helped me very much," he answered.

With her knees underneath her, she half reclined beside him, and her expression became serious. "You shouldn't sit like that; you'll destroy all my hard work."

"And you should lie down, or you'll destroy all of mine."

Karly wrinkled her nose at his jest, but there was the hint of a smile at the corners of her lovely mouth. Lying, she found the crook in his shoulder and moved until she was comfortable, her gaze on the ceiling above. "Thank you for the trousers."

Warrick glanced sideways at her. She was in his arms, finally. He savored the pleasure of holding her. It could have been sooner. He had been too angry to fight further and too stubborn to admit she could have a point. He needed to walk through his emotions alone before he could come here, and talk through them with Karly. "I thought about what you said; it made sense. You could have been killed over something so inconsequential."

"I felt so helpless."

Warrick drew an uncertain breath at the pain in her voice. He plunged on. "That would be your biggest fear." She shivered, her gaze locked upward. He feathered his fingers over her cheek, arranging her hair over her shoulder and then across the pillow.

"If I'm in control I am strong. I can protect myself."

"I can take care of you."

"It's not your job."

He wanted to snap at her, but the consequences would be disastrous. He felt her shift as she propped herself on her elbow and peered down at him.

"I mean that I should be able to handle everything myself."

He pulled a long breath through his nose before meeting her gaze. "We should look after each other, now that we're married."

"Then I have a confession." She caught his hand and

pressed it to her cheek. "You might get angry, but I want you to know. I trust you with my life."

She meant it. He rested his hand over her healed one. If only he could wrap a bandage around her hidden injuries, the ones around her heart and soul. But they required time.

"I have been diverted by many things. Maybe I was not fair to you, offering to let you pilot and then placing restrictions. I was cruel in allowing you to doubt your position."

"I appreciate that, but this is something different."

"I'm listening." He didn't move, not certain that he could. More secrets would be hard to hear at this point.

"I want to stay pilot, no matter what. Will you promise?"

He paused and considered. Words of love would sound false, and more reassurance might frighten her further. Karly wasn't ready to hear his heart. All that he had said would vanish like the morning mists. He did love her, and he had wronged her. He had cared for her, but if she hadn't always been honest, he was as much to blame as she was. As it was, he could see her silent struggle. He hoped she wanted to believe him, that she would agree, but feared the worst. Then what would he do?

"I made you pilot because you were qualified."

Karly dropped her gaze to where his hand touched hers. Her hair was cascading about her face and hiding her expression. With her hand she swept it behind one ear. "I am happy with you. I feel safe, and when you touch me . . ." she paused and lifted her head, "it's never enough." She smiled and bit her lower lip.

"You aren't planning on leaving me again?" Her manner turned guilty, and he raised his finger to her lips. "I am willing to accept anything but that."

"My balance has changed," she admitted hesitantly.

Warrick took her into his arms as his heart cracked. Brushing a kiss on the top of her head, he held her closer until she relaxed against him. "Your sea legs will return."

Chapter 23

"Go below and change into men's clothes, and hide your hair," Warrick ordered, forcing his voice even. It wasn't the time to worry. Not hearing movement from Karly, he lowered the glass and peered down at where she had her reports laid out around her on the deck, Karly's skirts making up the rest of the circle. Instruments held the corners of the reports.

"That wasn't a request, Pilot."

"I haven't finished updating my logs."

"Hurry, then come back."

Folding everything and tucking it neatly in her makeshift bag, Karly took his outstretched hand and got to her feet. She looked around at the crew now hurrying about their tasks, and then to the sky which was crystalline blue. Then she too saw the frigate in the distance, her white sails filled and headed directly for them. "What flag is she flying?"

"She just hoisted a black one."

"Pirates."

"I've heard more concern in your voice when studying the *Moorea*. Keep low, in case they're observing us."

"I won't be long."

Warrick watched her disappear. This time, he would stand

between her and fate. He returned to the helm, the other ship growing steadily closer. She was faster, and from her lines, she appeared French built. Peering through his spyglass, he studied the crew of the other ship as they worked, driving their vessel closer. Most of the crew were poorly clad, their heads covered against the harsh sun, typical of those who spent a great deal of time in its presence. They were busy preparing grappling hooks, riggings, and cannons. He followed one man he assumed to be the captain moving, directing and ordering, a spyglass much like his own in hand. Then he raised it, pointing it in their direction.

Warrick hoped he had not seen Karly. Where she had been, curled up and lower than the railing, it was unlikely. He would've had to have been looking at the precise moment she stood. Still, it was possible. All this time he had been against her wearing trousers, giving them to her reluctantly. She had refused to put them on, clearly picking up on his disdain. Now he wished he had insisted. Warrick frowned as William adjusted their course to try to capture more wind in the sails; evasive maneuvers wouldn't matter in a very short period.

"They'll be on us soon," Warrick said.

"How many do you believe are onboard?" William asked.

"Sixty, maybe seventy. And they're well armed, from the looks of them. They're preparing to fire a warning shot." No sooner had he finished than the other ship's cannon sounded, the roundshot crashing into the ocean short and off the port bow.

"Eager, aren't they?" Trent quipped.

"They have no intention of hitting us, unless we put up a fight. There's no treasure in a sunken ship," Warrick muttered.

"Why can't we outrun them?" Trent asked, unable to hide the concern in his voice.

"Their ship is built for speed; she's easily doing twelve

knots." Warrick paused as someone from the other ship shouted to drop their sails.

"What do we do?" Trent asked, his voice tinged in panic.

Warrick exchanged knowing looks with William, and then gazed over his crew. "They're hoping to intimidate us; maybe we can return the favor. See if our cannons don't make them rethink an attack." At the ready, he watched as five of the *Moorea*'s guns were prepared and aimed. Wreck called the order to fire. The guns rumbled to life, sending mortar crashing through their hull and deck. The response was immediate: cannons on the other ship thundered, but they missed the *Moorea* completely, landing wide.

"If they don't change course, we should fire," William offered from the helm.

Warrick raised his hand, holding the order and hoping the other ship would turn. Her course remained true, the distance narrowing rapidly. Nodding to Wreck for a second volley, Warrick watched as five more cannons sounded, their effect devastating, shredding a sail and breaking the top of the foremast.

"You got them! Fire again!" Trent shouted.

"This is not a game. I don't fire unless I have to," Warrick said irritably.

"They're pirates!" Trent argued.

"And possible allies," Warrick corrected. "Ideally we'll disarm them, and when they come alongside, we talk."

"But . . ." Trent's voice faltered at a loud boom, a whistling, and then the planks beneath their feet quaked, throwing them all to the deck. Another series of explosions cracked through the air, the *Moorea* shuddering with each progressive impact.

William staggered to his feet and grabbed the wheel. "We're hit."

"Can we get out of their line of fire?" Warrick demanded.

"They tore the mainsail; she's becoming sluggish," William said with a shake of his head.

"Bring her around," Warrick ordered. He watched the crew work as they hurried to repair what they could, and drew a deep breath. "Drop the sail; prepare to be boarded."

"Are you insane?" Trent argued.

"No, nor do I want my ship torn to pieces. Just because I'm letting them board doesn't mean I don't have a plan. I'm going below to find Karly. Secure what you can," he said and started below.

"You're leaving?" William asked.

"Karly should have returned by now," Warrick said. He barely lost a step as he clambered down the stairs and burst through the door into the great cabin. Heading toward their sleep quarters, he was almost at the second door when movement at the far end of the room brought him to a halt, the sight stunning him. She was standing on a chair, having removed a plank from the wall, and all he could see of her was her skirts, her upper torso hidden deep within the opening.

"What are you doing?" he shouted, striding toward her and grabbing her waist. She startled at his touch but didn't respond for a long moment, and he began considering what to do if she was stuck.

"Almost done, pull me up," came her muffled voice.

He didn't need to be asked twice, hauling her off the chair and into his arms. "You're supposed to be changing! Why are you still in a gown?"

"I thought this was more important. You told me to help you."

"By disobeying another direct order?"

"No, by hiding your letters from the king. They are private."

"If pirates see you . . ." Warrick drew a worried breath. "Do you have any idea what they do to women?"

Placing her hands on her hips, she tipped her head at him.

"That is the silliest thing you've ever asked me. All pirates are not the worst sort. I used to live with them."

Warrick gaped at her, and then heard the unmistakable scrape of ship-to-ship contact. Shouts, running, and shots sounded from above. Pirates were now onboard. They would find little treasure to satisfy them, and Karly would be an easy target. He hurried to his desk, and tore open the drawer and took out his pistol, only to have Karly grasp his hand. Glimpsing her worried expression, he took her wrist with his other hand, freeing himself. "I won't use it unless I have to. Hopefully they are willing to talk."

"If you come out armed, they might kill you without question."

"Not the worst sort?" He raised a brow. The worry in her voice was touching, but he could not allow himself to be swayed. "I'm not going out there without something or you won't stand a chance."

"What about you? Watching them murder you won't change anything. I can't let that happen," Karly said simply. "If you want to arm anyone, arm me. I can shoot myself."

"They'll have to kill me first," he said solemnly.

"That makes no sense."

"Nor does thinking I'm going to stand and watch you commit suicide."

Karly opened her mouth to disagree, but before she could, the heavy door splintered open. A horde of coarse-looking men pushed into the room. Warrick thrust her protectively behind him, but it was pointless. They were surrounded, overwhelmed in a matter of seconds. The pistol was wrested away, and then they were separated. Her hands held by men on either side, he lost sight of her as they dragged him into the corridor. Fear crested through him for her sake.

Forced into the sunlight amid raucous cheers, he could see that William, Wreck, Trent, and the rest of the crew were on their knees, bound or in the process of being tied. With a pistol to his forehead, he was forced beside them. Through the crowd he saw Karly. In her blue silk, she shone amongst the sea of dirty bodies that surrounded her. A tall black man moved before her. He placed his hands on his hips and threw his shoulders back. Around him the men broke into raucous laughter at whatever she had just said. Warrick thought about his father's dagger tucked away in his bureau. He should have kept it on. Then again, against so many he would not have a chance, he would be dead. He would have to wait for the right moment.

"So you don't like my ship, missy?" the pirate captain laughed.

Karly smiled and shook her head. "It's not the ship. You need to do a better job sailing her."

The pirate captain's smile faded even though the laughter around them became louder. "You would do better to remember my crew bested you. Money doesn't always buy the better."

Karly shed the pirate holding her arms. "The wind was in your favor." Then she gestured the men aside and walked past Warrick toward the captain. Unafraid, unarmed, her head high and her hair loose. She was glorious, and going to be murdered before his eyes, or worse. Warrick wanted to shout for her to abandon her plan. Her odd expression knotted his concern further. She reached the captain, took his arm, and raised it, her concern apparent.

"How's your arm? Did it heal all right?" Karly asked the pirate captain softly.

Warrick saw the man visibly start. He grinned and took a step toward her. "Who told you about my arm?"

"I wrapped it myself, and then brought you dinner. 'Course I dropped the tray. I was always dropping things, but you forgave me," Karly said. "Let's see if I remember, white fish, biscuit, and sea grape jam."

Warrick glanced up at the pirate flag on the mast of the other ship: a skull, crossbones and double hourglass. He'd never asked Bane for his insignia—no doubt this was it. This was Bane's crew, and the man before her was more than likely Hack.

"Oh, my lord. Karly?" Hack asked.

Karly smiled and nodded encouragingly, and Hack swept her into his arms, hugging her ferociously. Warrick tried to stand, but his guards forced him to kneel, bruising his knees on the deck. Karly's feet were no longer on the ground. "Put her down," he said as evenly as he could manage. No one seemed to notice, not even Karly, but Hack eased Karly to her feet.

"I missed you," Karly said.

"Not more than we did you," he huffed, planting her away from him and staring at her in disbelief. "You are a sight!"

"Thank you very much," she said, her eyes filled with hurt.

"In a good way—all decked out, prettier than I could have imagined. Pretty as your mother."

She beamed and blushed. "Thank you."

"Where's your father? Is he here?"

"No, he's in England," Karly said awkwardly.

"So how did you manage to escape the black-hearted beast that Angus sold you off to?"

Warrick had tried to get her attention. He felt her glance at him, but he was watching Hack. The man had not figured out whom he was, or why Karly was here.

"Who told you I was 'sold'?" Karly asked, her voice suddenly higher.

"That cretin uncle of yours showed up couple days ago at The Black Horse Tavern. You should have seen the look on his face when I asked about you. I thought he would faint. I got the story though. Did he hurt you?"

"Uncle Angus?'

"No, that overstuffed, self-indulged aristocrat, the Duke of Ralstead."

Warrick collected himself and prepared to defend the situation when Karly moved between them, possessed of a sudden coughing fit. He glanced at William, whose blue eyes were bright beneath his knotted brows. "Do nothing," Warrick warned and looked to Karly, not certain if he should thank her or strangle her when they finally had a chance to speak.

"He's not the duke. He's the duke's son, and this is his ship," she said.

"He's here?"

Karly reluctantly nodded toward where Warrick kneeled. "There." Hack brushed past her and stormed toward where Warrick and William were bound. Warrick pushed to his feet, thankful for the introduction. This time there was no resistance. His captors stood aside. Karly grabbed his arm and tried to slow him with no effect. In horror he saw her leap in front of him just as Hack clenched his fist. His hands tied, he could not stop her. "Karly, move!"

"It was my choice; I could have said no. He didn't force me," Karly said.

"Don't protect him, Karly. I won't kill him. I plan to teach him a lesson."

"No," Karly answered.

Hack's gaze fell on her and narrowed. "You're not making sense. He must have threatened you." Hack looked beyond her to Warrick. "You don't frighten me, and she isn't yours."

He wanted to push Karly behind him and protect her, but all he had were his words. "I have no desire to frighten you."

Karly touched Hack's arm, stepping closer. "I don't belong to anyone. I stayed because I wanted to."

Hack frowned and took her shoulders, studying her, and

sighed. "Are you carrying his child? I know when someone's not rightly themselves."

Her poise had vanished. Warrick watched her fight to regain her composure, but it was taking too long. Something was wrong.

"Karly is herself," Warrick intervened as his mind raced back to what had caused her to lose her focus. "She is herself and she is my wife, but I would never hurt her. She is the pilot for this ship, and, unless I am mistaking, she is the one who piloted us here to find you."

Karly wrenched free and faced him. "I thought it would be better if we found them first. I know I should have told you."

Hack caught her arm and started toward the other ship with her in tow.

Warrick saw her struggle, pivoted, and kicked the man holding him. It was the only signal his crew needed. The ones that had not been bound surged forward. Someone cut his bonds. He heard a pistol shot, but did not turn. His concentration was on Karly. Hack halted at the railing, stepped up on a wooden crate, and reached to pull her alongside him. Karly swirled her skirts and petticoats and stumbled. When Hack caught her, she caught him. His pistol was in her grasp before he could act. The clamor around the deck ceased as quickly as it had begun, and all eyes turned to Karly.

Raising the weapon to Hack's eye level, she cocked the lever. "There's nothing wrong with me."

"You took my pistol!" Hack yelled at her, but halted as her fingers closed around the trigger. He studied her and raised his brows innocently. "You wouldn't shoot me."

"Nothing fatal," she said, lowering the gun toward his foot, then raising it toward his groin.

Hack yelped, jumping backward. "Are you mad? I'm trying to help you."

"I don't want to be rescued; you need to listen, then you

can do what you please. But don't force me. You should know better than that."

Hack considered her with care before answering. "What will I be listening to?"

Karly drew a deep breath. "We'll take both ships to the cove, and then Warrick has some things he needs to talk to you about, including Bane. But you have to promise safe passage."

"How do I know he'll promise the same? More than likely he'll have his friends arrest us first chance they get," Hack said and jerked his thumb. "We'll all end up in prison, hanged no doubt."

"You have my word I won't turn you in," Warrick said.

"He means that," Karly said.

"I have no objections to discussing this here," Hack said uneasily.

"Both ships are damaged. The sooner we get them out of open water the better. The cove is protected."

Warrick watched Hack balance from one foot to the other, then stuff his hands in his hole-filled pockets. As Karly glanced around, it seemed the rest of the band was equally uncomfortable, and she lowered her pistol. "Did something happen?" she asked.

"No, the cove is fine," Hack said quickly.

"Is he there?"

Hack met Warrick's gaze for the first time, his face etched with concern. "No, child, not him. He's left us alone for the most part." Hack sighed and shook his head. "I can't do it. Was you who always brought the *Triumph* in. Since you've been gone, I can't manage the reefs. I tried once and nearly wrecked her."

"You've been at sea, all this time?"

"'Course not. We anchor a ways out and row in," he admitted.

"Let Warrick and the crew go, agree to talk, and then

I'll guide the *Triumph* in and teach you how." She didn't wait for an answer. She stepped to Warrick's side and took his arm.

He had said little, and he knew Karly felt the matter was settled. Directing the pirates onto the *Triumph*, she followed. While he was sure she had the situation under control, he decided to take a few of his own precautions. She could hardly object. He motioned for Wreck to join him, and turned to his brother. "The *Moorea* is yours. Follow our course precisely. If anything appears out of the ordinary, take her on to St. George and ask the governor for reinforcements."

"We may be nowhere near Bermuda," William said, frowning and glancing across the horizon.

"I doubt it's more than a day's sail, or Karly would not have found the *Triumph* so easily." William lifted an eyebrow, and Warrick shook his head. He did not want to explain further.

"Be careful then," William said and slipped a pistol into his hand.

"I intend to."

"And bring her back in one piece," William added.

Warrick paused at the railing and peered over his shoulder at his brother. "Oh, I intend to do that too," he said with a wicked grin. With the sound of William's laughter in his ear, he made his way to the quarter deck and stood beside Karly. It was nightfall when he felt Karly's hand in his. With a small squeeze and a tug she drew him to the railing. In the darkness, he could not see her well. The moon shadows were a curse and a blessing, as she could not see him either. He did not want to be angry at her, not again. He wanted to understand. "How much farther to Bermuda?"

"Tomorrow afternoon. You could get some sleep if you like."

"I would prefer to stay with you."

Karly gave a slow nod. "I owe you an explanation. I wasn't certain I could find them. Then I wasn't certain you would agree to asking for their help. I wanted the chance to try to persuade them."

"You believe they will help?" he asked. Karly blinked but did not waiver.

"Bane did, once you spoke with him."

"So you want me to speak with them?"

Karly turned and leaned on the railing, staring at the *Moorea*, which was still within shouting distance behind. "It would be better if you did. You saw how Hack reacted. He thought he was protecting me, and so did Bane. They don't mean harm."

"I will see what I can do," he said, combing his fingers through her hair. Then she was in his arms holding him tightly, her face pressed to his chest.

"Thank you."

Guilt washed through him as he kissed her hair. Her intentions to try were there, and for that he had much to be grateful. She had been raised among demanding men. He had been no different, until now. He needed to make certain he keenly listened and understood her in the future. With Wreck on watch, he moved and settled with leaning against the mast while Karly dozed in his arms. Hack and his crew moved about the deck as if they had always been there, a part of the large family.

Afternoon found them at the entrance of the cove. He could feel the excitement bubbling through Karly as she stepped to the wheel, and then it vanished. She was like an old soul, her eyes moving knowingly from the ship to the gap in the reef as if they already had the answers. In a tone he had never heard before she gave instructions the men never questioned. She was the captain, and they were her crew. They acted as if they had been drilled and this was no more than an exercise in perfection. The *Triumph* came about, then turned and reached for the cove, sliding past the whitecaps as if they did not exist.

The cove was deathly quiet, deserted, and lonely with no sign of life except the *Moorea*. Warrick scanned the shore, then raised his glass as Karly ordered the sails taken down. The pale pink sand looked all the brighter as it caught hints of the setting sun. There were no signs of footprints and no evidence of fire or shelter. If there were inhabitants, they had managed to obliterate any clue as to their comings and goings. To listen to the men onboard however, it was as if there were hundreds within shouting distance. Warrick raised the glass again, beginning at the turquoise waters to the right and panning slowly.

At the edge of the cove sat a crumbling building of limestone blocks that extended outward into the water. It could be a relic. Then again, it could serve as a boat dock. It stood, solitary and gray against the mighty walls of nearly black rock that flanked the bay on either side. Against them, the pair of ships seemed almost tiny, even their masts well hidden from prying eyes unless someone was directly outside the cove and looking straight in. Thick brush and trees were all along the beach, and Warrick got the distinct impression that beyond the shadows, eyes watched. He lowered his glass and frowned.

"Why don't they come out?"

"Because they don't have to," Karly shrugged.

"Drop fore and aft anchors," Hack called. Splashes sounded and the *Triumph* drifted slightly, turning with the wind, and stopped; the *Moorea* was a mere ship's length away.

"You're a natural," Warrick managed, keeping his eye on the land, his senses warning him to stay alert.

"You should see her when conditions are bad, or how well she can bring a ship in at night," Hack muttered, as he descended the ladder to join them. "Never misses a turn, never hits a rock. Been that way as long as I've known her."

"Even in nighttime?"

"It's not as hard as you think." Karly blushed "Isn't it beautiful here?"

Warrick surveyed the landscape. "Where is everyone?" Warrick asked, unable to contain his uneasy curiosity any longer. "Shouldn't there be someone to greet us?"

"Out of sight 'til dark," Hack grumbled. "It's when we do most of the work. There's less chance of being observed if you know what I mean."

"But the island isn't that big. Surely the authorities know where to find you?" Warrick asked.

Hack gave a throaty chuckle. "Knowing where we are is one thing. Knowing what we are up to is another entirely."

Karly stepped to Warrick's side. "You can't see the camp, but it's beyond the beach. There are homes and even a small chapel, although it isn't used very often."

"For deaths mainly," Hack offered.

"Do many die?"

"No, but we aren't allowed in town, so there had to be somewhere to pay respects. It used to be a hut, but a few years ago the winds were bad for almost a month so we couldn't sail. Everyone pitched in. It's much nicer now."

"Why . . ." Warrick began, shifting his gaze awkwardly from Karly to Hack.

". . . haven't they arrested us?" Hack finished his sentence and shrugged. "And do what? Hang us? They threaten, they come and go, but we don' bother the islanders and we keep among ourselves. Since we work at night, most of the time they have no clue what we're doin'. The only real trouble we've ever had was with Landgon, and you know the likes of him. Truth is, I don't think it sits too well with the governor that we're here, but then neither does the price of gettin' rid of us."

"We've got everything we need here," Karly added. "It's the perfect shelter from almost any storm. Up there," she said, pointing to the towering rocks to one side, "is ideal to watch for intruders. And the undergrowth beyond the settlement is so thick that there is no way you can sneak through without making a ruckus. We always know when someone is coming." She dropped her voice. "I'm rambling, aren't I?"

Warrick's smile softened at her enthusiasm even as he noticed her main points were the safety features of the place. "Ramble away. This has been your home."

"This place, this ship, and these people; I didn't realize how much I missed all of them, until now."

"Can I escort you ashore?"

"What about the *Moorea*?"

"William is overseeing the *Moorea* for the moment. And I have some things to discuss with Hack. It would help if you would stay with me." He expected she would find it hard to contain herself. To his surprise, she allowed him to help her into the boat and then ashore. They climbed the beach, toward the sea grapes, when he heard her gasp. He was in front of her, his pistol in his hand before she could react.

"Don't shoot! He's one of Hack's men."

Warrick didn't turn to her to ask, but simply watched as the man passed them by, following the shadows to the beach. Behind him were three others. None of them spoke, casting glances in their direction as they passed. "Talkative," Warrick muttered after they had gone.

"No one here would hurt me."

"You know them all so well? Trust them all so much?"

"Yes," she said. "Trust is the basis of our group. Through the trees is the clearing around which are the houses. I want to visit with the others. It will give you a chance to talk to Hack alone. Ask him about Landgon and the chest."

She was wringing her hands, her look of guilt back.

Warrick noticed a group of women in the direction Karly had glanced.

"Yesterday he wanted to kill me. I'm not certain I'll get very far."

"You're better with people than when we first met. You'll do fine. I'll join you later."

She wanted to talk to the women, alone. Her hand in his, he raised it to his lips, and brushed it lightly. "As long as you remain close, nothing will happen to you." She nodded, and he watched her go reluctantly. After weeks together, separation made him uneasy. The situation they were in was not helping the matter. Her suggestion made sense, and for that reason alone he followed it, seeking out Hack and helping him unload several crates.

Darkness fell, and they walked through the trees. Warrick expected to find a collection of small huts, possibly shacks. Here, nestled around an almost center square sat cottages of limestone, their colors a shocking array of pastels. Quaint and pretty, it could easily be mistaken for any small well-tended settlement, its members of the most upstanding sort. Crackling fires dotted the small settlement, completing the cheery atmosphere. The night was still warm, the salty tropical breeze soft, and he could hear the ocean in the distance moaning softly. He caught sight of Karly sitting by the large central fire, surrounded by what appeared to be a collection of ruffians and looking perfectly at ease, swapping stories and trading tales as if she were having tea with the ladies. He now understood Karly and Bane's protectiveness of this group. They were a surrogate family to each other, with boundaries and rules for how to live. It was only under those rules Hack was speaking to him now, Karly vouching for him as he had for her in England. Hack handed him a mug of coffee. Then he sat, and his eyes drew to narrow slits.

"You mind telling me why Bane didn't make the trip himself?" Hack drew on his pipe. "He said he was coming back."

The man was direct. Warrick knew it was best to be equally direct. "He was shot after kidnapping Karly. I found her locked in a ship's hold. I suppose he could have still made the trip, except he was ordered to stay in the country until we settle this matter. Once we find the gold, he claims there are documents with it to prove him innocent." He paused, considering the man before him. "Karly will verify all of that."

"You always honest, Mr. Barry?" Hack asked, raising an eyebrow.

"When I can be, yes. When I can't I prefer silence," Warrick answered.

"You would think, after having Caroline kidnapped away from him, he would have the sense not to do the same misery on someone else." He took another long draw of his pipe and chewed thoughtfully. "So, you'll be lookin' after Karly then?"

"Yes. I would appreciate it if you would tell me about Commander Farris."

"She told you about him, did she? Although not everything or you'd not be askin' me. Karly wouldn't talk to no one about him. But I have eyes. I saw what that man's about. He's in charge of the fort, the main one you be trying to protect. You'll be speaking to him about your plans and all since he's in charge of the ships here and their officers. Don't let him bother Karly no more."

Warrick's heart skipped a beat. He forced his expression to remain blank. "Tell me what happened."

"Farris is Lady Wessington's brother. It got him the post. Bastard came around a number of times. Checkin' up on us although his lieutenant could have done as much. 'Can't hide a pretty face,' I told Bane. Claimed he was doing inspections, keeping us from trouble. But we all knew different. When we was arrested, all the commander was interested in was her.

He offered to let us go if Karly turned her fancy his way, became his mistress." He watched the fire, lost in thought.

"Karly refused him."

"He's scum, and Karly played it. She got him to release us. Bless her heart. There was no way to keep so many of us, but she wanted us free. Then Lady Wessington heard about Karly and her husband is the governor. Next we hear, Karly's uncle has been told to get her off the island. I got to see her once. She was pretty scared, poor little thing. Losing her father, then stuck away from everyone. Farris left her in the dark part of the prison, too. I guess he figured she would be more likely to agree the worse he made it. Only he don't know her so well; a stubborn streak runs in that girl as deep as the sea," he sighed loudly and shook his head. "I bribed the guards to take food and messages."

Warrick caught evasiveness in Hack's voice. "Every day?"

Hack slowly smiled and nodded. "You're smart, Mr. Barry. Karly will do you good."

Warrick looked for Karly. She hadn't moved, hadn't changed her position, nor had those around her. But she seemed smaller and less certain. Hers had not been a kind world. That didn't explain her expression. The tendril of suspicion that had begun to wind through his brain started to itch. Her behavior had been odd, and then there was Hack's question if she were with child. She saw him then. Warrick gestured for her to come to him. One of the women bent and spoke in her ear. Even from a distance, he saw her tense. He would set her mind at ease about the commander. Then it was time to discuss the future.

Chapter 24

She had to tell him. The women had said what her heart already knew. The child might be within her, but it was theirs, hers and Warrick's. Warrick needed to understand what would happen, that she was going to leave him, but not by her choice, that the child would be alone, as she had been. But she wanted her baby to have a mother, Warrick to marry again. The thought ripped at her. Hers were not the needs that mattered.

Someplace dark, where she couldn't see his eyes as she told him, would be best. If there was pain, she didn't want to know—it might snap her own control. The rocks at the edge of the bay would do nicely. She approached the fire where Warrick and Hack sat. "What are you two discussing so secretively?" she asked.

Hack's chin came up, and he flashed a toothy smile. "Catching up on gossip, like you was doin'."

Karly smiled back and looked to Warrick. She twisted the band of metal once around her finger and offered her hand to Warrick. "Will you walk with me?" With a nod, Warrick stood, his touch a link to her soul. Her doubts ebbed. How could she not give him all that was possible? He was a part of her; to deny it was to deny part of herself. He had to know what she did.

She led him through the wooden path to the edge of the beach, while she sought for some conversation that wouldn't give her away, until she was ready. "I would like your advice regarding my uncle," she began.

Warrick stopped abruptly, pulling her to a halt. "Has he tried to contact you?"

"No, but I heard he is in St. George," she said and began to walk again. She glanced back. Warrick was following, but his arms were crossed. "I realize he has not treated me well in the past."

"Nor did he treat your mother well."

The rising moon silvered the landscape and washed the color from Warrick's face. "He never hit me. He is part of my family."

"It depends how you define a family."

"How do you?" Karly asked.

Warrick drew alongside her and with his hand on her shoulder, stopped her. He cocked his head as his brows came together. "He is not my uncle."

Her stomach suddenly felt very cold. "You're correct," she said with a quiver in her voice.

"He is my uncle," Warrick corrected, with dawning realization. "As my wife, your relatives are now mine."

"They don't have to be," she said and backed a step.

Warrick scooped her in his arms, his grip suddenly fierce. Karly met his searching gaze, stunned at his ferocity. "I'm sorry," he said with a rush.

Self-conscious, she was sorry she had brought it up. She needed to talk to Warrick about other things, not this. "You needn't be sorry. I wanted your advice, not an apology."

"You are welcome to both."

She wanted to sound confident, but it was taking all her efforts. But they were talking—that was something. "I thought you might be able to give me some guidance. You have more experience. You have both parents and your brother. What would you do if this was one of them?"

"I am not a good source of advice, Karly."

"Why?" She watched as he raked his fingers through his hair. In the dim light he pursed his lips and sighed.

"Because I find your uncle's actions hard to forgive. I realize he did come with your grandmother when he might have refused to escort her. That could count for something, provided he remains sober. Drunk he is volatile."

"Yes," she whispered, glad the bruise on her cheek was no longer a reminder.

"You should not be alone with him, but if you want to see him, I will go with you, although I would not expect great things."

"I don't. My mother's family has hurt for so long, if I can heal even some of the pain by visiting him, I believe she would want that. I know that is ridiculous since I never met her, but my grandmother reached out to me. I want to try."

"I will do my best to help."

Karly glanced toward camp. They were far enough away now that no one could hear them. Her courage stumbled. She caught his elbow. "I want to show you something."

"All right, and there's something I want to discuss."

She led him down the beach. The ground softened under her feet, and she dipped, kicking off her slippers and happily clasping them in her hand. "I missed this," Karly sighed, wiggling her toes in the cool sand. Reclaiming Warrick's hand, she led him out onto the beach and to the water's edge.

The silver bay lapped on one side of them while the shadowed outlines framed the landscape on the other. "Where are we going?" he asked.

"I told you, I want to show you something," she said, putting her slippers on.

Warrick stepped around a large collection of brush and paused. "So this is how they keep the beach clear of footprints—they use branches to wipe away the tracks."

The black rock sprung from the sand before her. Karly scurried up the near hidden trail to the first small ridge, calling for Warrick over her shoulder. She continued on, using her hands to help balance over the sharp rocks. It had been months since she had been here, and she was proud she could remember each stone, not setting a foot wrong. Warrick called her name, and she answered without turning. His second call was more urgent, and she stopped until he reached her. "It's not much farther."

"Good, then you won't mind holding my hand the rest of the way," he said in a clipped voice.

She could see his silhouette, dark against the dark sky, no trace of expression, and yet she knew exactly what it would look like in the bright of day. He was frustrated with her again, and her confidence faltered. "I'll take you to the *Moorea*." But as she tried to pass him he stopped her, placing his hands on her hips.

"No, it will be fine. Show me why you brought me here."

Nodding, she turned and continued her ascent, guiding him as they went. Karly continued along the rock outcropping along the narrow path that cut to the top. Bordered on three sides by water, it jutted far into the bay now bathed in silvery moonlight. Reaching the end she stopped, admiring the *Triumph* and *Moorea*, neatly tucked where she had left them. Small lights twinkled from the decks and reflected in long tendrils across the water. "This is one of my favorite times of the day," she said with a sigh. "Look across the cove. Can you see them?" she asked as Warrick's arms slid around her waist, tugging her to his chest.

"Do you mean the ships?"

The heat of him was a distraction. She heard his question,

ut her mind had trouble focusing beyond the sensation of
eing held. "The reefs, below us—can you see them?"

"It's high tide and dark. Of course I cannot see the reefs."

"Look again," she instructed and pointed him toward the
ntrance to the bay. There the night darkened further. The
noon had fallen behind a cloud, and the blackness around
hem was almost complete. She could feel his breath against
er back and on her shoulder as he searched. She knew
rom the tension in his touch when he saw the tinge of green
oftly illuminating a long band in the water around the reef.

"What's doing that?"

Karly shrugged. "When it's dark you can bring a ship in
sing them and nothing else. Somehow the water crossing
he reefs makes them glow. It is some kind of night fish or
eaweed," she whispered.

"You discovered this?"

"I noticed them one night while I was hiding up here."

"From Commander Farris?"

She flinched and felt him tighten his hold. "I left you
vith Hack so you could discuss Bermuda, not me."

"Sometimes it's better to let others talk when you can't."
Warrick softly cupped her cheek.

"He doesn't bother me anymore." Karly distanced herself
rom him with a step.

"Except you still have nightmares."

She had to fight not to lash out. "They're gone."

"Are they?"

Her breath was shallow; she was trapped. She couldn't
stay, and there was nowhere to run. She stared at him, furi-
us and terrified, while she tried to put the pieces together.
What he knew, how he knew, what he thought of her, and
now she would handle it. She realized he was steadying her,
drawing them both to the soft ground covered with soil and
grasses. He offered soothing words. She focused on stop-
ing the tears that threatened. "It's over."

"I know. He won't hurt you again."

"I told you, I don't expect you or anyone to protect me; can look after myself. You have other things to worry about And you'll need his help."

"I have a lot of things to worry about, and I will require his help. Never doubt that I will not compromise you ir the process."

His voice was full of assurance, but she felt none. She covered her mouth with her hand and fought the storm tha threatened to overwhelm her.

"He won't bother you. No more nightmares."

"It's not that. Warrick, I think I'm with child." The word: spoken, she began to shake. Worse, she started to ramble over her suspicion. It all came out in a blur. Warrick touchec her shoulder, but she shook him off. "I didn't want to tel you, not yet. But the women said I should."

"They were right."

Karly gasped a sob and bit the inside of her cheek tc force calm. "I wanted to wait until this was over, until we had stopped this . . . threat. You won't want me to help now and I have to."

"Your safety is important to me."

She swallowed hard. "Yours is to me as well. Don't make me stay on the *Moorea*. You need my help, you know you do." The sobs won. Karly bent her head and tried to bury the sound. Warrick scooped her into his arms and began to rock

"I'm glad you told me."

Karly looked up. The smile on his face had a mysterious quality she couldn't place. He wasn't angry. Not even a little. She had told him most of her fears. She decided she might as well tell all. "My mother died having me. What it I don't survive and you are left with the baby, like my father was with me?"

Warrick was silent for a long pause while he stroked her hair. "We can return to England before your time. My mother is there. She has attended more than one birthing. Or we can find a midwife here if you would prefer. You will have the best care."

"England. Your mother is kind; I would like her there too."

"England it is," he said and kissed her cheek. "And nothing is going to happen to you."

"You are going to make me stay on the *Moorea* aren't you?"

"I would like to." His expression turned grave.

"My stomach is flat. You can't see anything." She placed his hand on her abdomen to demonstrate. "I could be wrong."

"In St. George, I want you to talk to a midwife. We should try and surmise one way or the other."

"And then?"

Warrick studied her and gave a heavy sigh. "You should stay out of this. You should stay safe, or as safe as possible. A woman with child has no business chasing down a traitor. But, I can't foresee you sitting still for anything. I will let you help, but you must swear you will take care."

"I swear." Her voice trembled, and she wasn't sure if he was angry. She hugged him cautiously, not ready to believe he didn't have more to say. His grip tightened around her, enveloped her in comfort. The torment battering her ebbed, and she was able to take slower breaths. He had recognized her nature.

Chapter 25

If Karly's uncle was there, that meant Landgon was also
After all, Angus worked for him. The questions were where
and what was his next move? Warrick surveyed the deck
of the *Moorea* and crossed to where William studied the
logs. "What's wrong, little brother?" William stood to em-
phasize the fact he was taller and glanced down at Warrick
Warrick grinned.

"The sails are fixed, but the damage to the deck is going
to need more work than we can possibly do here," William
reported.

"Fortunately we are within a few hours of the shipyard
where she was built. Hasings will make her right, provided
she is safe enough for us to sail her," Warrick said.

"She'll get us there. She could get us to London if she
had to."

"St. George will be far enough. I'll go speak with the
governor, but I have a personal favor to ask."

William cocked his head, puzzled. "Oh?"

Glancing around uncomfortably, Warrick took his
brother's arm and led him to the railing. He took a deep
breath and lowered his voice. "I want you to stay with Karly
Don't let her out of your sight."

"You think Landgon will try to kidnap her?"

"I don't know," Warrick said and started to leave.

William stayed him with his hand. "Is something wrong? You don't seem yourself."

It was a private matter. However, William was his brother. He would help keep Karly safe. "I need to find a midwife."

"A what?"

"A woman who helps with babies," Warrick said, becoming flushed.

"I know what a midwife is. What do you want one for?"

"For Karly," Warrick muttered and then met his brother's baffled gaze. "She's pregnant." The look on William's face was too much. Warrick grinned. "You're going to be an uncle."

"She's so slim," William said with amazement.

"The baby is not due until winter—of course she's slim."

"Then why . . ."

Warrick glanced to where Karly stood a short distance away talking to Hack. He lowered his voice further. "I want her to speak with someone. She doesn't know what to expect, and she's scared." William's brows came together, and his mouth pursed. "Her mother died in childbirth. Will you stay with her?"

"I don't want to overhear anything about midwifing, but I'll keep her company," William assured him. Dirty water sloshed across the deck and over their boots. Looking up in annoyance, he spotted Jenkins. "Maybe while we're in Bermuda we should look into getting some more hands. Trent has many strengths; hiring sailors isn't one of them."

Warrick watched Jenkins. Bent over his bucket, he was mumbling his irritation beneath his breath. The lad hated work. Warrick decided he would offer to relieve him. If the lad wanted to disembark, he would cancel his obligation. "Trent didn't have a lot of time."

"He doesn't have a lot of experience."

"What's done is done. See that the ship is ready. We'll sail as soon as our guests leave." Warrick walked to where Karly chatted with Hack, her stance animated. So much depended on her, perhaps too much for anyone to have to carry, and he felt guilty. There was no help for it. Hack fell silent as he joined them. The man was comfortable with Karly, so that was the way it would be. One more item for her to carry.

"You almost ready to get this ship underway?" he asked her sweetly.

Nodding, Karly exchanged looks with Hack. "Hack has a suggestion." She placed her tongue in her cheek and waited.

"What kind of a 'suggestion'?"

Hack cleared his throat to speak, but before he could, Karly inserted herself partway between the two men, not giving him the chance. "Hack thinks Landgon may try to slip a ship in, perhaps off the north shore." She turned to Hack, who nodded.

"Wouldn't that be risky?"

"The reefs aren't as bad, not as far out, but the landing is tough. If you want to get a small rowboat in, it could be worth the risk. You could launch from quite a ways out, and the current would bring ye' in. The island would be defenseless by the time the rest of the fleet arrived. If we go overland, and find 'em before they can strike, we can cut 'em off." Hack said, grinning.

"I take it you plan to help us?" Warrick asked, keeping his voice even.

"Karly's vouchin' for ye', and I be tired of runnin'. If you be good to your word, help us with Bane's gold, and get us a pardon so's we can go about our life as regular people, yeah, I be willin' to help. The whole group agreed to help, provided when this is all over, the money we captured is ours."

"I believe I can broker a deal for you, provided there are no tricks."

"You have my word," Hack said and offered the palm of his hand.

If Hack expected him to slice his hand open to seal his word, he was mistaken. Warrick took his offer, turned it, and shook it affably. "Send word if you see anything."

"We'll head out to scout the north shore tomorrow. If you be needin' us, that's where we'll be." Karly's hand he squeezed tightly, and then he faced Warrick one last time. "You watch after her. From time to time, she has been known to get in a bit o' trouble."

Warrick knew better than to comment, and nothing good would come from a laugh. He pursed his lips and looked on as the older man climbed out of sight, catching a rowboat to shore. Regaining control, he cleared his throat. "Are you ready to sail this ship to Northington Shipyard?"

"I got her in here, didn't I?" Karly asked, lifting her chin,

"Yes, you did, and most impressively." Karly beamed, accepting his hand as he led her toward the bridge. He saw her smile fade as he took the helm. He knew she was disappointed, but it would have to wait. "Call your instructions to Trent. He'll take it from there."

Karly took her post and studied the sails. "Sound out when we are within a boat's length of those rocks." She pointed to the outcropping that guarded the bay.

He wasn't sure what to expect from the crew. Sailing into the cove, they had been flanked by a pirate ship, but clear of any threat, Karly was not necessary. Warrick saw Trent's frown. Wreck's back was turned, and his manner was brisk. He said nothing, nor did he even share a glance. Clearing the reef with no room to spare, she directed the ship north and smiled brightly at Warrick.

"You managed that very well," he said.

"Do you always compliment your crew?"

Warrick decided not to fall into her verbal trap. He had the right not to explain himself. He reached and turned her until she was facing the wheel, caging her on either side with his arms.

"You can't steer if you hold me like this," she muttered.

"I don't have to steer, you do," he said in her ear, guiding her hands to the wheel before settling them at her waist.

Karly glanced over her shoulder, "Me?"

"Yes, and if you don't face forward, we'll need even more repairs by the time we reach St. George," he said. She whirled away in an instant, pinning her eyes off the bow.

He started with the simplest of instructions. The *Moorea* was not a difficult sail, and Karly had the basic knowledge, but she lacked experience. What she knew she had learned from watching. More than once when he spoke she startled. After a half hour, she was close to tears, hiding it as best she could.

"I'm failing this badly," she muttered under her breath.

"If you're ready to stop, you can." She wavered in silence, and he surged with pride at her courage. He bent closer to her ear. "Remember, you have a talent. That should never be wasted."

"I don't want to stop."

"Then we'll continue," he said, smiling inwardly at her spirit. A gust grabbed the sails, keeling her to one side. Karly sucked in a quick breath, sending the *Moorea* closer with the wind.

"When the gust drops, turn her to starboard," he directed.

"Yes, sir."

"Hold her steady until we pass St. David's Island."

"And after St. David's Island, I should tack northwest."

"After St. David's, you will hand her over." His words were curt, not that he expected an argument from her. When the time came, she ducked under his arm, remaining beside him as he brought her about.

"That was wonderful."

"That was your talent," he said evenly. It was not easy to

conceal his pleasure, but he managed. He did not want to be caught grinning at his wife like a smitten schoolboy. The crew would never let him live it down. "When you're ready and not on duty, you may try again," he said, pretending to be distracted by the sails. Karly took up her position by his side, giving instructions until St. George came into view.

He heard the change in her tone. The crew did too because they looked up as she lowered her voice, her commands becoming crisp and authoritative. There was no time to admire the white buildings set against the green and blue background. He caught the scent of bread on the sea breeze and saw the flutter of banners from market day. Karly did not look at all. She ordered them on, past the gaiety and around the peninsula, until Northington Shipyard came into view. Guiding the *Moorea* carefully between two hidden reefs, she completely ignored the hails of two smaller boats that approached to pilot them in. Instead, she directed the *Moorea* straight, ordering a come about at the last moment. Within line-tossing distance of the pier she ordered the anchor dropped. Warrick glanced first to William's pallor and then to where Trent sat on a pile of rope, nodding compliance to Wreck's suggestions. "A rather extravagant entrance."

"I prefer not to waste time or sail," Karly said quickly.

Warrick closed the distance between them. "I prefer you take into consideration the delicate constitution of my crew."

Karly blinked and looked about her. "It was a bit showy of me."

He held her gaze, watching as her cheeks flushed with embarrassment. But just when he thought he might have to intervene, she nodded thoughtfully.

"Are you ready to go ashore?" Warrick asked.

"I could stay on the *Moorea* and help fold the sails."

"No, you cannot. Only a few crewmembers will stay aboard

while the ship is repaired. Hasings provides cottages for the rest of us." Her confidence vanished, and he recognized the distant look in her eyes. "Are you expecting trouble?"

She shrugged and started for the ship's boat. When he did not follow, she retraced her steps. "I never told Mr. Hasings who my father was. I was not sure he would want the daughter of a pirate working for him. I was certain his clients would not want me at his shipyard."

"He must have suspected something."

Karly flicked a glance toward the shore. "If he did, he never said. I would come when I could and he would pay me for a day's work and then I left. No one was the wiser."

"Your father let you come all this way and never spoke to the man?"

"I didn't tell Bane where the money came from, and the two of them never met. They had no reason to. But after the crew and I were arrested, Mr. Hasings may have guessed the truth. He'll think I have betrayed him."

"He might. It is also possible he will understand."

Karly released a shaky sigh. "I should stay onboard, at the very least until you have negotiated the repairs."

"I have ordered four of my ships from him. He is a man of business. He will treat you with respect. If you are worried about him being angry, I will make the arrangements here and we will stay somewhere else while *Moorea* is being repaired."

"You wouldn't mind?"

"Not if you are truly uncomfortable, but you shouldn't avoid him, not until you are sure," Warrick cautioned.

"I suppose I do owe him the chance to shout at me. Then again, you may be right. He might not even recognize me; Hack didn't."

He had to chuckle, not to be cruel, but because she was so certain the outcome had to be negative. Taking her hand and draping it over his arm, he helped her into the boat.

Waiting at the pier was Hasings. The older man looked downright furious. His face was scrunched in a scowl. His hair was wild. Warrick couldn't remember a time he had seen the builder more disheveled. With each step, Karly pressed her body tighter against him. He was considering turning around when he caught the ghost of a smile at the corner of Hasings's mouth. Warrick readied himself to jump in the bay after Karly if she chose to try to swim. He stopped before Hasings and forced his expression to remain bland. "I'm afraid I ran into a bit of trouble with the *Moorea*."

"What have you done to my ship?" Hasings gasped.

"Pirates," Warrick answered.

"So I see," Hasings quipped, his eyes on Karly. "You and that gang of yours broke my ship?"

Fidgeting, Karly pulled her shoulders together. "It was a misunderstanding."

Mr. Hasings stood in front of her as she held her ground, and Warrick's hand. He didn't yell. Much to Warrick's surprise, Hasings touched Karly's chin with extreme gentleness. "As are a great many things when it comes to you, are they not? I saw you bringing in the *Moorea* and was glad you decided to come."

"How did you recognize me?"

"Who else would bring a ship in straight on, taking the turn to the left of the inlet? No one but you could have executed that maneuver without ripping the hull wide open on the rocks. I knew it was you before you docked. We missed you."

"I missed being around here, too."

"So, you've come to work?" Hasings smiled. "I've got a lot of orders. There's plenty for you to do."

Reclaiming her arm, Warrick shook his head. "I'm afraid you'll have to do without her. Mrs. Barry has other obligations."

Hasings stared in surprise, his wizened face suddenly

less certain. Then he laughed loudly, placing a hand on one hip and extending the other to Warrick. "Well, that beats all If I had known you were looking for a proper wife, I woul have introduced you two a long time ago rather than protecting her from you. It would have saved everyone a worl of hurt and a bit of time."

"I was hardly looking for a husband," Karly said simply

"Maybe not, but since it has all worked in the end doesn't matter does it? You're staying with me, of course?'

"If you've got the room."

Hasings chuckled. "For you, I always have room. You car have the cottage by the bay, perfect for a young couple and very private."

Chapter 26

Warrick felt guilty. He wished he could have stayed with Karly rather than attending to business, but there was no one else. Diplomacy and William were hardly the best of friends, his brother prone to more emotion than the practice dictated. In the end, he needed to be the one to talk to the governor; he had no choice. Mrs. Morrison, the midwife he had sent for, had agreed to call that morning but had been late. He had delayed as long as he could to meet the woman personally and ask a few questions, although he was at a loss as to what constituted a good midwife. She had seemed well mannered, easy in nature, and reasonable. She was older with graying hair and a pleasant smile that never dimmed. Her recommendations had been the deciding factor. Her name was known among the elite socialites of the island. Warrick had sent letters by messenger to two of her patronesses, a viscountess and the wife of a marquis. Both suggested her highly, their children born without incident. No longer able to postpone his trip to Government House, the governor's residence, he had left Karly in her care, assuring Karly he would return before dark.

The sun had already disappeared behind the trees, hiding its splendor until the morning. While their cottage was full east, in the four days they had been there they had yet to see a complete sunset, the island in the way. Perched on an out-cropping of rock that dipped to the beach below, it was quaint and almost remote. Shielded by trees he could see the terrace of Hasings's home.

Entering the small foyer of their cottage, Warrick paused and listened for movement, then crossed the Spanish tiled floor and ascended the wooden stairs to the second floor. Opening the door to their bedroom he glanced around, first to the massive four-poster bed neatly made and empty, to the small sitting alcove, also abandoned. Warrick quickened his step. She could not have gone far. There were guards around the property. There was the beach, and Karly had made an offhanded comment about a swim.

He peered into the floral-patterned dressing room, think-ing perhaps she was indulging in the warm bath he had en-couraged, but there was no one. Everything was neatly in its proper place. He was about to pivot and make haste to the main house when a small sound stopped him. The French-style doors were wide open, ushering in the ocean breeze. He stepped through, onto the terrace that stretched outside between the two rooms.

Kneeling, with her head tucked between the heavy lime-stone supports, Karly leaned, peering over the side. She was so engrossed in something that she had not heard him enter. Remembering the near tragedy on the bowsprit of the *Moorea* he edged closer, deliberately scraping his boot to make her aware of his presence. His hand simultaneously grasped her forearm to be safe. She cocked her head, then lifted her chin and turned to meet his gaze. "What are you looking at?"

"A nesting pair of longtails," she said with whispered rev-erence, gesturing with her hand for him to join her.

Warrick sank beside her, and followed the direction of her hand. Sure enough, a small nest was on the rocks to the side and below, tended by an elegant white bird, dark marks about its head. Its tail was far too long for its own good. "I don't think I've ever seen one this close."

"Nor will you; they rarely sit still. I think she is tending her eggs. They must be near hatching because she hasn't moved. Her mate's been looking after her. Here he comes again with something in his beak." No sooner had she finished her sentence than a second bird swooped, landed for a moment, and took flight again.

"You think he's trying to impress her?" Warrick smiled.

"Longtails mate for life. He doesn't have to."

Reaching over, he ran his hand over her hair. Freed from any clips or braids, the brown locks tousled wildly about her face. "How did it go with the midwife, Mrs. Morrison?"

"Fine, she's very nice. She asked many questions, explained her reasons for each, and then gave me advice."

"Did she say anything of interest?"

"She believes it's a boy."

Before she could withdraw, Warrick placed his hand on her shoulder, only to have her turn her head. Something wasn't sitting well, but he couldn't place it. "How did she know that?"

Karly shrugged. "She seemed cónfident." She didn't want to discuss the matter any further; it was already difficult enough. "Any word from the governor?"

Warrick drew her back to the safety of the terrace and helped her to her feet, buying himself time. The governor hadn't been keen to listen, but he had his reasons. To admit Warrick could be correct regarding Karly and her band would mean that he had been wrong in condemning them. It took a great deal for any man to bow to his own ego.

"Yes, he agreed with the king's recommendations and mine. Provided Hack and the group are of assistance, he is willing to look past their history, and allow them to keep the booty from the French ship. And he invited us to the

Government House. There is a gathering, a party. It's the perfect opportunity to get the leaders together and discuss the situation."

"He invited 'us'?"

"Us," he affirmed. "I told him you were here, and about your father. I told him nearly everything." She tensed at his words, but he decided to press on. "And he admitted to me that he regrets some of the things that were said in the past."

"I can stay here and watch the *Moorea*'s repairs."

"That is Hasings's job."

"Warrick, I don't see how me attending will make any difference."

"It will to you."

"How so?"

"Commander Farris will be there." She paled before his eyes. He grasped her other shoulder to steady her in case she should faint. Her weakness passed quickly. He took her hand in his, considering it and his words carefully. "I want him to see you, know you are out of reach, off limits. And it's important you see him too. There will be no more nightmares."

"I haven't had any recently."

"That does not mean the matter is closed. You need some peace, and you will have some, I promise."

"You talked to the governor about this as well," she stated flatly.

"I clarified, that perhaps the governor was not told the entire situation, and asked, if it were his daughter on whom unwanted advances had been made, what would he have done? I also asked him to consider what would happen if there was no one there to protect his daughter, or defend her. He's a reasonable man, Karly, who has been given unreasonable facts. He should err on the side of the unprotected, but in this case, with his wife involved, he acted hastily."

"I would rather it be over."

"It will be, after tomorrow night. Trust me," he said gently, but she jerked away.

"Don't," she said, taking a step back. "Don't ask me to trust you. If I didn't I wouldn't be here; I would have never spoken to Bane about helping, or Hack or done half the things I have," her voice choked with emotion, and she wrapped her arms around herself. "If I didn't trust you, I would have never seen that woman in the first place, or let her bleed me. This isn't a matter of trust."

"Bleed you? What are you talking about?" he demanded.

Karly backed away and shook her head. "You're changing the subject."

"No, I think I discovered it," he declared. "Let me see."

She turned and stared out the window. "She said I was weak, and it would help improve my vitality by getting rid of any poisons in my system."

"Let me see." With slow deliberation she unlocked her arms and extended them.

Warrick took the right and cradled it while he unbuttoned the cuff.

"You've never seen someone bled before?"

"Not for being pregnant," Warrick said. He could feel the bandage. His anger soared.

"She didn't do it because I was pregnant; she did it because she said . . ."

"I heard you the first time." He managed to get her sleeve past her elbow. The white cloth was neatly tied in a large, bunched knot. He wanted to rip it off. Karly tensed, and he realized she was reacting to him. He counted silently to five and removed the dressing. Warrick sucked in a painful breath at the deep gash and purple-blue bruising. "Oh my

God," he exclaimed, and she flinched. He held on, guiding her toward the washbasin. "How much did she take?"

"I don't know."

"How long did she do this for?"

"I don't know," Karly repeated, her voice rising.

"Why would you let her do that?"

"You asked me to cooperate. You said she knew what she was doing."

Warrick was horrified. He had asked for her confidence and failed her. "I should have been there," he grated as he pressed a cloth over the raw wound.

"You wouldn't have been allowed to stay. She insisted on seeing me alone. William had to wait outside."

"Did you tell William about this?"

"No. What would he have done? And you needed to go; it was important."

"So are you," he said, consciously unclenching his jaw.

"Does this mean she isn't coming back tomorrow?"

"She isn't coming near you ever again. And you can be sure I plan to ask how anyone could recommend her."

"She's very attentive, and for some women, it's probably nice to be fussed over. But I don't have that problem."

She was defending the woman. He had to get control of his anger before she became upset. "No, your husband hovers all by himself."

Karly released a tremulous sigh. "Perhaps a bit."

"Except today, when you needed me."

"You're here now. That's what matters. That and agreeing I don't have to see her again."

It was his turn to chuckle grimly. "We'll get through this, and then I am taking you back to England, to a doctor we know, and my mother, whose judgment I trust since I am worthless to you right now. In the meantime, I have some medical books on the *Moorea*. One of them may come in handy."

"A book?"

"Would you prefer I find you another midwife?"

"No. A book and you will do fine. I'm sure nature knows what it's doing." Karly's voice drifted away.

Warrick searched her face. There was color in her cheeks. The midwife may have been a butcher, but she had not taken too much. "Nature may know what it's doing, but I still would prefer you and our child are somewhere comfortable when your time comes, with the right help, provided you will trust me again."

"If I agree, do I have to go to the party?"

"You wouldn't deny me the chance to show you off, would you?"

She blushed. "Flattery isn't fair; I'm not used to it."

"It isn't flattery. It's the truth. Hiding here won't solve anything. You'll spend your entire time worrying about the first time you will run into him, and you will. . . . The island isn't very big, and our mission is very specific. He will be involved. Better that we chose the time, place, and setting, rather than leave it to chance."

"You're very good at this," she said quietly after a long pause.

Warrick finished tying a new bandage and ran his fingers through her hair. "I'll try not to let you down again," he whispered.

"After all the things I've already put you through, you needn't worry."

"It's not a contest."

"Then stop keeping score." She tried to smile at him.

He dropped his arms to her waist, guiding her body flush with his. "It's in my nature, but I will try to improve." She laid her head on his shoulder, and for a fleeting instant, all was right again.

"Do I have to dance?"

"Only with me. The rest of the evening you can say you are tired. After today, that will be the truth."

"It's not your fault," she reiterated.

Warrick wove his fingers through the long brown mass, letting it cascade between them. Her hair was so soft. He tried to decide if it was her best feature. There was so much of her that was beautiful. He set aside the contemplation for another one. "After dinner I wanted to take you for a swim. I thought it would be refreshing. But I think we had better wait until your arm is better."

"If we wait, something else will happen. I would prefer to go tonight," she blurted. "I miss being able to swim on a real beach. Where did you have in mind?"

"The small cove on the other side of the house." He had pleased her, although he wondered if she would still be pleased when the adventure was over. Her near drowning may have washed from her mind, but not from his. Through the dinner of roasted pork, poached fish, corn custard, and asparagus, he managed to keep the conversation light and refine his plan. She was too keen not to notice, and he caught her staring at him several times.

Warrick led her past their cottage down a small path down to the beach. They crossed stone to another tiny beach beyond. The cove was in miniature, more bathing pool than ocean. It was surrounded almost completely by dark rocks, high enough to block them from view. Tonight, the full moon was above. They were its only audience. He removed his shirt and helped her from her gown, leading her to the water's edge, where she halted.

"These petticoats will get tangled again."

"I won't let anything happen to you," he said and cursed himself as her chin came up. His tone was too tight. She knew what he was up to.

"I need to remove my slippers and stockings."

Warrick waited as she sat and bent over, removing each

with definite care. Her manner had turned cautious. When she took his hand a second time, her hand was like ice. "Just a small swim," he assured her.

Stepping into the warm water, Karly halted abruptly, letting it lap over her feet. "Maybe this is not such a good idea."

"Place your sore arm over my shoulder."

"I don't like games," she said weakly.

She knew. She knew him, understood him and despite himself, he broke into a grin. He loved her for her intuition.

"If this is not a game, why are you smiling?"

"It is a long story," he said, concentrating on her wide eyes. "At the deepest end you can still stand. I promise things will be better if we confront this now." She hesitated. He could feel her hands begin to shake. When she moved forward it was in half-steps. He escorted her slowly. She gripped his hands tight as the water went knee deep, then waist. Her breath shallowed as he sank onto a bended knee, and she sat reluctantly. "Good."

"Then we're done?" she asked and made to stand.

Warrick held her to him. "Not yet. But I will wait until you're ready."

Karly turned her head back toward the shore, offering only her profile basked in silvery light. "I've swam all my life."

"How many times have you nearly drowned?"

"That was the first."

He was proud of her for fighting her fear. "You have every reason to be uneasy. I won't leave you."

Karly turned her face to his and adjusted her seat. "What next?"

"I'm going to lay you back. Close your eyes and imagine I'm carrying you." Her arm tightened across his shoulder. Her grip turned to iron. She complied until her head touched the water. She jerked forward with a splash and had to start again. It took several attempts. He could feel her breath deepen, quicken, as if any moment she expected to go under and needed to hold her breath. Silent, he kissed her, and her lips warmed. Her body eased farther into his embrace, her eyes trained on him, wary. "Relax; the seawater will do you good." He began to move through the water as she locked her gaze on his. Her legs came up, and he felt the swirl of her kick. She could swim.

Karly looked past him at the heavens beyond. "The stars are more brilliant here, and the moon seems . . ."

"Bigger," he finished for her, rewarded by her eyes settling back on him. They were at the deeper end of the pool where he was able to stand. Turning her gently, he could feel her hair brush over the bare skin of his abdomen beneath the water. She had calmed and was actually smiling.

"I really can swim."

"I believe you."

"You weren't sure. You can't fool me," she breathed.

"So I should stop trying?"

He lifted her free hand from the water, and she reached behind his earlobe with a soft caress. She guided his face to hers, his lips to hers, relaxing, tensing, until he raised his head, gazing down at her. "I don't mind you trying."

"There's hope for me?"

"I didn't say that; I said I didn't mind you trying."

"Tell me what Mrs. Morrison said that upset you so badly."

"She kept saying how weak I was. She told me all the things I would need to do to care for myself and about pregnancies that had failed. I feel guilty for getting pregnant. I probably won't make it through delivering this baby. I had to grow up without a mother. Now I'm placing our child in the same situation. It's too late, but this is my fault."

"If there's fault to be found, blame me. I had a better sense of what we were doing than you did."

"No. My father used to blame himself, but it wasn't his fault. Some women have the strength while others do not."

"You are hardly a wilting violet, Karly. You will be fine."

"You're awfully sure of yourself," she sighed quietly.

"Yes, I am," he assured. "I have every reason to be. Look at all we have already been through together, how much we have overcome. It's hard to see all of that at this time." He guided them back to shore and helped her to her feet. "Things will get easier."

"And if they don't?"

"Then we have each other to lean on. I didn't drop you in the ocean, and I won't let you fall." Returning to the shore, he placed a towel around her shoulders.

"I won't let you fall either," she said, placing a second towel around him and forming her body to his seductively.

"I'll remember that," he said, nuzzling her neck.

"And if you forget, I'll remind you."

At her ease, he was able to release the tension he had been carrying since dinner. He could stay here and be happy. It wasn't possible; it wasn't even close to possible. Embracing her, he closed his eyes, and wished tomorrow was not so soon. They would need every bit of strength to get through what was ahead without shattering what they had built tonight.

Chapter 27

Government House was built to be imposing, and it was. Nestled within St. George, Karly had seen its tall gray facade from the water and from the gates, but never from the front doorstep. She reminded herself she was here by invitation. By Warrick's side she stepped confidently across the threshold into the main hall awash with pageantry. Then she spied the governor. She shrank back behind Warrick, who immediately turned, as if she had called his name, and frowned.

"What are you doing?"

"I can't speak to him," she said, indicating where the governor stood. "I'll wait here while you sort things out."

Warrick shook his head and slid his hand behind her back. "We came here to sort this out. He wants to meet you. I promise he will be civil."

She considered his words, what he had said and what he had not. She could not imagine the governor had recounted exactly what had happened in that prison cell. He had not been the one shouting, demanding, threatening, and leering at her. But he had been there. She could close her eyes and see his distant stance as he watched her interrogation. To him, she was a pirate. Karly gave a shudder, and Warrick tugged her closer.

"I know that is one of the reasons you brought me here, and I thought it wouldn't bother me. I need more time."

He searched her face and glanced over her shoulder. "It appears we may have a small distraction," he said.

Karly turned as a small group of men and women swept toward her. She recognized them as some of the same islanders who had been quick to condemn her father. If she could avoid them, she would, but she considered Warrick. He was the son of a duke, and she was his new wife. She could not shirk her duty. Straightening her spine, she forced herself to relax. "The tall man is Mr. Cunningham. He earned his money in salt. Mr. Benton and Mr. Norwich are both privateers, and the lady with them is Courtney Norwich." She saw the amusement in Warrick's eyes and realized immediately he already knew who their visitors were. But before she could retort he pulled her to his side and faced the small group.

"Ms. Norwich, gentlemen, it is a pleasure. I would like to introduce my wife, Karly Barry."

Karly ignored the look of surprise on Courtney's pretty face, even as it narrowed to irritation and she dropped a small curtsey. Karly returned the gesture and smiled up at Warrick. She decided it was better if Warrick spoke and she stood by as the dutiful wife.

Mr. Cunningham cleared his throat. "Let me be one of the first to offer my congratulations. I must admit I was surprised to hear of your visit."

Norwich nodded. "Rumor has it that you are here on business."

"I am not a great believer in rumors," Warrick answered.

Norwich and Cunningham exchanged pained looks, and Benton clenched his jaw. "Your lordship, there is talk of an invasion. Is it true?" Cunningham said.

"Rumors of an invasion have been around for years," Warrick said. "Why would you give them strength now?"

"Your visit," Norwich said quickly. "Then there are the French privateers. They have become a damn nuisance."

Warrick's expression became grim as he looked between the men. "Should you find any information of merit, I would ask you inform me directly."

Karly watched the men nod vehemently. Mr. Cunningham actually smiled at her. She didn't need to defend a thing. They would accept her on the merits of her husband. There was a part of her that was outraged. She wanted to point out the unfairness of it all. But it would serve no purpose. They would not change. She realized they would not have to. She had placed far too much emphasis on their opinions.

Courtney gave a brilliant smile and swayed her hips as the music began to play, her eyes on Warrick. The woman was a flirt. Karly pressed closer to Warrick and was considering saying something when she caught sight of the governor and his wife approaching. She was surrounded.

"Lady Wessington," she blurted and dropped a curtsey even before Warrick could introduce her formally. She needed no introduction. She stood at the pressure in Warrick's fingers and regarded the lady directly. There was no malice in her expression at all. If anything she seemed almost nervous, her blue eyes searching Karly's face intently. Karly knew better than to gape, but she couldn't stop herself.

Lady Wessington smiled and inclined her head. "My husband tells me you are an artist."

"I am more like a dabbler, my lady. I cannot paint."

Lady Wessington gave a watery laugh, and appeared to relax. "A good term and one I can identify with. I am a dabbler as well. What subject do you prefer?"

"I draw mostly ships and wildlife, nothing of consequence."

"Indeed? That sounds enchanting. I prefer dogs . . . my dogs actually. I have spaniels. My favorite had puppies a few weeks ago. Would you like to see? They're really very dear."

Karly's heart quivered. Lady Wessington sounded kind, and her manner appeared genuine. But her nerves crackled. She needed to steady herself.

"I've never seen young puppies," she admitted.

"Karly would be delighted," Warrick said from beside her.

Karly looked to Warrick. His voice sounded odd, but his expression was even odder. She could see the concern in his expression and was touched by it, but there was also a hint of warmth. She was about to ask him what he was up to when she remembered their conversation about pets.

"My husband is concerned I do not know any animals," she said, looking deep into his eyes.

Lady Wessington's smile softened. "You may pick one."

Karly heard her, but she was watching Warrick. "Why would you want me to have a pet?"

"For the same reason I want you to have a home. Consider it a wedding present," Warrick said.

"The home or the pup?" she breathed and stepped closer.

"Both," he smiled.

She remembered where she was and blushed at the governor, who cleared his throat.

"I have made a few inquiries," he said. "Warrick, I would like a word in private, if I may."

Karly gave him an encouraging smile. "I will be right here when you return," she said.

Warrick still appeared uncertain, but finally nodded his consent. "We'll be in the library if you need anything," he said and brushed the back of her hand with his lips.

She didn't want to give him a chance to reconsider; he did need to go, and she to stay. She turned, following Lady Wessington without looking back, but also without dropping her guard. But time passed and nothing happened, their conversation easy. She began to finally relax. Seated in her intimate reception room, a puppy in her lap, she couldn't stop the smile that broke on her face. The other woman was many years her senior, but in many ways her life was comparable—a love of art and sea.

"Aren't you going to miss the puppies when they are grown up?"

"Not really, I find them homes where I know I will see them from time to time. And I always keep one for myself. That one seems to like you. . . . You should keep him."

"I've never had a pet," she said and swallowed hard.

"All the more reason you should. They make superb little watchdogs. Besides, your husband says you are wonderful with dogs . . . something about you charming his guard dogs shortly after you met?"

Karly giggled and peered down at the brown and white bundle in her lap. "What would you do if you saw an intruder?" she crooned and stroked the little head that lifted and looked up at her.

"See, he listens to you already."

She sucked in a deep breath. "I don't know how to care for a puppy."

"You are kind and a quick learner; you will do fine. And he can stay here until you are ready to return to England."

"He is lovely," Karly said, running her hand over the silky fur. "Thank you for your kindness."

"I should thank you. I should have done more. When my brother accused you of trying to seduce him, I assumed he was telling the truth."

"This isn't necessary." Karly began to stand, only to have Lady Wessington grip her elbow.

"My brother is good at his post. I didn't want to believe that there was another side of him, one that would take advantage of a woman. I assumed you were trying to manipulate your way out of trouble, into his bed."

Her knees weak, she sank to the ground. The warmth gone, absently she watched the pup circle and nose her leg. "I did."

"You tried to save your friends. Warrick explained what really happened." She reached out and took Karly's hand before continuing. "I am sorry for the way my brother behaved."

Her throat too tight for words, she nodded and turned her attention to the pup. She brushed away the tears, hiding them as best she could. The little creature nibbled on her finger and let out a small whimper. "I think he's hungry."

"When you name him, you should consider his favorite food. Take him, he'll bring you luck. We'll let him eat. You can pick him up before you leave. Besides, I should check on the other guests."

Setting the puppy back with the rest, she stroked his head and shook her own. "I hope Warrick won't mind."

"I'll tell him it's a governor's order."

Karly returned to the party reluctantly. She found a seat in the corner of the ballroom away from the other women and behind a rather large display of sugared fruits, content to watch her new friend. Buried in a cup of tea, she hoped she would remain unnoticed until Warrick returned. Unfortunately she had placed herself in the position where someone could corner her, and it didn't take long.

"So how did you manage it?"

Karly winced at the familiar voice. She kept her expression placid as Courtney Norwich sat down by her side. She had no excuse to leave, nor could she ignore the woman. The Norwiches were too important, and she was considered a member of the gentry. Being respectful was part of her duty. She thought of how graciously Jaline had behaved toward guests at her party. She lifted her shoulders and forced a distant smile. "Manage what?"

"Why, catching Warrick Barry without dowry or connections. You hardly travel in the same circles. Last I heard, you were being tossed off the island. How did you meet him?"

The woman was simply rude. Or perhaps she had once had designs on Warrick. The reason didn't matter. But she had chosen to challenge her here, at a public gathering. That was rather telling. Courtney's glance across the room to where a group of women stood tittering was the other piece of the puzzle. They wanted to embarrass her. To make her say or do something they could use against her. "He stopped me to ask a question."

"At a party?"

She kept her expression as serene as a field of flowers. "Yes, a small party."

"I see, and so the marriage happened quickly then?"

"He didn't want to wait." Karly look another sip of her tea. Another half truth, but they were hardly interested in the real story.

"I never thought, what with your father's scandal, that you of all people would end up a duchess."

"I'm not; his mother is."

"Still, it must feel rather nice to have done so well for yourself. You must be proud."

Karly placed her cup to the side. It was better there than throwing it at Courtney, which was her first thought. She could see the door through which Warrick was no doubt deep in discussion. That was not an escape route. Nor was this a battle worth fighting. "I remember seeing a charming garden. Please excuse me; I'm going to take a short walk." Proud, her ribcage high, she walked through the terraced doors and into the gardens without another word, filling her lungs with the scent of jasmine. Fortunately, no one had offered to come with her, and she continued down a small path well-lit by torches, toward the soothing sound of the waves below.

Thinking back, she should have told Lady Wessington where she was going. But that could lead to more trouble. She would want to know why, and the Norwiches would be difficult. No, she was pleased with the way she handled the situation. She reached the moon gate, its arched, almost circular shape appearing a portal to another place. Passing through, she halted at the small terrace, the ocean visible and comforting. The evening wasn't as bad as she had expected. It would be over soon, and they would leave. Hopefully Warrick had obtained what he needed.

"I was wondering when we could talk."

Karly whirled, facing the man standing in shadow. She needn't see his face to know his voice. "Commander Farris."

He stepped into view looking much as he had in her nightmares. He was tall, his face angular and his mouth thin. His eyes glinted in the dim light. They swept over her. He was dressed in full uniform but was missing his hat.

"I always knew you would be stunning in blue silk."

Karly brushed her hands absently over the dress. It was more skirt than she was used to, and yet she felt minimally clothed before his eyes. It was the way he looked at her. "Blue is Warrick's favorite color."

"Married and safe from me, is that it?" He chuckled softly.

"It's for the best," she said with finality, but he made no move to go.

"The best? For whom? Somehow I never considered you the socialite type. At least the life I offered you would have given you freedom to do as you please."

"I would never have been able to hold my head up in public. I couldn't do what you were asking. Excuse me." She started away when his next few words stopped her cold.

"David Landgon is back."

"Are you sure?"

"Quite, although where, I'm not sure. Someone said he arrived on a merchant vessel, but we searched them and found no trace. A lot of people are scared."

"I'm not."

"No, can't imagine you would be. If you had any sense, you would reconsider."

"Thank you for the warning." She made to turn, but he caught her arm. Stepping back, she kept as much distance as his contact would allow, glaring at him.

"I may have handled myself badly in the past. I wanted you to know, if you do find yourself in trouble, you can come to me."

"To you or to your bed?"

"Honestly, Karly, do you have to be so blunt?"

"Seems as if the matter requires it, wouldn't you agree? And to be blunt, I doubt my husband would approve, not that I am slightly tempted."

"You've changed. You're more confident," he mused and then seemed to shake himself. "If the need arises, you can approach me as an old friend or political ally. It really doesn't matter. I will receive you regardless."

She didn't trust him, not even a little. There was nothing specific that screamed out to her. It was her sense of the man as a whole. She may have changed, but he had not. He had sought her out for a reason, waiting until she was alone. Although he wouldn't say it, she felt very much the prey, and she prepared herself for what might come next.

"I'm quite stocked with allies for the moment. If I need another one, I'll send my card." She stepped back when his grip tightened painfully around her arm. Pivoting, she broke his hold. "You can't bully me anymore."

He lunged and she kicked, her aim true, his kneecap sounding with a pop. Then he cried out, staggering before her eyes. It was more than was warranted, and then she saw the arrow embedded in his shoulder.

Spinning, she caught a glimpse of the figure before it disappeared behind the hedge. "Commander?"

"It's deep, but it's not bad," he gasped.

"I'll be right back," she said, gathering her skirts tight around her and breaking into pursuit. Sounds of crashing underbrush were her clues, and she couldn't help but realize the attacker was not terribly skilled. He was giving away his position as clearly as if he were calling it out with his voice. The moon helped to light her way. She thought she was gaining, when suddenly the trees cleared, and she found herself on a road of crushed stone, very much alone. Circling, she found no trace of her quarry. The attacker had simply vanished. Karly shuddered, recalling old ghost tales from firesides gone. The arrow was very real and probably intended for her. If she studied it, she was sure it would be similar to the one used on Jaline. Having no choice, she turned back. The walk was farther than she thought as she picked her way through; then she heard someone approaching. Ducking into a thicket, she waited. The moon peering through the trees gave her a shadow, and then Warrick's silhouette.

"He got away," she said, showing herself.

Grabbing her by the shoulders, he shook her, furious. "You shouldn't have run after him. What would you have done if you'd caught him? Did you think of that? You could have been killed!"

"I could have been killed if his aim was better. I'm sure it was me he was trying to hit."

"Of course it was you. If it was the commander, he could have tried a dozen other times or places."

"We needed to know who it was. I can't let anyone else suffer on my account."

"Does that include me? One moment you're safe at the

party, the next with a man who has terrorized you to the point of nightmares. I promised you I would watch over you, but you're not making this easy. Did he lay a hand on you? Karly? Are you even listening to me?" he demanded.

She wanted to answer him, but for some reason, she had begun to shake. It was weak of her and she fought the inclination when he wrapped her in his arms.

"I'll take you back," he soothed. But as they passed the scene of the attack, she nudged him toward where the governor stood peering hard at the ground.

"They may have found something," she murmured.

Warrick shot her a thunderous frown, which vanished as the governor approached.

"Are you all right?" the governor asked.

"She didn't manage to stop whoever it was," Warrick answered.

He still sounded so angry. He might not accept her apology, but she felt she owed him one all the same. Even if she had succeeded and caught the man, she had been reckless. She set aside the scene, the governor, and even her own terror.

"Warrick, I really am sorry. I should have waited." She saw his jaw tense, but he gave her a curt nod.

"It appears he stood with his right foot forward," the governor said after a long pause.

"Which would mean he was likely left-handed," Warrick said.

"Would have been nice to know who was behind all of this. Commander Farris is furious. Oh, he'll recover soon enough, and it won't upset any of our plans. It serves him right," the governor said with a sigh. "He should have never been out here in the first place. I warned him to leave Karly alone. Still, I guess if he hadn't been here, the outcome would be rather different."

"The commander didn't hurt me," Karly said shakily, lifting her head.

Warrick exchanged glances with the governor as he tucked her closer to his side. "There wasn't much of an opportunity; you weren't gone that long."

"There never should have been any opportunity, now or in the past," the governor said. "That's my fault. The man has a poor disposition in everything but naval strategy. I should have followed my own counsel, trusted my instincts. If I had, Landgon would have never been able to carry this scheme as far as he has. This whole thing is more my mess than yours. For what it's worth, I am sorry. I should have listened with a better ear when you said your father wasn't involved."

"Thank you," Karly whispered. "Does that mean you'll pardon them?"

"I'd prefer proof. I need to see this letter. But don't worry, your husband has a plan to help clear all this up."

Karly nodded, and, focusing within, she blotted out the rest of their conversation. There was nothing else to say, nothing else to offer for the time being. She needed to prepare herself for the tempest that was bound to come the moment Warrick got her alone.

Karly was at a complete loss over Warrick's silence. Alone in the carriage, he made no attempt to chastise her. At first she took it for anger, then indifference, but neither theory made any sense the more time that passed. She found her own temper flaring, fueled by frustration and an inability to decide what to do next. The carriage halted. He climbed out, helping her down with minimal conversation. Settling the puppy in the stables, he walked by her side to the cottage, not looking at her. She entered first, waited for the door to close, and turned back to face him.

"I should not have gone after him alone, I know." She waited as he nodded thoughtfully.

"We should get some rest."

Her anger soared at his lack of engagement. Unsure what else he expected of her, she whirled and ran up the stairs, retreating into the side room and shutting the door. Removing her ball gown was a fight that took all of her concentration and more patience than she possessed for the moment. Aggravated at her lack of progress, she sank to the floor in the corner and buried her face in her hands, masking the sound of her sobs and losing track of time. Regaining control took fortitude. Reminding herself to be patient, she set to work again on the elegant gown, the silk slippery in her hands.

She paused from time to time to listen for any hint of Warrick's state of mind, perhaps even an attempt at conversation. Songs of the night, the chirping of frogs and insects were her companions. In the end, she decided he had most likely gone for a walk nearby. Relieved as the dress finally came free, she laid it carefully over the chair in the corner to be pressed and cleaned in the morning. Tugging a nightdress over her head, she tied the silken cord in the front over her breasts.

She was torn. To approach him was to invite criticism, criticism she wasn't prepared to hear. But to ignore him was unacceptable to her very nature. Retreating to the bed, she arranged the duvet, sheets, and pillows, giving him every opportunity to bridge the void. Sensing movement, she looked to find his dark eyes upon her. His face drawn in unspoken sadness, and he turned away.

Chapter 28

It was the middle of the night. He couldn't be sure of the exact time. Sleep was his enemy. He got out of bed, covering Karly, and dragged a chair in front of the open French doors. There he sat with his back to the room, watching the night-shrouded horizon. He had promised to let Karly help him. For that she could have been killed. What was disturbing was her continued lack of concern for her own safety. Or was this all his fault? A soft breeze stirred the curtains, leaving him untouched, as if not wanting to disturb his ponderings. He heard her rouse from the bed and approach. She knelt by his side and laid her hand over his on the armrest.

"I'm sorry. I shouldn't have gone off on my own. I was reacting the best way I knew how. I was afraid if I went for help they could have killed the commander. Despite what he did to me, he doesn't deserve to die. It didn't occur to me I was the target until I was halfway into the brush," she said, her voice tight.

"Would it have made a difference?" he asked.

"I would have gone to solve the mystery. It could have been a trap, there could have been someone waiting to kill me. I didn't think. As for Commander Farris," she continued, "you told me that seeing him would be good, make the nightmares disappear. I didn't intend for us to be alone. I went for a walk. I never even saw him at the ball. He followed me."

Removing her hand, she started to rise. He caught it back and she sank again beside him. "You don't need to apologize; I should be the one to offer apologies. Since the beginning I have said I appreciate you as you are. That is true. But I have expected you to change in many areas."

"Not really," she whispered after a cumbersome pause.

"It's your life that's altered far more than mine. What did you do tonight that wasn't part of who you are? You attended a party for my benefit not yours, dealt most gracefully with people who were not your friends, and placed your life in jeopardy for a man who nearly raped you. You did this because you are more loyal to your heart than what is logical."

"I can be logical."

"Yes, but it is not your very nature." He feathered his hand across her cheek, pausing on a tear.

"Your life is different too," she said faintly.

"It has changed for the better. I should be telling you that instead of making demands and lecturing you at each hitch in our journey."

"You've been understanding."

Warrick chuckled. "No, Karly, not really. Patient perhaps, but understanding? I've been trying to figure out how to convince you not to run off. If the roles were reversed, I'm not so sure I wouldn't be trying to leave myself."

"It may be for the best," she said, her lashes sweeping downward.

"No."

"But you said . . ."

"I am wrong. I'm sorry for not recognizing sooner how poorly I have cared for your feelings. I won't agree that you

:aving is for the best. Why do you think I have tied myself
nd you in knots trying to convince you otherwise?"

"We're just so different."

"Not precisely. We approach life and people similarly. We
oth love the sea, ships, and adventure."

"You hate heights."

He blinked at her and pursed his lips, somewhat be-
1used. "Heights?"

"I was merely pointing out where we are different." She
hrugged.

With his finger he lingered over the soft outline of her
ps. He traced their contour in a long, stroking caress, ef-
:ctively silencing her. Her protests were from fear, and he
eeded her to understand his point.

"I don't like heights. I especially don't like you and
eights, but then I have my reasons. That aside, we rather
omplement each other. I never sought to force you. I
anted you to want to stay. I thought I was helping make
1at possible, but I've only made it more difficult by not
oing right by your needs."

"You're helping my father and Hack. You're helping En-
land. Those are all important reasons."

"And where does Karly fit into all of that?" She drew
ack, got to her feet, and retreated to the far side of the
oom. He let her go and remained seated, following her
ith his eyes and heart.

"Warrick, there's no reason for this. I'm here," she said
ith a shake of her head.

"Yes, there is. It's time you knew the truth."

"I'm not sure I like the sound of that."

"Why?"

"Because look at the truth of my grandparents or my par-
nts. There are times when it's best not to know all. Espe-
ially when it changes nothing." She gritted and wrapped
er arms around herself.

"Love does change things," he said softly.

Whirling on him, she remained at the far end of th
room. "Love?"

Warrick drew a long breath and nodded. "I have love
you in so many ways. You've become part of my life and m
heart. Karly, I'm not much for words, not the right ones.
do know what I am feeling. I have handled it badly, bu
don't doubt for one moment it's there." He stood and took
step toward her, and she shifted uncomfortably.

"I love you too," she said. Releasing a slow shaky breath
she met his gaze and looked away. "I've loved you longe
than I could admit. It's not that easy. You wish I were dif
ferent."

"You misunderstand. I wish you were more careful," h
whispered, standing before her. Gently, he touched he
cheek and followed the line along her jaw. There he coul
feel her heart hammering. It gave him courage to press or
"I don't want to live through a future without you in it."

"That could happen anyway."

"Because of something a poor excuse for a midwife said
There is nothing wrong with you, Karly, except a lack of in
formation. Anyone who can climb mainsails, not to mentio
trees, is hardly sickly and weak. We've gotten through s
much together. We'll get through this too." He ran hi
thumb in a light caress, resisting the urge to embrace her.
was a distance she needed to cross willingly. To join hir
in spirit, not simply in presence. "I need you. I think yo
need me too. Maybe not for your basic survival, but life i
not simply surviving, is it?"

"No, it shouldn't be."

"You're as much a part of my life as I am."

Karly entwined her arms around his neck and hugge
him tightly. "What do we do?"

"Love each other, and don't let go," he said and found he
kiss. He lifted her in his arms and tugged her nightdress fror

er. When he went to remove his own garments, she nudged
is hands away. Clumsy but determined, she managed his
hirt but faltered on his trousers.

"These are much easier when I'm wearing them." She
aughed nervously.

Taking her hands in his, he brushed each to his lips. "I
an manage," he soothed, freeing himself. She sat waiting
or him, reaching to close the distance as he knelt on the
ed beside her. His hands to her shoulders, he drew her into
is embrace and kiss. She pulled him to lie down; he chose
place beside her.

She ran her hands over his chest and back. Locking his
assion and ardor behind steel bars, he pressed her back
hen she tried to guide him to enter her.

"Too soon, love," he said and caressed her curves, sa-
oring the taste of her through their kisses. She was perfect
or him, in all ways. He would never tire of the feel of her
eneath his hands. He nibbled across her breasts, suckling
nd playing until she gave a sexy whimper. He had no stam-
na tonight. He wanted her, so badly. He was hard, his need
rgent.

"Don't tease me," she said and arched toward him.

"I'm not."

"I won't break."

Her hand cupped his backside. She all but pulled him
loser. He could stand no more. Warrick slid between her
highs and rose over her. She met him halfway, rising to his
hrust, harmonizing his rhythm. It didn't last, his need spi-
aling out of control. He was fierce, his passion unfettered.
nd then he fell, over the edge of reason and into her arms.

"I hurt you."

"You didn't."

Warrick turned his head. "Are you sure?"

"I'm happy."

He didn't have to pretend, although next time he would

be gentler. He gathered her to him, her cheek to his chest
her form to his, and let their spirits intertwine. His prayer
were answered. Slowly with reverence he asked with hi
body. She answered with strokes of her own.

"I love you."

"I love you, too," she said with a hitch in her voice.

"That is a good thing."

"Love will not solve our problems."

"But it will make the road easier. I only wish I had rec
ognized you for who you were years ago on Hasings's dock.

"Back then I thought you were handsome, perhaps a bi
arrogant."

"Arrogant or not, it would have saved you from so muc
pain."

"Perhaps I had to go through that. My experiences hav
served some purpose in you catching Landgon."

At times she was too logical, but he could fault her noth
ing tonight.

"The past cannot be changed," he admitted, skimmin
his hand over her bare shoulder. She snuggled closer, an
her breath tickled over his chest, becoming more even. Sh
had fallen asleep, but he was unable to settle, despite th
comfort of their bed. Warrick's mind sped and slowed, re
playing and savoring the evening. She had a point regard
ing her past. He could not change it. However, he felt he ha
let her down. The odd thing was, she did not care. She mus
love him, love all of him as he did her. He wished she wer
awake, so he could hear her say the words again. He wante
to tell her one more time and then make love to her, whis
pering his heart in her ear. She gave a soft moan. He waite
tense, but the nightmares that had haunted her were siler
tonight.

He was caught in his own musings when somethin
brushed his mind. Halting all thought, he strained for th
source. The night sang its usual song, and Karly stirre

easing her leg farther over his. His heartbeat quickened as she nestled under his chin. Lovingly he tightened his hold and then heard an odd sound. Moving with caution, he reached behind his second pillow where his pocket pistol was hidden, wrapping his finger around the trigger. His senses prickled a warning at the snap of a branch outside their window. With no further warning, the dark shadow of a man climbed silently from the shade tree onto the terrace and crept toward their bed. Lifting the weapon, Warrick took aim.

"That's close enough," Warrick hissed. The intruder froze, and Karly woke, her cheek to his bare shoulder sending a quiver of contact down his spine.

"Warrick?"

"Karly, don't move," he ordered.

Karly turned her head toward the stranger and shied, pressing closer to Warrick and pulling the blankets over her nakedness. "What do you want?"

"Hack told me to fetch ya'," the man muttered, lifting his hands.

"Then why not use the door?" Warrick growled as he sat up very slowly, keeping the pistol leveled.

Struggling up with the blankets, Karly lit the candle on the bedside table. The man blinked as the light flickered awake, but he kept his great eyes on Warrick. "It's all right," she said, laying her hand on Warrick's wrist. "Bug is one of Hack's men from the camp. What did Hack say, Bug?"

"Says there's something ya' need to see about that man Landgon. That I was to bring ya'," Bug answered, stuttering over Landgon's name. His eyes flitted from Karly to Warrick.

Disregarding Karly's subtle request, Warrick kept the gun leveled at Bug. "Would it be too much to ask for everyone to use doors?"

"Trees are safer," Karly said.

"No, trees are not safer," Warrick said. He decided the man was not a threat and lowered his weapon. "Bug, you can wait in the hall; use the door. Karly and I will get dressed and meet you there."

"I'll wait in the hall," Bug said simply, opening the door and peering suspiciously. He looked back to Karly with uncertainty.

"It's all right. The hall is safe," she said softly, giving him a reassuring nod. She waited for him to close the door before gathering the sheet and heading for the armoire. "You don't have to come. It is the middle of the night."

"If you think I'm going to stay here while you head off with a man named Bug, you are mistaken." Warrick said, tugging on his britches and buttoning his shirt.

"He can't remember his real name, and he likes bugs," Karly returned and started for the door.

"You will wait," Warrick said, taking out a parchment and penning a quick note to William and watching her from the corner of his eye. Thankfully she did not move. He was beginning to understand her, even appreciate her tendencies, even when they caused him worry. She cared about her friends and wanted to help them. It was admirable. She did not know her own value. That she was becoming more important to him than his own safety was something she had yet to grasp. He found himself anxious for what lay ahead. He did not want to lose her, and he could feel the prickle of danger. He had folded the note, but reopened it, added an extra warning to William before blowing out the candles and proceeding into the night.

Chapter 29

"Where she goes, I go," Warrick said. He walked forward and took one of the horse's reins from Bug.

"Hack said Karly." Bug gave a bewildered shake of his head.

Karly took Bug's hand in her own and patted it. "He'll understand. I'm sure he didn't mean to leave Warrick out."

"I'm not as certain," Warrick said irritably. "He only sent two horses." She shot him an annoyed look, which he mirrored back at her. He mounted the bay and offered her his hand, pulling her up in front of him.

"Hack gave you his word he would try to help," Karly said in a quiet voice.

Warrick gave the animal a gentle squeeze. It launched into a brisk trot, throwing Karly deep in his arms as it tried to keep up with Bug's mount. She glanced back at him, then turned in the direction they were heading. The silence became near painful. They had only just made love and declared love. He hadn't imagined it, or her. Each caress was etched in his memory. Was that her hope, or her fear? He wasn't sure. He wondered if she even knew.

"I did not want to argue with you," he said.

"Nor I you."

"You're a thousand miles away," he said in her ear as his horse broke into a canter. He felt her take a deep breath.

"Actually I am only a few miles, down this road. What do you think we'll find?"

His mind was back in their cottage. Although Karly was again in his arms, he had not adjusted. He had to force himself to concentrate on something more than her warmth. Hack had roused Karly for a reason. Whether or not he was expected was another question, with many answers. If this involved Landgon, why would he not be summoned along with Karly? They were on a road heading through shrouded darkness, possibly into a trap. Warrick could feel his pistol, but that was no match for several men. He rode on, his sense of direction askew. He caught glimpses of the sea, but it was a long time before Bug slowed his horse to a walk. Warrick felt the wind on his cheek and caught a glimpse of silver water broken by whitecaps.

"We're on the north shore."

"That is where Hack said he would be," Karly said, keeping her voice low.

Bug veered off the road, and down a narrow path of murky darkness.

The trees thinned. They were approaching their destination, and he didn't feel prepared. It was too late now, but he wished he had more time before they left. Warrick studied the shoreline below. There was almost no beach to break the black rocks and no ships. After another few minutes he dismounted, tying his horse to a tree.

"Must be quiet," Bug whispered, placing his finger to his lips.

The man was cautious. Warrick let him lead and took Karly's hand, keeping between them. He heard her exasperated breath and knew she didn't approve, but she did not argue. She did what he would have hoped: trusted him and his instincts. It had only been a few days since he had

handed her the helm of the *Moorea*. He could not know
unless he asked her, but he wondered if placing the lives of
himself and his crew in her hands had not made a difference
in her mind. She was his in so many ways: his wife, his con-
fidant, the pilot of his ship, and his lover. Inside her grew
their child. She had told him she loved him and then fretted
over the admission. He gave her hand a gentle squeeze and
raised it to his lips, kissing it through the darkness. If he
could not speak, he would show her how much it all meant
to him, how much she meant to him. Bug motioned them to
bend, and he kept low as they climbed through the undergrowth. Then he stopped and squatted, Bug pointing to the
cove below.

Small and well sheltered, he had an excellent view of two
longboats drawn on the beach. No flags or uniforms were
visible, but Warrick didn't doubt for a moment these were
foreigners. There was no sign of Hack, or Landgon. He
could see a small campfire and hear the murmur of many
voices.

"How many men do you estimate?" he asked.

"Twenty-five, plus five more on the rocks," Karly said.
"Where's Hack?"

Bug shrugged. "Dunno. Said to meet him here."

Warrick was more concerned by the voices. They were
speaking French, he was sure of it. If Hack had not been so
secretive regarding their purpose, he would have brought a
glass. He would have been able to see much more. He
would also have brought help. "He's probably closer; we'll
go see. Karly, you stay here and out of sight. If anything
happens, take a horse and go get help, understand?"

She gave a reluctant nod. "Perfectly."

His tone had been clipped and precise. He gave her a
hard look to be sure before he leaned forward and kissed
her cheek. "I'll be back shortly."

"I'll hold you to that." She held his hand longer than necessary before releasing him.

He could not pretend not to hear the fear in her voice. It was oddly heartening because he knew it was for him. Reacting was impossible, with a French scouting party within shouting distance. He looked once more at where she hid. She seemed too small and too vulnerable. He set off after Bug over rocks and through the scrub until they reached the edge of the open space. Warrick caught Bug's sleeve, opened his palm, and motioned for him to stay. The large man nodded; then his eyes flickered over Warrick's over his shoulder. He realized they weren't alone just before he was hit, stars exploding before his eyes. He fell, and someone kicked him hard. He heard Bug struggle and then fall with a grunt and lie still. Then they were both dragged across the sand. Hauled like a ragdoll, his hands and feet were tied and he was shoved into a seated position next to Hack. He blinked blood from his eye as Bug was dumped beside him. Warrick saw Landgon directing the men in French.

He finished and stood gloating at them with his legs apart and his hands on his hips. "My dear Lord Ralstead, whatever are you doing here, in the middle of the night?"

"Botanical research."

"In the dark?"

"It is the only time you can be certain to find non-native species," Warrick said with a ghost of a smile. He braced for Landgon to hit him. Instead the man crouched like a big cat toying with its prey.

"And where is the lovely Lady Ralstead? Back at Northington Shipyard? It would be like you to leave her there for safety. I would like to pay my respects."

Like hell, Warrick thought. "It seems you have bigger issues than a social call." He jutted his chin toward the second longboat.

"Not exactly. You see, I will need her help if I am to bring in my French friends waiting just over the horizon. I should have known better than to assume she would map a true key. Fortunately I had the sense to test it on a schooner. We had to leave the frigates out of sight."

"You sent the message," Warrick said with dawning realization. "That is why you asked for only Karly to come."

"It was easy with the help of that oaf," Landgon smiled and pushed at Bug with his boot. He motioned a soldier over.

Warrick listened as Landgon gave directions to capture Karly. Anyone who interfered would be shot. They knew about the guards and how to avoid them. He hoped Hasings was in bed. William was on the *Moorea*. "You will never get past the guns at the fort."

"Not without the poison that I managed to replace. The regiment at the fort will be dead long before we arrive. With Karly's help, my friends will be able to sail directly into St. George's harbor uncontested. I will be declared governor. Before England can react, the deed will be done."

"It will be war."

"War is only a matter of time anyhow. There is one matter you can assist me with."

"I have no intention of assisting you at all."

"Ah, but in this case I think you will make an exception. I need to know the location of the chest that Bane took from the French ship. It was intended for me. The money is to pay my troops."

"I don't know what you're referring to," Warrick said, but he let his voice falter. If he had some use, Landgon wouldn't kill him.

Landgon's smile broadened. He stood to his full height and turned to the French commander, pointing to the boat. "Place them in the second boat. Once we get offshore, we'll throw them overboard along with their pirate friend." Bug had not regained consciousness, but they gagged him anyway. Warrick kept his mouth closed against the rag that was tied far too tightly while Landgon looked on. Then Landgon bent so that his face was only inches away. "I am pleased you didn't help me. As much of an inconvenience as you have been, Karly has been far worse. Getting the truth from her is going to be very satisfying."

His knees were already bent. Warrick kicked out in fury, catching Landgon in the groin on purpose the way Karly had caught him when they first met. Landgon fell while two guards lifted Warrick bodily and dropped him into the boat, shoulder to shoulder with Hack. Bug was thrown on Hack's other side. Warrick tried to move when Landgon leaned into the boat and closed his hand around his throat, choking him until his vision dimmed. He fell back and wondered if the man would kill him now, but he let go and disappeared.

Exchanging a pained look with Hack, he considered their options. There was no easy escape. Orders were shouted. He heard the first boat scrape across the sand. Men grunted as they climbed aboard, and then there was the splash of oars as they headed into the bay. That would be the first launch. On a horse he could outrun them and warn the fort if he were free. Then he could help Karly. With luck, she had seen the struggle below her and had carried out his instructions. By now she was on her way to St. George for help. It might be too late for him, but not for Bermuda. She would be safe.

He should be comforted, but his stomach began to knot. He wanted to be the one to bring Landgon to justice. For the threat he represented and, on a personal level, for all he had done to Karly. A small vibration shook the boat as the men loaded cargo. Their hushed banter sank his spirits even lower. And then he heard Karly's voice, sweet as a spring wind through a meadow just above his ear. He hoped he was dreaming. He looked up into her beautiful face, the last one he wanted to see at this moment. She was

peeking over the edge of the boat. Then she disappeared as
a man approached, deposited his supplies, and walked
away. Any minute they would see her. Karly dropped into
the boat beside him. She seized a man's coat lying within
reach and draped it over her head, hiding her from all
views but his. Passersby would see a bundle by his side,
nothing more. She pulled off his gag and began picking
apart the leather thongs that bound his wrists.

"Leave now!" he said under his breath.

"Not without you."

Freed, his hand caught her hand, his head pounding in
fury. "Leave!"

"Not without them." She jerked free, and crawled to Bug.

Warrick untied his ankles and then helped Hack, who sat
rubbing his wrists. Another man approached, and they huddled close, blocking Karly from view with their bodies. As
soon as the man turned, Warrick indicated for her to follow
Hack out of the boat with a flick of his wrist. He waited
while Karly climbed out, and then helped Bug before going
over the edge. Karly was waiting for him. He gripped her
wrist and listened for the patrol. When backs were turned,
they dashed for the cover of the woods, and up the slope to
where the horses stood quietly.

"I told you to go get help if anything happened."

"You told me to get a horse and get help. I always intended to do just that," she said and swung up into a saddle.

"That was not what I meant," he snapped, keeping his
voice low.

"I wasn't leaving you."

"It's just as well," Hack said quickly. "Landgon is looking for you."

"Landgon lied," Bug said as Hack patted his shoulder.
"He said Hack asked for her to come here."

"Take the second horse. Go and warn your camp about

what is going on." Warrick climbed up behind Karly and slid his arms around her waist.

"First my camp, then your brother," Hack agreed.

Warrick reached down, took Hack's hand, and gave it a firm shake. Then he didn't wait. "Hold on tightly," he whispered in Karly's ear.

"I intend to." She slid her arm over his thigh to anchor herself.

Chapter 30

Warrick already hated the commander twice over for intimidating Karly. It was not enough he was in a sling. If he had his way Farris would have been removed from command. Standing before the British flags, Commander Farris was not a suitable representative for the country he was trying to protect. But he was in charge of the fort.

For his part, Farris remained quite still since their arrival, not moving from the very center of the reception room at the fort. Beneath his feet lay a large Turkish rug and in its middle, a flowery pattern. Warrick wondered if Farris had consciously chosen the place as his position of command, a prop of authority placing him at the very hub of any discussions or action the room might witness. It was clever and almost subtle. He watched the man's eyes drift from him to Karly as he considered their story. Then his eyes lingered on Karly. Warrick reached for her hand, clasping it firmly in his own. He waited as Farris walked to the window, staring out at the darkness that cloaked the fort's courtyard below, his back to them.

"I estimate they will be here shortly, if not already. They had a pretty good start on us," Warrick said.

"So if I understand you correctly, this boat full of French

spies has somehow managed to row past over a hundred waterfront homes unseen and sneak up on my fort, where they intend to poison my garrison unnoticed. Then they plan to kidnap Karly to help navigate an invasion force. Is that the crux of your warning, Mr. Barry?"

Warrick could see Karly shift uncomfortably, but he was unfazed. "That, and the fact I have the full authority to order your cooperation."

Commander Farris turned slowly, his eyes narrowed. "Order me, is it?"

Karly cleared her throat. "There's no moon, and the Moorehams are having a party tonight, so most of the waterfront homes would be empty. Also, it started raining a short time ago. No one would be out to see them. It is possible to get here from the sea without being seen."

"As you well know we are surrounded by a barrier reef," Commander Farris answered in a stiff voice. "And Karly is now safely within these walls and out of reach."

It was either the tone or Farris's expression that unsettled Warrick. Farris's suggestion that Karly was in his care pierced his soul. He took a step forward. "I will look after Karly."

"The adjacent cove has no barrier reef," Karly said. "They could land there and, with a simple climb over the rocks, be within striking distance within a matter of twenty minutes."

"Suppose you are correct, and they did manage to get this far. The fort is impenetrable. There is a hundred-foot cliff on the ocean side and then the wall on top of that. Guards patrol along the entire perimeter, which incidentally has a rather deep moat fortification, and our water supply is also secured." His shoulders slumped. "It's not like I haven't already taken measures to prevent an assault."

"I'm sure you have," Warrick said. "But perhaps they are aware of something you are not."

"Or possibly you are wrong, and they have chosen another target." Farris walked decidedly to the large oak desk that occupied the entire corner of the room and seated himself in its heavy accompanying chair. "I have taken the liberty of posting patrols around Government House as well as the homes of several of our prominent citizens."

"If you've deployed troops, how many are left here?" Warrick asked.

Farris sniffed and rubbed his nose. "Half, enough to arm the cannons if ships were to appear."

"You have twenty cannons. There were at least ten men in that boat," Karly said. He stared at her in silence. "It would not be an easy fight."

"I thought they were relying on stealth. What makes you think they are going to fight?" Farris asked, looking to Warrick.

Warrick was growing tired of the man's arrogance. His pride was placing his regiment, not to mention the island, in jeopardy. "You said the water supply was fortified. What if they've changed their plans? Time is short. Landgon knows we are aware of the poison. He also has to be getting desperate. What if he plans to simply take the fort while half the men are gone, using the timing to his advantage?"

"Even if that's so," Farris said cautiously, "it doesn't change the fact the fortress is well prepared. Getting inside would hardly be an easy task. Reinforcements could arrive before they ever accomplished their goal."

"It's easier than you think," Karly whispered.

"Oh? Explain," the commander ordered, staring at her unabashed.

She glanced at Warrick, who gave her a tiny smile of encouragement. "Through the tunnels, underneath, you can get in and out."

Farris gave an indifferent snort. "If it's so easy, why didn't you walk out of here when you had the chance?"

"If I used it to escape, would you know it existed?"

"Then what purpose does it serve?"

"It is there to help feed and take care of those you have left or frightened. Some of the guards even know about it. No one has told you because no one knows who's next."

Farris advanced from behind the desk as Warrick stepped in front of Karly. "You chose to remain here. You refused to cooperate to find criminals against the crown of England."

"I stayed because I had no choice. The prison you held me in wasn't down below us. It was all around and the bars weren't iron; they were the rumors and lies you told."

"Don't press it, Karly," Farris growled.

"Enough," Warrick said, narrowing his eyes at Farris. "Any other place and I would gladly challenge you."

"Then do so."

"It would be a pleasure. Once we have dealt with this, I will send my second to settle the arrangements."

There was no doubt in her mind Warrick meant to finish the matter. Karly inserted herself between the men, and shook her head. "There will be no duel."

Over her head, Warrick caught Farris's eye, exchanging what he hoped was a look of understanding. Then he steadied his temper. "Assuming there is a passage, the question is how to stop them from getting in."

"From the top of the stairs," Karly said quickly, walking to the map of the fort on the wall. "They have to pass through this narrow passageway to get into the main section. If you place some troops there, and a few at the top of the wall above the cave entrance, you can pin them down, until they surrender."

Farris's expression hardened, but he said nothing, considering his hand in the sling finger by finger. Without warning, he let out a shout for the lieutenant on duty. Speaking as soon as the man entered the room, he ordered him to do as Karly suggested, along with arming the cannons.

"This will have to do since I don't intend to recall troops from elsewhere. You may well be wrong. I have assigned my troops as I see fit."

"Karly is rarely wrong, and Landgon is out there somewhere."

"I'm not a fool, Lord Ralstead. Personal differences aside, I want the same thing you do: the safety of those people I have been assigned to protect."

"I consider you and your behavior toward Karly beneath contempt," Warrick said. He wished the night were over. He would like to wrap his hands around the man's throat. "Threat or no, do not bother her again, or I will have no qualms showing you exactly what I want. If you'll excuse us, I'm going to accompany the troops." Taking Karly's arm, he escorted her unabashed to where the lieutenant stood gaping by the door and gestured for him to lead.

As they walked down the stairs and crossed the courtyard, Warrick asked about operations and defenses. For his part, the lieutenant gathered troops, ordering them to the ready. They crossed to one of the darkened limestone tunnels, and Karly took Warrick's hand. Hers felt like ice. He rubbed it as they continued down the darkened hallway lined with supply crates and cannonballs. With regular intervals they passed splashes of moonlight, openings in the fort wall to the sea below. Each was filled by a cannon pointed at targets yet unsighted. Then the lieutenant halted, directing the soldiers to take up positions on each side of the hallway.

"Wait here, I'm going to get some more men," he said. "Perhaps you and your wife should return upstairs?"

"Thank you, Lieutenant, but I believe we will stay," Warrick said and pressed her back and down behind him and drew his pistol. Karly was shivering. He took her in his arms and held her to his chest. "Everything will be all right, but you must stay with me. I don't want you on your own with Landgon and Farris nearby, and I need to be here."

"I could be wrong. Landgon might not know about the tunnel."

"You knew about it."

"I was held prisoner there."

"Yes. I know," he said tightly and caught her chin, looking deep into her eyes. "But never again."

"You can't duel him"

"Karly . . ."

"He is a terrible shot. It would be like murder."

"The man is a commander. He must have some marksmanship."

"None. He can't fight with swords either. He loses his balance."

"What the devil is he doing in charge?"

"He knows strategy, and his sister is the governor's wife."

"I will find a way to let him out of the obligation," Warrick said with a shake of his head. "And he should be removed from active duty." Warrick was thinking of the letter he would pen to Admiral Howarth when they returned to England when he heard the approach of footsteps. Warrick swept Karly behind him. Deploying his soldiers around the tunnel, the lieutenant again faced Warrick.

"If you would like, I will have two of my men escort Lady Ralstead out of harm's way."

"Lady Ralstead would prefer to stay with her husband," Karly said, gripping Warrick's free arm.

Warrick saw the lieutenant frown as he returned to duty. Then he gave Karly a pointed frown. "When someone addresses me, you should let me answer."

"Even when it is about me and I am standing right there?"

"Even when." He was prepared to say more when the lieutenant hissed and Warrick turned. A sinister shadow was moving up the stairs, the torches from down below distorting it to gruesome proportions. It was joined by others, until they filled the wall. "Stay behind me, no exceptions."

Hushed whispers drifted up from their location. He crouched lower. The first man appeared when the lieutenant called out a warning. Shots were fired almost instantly, coming from all directions and ricocheting off the walls. Caught uncertain, there was confusion, and although they appeared at the top of the stairs, many disappeared for the safety below. He heard the lieutenant order pursuit and instinctively grabbed Karly.

"I thought we were following."

"Not down there. Better to wait. The lieutenant knows his men."

"And you're afraid I'll get into trouble."

"It had crossed my mind." It was some time before he heard returning footsteps on the stairwell. Moments later, stunned prisoners, triumphant soldiers, and finally the lieutenant emerged. "Is that all of them?" Warrick asked.

"I believe so, although, if you wouldn't mind, I would be grateful if your wife would show me the location of the hidden passageway. They must have shut the door. I'd hate to think we missed a few, hiding somewhere in between this location and the soldiers below. We don't know how to check."

"Of course," Karly said, and reached out to clasp Warrick's hand.

He wanted to tell her she didn't have to do this, but he knew she did. He kept close beside her as dank, stale air greeted each breath, and shallowed his breathing. They passed rows of muttering prisoners hidden behind iron grates lining both sides of the hall. Karly hurried forward and down the second flight of steps to the narrower and darker lower level. There was no room beside her. He had to follow single file. He placed his hand on her shoulder.

She immediately covered it with her own. There were no grates here, only solid doors with iron bars that offered little light or hope. Even the torches were smaller, reflecting less interest in the comings and goings of the occupants. She walked a bit faster, until she reached the end and solid rock, resting her hand against the stone.

"Are you sure you are in the right place?" the lieutenant asked gently after a long pause.

"Yes," she whispered.

Hearing the strain in her voice, Warrick gave her a small squeeze. She cocked her head to look at him. Her eyes were hazy, and she seemed as lost as that first night he had met her. "Take your time," he said, although he didn't mean it. What he wanted was to leave, to remove Karly from this place of nightmares and terror and never let her return.

"Things are rarely as they appear."

"That appears to be a solid rock wall," the lieutenant said from behind them.

"Yes, it does. It is completely solid, but that's not the way in." Karly turned to the cell to her right and pushed its unlocked door inward. She winced at its protesting groan. Stepping inside, she reached around behind it and pulled on the old iron latch. Where moments before the entire door and frame had appeared a fixture of the wall, the frame now swung loose. It filled the narrow aisle with its bulk and revealed a tunnel, with steps of stone leading down into darkness. "Through there, you'll find what appears to be a dead end. When you reach it, look down: there is a stone poised on its side. Slide it to the left. You will be in the cave below. It's hidden from the other side by another large rock, so you wouldn't find it unless you knew where to look."

"Very clever." Warrick drew her back and to him. "If you don't mind, Lieutenant, I'd like to take her out of here."

"I quite understand. My men and I will handle it, thank

you." The lieutenant motioned his accompanying soldiers forward and into the passage.

Warrick began guiding her back the way they had come, too angry to speak. That Karly had been in a place like this to begin with was upsetting. That she could have left and didn't was even more so. Regardless of her heart or sentiments, he would have hoisted her over his shoulder and dragged her out. The fact Hack didn't was infuriating. Her logic was both noble and flawed in his opinion. She stopped to stare at one of the doors, and he frowned impatiently at her. "We should keep moving."

"This was where I was held," she said hollowly and walked to the heavy door, standing on her toes to peer in through the bars. It creaked and swung inward. She paused, and he reached to take her arm when she walked across the threshold to the center of the room, or cell. "It really is over, isn't it?"

"Yes, Karly, it really is."

"And you want me to stay, despite everything, even this?" she asked, looking pointedly around and then back to him.

"This, you, everything, and all things I have yet to discover, which I happen to be looking forward to."

"I could die having this child," she hedged.

Warrick sucked in a breath. He wanted to argue with her, but decided against it for the time being. She had reason to be afraid. He was too. Babies were supposed to be joyful things, but the thought of losing Karly made his stomach knot. "I'm going to do everything I can to make sure that doesn't happen."

Karly walked to the far side of the room in three strides. "There was a time when I thought this was all my life would ever be and I accepted it."

"And now?" he asked as his heart leapt to his throat.

"I know I've said I want to leave, to move on, that it's

for the best," she admitted and took a tiny step closer to him, "but now, all I want is you."

"I'm right here." He lifted his hand toward her. She took small, hesitant steps and stopped out of reach. "Let me take you out of here."

"I love you," she breathed.

"And I love you," he said with a hard swallow as she battled the last of her demons.

"What if it's a girl?"

"Then I can only hope she'll turn out half as wonderful as her mother. Can we go home?" he asked, eyeing the darkness around them.

"After we help Hack, and find the documents to prove my father had nothing to do with any of this."

"I had no intention of forgetting Hack or your father, or the bounty on you. I just want to get you out of here."

"Oh," she said, taking another half-step.

"And somewhere a little more private . . ."

"Oh," she said, moving even closer.

". . . where we can pick up this conversation," he whispered.

"I'm sorry I interrupted you."

As he again offered his hand, she reached out, took it, and stepped into his arms. "As you should be," he said gently, kissing her hair.

"I forgot about the bounty."

"I have a theory, but we will help Hack first," he offered. Her head came up, and she met his gaze.

"You are taking on too much on my account."

"Not too much—as much as is necessary."

"You have my heart."

Feathering his touch across her chin, he cupped it and kissed her cheek. "We have a long, good life ahead of us. You don't have to worry anymore."

It was enough for her to leave with him and he felt his

...eart swell at her words. They were so close to an end that ...ad seemed out of reach. Had he not taken measures to help ...ngland, whatever his reasons, he would not have found ...arly. But as they walked the stairs into the fresh air there ...vas no sweetness, and a weight settled over his shoulders.

Chapter 31

As far as she was concerned, they were wasting time. Karly had been ready to enter the cave Bane described the minute they arrived. Negotiating with the governor, William, Farris, and the lieutenant had no merit. Hack had to come as did she, since Bane had described the traps to her. The rest of the party was irrelevant. They needed the letters to show the crew's innocence in the conspiracy. As far as she was concerned, Landgon had already proved his guilt beyond a doubt; no further evidence was necessary. The governor's point that it mattered who signed the letter was irrelevant. Landgon belonged in prison.

It was for Warrick that she stayed. The toll on him from supporting her had been great. He looked tired; the bruise on his head from yesterday was darker. If he wanted to work out the demands of various parties, she would wait.

"If Lady Ralstead is going, then I am, too," the governor said, his hands imperialistically on his hips as he glared from Karly to Warrick.

"Karly is going because Landgon was not captured at the fort. Also, she knows Bane better than any of us. She may be able to help if we get in a bind down there," he said, gesturing toward the cave mouth with his torch.

"Even so, you require my signature to void the sentences for Bane and his crew. I should be present for evidence that I discovered proving their innocence. I do not wish to be difficult, Warrick, but you have a vested interest, as do your brother, Karly, and Hack. You need someone with you who can vouch for the authenticity of any papers, should it ever come into question back in England."

"I should come as well," Trent began.

"No, you stay here and keep watch along with the commander. The lieutenant will be accompanying us," Warrick corrected. "As for you, your lordship," he said, turning to the governor, "if you wish to come, I cannot stop you. You must remember this is my endeavor. You will need to follow my directions; if that is a problem, then you'd best stay here. Bane has several booby traps, and the footing is poor."

"I'll manage," the governor said. "Lead on."

Warrick nodded and lit his torch and then Karly's. She waited only long enough for the others to ignite theirs before turning and leaving the sunlight behind them. The narrow entrance wound and dropped before quickly opening into a large gaping cavern with no apparent direction of where to head next. "He mentioned to look for marks he left in the wall: a circle, in blue. He said he left more each step of the way."

"Do you recognize this corridor?" Warrick asked.

"So far, but it's very easy to get turned around down here. That's the reason for the marks. We must follow them to be safe." It would be just like Bane to change markings around, not to prevent her from finding her way, but to keep anyone else from unraveling the puzzle. Checking for the circles, she refused to proceed past a juncture without one. Bane had warned her to watch for his Jolly Roger, the same as the one she had designed for his flag so long ago. What she wasn't sure of was the exact location of his traps. Despite her nerves, she couldn't help but find the humor in her

entourage. The men followed her very steps. When sh
stopped, they all halted at once. Had the stakes been lowe
she might have giggled. She spotted the glint of metal an
froze to the sound of many boots scraping on stone behin
her. "Bane's first trap: one sword dipped in poison an
spring-loaded. To disarm it, look for a string on the groun
or a stone that seems out of place."

"I found it. One string, just about ankle level," Hac
called from his position to her left and low to the floor.

Karly crouched beside him, but when Warrick reache
out with a small dagger, she grabbed his wrist.

"Seems easy enough," William said.

She examined the device, nodded, and Warrick cut. Re
alizing she was holding her breath, she released it an
smiled at him. "That's one. Each will be more difficul
That's how he surprises you." She got to her feet. "You sti
want to do this?" She swept the group with her eyes. Whe
no one spoke, she faced the path. "That's what I thought."

Karly kept her steps small as the path was uneven an
slippery with water leaking from the surface. The deepe
they went, the damper it became. While at first there wer
merely puddles, soon there were small ponds for them t
traipse through.

"Nice location. I can see why your father picked it," Wa
rick said, his face etched in worry.

"We're close. It won't be much farther. Then we'll get ou
of here."

"Sooner would be best. I don't like this."

A pool blocked their path. "Search the walls. See if ther
isn't some marker." She listened as the men began the
search. Something wasn't right here, but the ceiling ap
peared intact. Karly peered at the surface of the water. Th
reflection was near perfect, too perfect.

"Here," William called. "He's placed a small Roger here.

Karly traced the pirate symbol with her fingertip. "It points to the right side of the path."

"Then we stay right," Warrick said, nodding to William.

"Right it is," William echoed.

They had agreed that while she would lead, Warrick would go first around the traps. But as Warrick inched forward past the drawing of a Roger in chalk, her instinct began to scream caution. Bane's warning would not be that simple. Why would he care which side of the path they went on? They could swim, and so could he. The Roger had to indicate something more sinister. She stared at the pool, then the walls, and grabbed for Warrick's arm, dragging him backward. "I don't think he is telling us how to cross."

"Can you be more specific?"

Karly shook her head. She picked up a small stone and tossed it in the pool. Ripples drifted outward from the impact. The pool appeared completely normal. She peered closer and noticed the walls. Karly pointed at the long, scraped marks. "It's covered in scars, as if something has been done here. Did Bane say anything to you, Hack?"

"When we came through here, it was fast. He told me he was comin' back to arm it, but I never knew what he did."

Karly inspected the edges of the pool, avoiding the water. It covered the entire path, spreading around the bend in the trail ahead. There was no way except through it. There was no way to gauge its depth; the torchlight was not brilliant enough. She was missing something, something crucial, and she backed up. "It's wrong."

Hack coughed. "This Jolly Roger is red, not white."

"Red?" the governor asked.

"It means death," Karly said, glancing at the men gathered around her.

"So what do we do?" William asked.

"We could swim it," the governor said, starting forward. Warrick yanked him back despite his bluster. "Perhaps

you should take a better look at the water." He gestured t
a dimly lit corner. Just breaking the surface was the skele
ton of a hand.

"It must be poisoned," Hack said.

"So much for the swimming option," William remarke
dryly.

"We need to go back," Karly said.

"But we already know what's back there," the governo
protested.

"Possibly, there could also be something on the trail tha
we can only see from this direction." She had not gone mor
than twenty paces when she spotted another set of drawing
this time looking very much like boxes. "There should be
door here, somewhere."

"Bane noted a lever, at least that is what he called it,
Warrick said, searching. "Ah, here it is." He pulled on th
large stone piece, and the door swung open, revealing th
passage behind it. "It's not much farther."

Karly entered and began to search the walls. She wa
looking from right to left. She should have been lookin
ahead. A noise startled her. Then she saw the light. Land
gon stood with a torch in his hand, his legs planted an
before him, an open chest. There was no sign of any docu
ments. "How did you get down here?"

He blinked, his eyes flickering around the group behin
her, and smiled. "I went to Hasings's home looking for you
What I found were Bane's notes to this cave. I assumed i
was where he had stored my money."

The governor started forward, but Warrick waved hir
back. "He's got explosives."

Landgon smiled, holding the stick of dynamite closer t
the flame of his torch. "I thought I might need it to brea
through a wall. Turns out I may have to use it after all.
you want to get out of here, you'll let me leave with the gol
that Bane stole."

"It's not yours," Karly said and moved closer. She could
ee inside the chest, but there was still no sign of the docu-
nents Bane had described.

Landgon dipped the fuse and smiled as it sizzled to life.
It most definitely is mine. I have more than earned it."

"You'll never get past me." Warrick advanced a step.

Landgon's smile faded as fear seeped into his eyes. He
ave a noncommittal shrug and looked at Karly. "I am a rea-
onable man. I will leave you the proof your father had
othing to do with any of this. Your freedom for mine," he
aid and pulled out a folded document from his left pocket,
ts seal broken. His eyes narrowed, and he waved the stick
f explosives before them. "Make up your mind."

"And how will the French react when they find you have
aken the money for bribes and salaries and disappeared?"

"They won't be back. As we speak they are sailing home.
imagine the government will deny that I ever existed. The
old is mine to start over with," he said, his tone becoming
trained.

"Take the gold," Hack said, extending his hand.

"I thought you might see reason." Landgon grinned. He
ropped the paper on the dirt and clutched the dynamite
ighter. "Warrick, you will take one end of the chest and
elp me to a ship. When our business is done, you can go
ree."

Warrick walked stiffly to where Landgon waited but did
ot bend. "Put out the fuse or we go nowhere."

With a short motion Landgon drew his pistol. He placed
he dynamite in the same hand and wet his fingers. Rais-
ng an eyebrow at Warrick, he waited with his fingers
oised. For a long moment he did nothing. He finally closed
is fingers around the fuse, snuffed it, and tossed the dyna-
nite to the side. "You take the right side of the chest and
ehave yourself, or I might shoot your bride instead."

"When I get you out of here, you're to leave. That's th end of this," Warrick said, his voice devoid of emotion.

"Naturally, you won't find me back here."

She couldn't think about Warrick in Landgon's hands The idea terrified her. She needed to get the document first. Moving slowly, Karly eased toward the paper. Warric frowned in her direction, but she didn't stop. She wa almost at her goal when she saw the spark. The fuse sput tered to life, skimming the gap to the explosives in a matte of seconds. Landgon hadn't been thorough enough. He heart froze, her stomach lurched, but luck seemed to b with her. Nothing happened, and then, time ran out.

The explosion was immediate and all around her. It threw her backward onto the dirt floor. Stunned, she lay trying t catch her breath and then struggled to sit. Across the scat tered debris she saw Warrick. His hands were on Landgon collar, and he had him backed against a wall. Landgon's fee did not touch the floor. William hovered nearby, and ove the chest were the governor, the lieutenant, and Hack. Sh coughed and stood.

"Karly?" Warrick demanded.

Karly sputtered and wiped the grit from her mouth. "I'r fine," she said and looked about her. She spotted the folde paper against the far wall. Her torch miraculously stil alight, she grasped it and picked her way over the rocks. rumbling sound began like thunder and built louder unti the walls around them trembled. Karly straightened an looked up. The cavern had come to life with sound an energy. She had just a few more feet to grab the paper. Sh took the chance.

Debris showered around her as the ceiling began to co lapse. She heard Warrick's cry, and then he had her wais He pushed her against the wall, sheltering her body with hi own. It seemed to last far too long. Dust choked her lung and her ears rang from the roar. Gradually it slowed. It too

moment for her to realize the deluge of debris was truly
ver. The air was thick with dust. Karly lifted her skirt and
eld it over her face, breathing through the gauzy fabric.
he nudged Warrick, but he didn't respond. She felt for his
heek, then his neck, searching for a life, when his hand
losed over hers and he began to cough.

"Put a cloth over your mouth." She heard him fumble and
is breathing evened. "I think we're trapped."

Warrick's answer was to give her hand a hard squeeze. He
elped her to her feet and started toward an odd glow. "I
ound a torch." He shook, and the flame danced, then grew.

She turned to where the exit had been, and her heart sank.
massive wall of stone stood where the passage had been
noments before. Picking up a stone, she moved it and then
nother as Warrick joined her, calling William's name.
Through the darkness came a muffled shout.

"Is everyone all right?" Warrick demanded.

"Everyone except Landgon. He's dead. Are you two all
ight?" William asked.

"We're fine," Karly said, her voice choked with dust.

"Stay there—we'll dig you out!" William cried.

A low rumble sounded, and Warrick jerked Karly back
gainst the wall as rock and sand fell from the roof, adding
o the barrier. "No. Get out. The whole cave could come
own any time," Warrick said.

"I'm not leaving you," William answered.

Karly shook her head. "They won't get us out that way.
's far too much."

"You wouldn't by chance know another way out, would
ou?" Warrick asked halfheartedly.

"Remember when I told you a secondary plan is always
ecessary to fall back on?"

"I'm not going to like this, am I?" Warrick's voice
ounded resigned.

"Deeper in the cave there's an underground lake that's fed

by the ocean. You have to swim out through an underwate
pass. The tide has to be right, or we won't get through i
time. The tide and current have to be in our favor. It's a risk
maybe too much of one."

"Our alternative is to stay here and then what? Have ou
child in this cave, provided it doesn't collapse on us in th
meantime?" Warrick turned back to the rubble. "William
get the others out; Karly and I have another way."

"Tell him to meet us by the cliff due north, overlookin;
the ocean. That's where it comes out." Karly waited whil
Warrick repeated her instructions. There was silence on th
other side. "They don't think we can do it," she said.

"Karly," Warrick hissed, but he quieted as William'
assent came back. He took the torch in one hand and face
her. "My brother was trying to think of options. He trust
you as much as I do."

"I suppose that is something I will have to get used to."

"Yes, you will," he said. "After you."

She took a step and then remembered the reason for thei
dilemma. Searching the ground she spied the paper an
snagged it with a grin. "All this trouble, we aren't leavin;
without this." She tucked it in the waist of her skirt. No
she needed to get them out. To that, she had to keep her wit
about her. She made a wrong turn and had to backtrack. An
other wrong turn and she stopped. All the passages ap
peared familiar. It didn't help her composure that with eac'
rumbling aftershock, Warrick pushed her against the wal
his body to hers, protecting her.

She couldn't hear the ocean. She was lost. Karly leane
into him. "I don't recognize anything anymore."

"You will. Just go slow. You're doing fine."

"No, I'm not. If I hadn't gone for that letter . . ."

"You would be in here alone, we wouldn't have it, and
would be beside myself."

"And safe," she added tearfully. Warrick touched her row, adding to her misery.

"Not my heart, knowing you were in danger and out of my reach. I'd rather be here with you, whatever happens."

She stared at him in disbelief, tears falling faster than he could brush them away. "Warrick, that's very sweet, and completely wrong."

"So much for my attempt to cheer you," he said forlornly.

She had to laugh, albeit softly. "It did help a little. The act you've had faith in me means a lot."

"I have more than faith. I know what you're capable of, good and bad," he said with a wink and then became serious. "I love you, Karly. That won't change."

She met his kiss with her own, then rested her forehead to his. "I love you, too."

He caressed the nape of her neck. Her tension drained. While she didn't feel confident, she had to try. Karly turned her senses past the torch and into the darkness. Aftershocks rumbled in the distance, but there was also a low repetitive roar. With Warrick's hand in hers, she returned to a passage they had already tried, but turned left instead of right, turned left again, and continued down the slope. The walls rumbled, and more dust fell. She kept her pace brisk, although she was tempted to run. They were far from Bane's marks, far from any direction they had taken. She was becoming nervous when they turned a corner and there it was, the lake. Stopping, she pivoted to Warrick. "Hear that sound?"

"Yes," he said and caught her waist.

"It's not a cave-in. It's the ocean waves breaking against the rocks. This is where we go out." Warrick planted the torch, which sputtered and became only half as bright as it had been. Soon they would be in darkness. They were short in time. She removed her petticoats and looked up to find him grinning at her. "Not a word."

"If you hadn't, I would have taken them off of yo⟩
myself."

She tossed them at him.

With a smile he caught them and let them fall to th⟩
cavern floor.

Karly held his gaze and slid her hands around his wais⟩
She wanted to say something meaningful. How much h⟩
meant, how thankful she was, even when he was difficul⟩
how much she loved him . . . but words were insufficien⟩
He bent forward and kissed her with slow strokes of hi⟩
mouth. It was enough. Taking his hand, they stepped int⟩
the water side by side. She shivered and then braced at th⟩
cold. "We need to feel for where the water is warmer; tha⟩
would be the ocean coming in. That's how we'll know th⟩
way out. Be careful. It gets very deep, with no footing."

She released his hand and began a slow walk, then starte⟩
swimming when the water dropped. The water was cold
and she began to shiver. Then the water changed, and sh⟩
knew she had found what she was looking for. "Over here,⟩
she called, and treaded water while Warrick swam towar⟩
her in long, languid strokes. Clearly he would have n⟩
trouble getting through, which meant the rest was up to he⟩
"We need to take deep breaths."

"And say a prayer," he added.

"Absolutely," she managed, meeting his gaze. "You hav⟩
the most incredible eyes."

Warrick choked and then coughed. "And you have th⟩
most incredible sense of timing."

"I just wanted you to know in case . . . well just in case.⟩

"Karly, we're going through, and when we are out of this
and onboard the *Moorea*, I intend to lock our cabin doo⟩
and continue this conversation to completion." He shook hi⟩
head and chuckled.

She drew a shuddering breath and took his hand. "We'll g⟩
on the count of three." She counted and wished for calm⟩

ut it wasn't to be. Three came far too quickly. With practiced
ontrol she forced herself to concentrate. A deep breath and
he was underwater, Warrick's hand in hers. She kicked with
ll her might. The current pushed like an invisible hand
gainst her face. Then, in a change of heart, it changed direc-
on and dragged them outward. Rocks scraped her sides, and
er breath burned like fire in her lungs. Warrick's hand was
orn from her grasp. The world around her grew lighter
ehind her lids. She opened her eyes against the sting of sea-
vater. Light filtered down toward her. She struggled toward
ie surface, breaking out and free, and sucked in a breath of
resh air. Spinning while treading water, she saw Warrick a
ew strokes away. Then she heard William's shout from the
liffs above.

"You did it," Warrick said with pride as a rope splashed
etween them.

She took it for his benefit, although the rocks were so
orous she could have clawed her way up the cliff. Collaps-
1g on the grass in the Bermuda sun, she eased closer to
Varrick. He settled her on his shoulder as she tried to catch
er breath. She looked up to see Hack and reached for the
aper in her waistband, but it wasn't there. Terror pierced
er heart. She bolted to her feet and for the edge.

"Where are you going?" Warrick demanded, seizing her
vaist.

"The letter proving their innocence, I lost it! It was in my
ocket. It must have come out when we were swimming."

"You can't go back. We barely made it through, and the
ave is unstable."

"I have to!" Karly tried to jerk free.

"It's gone. It could be anywhere," Warrick said in her ear.

"Hack, the crew, my father—they're all counting on me.
have to tell the governor something. What's going to
appen to them if I don't?" She clamped her mouth shut as
ie governor reached them. It was unfair. All they had been

through. "I lost the papers. Maybe if you look over the clif
you'll see them."

"That's not necessary. Bane and his crew are going to b
found innocent," the governor said. "I gave my word."

Karly watched him in disbelief. "But I lost the proof."

"I saw the letter."

"But you didn't read it," Karly protested.

"I don't recall that being part of the deal. Do you, War
rick? Seems to me I asked to see it, so fair's fair. I'll sign th
documents in the morning. I have no need for more pris
oners," he explained. "Your father shouldn't have acte
without authorization, but in light of what has happened,
will overlook it."

Hack cleared his throat and gave an apologetic sniffle
"Do you mind my asking about the gold?"

The governor shuffled, but gave a nod. "It will be dis
persed among you and your crew as promised."

"And as soon as it is, we're bound for England, as I prom
ised," Warrick said.

"So, it's over?" Karly asked, facing Warrick.

"Except for a few details, we have the rest of our lives t
look forward to," he told her softly.

Chapter 32

Karly stepped out into the sunshine and grinned. The height of the lighthouse was exhilarating. Here was her break from helping Hack and the others plot their homesteads, a grant from the governor to get started on the right foot. The air, freed from the earth, danced and played about the lighthouse and through her hair, teasing her like a small child. It was vastly different from the heaviness in London. She would miss the scent of the open sea accented by the cries of longtails soaring above her head. Perhaps Bane would return here, too.

She almost forgot her reason for the climb in the first place. But her lapse was momentary. She walked around the small balcony to where Trent stood, somberly watching the horizon. He seemed so sad. Karly leaned against the railing beside him. She pondered the view when he startled, looking at her with surprise.

"Did you know that ships can see this lighthouse for almost thirty miles?" she asked.

"What?"

Karly smiled, hoping to cheer him. "And if you look due northeast, you can see where they are planning to move the capitol to Hamilton from St. George."

Trent frowned and looked over her shoulder. "Does Warrick know you are up here with me?"

"No. He's helping Hack. I didn't want to bother him. Besides, I wanted to talk to you. So when I saw you up here, thought it would be a good time."

"Oh?"

Karly placed her hand over his. "You and Warrick seem to be avoiding each other. I thought maybe I could help. You have been friends for so long . . ."

"It's not necessary."

She wasn't convinced. "You're going to be on the ship together for the entire voyage to England. There's a lot less privacy there. It would be better to talk here. Wouldn't you agree?"

"I'm not going to England, Karly. I'm staying here." He slipped his hand from her grasp and shook his head, moving away from her.

Her heart sank. "This is my fault."

Trent stiffened and jerked back toward her. "I never said that."

"It is. Since the storm, you two haven't gotten along. told Warrick the accident was my fault. That you asked me to go below deck and I refused. He doesn't blame you."

"Whether he blames me or not, you were nearly killed trying to save my life."

"That's what friends do for each other."

"And when have I ever been your friend?" he snapped. " have done nothing but try to turn Warrick away from you since the day you fell out of that tree."

Karly was quiet but watched him until he looked silently away. "I know I am an outsider, but that doesn't change the fact that you mean a great deal to Warrick and William and me, too. I know they would be very upset if you were to simply walk away."

"As I recall, you tried several times to walk away. *Run*

way, if memory serves me correctly." His voice was filled with sarcasm and anger. But there was sadness too. It made no sense.

"I've learned it's hard to share your life. But I'd rather struggle than be alone."

"And it doesn't hurt that you happen to be deeply in love."

Karly blushed. "I do love Warrick, very much. I'm glad he stayed with me long enough to let me figure that out for myself."

"He's loved you for longer than he will admit. I could see it in his face before we ever left England. You two are right for each other. I nearly destroyed that. I have no business in either of your lives."

Puzzled, she almost reached for his hand to comfort him, but thought better of it. He would most likely turn away again. "It's been a stressful time for all of us, but you haven't destroyed anything. Warrick and I are fine, as is the baby," she said as gently as she could.

Trent's eyes fell to her abdomen. "I want you to know I am genuinely happy for you. Love is not easy. You are lucky to find someone who loves you. That is a most precious treasure."

"You are speaking in riddles," Karly said.

"Better than confessing truths, although I think Warrick already suspects . . ." His voice drifted away with his gaze into the distance. "You had better go before he finds you missing."

"Suspects what?"

"Suspects that Trent may have had something to do with your 'accidents,'" a voice from behind her said coldly.

Karly pivoted. There stood Jenkins, the untried deckhand Trent had hired in London. In his hand was a pistol at the ready, and he was pointing it at her heart. His cap was pulled down over his forehead, his face soiled and his

clothes ragged, but she could see his eyes clearly. They were
narrowed in hatred. Her hand fell protectively to her belly
"What are you talking about?" The next instant Trent had
jerked her backward, placing himself between them as a
human shield.

"It's over, Amanda," Trent snapped.

"Amanda?" Karly asked and looked closer.

"It was you who gave me the idea," Amanda sneered a
Karly. "After all, you dressed like a man."

"Why would you need to disguise yourself?" Karly
asked.

Amanda gave an eerie laugh and addressed Trent. "From
this height we can throw her over the balcony. It will look
like a suicide."

"I told you, I'm not helping you anymore," Trent said
stiffly. "Your plan won't work. She's pregnant with Warrick's child. Even if she dies, he won't marry you."

"That's not your problem," she said, her voice rising.

"No, I'm your problem," Karly retorted and stepped to
Trent's side. He caught her arm and tried to wrench her
behind him again, but she held her ground. "Why did you
do this?" she asked him.

Trent dipped his head, even as his gaze remained locked
on Amanda. "I'm the third son in my family. I've never had
much wealth. It never bothered me until I made the mistake
of falling in love."

"I never said I loved you," Amanda interrupted.

Trent gave a hoarse laugh and flickered a glance toward
Karly. "I thought she loved me too, but she wanted afflu-
ence. I don't know why it made sense, but when she suggested she marry Warrick but still remain a part of my life
it seemed the best solution. It was the only solution that
would work. I didn't want to lose her; she meant everything
Amanda said you were an upstart looking for a way to trap

the right prize. I assumed she was telling the truth. The sooner you were gone the better, whatever it took."

"You set the bounty?" Karly asked.

"I set the bounty," Amanda returned. "But it seems the criminal element of London is not as good as I hoped."

"You should have given up marksmanship when you hit Jaline instead of me. Why did you run off when you could have finished me then?" Karly chided. If she could draw her out, Amanda might make a mistake.

"I didn't mean to hit Warrick's mother. I always liked her. When this is done, she is going to be my mother-in-law. I could not forgive myself if I had killed Warrick's mother," she said, her voice rising into a singsong tone. "I couldn't let her see me, find me, so I ran."

"You pushed me overboard."

"Yes," Amanda said with some pride.

"That was when I told her I had enough," Trent said. "I saw how much you and Warrick meant to each other. He risked his life for yours. I had no right to destroy your happiness for my own. When we got to Bermuda I told Amanda I wanted nothing more to do with the whole plan. I begged her to simply sail away with me."

Amanda's expression turned icy. "Sail away, penniless, to be some merchant's wife on a small island? I regret I'm not a better marksman or I would have killed you at the governor's ball instead of hitting that ridiculous commander."

Karly felt ill as she watched the same madness that had seized Landgon glow in Amanda's eyes. Her need for wealth was no less desperate than his had been. And she was just as desperate. There would be no reasoning with her. Karly's one hope was to distract her long enough to overpower her. But how? There was little room up here, and only one way down. It was like being trapped in a crow's nest with a madman. And then Amanda leveled the pistol.

Karly prepared to spring when she was shoved aside as

Trent lunged forward. She twisted, avoiding a fall, and regained her balance to see Trent struggling with Amanda, the pistol between them.

"Get out of here, Karly!" he ordered.

She wanted to help him, but as she started forward, his expression became fierce.

"Go now!" he roared.

She needed a weapon. Karly ran for the door and darted inside. There she seized a long pole used to light the beacon flame each night. Her hands gripped the iron when a gunshot made her flinch. Her heart hammered in terror for Trent. He wouldn't shoot Amanda; he loved her. It had to be the other way around. He could still be alive though, and she wasn't about to desert him. Karly clenched her teeth and lifted the bar like a sword in front of her. She stepped outside just as Amanda came around the corner.

Karly swung and caught her by surprise. She hit her forearm, and sent the pistol flying over the edge and into the rocks below. Pointing the pole directly at Amanda, she braced it against her hip. "Trent's right: it's over." Amanda appeared scared, and Karly felt a pang of sympathy. She eased her grip. Someone must have heard the gunshot and would be on the way. It would not be long. Then the corners of Amanda's mouth lifted cruelly. Steel glinted in the sunlight, and Karly saw the knife.

"I learned a few tricks of my own below decks on the *Moorea*. Never have just one weapon. Funny how such a simple sailors' game of target throwing could come in so useful," Amanda sneered.

She took a step, and Karly raised her makeshift sword defensively. She had to be close enough so she could spring and knock Amanda down before she threw. Timing needed to be her friend. She concentrated when Warrick's voice filled with raw emotion pierced her consciousness. The gunshot must have alerted him. He was coming to her rescue.

Amanda seemed to be thinking the same thing because she gaped about her, as if looking for an escape. Karly changed tactics. Not dropping her guard, she softened her features.

"Amanda, it's going to be all right," Karly soothed.

"Don't talk to me!" Amanda screamed.

Over the pounding of her heart Karly heard the hurried steps ascending the spiral staircase inside the lighthouse. Warrick was not alone. Several men were on their way. It would not be long, she told herself.

"Put the knife down, and everything will be fine."

Amanda backed a step away from her and glanced desperately around.

"There are people who care about you like Trent and your family. Drop the knife, and we'll go help Trent."

"I shot him," Amanda said, her voice shaking.

"Yes, but he could be all right. We should go check." Karly waited. Her knees began to quake as the knife clattered to the ground. Amanda backed away as Warrick burst through the door between them.

"Karly?" he gasped.

A single step and she was in his arms and he in hers, her face buried in his shoulder. She heard him ask if she was hurt, but before she could answer, he called out in alarm. Karly looked up to see Amanda climbing over the railing. "Amanda, no!" she cried, but Amanda's head never turned; she simply disappeared from view. Karly started forward, but Warrick hauled her back.

"It's almost a hundred feet to the ground," he whispered thickly. "Don't look."

Horrified, the tremors started at the deepening realization of what had happened. "Trent's shot. He tried to save me," she managed, her voice trembling.

"I'll go."

Karly recognized the voice as William's, but couldn't turn, her eyes frozen on the last place she had seen Amanda.

"She's the one who tried to kill me, from the beginning. She manipulated Trent into helping her." Karly blinked and turned toward Warrick. "Can we go please? I think I've had enough of heights for a while."

"For a while? How about forever?" He clasped her to him.

"When did life stop being fair?" she asked, her words almost stolen by the wind and his coat.

He kissed the top of her head. "When was it ever? All the more reason to hold on to it tightly. Every moment is precious."

"She didn't have to do that. Trent loved her."

"She couldn't see anything else, even though there was so much else *to* see."

"Sometimes it's hard to see more."

Warrick slipped his hand through her hair to the back of her neck, running his thumb lightly over her cheek. "If you ever have trouble seeing more, find me. I'll set you straight."

"You just did," she whispered, then hugged him and felt his lips on her tears. His arms were like a familiar melody, anchoring her mind. She welcomed their comfort.

Epilogue

Warrick didn't have to search for her. The music room at Greythorne was Karly's favorite. She had confided once she liked the height. She could see half the basin from its vista. By her side sat Crumpet, curled and half asleep. The dog lifted his head as Warrick entered, glanced at his mistress, and gave a low whine. "Is it still snowing hard?" Warrick asked. It was a rhetorical question, mighty flakes descending from the heavens simultaneously brightening and darkening the landscape of Greythorne Hall.

Karly glanced toward him, her silhouette revealing her well-rounded abdomen. Then she turned away and faced the windows. He placed his hands on her shoulders, drawing her into his arms, warmth to warmth. She nodded in his direction with a gentle smile, and then returned her focus to the courtyard below.

"You shouldn't be up here," Warrick said. "The fire is low, and it's cold. Your father and grandparents are downstairs wondering what happened to you."

"Are they arguing?"

"No. The moment you left, your father started telling stories about when you were little. Everyone is delighted."

Karly shook her head looking down at the floor. "Even Uncle Angus?"

"Your uncle is the one you can hear laughing from here," Warrick said with a grin.

She leaned into him and relaxed. "I owe this family to you. Without your . . ."

"Interference?" Warrick asked.

"I was going to say insistence," she corrected. "Without your insistence that they strike a peace, they would still be arguing and hating each other."

"I had help. Your grandmother was determined as well. And then there's the baby. They all want to see it grow, see their family continue." She flinched and looked up at the ceiling. He waited for what she might say next. He had learned so much of and from her these last few months. She was certain of her own death. The baby would come, and she would leave. He had tried to reason with her, but Karly held little faith in logic, even his. It unnerved and even frightened him, although he would not admit it to her.

Enlisting his mother's help had not lessened Karly's fear, just buried it. Unspoken, he glimpsed it in fleeting moments from the corner of his eye. A nursery suite was built off their bedroom, but she never stepped inside. It had been his mother who had handled the arrangements. Fear had paralyzed and resigned Karly, and he had no action but to be persistent. Time was on his side. "Karly?"

"Do you think the snow will slow the doctor?"

He wrapped his arms around her waist with his own sigh. Then the meaning of her question began to needle through his mind. His eyes fell over her shoulder to her swollen abdomen while his heart continued to his knees. He stepped around and turned her at the same time, studying her intently. Pain etched her features into deeper relief. "Tell me."

"The pains started a while ago."

"The baby's coming, now?" he said, his mouth suddenly dry.

"I wasn't certain, but they are regular, and a bit worse. It won't be long."

He had expected panic or tears. Karly met adversity with strength, but facing what she deemed as her death with quiet resolve was unnerving. Warrick quelled the fear. He could not lose her. "I'll get you to bed."

Karly blinked as if coming out of a dream and frowned. "You should fetch the doctor first, for the baby's sake."

"You first, then I'll send Trent. He offered to go, and the village is not far."

"It is good of you to forgive him," she said and attempted a smile. Then she gasped.

As she bent, Warrick gripped her hand, her hold becoming tenacious. She began to tilt to one side, and he caught her waist. Clinging to him for support, she halted and gasped another breath and then shuffled a step. He bent to scoop her into his arms, but she pushed his hand away.

"I can walk."

"I know; I've seen you do it. But we still have a long way to go."

"If I'm too slow, go ahead. I'll meet you there," she chided.

Warrick felt his patience begin to thin by his concern for her. "Why didn't you call someone?"

"I didn't want to shout, and no one was nearby," she said.

Warrick barked a raw shout, relieved when Briggs appeared moments later, flanked by three staff. "Send someone for my parents."

"You don't need to bother them if they're enjoying themselves," Karly said.

"Pay her no mind, Briggs. Tell my mother, and send Trent for the doctor."

Karly shook her head as Briggs hurried away. "You really

should say please when you ask him to do something. He is a part of the family. Besides, it sounds nicer than an order."

Warrick listened with half his attention to her chatter as she went from lessons in human kindness to venting frustrations as more people arrived. The other half of him was forging a plan. Getting her changed, helping her to their bed, and arranging pillows so she was comfortable wasn't difficult. Trying to organize the well-wishers was. He turned the responsibility over to his father, who managed to send everyone, with the exception of his mother, back downstairs.

"Are you leaving?" Karly asked as her fingers clenched his hand.

Warrick sat on the bed beside her. "Not unless you want me to."

"You promised to stay."

"Then it's settled. I will stay." Warrick clasped her hand between his two, raised it to his lips, and kissed her fingertips. She didn't answer him, her face pale and eyes closed. He touched her cheek, questioning.

"It hurts," she said, drawing a breath, and peeked up.

"I'll order some brandy."

Karly shook her head. "No, I can't drink anything."

"You could try . . ."

"No!" she cried, cramming her eyes shut and pursing her lips.

He was helpless to stop her pain. Warrick pressed a kiss to her forehead to steady his own nerves as much as hers. "Let me do something," he whispered against her skin. Her ragged breaths slowed, and he felt her give a small shudder.

"Talk to me about anything. I want to hear your voice."

He looked at her and tried not to worry. Karly was reasonably healthy, he reassured himself, even as he noted the dark circles under her hazel eyes. She had not slept well in weeks. She claimed the child was restless, but he knew she was frightened. True to her spirit and nature, she pressed on and refused to discuss it. He had promised to be her strength. Now he was crumbling. The prospect of losing her was all too real. He couldn't pretend he didn't feel the same terrors she did. There was a difference, however. She would make the journey, and he would watch. He would not let her make it alone, however. Warrick tightened his grip on her hand and smiled. "We can't delay any longer. We need to pick a name for this baby."

"The midwife said it was a boy. You pick."

The falter in her voice was nearly as pronounced as the one he had heard in his. Warrick shook his head and forced himself to calm. "I hold no faith in anything that woman in Bermuda said."

"It's your decision," she persisted.

Warrick lifted his shoulders and gave her his sternest look. "It could be a girl."

"Girl or boy, as long as it is all right."

Warrick swore to himself. She was giving up and giving in to the fear she would die like her mother had, in child-birth. He needed her to come back to him, or he was worried he would lose her. He fought back his rising panic and gave an exaggerated shrug. "How about Mortimeriton?"

Her reaction took a long moment. Then Karly choked and flickered a glance at him. "That's not even remotely funny, Warrick."

"Then help me."

"I don't know any boys' names," she whimpered.

"You managed to find one for Crumpet."

"Crumpet's a puppy, not a baby."

"All right, since you don't know boys' names, we'll try girls. What about Caroline, after your mother?"

Her eyes opened. She gave a small tremor, then a nod. "I think everyone will like that," she said between clenched teeth.

Peace settled between them as warmth returned to her eyes. Warrick brushed a kiss across the back of her hand. The danger wasn't over. He heard footsteps and prayed for the doctor. It was his mother who swept into the room with two servants in her wake. At least he was not alone. He glanced down at Karly, who seemed paler. A sheen of sweat now covered her brow. "Since we've settled the name if it's a girl, we're back to boys' names."

Karly shook her head. "You can't use that horrid name."

Warrick wanted to smile with relief. She was still very much with him. "What if I said it belonged to my great-grandfather?" he deadpanned.

"Not Mortimeriton?" Jaline demanded with a small snort as she presented Warrick with two large blankets. Her ebony eyes were bright even as she held her tone even.

"It is a good name," Warrick teased and felt Karly yank hard on his hand.

"Pick something else," she commanded.

"I will go see what is keeping the doctor." Jaline smiled.

Prepared to jibe, he noticed Karly was no longer paying attention to him. Her expression had hardened. She was looking toward the window. He held her hand and gave it a rub. "It is a family namesake. If you don't want me to use it, you need to come up with a better one."

"I can't think."

"You are one of the quickest thinkers I have ever met."

Karly heaved a sigh and drew her brows together, glowering. Then with a sigh, she shook her head and wet her lips. "I know you are playing with me. Thank you," she whispered.

He raised her knuckles to his lips, brushing once, twice, and then three times before he pressed his kiss and held her gaze. The moment was broken with more pain.

"It's supposed to hurt more as it gets closer," she said.

"I don't like seeing you in pain," he answered.

"Then pick a different name," she minced between breaths.

He couldn't help but laugh. "You are, without a doubt, stubborn and relentless. Promise to never change."

"I'm going to remind you that you said that when this is all over," she said, grimacing.

"That is the first time you have mentioned after the baby is born," he said softly. She appeared uncertain. He thought he had just made an error when she relaxed, accepting brandy and resting between contractions. Warrick lost track of the time except for the fact it seemed to be moving far too slowly. Relieved as he was when the doctor arrived, he nearly sent the man away when he demanded Warrick wait outside. Ordered to work, the doctor countered his mother's disapproving glance with his own at Karly. Thankfully, she didn't argue.

It was evening before the pains made it clear the birth was imminent. He expected Karly would panic. What he wasn't prepared for was the effect her cries would have on him. His agony was complete. The only thing that kept him in check was the fact that Karly fared far worse. She was beyond his help.

"Just a bit longer sweetheart," he said. The words sounded hollow. The doctor had already made that pledge several times. Even as he fought on he was beginning to wonder if something was wrong. "Think about when this is over. You are going to have to teach our son or daughter how to read secret codes. After that they must learn to pilot a ship and . . ."

"Climb a tree?" she interrupted.

He was supposed to laugh, but the pain took her away. He could find no more humor. He watched as she alternated between exertion and rest. When she buried her head in the pillow, he knew it was for his benefit. "Go ahead and scream." She shook her head. He switched from teasing her to the most tender words he knew. "You're doing fine," he said. Her answer was a mere breath. He heard her say his name before she fell into a near-unconscious stupor. He touched her face and cheek, felt her breath, and, feeling it steady, glanced at the doctor.

His back was to them, and Warrick heard the small cry of the new baby, saw his mother mouth the babe's sex, and turned back to Karly. He bent to her ear. "I love you."

"I love you too," she murmured, her eyes half open. "You look tired."

"I am," he breathed with relief as she slowly regained consciousness, "but not as tired as you."

"Is it over?"

"Yes, and you're going to be fine."

She was alert now, the blood draining from her face. "And the baby?" she asked anxiously.

"Caroline is fine."

Warrick helped her to sit while she expectantly watched the doctor and Jaline with her daughter. But when Jaline approached and offered the tiny bundle of fluffy white blankets, Karly shook her head. "I'll probably drop her."

Jaline eased the baby toward her and lowered her into Karly's arms. "You'll learn. I'll go tell the families. They'll want to know you are all right."

Karly glanced at Warrick, then the doctor. She swallowed hard, as if that would make a difference. "She is healthy?"

"Very much so. Resting is normal at this age, which is what you should do," the doctor said and patted her hand. "I'll be back shortly to check on you."

The door closed, and they were alone, at least for the moment. Soon well-wishers demanded to see the baby. He watched as Karly's gaze dropped slowly to the baby.

She risked a quick touch of the tiny hand before lingering. "I wager you're glad you're not a boy," Karly whispered to the infant and looked at Warrick. "You didn't leave."

"I promised I wouldn't."

"And you have been good on your promises, most of the time."

The spark had returned. Warrick brushed her hair back over her shoulder, draping his arm about it. "You aren't really going to teach her how to climb trees, are you?"

"Look how useful it has been over the last year," she grinned, but suddenly paled and searched his face. "You were hoping once the baby was born I would change."

He had thought her pain had returned. Relief poured through him. She was all right. Warrick gathered Karly and their daughter in his arms. "You're correct."

"I am?"

Warrick laid his forehead to hers and kissed the tip of her nose. "I hope you will change into a wife and mother who knows I will always be beside you."

Her smile was slow, but it reached her eyes and sparkled, igniting the flecks of gold within them. "You realize if you get your wish, our lives could become even more exciting?"

"I was hoping you would say that," he said and kissed her, soul to soul.

More by Bestselling Author

Janet Dailey

Bring the Ring	0-8217-8016-6	$4.99US/$6.99CAN
Calder Promise	0-8217-7541-3	$7.99US/$10.99CAN
Calder Storm	0-8217-7543-X	$7.99US/$10.99CAN
A Capital Holiday	0-8217-7224-4	$6.99US/$8.99CAN
Crazy in Love	1-4201-0303-2	$4.99US/$5.99CAN
Eve's Christmas	0-8217-8017-4	$6.99US/$9.99CAN
Green Calder Grass	0-8217-7222-8	$7.99US/$10.99CAN
Happy Holidays	0-8217-7749-1	$6.99US/$9.99CAN
Let's Be Jolly	0-8217-7919-2	$6.99US/$9.99CAN
Lone Calder Star	0-8217-7542-1	$7.99US/$10.99CAN
Man of Mine	1-4201-0009-2	$4.99US/$6.99CAN
Mistletoe and Molly	1-4201-0041-6	$6.99US/$9.99CAN
Ranch Dressing	0-8217-8014-X	$4.99US/$6.99CAN
Scrooge Wore Spurs	0-8217-7225-2	$6.99US/$9.99CAN
Searching for Santa	1-4201-0306-7	$6.99US/$9.99CAN
Shifting Calder Wind	0-8217-7223-6	$7.99US/$10.99CAN
Something More	0-8217-7544-8	$7.99US/$9.99CAN
Stealing Kisses	1-4201-0304-0	$4.99US/$5.99CAN
Try to Resist Me	0-8217-8015-8	$4.99US/$6.99CAN
Wearing White	1-4201-0011-4	$4.99US/$6.99CAN
With This Kiss	1-4201-0010-6	$4.99US/$6.99CAN
Yes, I Do	1-4201-0305-9	$4.99US/$5.99CAN

Available Wherever Books Are Sold!

Check out our website at **www.kensingtonbooks.com**

More by Bestselling Author

Lori Foster

Available Wherever Books Are Sold!

Check out our website at **www.kensingtonbooks.com**

Books by Bestselling Author
Fern Michaels

___The Jury	0-8217-7878-1	$6.99US/$9.99CAN
___Sweet Revenge	0-8217-7879-X	$6.99US/$9.99CAN
___Lethal Justice	0-8217-7880-3	$6.99US/$9.99CAN
___Free Fall	0-8217-7881-1	$6.99US/$9.99CAN
___Fool Me Once	0-8217-8071-9	$7.99US/$10.99CAN
___Vegas Rich	0-8217-8112-X	$7.99US/$10.99CAN
___Hide and Seek	1-4201-0184-6	$6.99US/$9.99CAN
___Hokus Pokus	1-4201-0185-4	$6.99US/$9.99CAN
___Fast Track	1-4201-0186-2	$6.99US/$9.99CAN
___Collateral Damage	1-4201-0187-0	$6.99US/$9.99CAN
___Final Justice	1-4201-0188-9	$6.99US/$9.99CAN
___Up Close and Personal	0-8217-7956-7	$7.99US/$9.99CAN
___Under the Radar	1-4201-0683-X	$6.99US/$9.99CAN
___Razor Sharp	1-4201-0684-8	$7.99US/$10.99CAN
___Yesterday	1-4201-1494-8	$5.99US/$6.99CAN
___Vanishing Act	1-4201-0685-6	$7.99US/$10.99CAN
___Sara's Song	1-4201-1493-X	$5.99US/$6.99CAN
___Deadly Deals	1-4201-0686-4	$7.99US/$10.99CAN
___Game Over	1-4201-0687-2	$7.99US/$10.99CAN
___Sins of Omission	1-4201-1153-1	$7.99US/$10.99CAN
___Sins of the Flesh	1-4201-1154-X	$7.99US/$10.99CAN
___Cross Roads	1-4201-1192-2	$7.99US/$10.99CAN

Available Wherever Books Are Sold!
Check out our website at **www.kensingtonbooks.com**